Emily's eyes softened and a lovely smile played around her mouth. 'I felt it again, my baby moved. Annie, it's mine, my own little baby. How could I ever have thought that I could give it away? It was the baby's way of telling me that I have responsibilities.'

'Yes, Miss Emily, your baby has a right to your love but what are you going to do about your parents? Maybe they will come around to your keeping it after all.'

'No, they won't, I know them too well. They don't want a grandchild born out of wedlock, they couldn't stand the shame. Keeping my baby will mean cutting myself off completely . . .'

'Do you want me, Miss Emily?'

Emily's eyes swam with tears. 'More than you'll ever know, but even if you are not prepared to be with me I would still do this on my own.'

Annie was openly crying. 'As if I would leave you. What do you take me for?'

Also by Nora Kay in Coronet Paperbacks

A Woman of Spirit
Best Friends
Beth
Lost Dreams
Gift of Love

About the author

Nora Kay was born in Northumberland but she and her husband lived for many years in Dundee. They now live in Aberdeen. *Tina* is her sixth novel.

Tina

Nora Kay

CORONET BOOKS
Hodder & Stoughton

To Bill and Raymond

Copyright © 1998 by Nora Kay

The right of Nora Kay to be identified as the Author
of the Work has been asserted by her in accordance
with the Copyright, Designs and Patents Act 1988.

First published in Great Britain in 1998
by Hodder and Stoughton
A division of Hodder Headline PLC
First published in paperback in 1999
by Hodder and Stoughton
A Coronet paperback

10 9 8 7 6 5

A CIP catalogue record for this title
is available from the British Library.

ISBN 0 340 68966 8

Typeset by Hewer Text Ltd, Edinburgh
Printed and bound in Great Britain by
Clays Ltd, St Ives PLC

Hodder and Stoughton
A division of Hodder Headline PLC
338 Euston Road
London NW1 3BH

Chapter One

The strident sound of the bell ringing was an unwelcome disturbance. Mrs Martin, cook-housekeeper at Denbrae House, had just that minute made herself comfortable in the only chair with arms and a cushion for her back. Her poor, swollen, aching feet were on the wooden stool.

'Would you credit that,' she muttered crossly and jerked her head to see which of the rooms was demanding attention. 'Annie,' she shouted.

A head popped round the door. 'What is it, Mrs Martin?'

'Anyone else there or is it just you?'

'Just me.'

'Then you'll need to take yourself upstairs and see what is wanted.'

Annie sighed but silently. She had been on her feet since half past five in the morning and this was supposed to be a quiet time. With luncheon over, the dining-room table cleared and the dishes washed, the maids looked forward to a short break before their other duties claimed them.

Denbrae House stood on slightly raised ground with the Perthshire hills swelling up in the background. It was a substantially built property which earned the description of a small mansion. Situated on the outskirts of the pretty little town of Greenhill in Perthshire the house held a commanding position. Greenhill was a quiet country town described by some as genteel. The well-off lived there and it also found favour with those seeking a pleasant place in which to spend their retirement. An added attraction was its nearness to Perth and with Dundee not so many miles away. Both cities were well served with quality shops and stores.

On the instructions of the master who felt it was more welcoming, the ornamental gates to Denbrae House were usually left open. The house was approached by a long drive lined with flowering shrubs and ending in a broad carriage sweep. Marble steps led to the heavy oak door and ivy and wistaria grew up the walls and circled the attic windows. Tall mature trees stood like sentries and were just far enough away from the windows not to block out the light. To the back of the house were smooth lawns and walkways and a flight of worn stone steps led down to a sunken garden. All were kept neat by two gardeners and numerous helpers.

Denbrae House was home to Alfred Cunningham-Brown and his wife Maud. After many years in India that had added greatly to their inherited wealth, they returned to Denbrae House in 1895 and now five years later were well settled and enjoying life. Too young to retire and happily enjoying good health, Alfred Cunningham-Brown was heavily involved in local affairs and chaired a number of committees. His wife, Maud, had agreed though half-heartedly it had to be said, to give her support to one or two organisations but rarely put in an appearance at the meetings. She disliked speaking in public and since her voice didn't carry she was in no demand as a speaker. Her donations, however, were much appreciated and all agreed that she was a charming and generous lady. She was quite incapable of making a decision and those that had to be made were left to her husband. The running of the house was left to Mrs Martin. There was no housekeeper, the woman once employed in that capacity had been a disaster. She would have made an excellent sergeant-major having the voice and manner of one. Mrs Martin could stand it no longer and threatened to give in her notice if matters didn't improve. The maids were frequently reduced to tears.

Maud, forced to a decision in this instance, decided a good cook would be more difficult to replace. In the end the housekeeper had to go.

Delighted with her victory, Mrs Martin had suggested to the mistress that she should take over the management of the house as well as being in charge of the kitchen. Maud found no objection to this and regarding extra staff Mrs Martin was given a free hand. There were three resident maids, Annie, Bella and Mary. A scullery-maid came in daily as did a woman who did the scrubbing. Mrs Rafferty, a widow who had once been a cook, came in for a few hours to assist in the kitchen. If there were little upsets they were never allowed to get serious and on the whole they all got on well together.

The Cunningham-Browns had three of a family. The children had been born in India and had spent their early years in that country before returning to Scotland to be educated. The eldest was eighteen-year-old Emily who after completing her schooling in St Andrews had refused to spend a year at a finishing school in Switzerland. Maud made mild protests but wasn't upset. It would be nice to have her daughter at home and she had no need to feel guilty since Emily had been given the chance and declined.

In appearance Emily took after her mother. She was quite tall and slender and had long, golden-fair hair that curled naturally. Her skin was perfect and looked like ivory touched with the delicate pink of a rose. Her eyes were a clear grey and fringed with thick dark lashes. Maud and Alfred were very proud of their lovely daughter. None of their friends' daughters were nearly as pretty, a few were decidedly plain and the despair of their parents who were frantically trying to marry them off when the girls had at least youth on their side.

There were no such worries for Alfred and Maud. Emily had more than her fair share of admirers and in time she would make her choice. The young men who came about the house were all eminently suitable and Emily's parents were in no doubt that she would make a good marriage.

The two boys, Michael sixteen and Robert fourteen, were at boarding school in Edinburgh. They were likeable but boisterous and Maud confessed to her friends that her head ached from the first day of the holidays to the last. Much as she loved the mischievous pair it was a relief to see the trunks packed and the boys despatched to school.

Annie could see that the summons had come from the upstairs sitting-room used by the family when they were on their own. It wouldn't do to keep whoever it was waiting and Annie left the kitchen and hurried along the passageway with its dreary brown linoleum and drab walls. The dreariness ended when Annie passed through a small archway. Then it was like slipping into another world. Paintings covered much of the cream-coloured walls and the carpet was soft underfoot. Annie caught a glimpse of herself in a mirror and patted her fine, flyaway hair into place. In another few moments she had reached the beautiful curved stairway at the front of the house. Out of breath after hurrying and climbing the stairs, Annie walked along to the family sitting-room, knocked and entered.

Annie Fullerton was twenty-three and Denbrae House had been home to her since the Cunningham-Browns had taken her into their employ. A member of the board of Craigieview Orphanage, Alfred, perhaps to show an example to others, had taken one of its orphans to be a scullery-maid in his home. A willing and intelligent girl who never complained or gave any trouble, Annie had quickly risen from the position of scullery-maid to house-maid.

She was neither plain nor pretty, just very ordinary. Her light brown hair was parted in the middle and swept back from a smooth forehead. She was very thin and her eyes, her best feature, were a soft brown.

At Denbrae House the custom was for the master and mistress to retire to their bedroom after the midday meal. This was a habit acquired when living abroad. A sociable couple they enjoyed entertaining and being entertained. Those guests staying for a few days or longer and who themselves had spent years in India, were usually more than happy to retire to their bedroom for an hour or so. Others who had only known the Scottish climate were not so accommodating. To them a rest in the middle of the day was unthinkable and a complete waste of time. There was a time for bed and it wasn't during the day. Only the very young and the very old could be excused.

Sometimes Emily took the dogs for a walk across the fields but if she didn't feel like it she left it for someone else and instead relaxed with a book.

She looked up when the door opened.

'Thank goodness it is you, Annie, I didn't want anyone else. Come in, don't stand there and make sure the door is shut. No, on second thoughts go back down again and bring a pot of tea. I know it is early but I feel like one. And, Annie?'

Annie turned round.

'Make that two cups.'

'Two cups, Miss Emily?'

'That's what I said, two cups,' came the impatient reply.

Annie was concerned. Miss Emily didn't look like herself, in fact she looked pale and troubled. 'Miss Emily, you don't look well,' she said, then wished she hadn't.

'Never mind how I look,' Emily almost screamed then pushed her knuckle into her mouth. This wouldn't do, she must pull herself together. The last person she wanted to offend was Annie.

Annie didn't take offence, someone in her position couldn't afford to.

'I'm sorry,' she said dropping her eyes. Then she left the room and retraced her steps to the kitchen. When she returned she was carrying a tray covered in a white, stiffly starched tray-cloth. On it was a small silver teapot, strainer, sugar bowl, milk jug, teaspoons and two rose-patterned fine bone-china teacups and saucers. She placed the tray carefully on one of the low tables near to the fire. Only a small fire burned in the grate since some warmth was coming from the April sunshine slanting in the window.

'Thank you, Annie, and I'm sorry I spoke to you like that.'

'That's all right, Miss Emily, and if that is everything—'

'Of course it isn't everything, the other cup is for you. I want you to join me.'

'Join you?' Annie said stupidly and her normally pale face crimsoned angrily. She hated to be made fun of and that is what Miss Emily was doing.

'Yes, join me. Do you see anyone else in the room?' She gave an exaggerated look around.

Annie looked stubborn. 'No, Miss Emily, it wouldn't be right.'

'For goodness sake, sit down and do as you are told. I have something I want to say to you and this will make it easier.'

Annie did sit down but the colour had drained from her face leaving it grey.

Emily looked at her curiously. 'Why are you looking so worried?'

Annie shook her head, she didn't know what to say.

'You have nothing to worry about, I'm the one with all the worries.' She gulped. 'I almost wish I were dead.'

'Nothing can be as bad as that,' Annie said gently.

'Can't it? Shows how little you know.' She waved a hand in the direction of the teapot. 'Pour the tea, will you?'

Annie put a little milk into each cup then poured the tea. Now that her own position didn't seem to be threatened she could cease worrying and give her attention to Miss Emily. Poor lass, something was very far wrong but for the life of her Annie couldn't understand what she could do about it.

Before lifting her cup Annie waited until Miss Emily had taken a few sips of hers. Silly to be nervous with the cups since she had washed, dried and put away the china often enough. But this was different, this was an ordeal. What if the mistress walked in this minute and saw her daughter having tea with one of the maids. It didn't bear thinking about.

Raising the cup to her mouth she drank a little. After being used to thick, white kitchen cups she had a real fear that her strong white teeth might break the delicate china.

'Annie, you are my friend, aren't you?'

'No, Miss Emily, I'm your maid.'

'But you would be willing to help me?'

Alarm bells were ringing and she would have to go carefully. 'I would do my best but I'm promising nothing until I know what it is.' She wouldn't risk her employers' wrath and why should she? Whatever predicament Miss Emily had got herself into she would be forgiven but it didn't follow that a maid would be treated as lightly.

Emily had grown quiet and was just staring into space as though lost in her own thoughts. Annie turned her eyes to admire the room. She liked it best. Compared to the elegance of the drawing-room and dining-room it was shabby. And it was this shabbiness and the lived-in look that made it look homely and appealing. Rich brocade curtains in shades of red and pale pinks hung at the double window and on the sill like a welcome touch of spring, were two bowls of hyacinths, one pink, one blue. The high ceiling had attractive cornices and the large sofa and armchairs had been bought more for comfort than appearance.

With a deep sigh Emily looked over at Annie and the maid was shocked to see such despair. She was no stranger to despair herself, in her short life she had seen too much of it. Miss Emily had everything or so it would appear. Apart from parents who doted on her she had beauty, lovely clothes and a splendid home.

'I was wrong then,' Emily said sadly, 'I really did think that you would do anything to help me.'

'Almost anything.' It would be dangerous to go any further than that, Emily thought. Once given, a promise couldn't be broken.

'Almost anything will have to do.' She gave a half smile.

'There is just a possibility that I may have to leave home.'

'Leave Denbrae House, Miss Emily?' Annie sounded shocked.

'It may well come to that and if it should I would want you with me.'

'Where would you be going?' Annie said cautiously.

'I have no idea other than it will be a fair distance from here. Does the thought of that frighten you?'

'A little.'

'Why should leaving Denbrae House upset you? It isn't your home.'

'The only one I've known, Miss Emily,' Annie said shortly, 'and a lot better than the orphanage.' She drank the rest of her tea and put the cup carefully back on the saucer. 'Miss Emily, if you would excuse me I must get back, there is work to be done.'

'Very well, you are excused.' She pushed back the half-empty cup and said abruptly, 'Get rid of this, then go.'

'Yes, Miss Emily.' Annie got up and hid her relief. This way Mrs Martin would know what was going on and not blame her.

Emily watched the busy hands as Annie arranged every-thing neatly stacked on the tray then balancing it on one hand managed to open the door with the other. A part of Emily's brain registered how difficult that must be but even so it would not have occurred to her to get up and assist by opening the door. That was just not done. One expected a well-trained housemaid to cope.

She had always thought Annie to be different from the usual run of servants. The young woman had a quiet dignity that was all the more surprising given her humble begin-nings. That the day would come when she, Emily Cunning-ham-Brown, would need Annie and not just as a maid, was laughable yet that day had come. In the months ahead she would need all the help and support she could get and that was unlikely to come from her parents.

Praying wouldn't do much good. She did have her faith

and it might give her the strength to face what lay ahead. She believed that God was fair but she also believed that He was severe. Sins would be forgiven but there would be a price to pay. How it would be exacted was what she was worried about.

That her parents would want her out of sight she had no doubt. She accepted it as inevitable and Annie was the one person she wanted with her. Strange that, but it was true. She needed someone quiet and sensible and most of all someone who wouldn't preach. Annie hadn't agreed as yet but she was hopeful.

Putting off the inevitable was only making it harder on herself. She would face them tomorrow morning. After breakfast would be the best time and before her father got behind his newspaper. She could imagine the look on their faces, it would be one of shock and horror and no wonder. She had done the unforgivable.

What loomed ahead was quite dreadful but would be much worse without the money she had been left. Thanks to darling Great-Aunt Anne she had the means to be independent. Emily managed a smile as she remembered. Her great-aunt had been a character. A spinster from choice she had deplored the way women were treated.

Emily was remembering the occasion when she had been asked to sit beside her great-aunt so that they could have a serious talk. Woman to woman she said. The old woman never spoke down to her. At the time Emily had been thirteen and spending part of her school holidays at her great-aunt's home in Newport across the River Tay from Dundee. It was one of the tall houses that had a wonderful view from the front windows of the river in all its moods. Neighbours considered the elderly woman an eccentric and she would not have argued with that. As a girl it had angered her that her brother's education should have been so important when it was perfectly obvious that she had the better brain. To her mother in particular her intelligence was an embarrassment and her outspokenness to be deplored. All that was required from a daughter of a good family was knowing how to conduct herself and the ability to read, write and do simple arithmetic. Music was important and piano lessons a must. At least two hours a day were set aside for practice and it was a proud moment for parents when their daughter was able to play sufficiently well to entertain guests. Even better if she could sing and accompany herself. The young Anne mastered the piano but had no singing voice.

'Are you going to tell me something special?'

'I am.'

'Is it something nice?'

'I would say so.'

They were sitting in a large, high-ceilinged room with a handsome bureau and two bookcases along one wall. The fireplace had a high brass fender that gleamed though not as brightly as the log box beside it. The larger pieces of furniture had been bought with the house and suited the room. The glass shelves in the china cabinet held exquisite porcelain figures and decorative plates. A silver rosebowl had pride of place in the middle of the centre shelf. Scattered around on various surfaces, including the top of the piano, were family photographs. And on the walls hung dull oil paintings of lochs and Highland cattle together with two pretty watercolours of local beauty spots.

'Emily, you are thirteen and very nearly grown-up.'

'I won't be properly grown-up until I leave school.'

'That is true.' The old woman nodded her head and said slowly, 'You are very fortunate, my dear, to be receiving a good education. I had a lot to do with the choice of school and without my interference you would have continued being taught at home.'

'Did you go to school?'

'No. In my day there was no choice, one had a governess. I was at the mercy of one who knew precious little as I very soon discovered. She could never answer my questions and got flustered and angry when I persisted. I was determined that wasn't to be your fate.'

Emily giggled. 'Were you a little horror?'

'From all accounts I must have been.'

'How do you know so much when nobody taught you?'

'I had an enquiring mind and the benefit of a good library.' She waved her hand in the direction of the book-cases. 'That was my school, Emily. Self-taught you could say. But I'm wandering and what I want to say to you, child, is just between us. It is important you understand that.' She frowned and looked stern. She had no difficulty looking severe; she had that sort of face.

'A secret? I can keep a secret.' Emily's face brightened in anticipation. Her parents could never understand why she chose to spend some of her holidays with her father's aunt. The rest of the family did their duty visits and kept those very short. They didn't want to risk cutting themselves off completely since they all had expectations and the old woman couldn't last for ever.

Only Emily knew how interesting her great-aunt could be and the wonderful stories she could tell.

'I hope you can because it is important that you keep what I am to say to yourself.' She paused and sat up straighter. 'What I want to talk to you about is independence. That, my dear Emily, is the greatest gift of all for a woman.'

'Like being able to do what you want without having to ask permission?'

'Exactly.'

'Is that why you didn't get married because you wanted to be independent or did nobody ask you?'

How brutal the young can be, she thought. 'Young woman, I wouldn't say tact was your strong point,' she bristled. 'What a thing to say to an unmarried lady. I'll have you know I had my admirers, not many I have to confess. But then I wasn't a great beauty like your mother or mine for that matter. Another thing to bear in mind is that most men do not like clever women.'

'Why not?'

'It makes them feel uncomfortable. They think, mistakenly I may add, that they are superior. From the time they are born boys are encouraged to believe that and some women, perhaps most, let them go on thinking it.'

'You wouldn't and neither would I.'

'Most certainly I do not share that view and it infuriates me that others still do. Unfortunately there was not a great deal I could do about it,' she said shaking her head and dislodging a few hairpins. 'I hope a woman's lot will have changed before it need concern you, though I suspect it may take longer.' She smiled. 'Find yourself a husband who appreciates you for yourself and not just because you have a bonny face.'

'Have I? Am I pretty?'

'Yes, but don't let it go to your head.'

Emily bent down to pick up the hairpins from the carpet and arrange them on the arm of the sofa. Later she would put them on her great-aunt's dressing-table. Emily had the freedom of the house.

'Is that all? Is that the secret?' Emily couldn't hide her disappointment.

'No, none of that is a secret, indeed most of it is common knowledge. The secret and remember it is a secret is that I am going to leave you all my money.'

'All of it?' Emily's eyes widened in shock. 'Nobody else is getting anything?'

'That is correct. Your parents won't like it.'

'Why not?'

'Because they won't like me favouring you and forgetting your brothers.'

'Aren't you going to leave anything to Michael and Robert?'

'Not a penny.'

'Don't you like them?'

'Of course I do, rascals though they are. They will be in line for plenty and won't need any financial help from me.'

'I suppose that is all right then.'

'Perfectly all right. I can do as I wish and don't keep interrupting or I'll forget what I want to say.' She paused and her face criss-crossed in lines broke into a smile. 'Best of all you won't have to wait until you are married or reach the age of twenty-one to inherit. No, my dear Emily, you will be entitled to draw on the money when you are eighteen. Should I still be in the land of the living when you reach that magical age, you shall have to wait a little longer. That isn't very likely,' she said suddenly sounding weary.

'You aren't going to die?' Emily said in a frightened voice.

'Not this minute,' she laughed. 'I would hope to get more warning than that.'

'You shouldn't joke about it,' Emily said looking distressed.

'Why not treat it lightly, we all have to go sometime and in the order of things I have had more than my allotted years.'

'I don't want your money if you've got to die.' Emily's eyes filled with tears. 'You could still live a long time, couldn't you?'

'Yes, of course I could but don't be distressed at the thought of my demise. I haven't done anything too terrible in this life though that isn't to say I haven't been tempted.' She smiled and patted Emily's hand.

'You will go to heaven when you die, of course you will. You are good and you are kind.' Emily had a vivid imagination and she couldn't bear to think of her great-aunt being refused entry into that mansion in the sky.

'Thank you, my dear and don't worry, I'm fairly confident I'll go to heaven and if not I'll have plenty of company wherever I do end up,' she said drily. 'With that distressing subject out of the way perhaps we could get back to the real purpose of this conversation. I want to make sure that whatever happens you will be all right.'

'Why shouldn't I be?'

'I can't answer that, none of us knows what is ahead. I trust that you will be happy but, should there come a time when you are in difficulties, it will help greatly if you have the means to support yourself.'

Emily was frowning and looking perplexed. What did her great-aunt mean? Her mother and father would always be there for her.

'You are too young to understand and I doubt if I could make it really clear. Still I must try. Your parents love you dearly and want only the best for you. Their best might not be the same as you want for yourself. If you are totally dependent on your parents the probability is that you may have to do what they want.'

'I see,' Emily said slowly. 'With money of my own I would have a choice in the matter.'

'Well said, I couldn't have put it better myself. All this is very unlikely, Emily. In all probability you will have a trouble-free life and marry someone you love who will be acceptable to Alfred and Maud.'

'This is just in case I fall in love with someone totally unsuitable.' Emily was beginning to enjoy herself. This was the most interesting conversation she had ever had.

'I hope you won't be silly enough to marry a rogue.'

'No, I won't.'

'What I had in mind was you perhaps falling from grace.'

'Doing something dreadful?'

'Not in your eyes only in theirs. Now I've got you totally confused.'

'No, you haven't. Do you think I might fall from grace?'

'I sincerely hope not, but being a much loved daughter would make your position all the worse if you were to do so.'

'Did you ever fall from grace or should I not be asking that?'

'No, you shouldn't but I'll answer it. I didn't do anything as terrible as anger my parents sufficiently to show me the door, but I was a great disappointment to them. Your mother was the kind of girl they would have liked for a daughter. Maud was everything I wasn't but they got the next best thing when she became part of the family.'

'You aren't a disappointment to me.' Emily flung her arms round the old lady's neck and hugged her. 'I love you and that's why I like to come and stay here.'

'Bless you,' she said as she gently removed herself from the stranglehold.

'Thank you very much Great-Aunt Anne. This will be our secret and I promise you I won't tell a living soul.'

'Such a silly expression, you wouldn't be likely to tell a dead soul, would you?'

Emily giggled and sprang up. 'Time for your afternoon tea, shall I ring for it?'

'Yes, do that. I hadn't realised it was that time but when you get to my age food isn't important. I'm never hungry but I daresay I would enjoy a cup of tea.'

Emily closed her eyes. How strange that she should remember it all so clearly. The years had just rolled away and for a short time she had been that happy thirteen-year-old. The holiday had been special and stayed with her because it had been her last in Newport. Three months later the old lady had slipped away peacefully in her sleep.

What would her great-aunt have thought of her now? She would have been disappointed. No, she would have been much more than that. She would have been deeply shocked. Her great-aunt would never have behaved in that way but then she had never been in love. Never felt that thrill of excitement and that strange longing run through her veins.

How could it be wrong to love? That's what she had thought and her ignorance and stupidity had brought her to this.

Until now Emily had given no thought to the money left to her. Now she saw it as a godsend. Whatever the future held she wouldn't be penniless. Well into the night and until sleep claimed her, Emily tried to marshal her thoughts and prepare the words that somehow she had to find the courage to say.

Chapter Two

As soon as Emily awoke all her fears and anxieties crowded about her. As she well knew her father could be cold and hard when he chose to be and what she had to confess was going to devastate him. Her mother, too, though she might be a little more understanding. Once he had got over the first shock she could see her father's orderly mind taking over. Alfred Cunningham-Brown would now concentrate his mind on how best to protect the family's good name. That could only be achieved by getting her away and out of sight as soon as possible.

Throwing back the covers, Emily got herself out of bed and tried to stem the rising panic. In her bare feet she padded across to the window to draw back the curtains. No blinds were necessary since the material was heavy and the curtains lined. Sunshine flooded into the room and as she laid her brow against the cold window there was a light tap at the door. A maid came in with a jug of hot water which she placed on the marble top.

Opening the window, Emily leaned out and breathed in the fresh, cold, clear air. Of all the seasons this was her favourite. She loved to see the trees newly in leaf and the splash of colour that came with the crocuses peeping through the grass. Others, mostly yellow and purple clustered around the tree trunks while under the hedges were clumps of delicate primroses. Beyond lay a whole field of golden daffodils that looked like a giant bedspread. And in the far distance the hills were faintly hazy though by mid-morning the haze would have lifted.

Emily's eyes filled with tears. It was all so heartbreakingly familiar. She loved her home and the surrounding country-side and never more than now when she would have to leave it for she knew not where. Scotland was a country of contrasts that never ceased to amaze. The Highlands had a harsh, brooding beauty whereas here in Perthshire the hills were softer and gentler. For a brief moment she forgot her troubles, the view from the window, especially in the early morning, always had the power to awe her. Then once again the present overwhelmed her, and shivering she closed the window.

After emptying the hot water into the basin, Emily pulled the nightdress over her head and let it fall to the floor. Her figure seemed the same, she saw no difference, but soon she would. Best not to think about it. Using the flannel cloth she gave herself a quick all-over wash then dried herself with the two fluffy towels to hand. Fresh undergarments were on the chair together with a skirt and high-necked blouse. The peacock blue skirt was old and if her mother had had her way it would have been removed from Emily's wardrobe. It had been a favourite and she had clung to it. Wearing something old and familiar might help her though she didn't know how. Sitting down in front of the dressing-table mirror, Emily tidied her hair and pinched her cheeks to bring some colour into them. Every moment was bringing the ordeal closer.

Shutting the bedroom door, Emily went downstairs and as she neared the breakfast room the smell of grilled bacon, usually so welcome, made her stomach heave. She had to stand still to fight the nausea. A maid passing by eyed her curiously then hurried away. Emily turned the door knob, put a smile on her face and went in.

Her parents were already seated at the table and looked to the door when she entered. Greetings were exchanged, her father's a mere grunt. First thing in the morning he was not at his best. In front of him was a plate of bacon, two sausages and scrambled eggs.

'Ring for more bacon, dear, if there isn't enough.'

'No, thank you, Mother, I don't want any. Toast will do.'

Her mother tut-tutted. 'That is not a proper breakfast for someone of your age.'

'Maud,' her husband said irritably, 'leave Emily alone, she isn't a child and she'll take what she wants.'

'I'm sure she will. I am merely concerned because just recently Emily has been picking at her food,' his wife said in an injured voice.

Emily remained silent and concentrated on putting a scraping of butter on her toast. She could feel her mother's gaze on her.

Maud was noticing the dark shadows under her daughter's eyes. The girl looked run-down, not a bit like herself and clearly in need of a tonic from Dr Young. Rather than have the good doctor come to the house they would see him in his surgery. Maud had great faith in the bottle of reddish liquid and just the look of it had the power to make her feel better. She didn't stop to consider why that should be.

Mrs Cunningham-Brown did not take a cooked breakfast herself. Toast was all she had. Picking up another finger of lightly toasted bread, she buttered it and added a little marmalade. Looking across the breakfast table at her husband's dour face, Maud would think of someone else sitting there. She didn't have any particular person in mind or maybe she did and kept it a secret. Life with Alfred had never been exciting but as her own mother had pointed out, it wasn't to be expected. Unexciting men made the best husbands and she was very fortunate to have Alfred. He was faithful, or as far as Maud knew he was. He provided a good home for his wife and family and all he asked in return was respect and obedience at all times. She really had nothing to complain about.

Maud's beauty was fading with the passing years but she

dressed well and was careful with her appearance. Alfred was proud of her and not in the least disturbed when admiring glances still came her way. Rather he was pleased. It was an endorsement of his own good taste and Maud had the good sense to know on which side her bread was buttered.

Maud liked to flirt, she liked to feel admiring eyes on her and her heart would flutter when she was in the company of a handsome man. Dr Benjamin Young came into that category. Maud was very fond of the middle-aged doctor with his thick greying hair, vivid blue eyes and his strong features. Unlike his brusque, outspoken predecessor, Dr Young had a charming manner and even the mildest complaint received his serious attention. Maud wasn't a hypochondriac, no one could accuse her of being that, but she was a great believer in having small health worries removed rather than go on imagining all kinds of dreadful diseases.

Maud had made up her mind. Emily would accompany her to the doctor's just to make sure there was nothing seriously wrong.

Directly after breakfast and as was their custom, Maud and Alfred got up from the table and went upstairs to the family sitting-room. Emily knew what would follow. Her father would get behind *The Times* and his wife would take a glance through the local paper until the post arrived. Quite a number of the letters were for Maud. She was a good correspondent. Emily seldom joined them but this morning she followed them upstairs. Her stomach was churning with fear and her mouth had gone dry.

She watched her father sink into his chair, the springs making a mild protesting clang at his weight. Her mother settled herself in the high-backed chair she favoured not for comfort but for the support it gave. Emily went over to sit on the sofa.

'What plans have you for today, dear?'

'I don't have any, Mother.'

'No?' Maud's eyebrows shot up. This was almost unheard of, the girl must be far from well, she thought worriedly.

Emily's nerves were strung so tightly that when she spoke her voice came out high-pitched.

'Please don't start reading your *Times*, Father,' Emily said desperately. 'I have something to tell you, something to tell you both.'

'Not now.'

'It has to be now, this is very important.'

'It had better be,' Alfred said frowning heavily and after folding the paper placed it at his feet. 'Very well, Emily, you have our attention and now we are waiting to hear what this is all about.'

Emily drew a deep, steadying breath. 'I'm pregnant, Father,' she whispered.

There was a terrible silent stillness in the room broken at last by the words forced out.

'What-did-you-say?'

Emily froze at the expression in his eyes.

'You can't be!' Maud shrieked.

'Be quiet,' her husband barked, 'I'll deal with this.'

'Are you pregnant?' His voice had gone dangerously quiet.

'Yes.'

'Are you absolutely sure?' Maud said brokenly as she twisted the handkerchief in her hands.

'Yes, Mother. I've been to see the doctor.'

'You've been to see Dr Young?' Maud said faintly.

'No, I went to another doctor, one in Perth.'

Maud breathed a sigh of relief that she had been spared that.

'And now, young woman, I want the name of the blackguard responsible.'

Emily shook her head.

'You'll tell me, my girl, or I'll shake it out of you.'

'Alfred, please,' his wife said fearfully, 'you must keep calm and threats won't achieve anything.'

'Keep calm, woman?' he roared. 'How can anyone keep calm in this situation? My daughter is no better than a street girl.'

Emily drew back in the sofa as though warding off a blow.

Maud was breathing heavily. 'I won't have you talking like that, Alfred. I'm just as shocked as you are but this is no way to go about it.' Turning to Emily her voice softened. 'You must tell us who he is, dear, you can't keep that from us.'

'I'm sorry, Mother, but I can't. All that I can say is that it is no one you know.'

'Which is as I thought, you have been seeing someone secretly.' Alfred turned on his wife. 'This wouldn't have happened if you'd kept an eye on your daughter instead of giving her so much freedom.'

'I'm to be blamed then?' She bit her lip and looked imploringly at Emily.

'I'm so sorry, Mother, so very, very sorry that I've hurt you and Father but I can't tell you.'

'Meaning he's cleared out?' Alfred said brutally.

She looked him in the face. 'He has gone that is true, but he knows nothing of this.'

'Then the sooner he does the better.'

'Emily, if you know where he is you must get word to him. He has a right to know.'

'I can't, I don't know where he is.'

Beads of perspiration were forming on Alfred's brow. 'We have our good name to think about and the boys, how are we going to explain this to them?'

'I'll go away, I'll do whatever you want.'

'Too true you will. You'll go away from here, nothing is surer than that. You aren't the first to bring shame on their family and sadly you won't be the last. There are places where your kind can go. Thank God we have the money and can pay to have you sent to one of them. I'll make discreet enquiries.'

Maud's face blanched. 'What do you mean, Alfred?'

'Obviously not what you are thinking. That would be criminal.'

Emily wondered what was criminal but was afraid to ask.

'She will be sent to stay with someone prepared to look after her until she has given birth. Don't look like that, Maud. Your daughter will be very well looked after. It will cost a great deal of money but will be worth every penny if we can keep this a secret.'

'I have my own money,' Emily said quietly.

'So you have and you may have need of it yet. The expenses for this I shall meet myself.' He was silent for a long time, *The Times* at his feet forgotten. At last he spoke. 'Explaining your absence is going to be a problem. Have either of you any suggestions?'

Emily shook her head.

'Maud?'

'Not unless a holiday, something like that,' she said nervously. 'I really don't know, Alfred. It is all so very difficult and people are very quick to draw their own conclusions.'

'In which case we must make sure that what we decide on rings true.' He looked thoughtful then nodded.

'You have an idea?'

'I think so. What is her name? Jenny's girl, what is her name?'

'Lily. Why? What about Lily?' Jenny was Maud's sister who lived with her husband Edward and their two of a family. They had their home in Inverness but there was very little contact since the menfolk didn't get on. Jenny and Maud exchanged letters and kept up-to-date with each other's affairs.

'Didn't you mention that Lily was to spend a year in Paris with a family?'

'I did, but I fail to see how that could help and it happens to be Lyons not Paris.'

'Makes no difference for what I have in mind.'

22

Maud frowned then her face brightened. 'You mean pretend that Emily is to accompany Lily? How clever of you, Alfred. No one would question that and the Inverness folk are not likely to hear about it.'

'You are the one who will have to be careful.'

'Oh, I shall, I'll be very careful what I write. It's going to be a strain but as I said I'll be careful.'

They were talking to each other as though they had forgotten she was there in the room with them. Emily felt it was time to mention her own money again.

'Since this is all my doing I don't want to be a financial burden and would much prefer to use some of the money Great-Aunt Anne left me.'

'I said no.' It had annoyed Alfred that his aunt had left her entire fortune to Emily though he knew he should be relieved it was kept in the family. It wouldn't have surprised him or anyone else if his very difficult and eccentric aunt had chosen to leave her money to a dogs' or cats' home. 'I'll make the necessary arrangements and pay for them and that way there will be no unfortunate slip-ups.' Money was the least of his worries.

'Mother?' Emily turned to Maud. 'You wouldn't object, would you, if I took Annie with me?'

'You can do without a maid.'

'No, she can't, Alfred. She will need someone though I would prefer if it wasn't Annie.'

'I don't want anyone else,' Emily said stubbornly.

'You are in no position to dictate,' her father said angrily.

'I am not dictating, Father, and this is between Mother and me.'

'It's all right,' Maud said hastily and anxious to avoid any more unpleasantness. 'Annie can go with you if she is agreeable and she may not be.'

'Giving in to her again,' Alfred said nastily.

'In this instance, yes, I am. Knowing there is someone with her I can trust will give me peace of mind.'

'I'm grateful.' She would say nothing about having already approached Annie.

'Mrs Martin will have to see about a replacement and how do I explain that? How do we keep this from the servants?' She put a hand to her brow.

'Good God!' Alfred exploded. 'Here we are in the middle of a family crisis of the worst kind and you are worrying about the servants. They don't matter. No doubt they will gossip among themselves but if they value their job they will make sure it goes no further. As for you, young woman, you disgust me and the less I see of you the better.'

Emily dropped her eyes. Once he had loved her and been proud of his daughter and now all he felt for her was contempt. Fleetingly she had seen something else in his eyes — pain and bewilderment — and that hurt more than anything he had said.

'Your daughter—'

'She happens to be yours as well.'

'More's the pity. See to it that she confines herself to the house and garden. She will dine with us but at no time is she to address me. Do I make myself clear?'

'Perfectly clear,' his wife answered.

As he reached for his paper mother and daughter left the room.

'I need some fresh air,' Emily muttered desperate to make her escape.

'So do I. I'll get my cloak and join you.'

In the garden they strolled around admiring the display of spring flowers as though nothing untoward had happened. Behind the sun it was chilly and Emily shivered.

'You should have brought a cloak,' Maud said wrapping her own around herself.

'I'm not cold.'

'You can't take risks with your health, dear, you must look after yourself,' Maud said kindly.

'You don't have to be kind.'

'I'm your mother,' Maud said gently and with a faint smile.

It was too much for Emily and the tears overflowed. 'Don't you hate me? You should.'

'I could never do that. You have been a very silly girl, not wicked just silly. I'm disappointed and shocked of course I am, but it has happened and life for all of us must go on.'

'Father will never forgive me.'

'No, I don't expect he will. And you are not helping yourself by refusing to name the person responsible. Surely you have some idea of how to get in touch?'

'I don't, honestly I don't.'

'How did you meet him?'

'We just met.'

'Are you ashamed of him?'

'No, of course I am not.'

Maud's voice softened. 'Love is a very strong emotion and sometimes it is difficult to – to hold back. You just didn't think of the consequences. The man doesn't suffer, he ruins your life but he gets away with it and you stupid, stupid girl that you are, won't say a word against him.'

'He was completely honest, Mother, marriage was not a possibility for him.'

'Because he was already promised or perhaps he had a wife.'

'No,' she almost screamed. 'You just don't understand.'

'Why shouldn't I understand?'

'Because you just wouldn't.'

'Meaning I've never been in love?'

'Not at all, it was simple for you. You and Father fell in love and got married.'

Maud was silent.

'There was someone else once upon a time,' Emily said softly.

'This is between us?'

'Of course.' She paused. 'Father wasn't the love of your life was he?'

'He is and has been for a long time. He is a good man,

annoying, pig-headed and impossible, but a good man for all that.' They were both laughing.

'Tell me, please, I would like to know.'

'Not a lot to tell. Like so many, yourself included, I fell in love with someone totally unsuitable. He was handsome, charming and penniless and I do believe I might have run away with him if he had made that suggestion. Young girls can be so impossibly romantic.'

'Don't stop there.'

Maud gave a sad smile. 'My parents, your grandparents, were comfortably off but far from being wealthy. I like to think he loved me and I do believe he did. Only the money I'm afraid was a bigger attraction. When my father made it clear that he wouldn't see a penny of it his ardour cooled.'

'Were you terribly miserable?'

'Broken-hearted and humiliated.'

'Then Father came along?'

'Yes, your father came along. He loves me and I think I have been a good wife.'

'No regrets?'

'None. Just memories and they don't harm anyone.'

'Money had nothing to do with mine. He wasn't interested in money.'

'You can't be sure of that.'

'Mother, I am very sure. If it had been for my money he would have married me.'

'I don't know what to think. But one thing I ask of you and it is for your own sake. Don't antagonise your father, try to understand his feelings and do what he asks without question.'

'I'll try.'

'When is the birth?'

'The beginning of October. The doctor said the fifth but to give or take a week either way.'

'You are taking this very calmly I must say.'

'I'm not. You couldn't be more wrong. I'm desperately sorry this has happened and I'm scared too.'

'No need to be scared. To give your father his due he will

make sure that you are in safe hands.' As she said it and sounded reassuring Maud thought back to her own experiences. Childbirth hadn't come easy and the first, Emily's birth, had been very difficult. At the time she had vowed she would never go through it again. Fortunately she'd had an easier time with the other two. They had reached the bottom of the garden and started to retrace their steps.

'I deserve to suffer after what I am putting you and Father through.'

'Too late for regrets.'

'I'm expecting a baby yet it doesn't seem real.'

'It'll be real enough when it comes but apart from giving birth, you will have nothing to do with the baby.'

'Of course I will. It is my baby and you should care it will be your first grandchild.'

Maud winced. 'That was cruel and unnecessary.'

'I'm sorry.'

'Let me carry on with what I was saying. As soon as the child is born it will be removed. A good home will already have been found. The woman may be unable to have a child of her own and be deeply grateful to you.'

'What if I want to keep my own baby?'

'Out of the question.' She paused. 'Before we go indoors I'll try and prepare you for what lies ahead.'

Emily's heart lurched. Her mother was taking her departure very calmly and making her feel like an outcast.

'Some women in exchange for money will open their house to an unmarried mother-to-be.'

'A sort of guest house?'

'Hardly that. You may be the only one and then again you may not. There will be a midwife living nearby who will be called on to attend when your time comes.'

'You'll come, won't you?'

'Your father wouldn't allow it.'

'It's a good thing I *am* going to have Annie then, isn't it?'

'Don't be too sure about that, you can't force the girl into a situation she doesn't want.'

Chapter Three

'You wanted to see me, Miss Emily?'

'Yes, Annie, I do.' Emily's voice cracked and she burst into tears.

Annie went in, closed the door and looked with concern at her employer's daughter. She longed to give comfort but knew it wasn't her place. Instead she remained standing where she was until the storm of weeping had ceased. It ended with a few unladylike sniffs and a dab at her eyes with the lace-edged handkerchief taken from the cuff of her blouse. A moment or two later Emily looked up shame-faced and gave a half smile.

'How dreadful of me to break down like that. I *am* sorry.'

'No need to be Miss Emily, there's time we all feel like that.'

'Even you, Annie?'

'Even me.' Annie wondered why she should be different. Wasn't she allowed feelings like everyone else?

'You always strike me as being someone who would just face what had to be faced without making a fuss.'

'I suppose I am, I haven't much choice but it doesn't mean it is any easier for me and,' she smiled, 'I'm one of those who thinks a good greet does folk a lot of good.'

'It won't do me any good I'm afraid. But don't stand there, bring over one of the chairs.' Emily swallowed and blinked away the tears threatening to spill.

Annie did as she was told and sat down with her hands folded in her lap.

'I hope I can trust you, Annie.'

'I hope so too, Miss Emily.'

'You can't but know there is something wrong?' Emily had been locking and unlocking her fingers. 'I'm going to have a baby, Annie.'

Annie looked at the lovely tragic face but kept her own expressionless.

'Well, aren't you going to answer? Or didn't you hear what I said?'

'You are going to have a baby, Miss Emily.'

'You did hear. I must say you don't appear to be surprised.' She paused and her eyes narrowed. 'Could it be that you already knew, that you perhaps overheard?'

No one was going to get away with saying that to her, not even Miss Emily. Annie's head went up and her eyes glittered angrily. 'I have never eavesdropped in my life,' she said indignantly.

Emily was quick with her apology. 'No, of course not, I didn't mean to suggest that.' Goodness, she hadn't expected Annie, a mere maid, to be so prickly. Even if she had been guilty of listening at doors, it wouldn't have been necessary. Her father had a booming voice, made louder if he was angry or upset and he had been both. 'Do tell me though why my – my news didn't come as a surprise or should I say shock?'

'You want to know, Miss Emily, well it was simple really. First you saying you were going away but you didn't know where and then you looking so pale and worried and—' Annie stopped.

'And what? Go on.'

'You with a good healthy appetite and not eating a cooked breakfast.'

Emily smiled weakly. 'Nothing much misses you. You are observant, Annie.'

'No more than anyone else, Miss Emily.'

Meaning – she must mean there had been talk in the kitchen. The possibility that there might have been shocked Emily. Though why that should be so she didn't know. It was a well-known fact that the servants were the first to know what was going on.

'My parents are in a dreadful state.'

Annie nodded. It was only to be expected. The maid did have some sympathy for the master and mistress. They were good employers and their much loved daughter getting herself into trouble must be very distressing. Strange too that in the circumstances there wasn't to be a rushed marriage. Whoever was responsible must be totally unsuitable. Annie recalled the young men who had, until recently, come about the house. They came from well-respected families all socially eligible and were welcomed by Mr and Mrs Cunningham-Brown. That could only mean that Miss Emily had been meeting someone secretly. The poor lass must have fallen for some good-for-nothing which just showed that when it came to love the rich could be taken in just like anyone else. Annie wondered if the mistress had ever warned her daughter of the dangers and thought not. She had a quiet smile to herself when she thought about Mrs Martin. The cook took a motherly interest in her girls and frequently warned them of the wicked ways of some men. It would be a foolish lass, she said, looking from one to the other who believed promises from the smooth-tongued and gave themselves before the all important ring was on the third finger of the left hand.

Annie had giggled along with the others but the laughter was not cruel. They all liked the woman and none of them believed Mrs Martin had been married. Cooks, for unexplained reasons, used the prefix Mrs before their name whether or not they had the right to do so.

Annie listened but didn't need the lecture. She was a girl who could look after herself. Being brought up in a hard school had seen to that and it would have been a brave lad who tried anything on with her. In a test of strength she wouldn't have stood a chance but the wee pepper-pot she carried in her coat pocket gave her all the protection she needed. Painful, cruel even, but you had to fight with the weapons to hand was how she excused herself. Thankfully it had never come to that, but she was prepared.

'In time I'm sure my mother will forgive me. Not my father though, he won't even speak to me if it can be avoided,' Emily said sadly.

Annie made no reply, she didn't think one was expected. Most likely Miss Emily was just talking to herself.

'It's so awful,' she continued, 'to have to leave my own home and it would have been alone if I hadn't insisted on you accompanying me.' Emily looked up with anxious eyes, 'You haven't changed your mind, have you?'

'I didn't promise anything, Miss Emily, but it is all right with me if the mistress will let me go.'

'She will. My mother is more than agreeable.'

'Then that's fine, Miss Emily.'

'Good! Mrs Martin will have to be told to find a replacement for you. Just a temporary one,' she said hastily.

Poor lass, Annie thought, it would seem her parents were less concerned about their daughter than the threat to the family's good name. Made you think really.

'Will that be all, Miss Emily?'

'No, you can't go yet.' She shook her head slowly. 'Annie, I can't feel this is really happening to me, it is like a bad dream. Fancy me telling you all my troubles, I mean you are just a maid but I do feel you understand and heaven knows I can't confide in any of my friends. Probably shun me if they were to find out,' she said sourly.

'Surely not.'

'Most definitely yes. What is the expression? Fallen woman isn't it? My father didn't call me that but something similar.'

'Don't, Miss Emily, don't torture yourself and that is all you are doing.'

'I know and I can't help it.' She gave a deep sigh. 'My

father is arranging everything. He is very good at arranging and he thinks he has come up with a plausible reason for my absence. Want to hear it?'

'If you want to tell me.'

'Might as well. The story will be circulating shortly. My mother thinks it is brilliant but then she always thinks that of my father's ideas.'

'Do you think it is brilliant?'

'I suppose so. Mother and I couldn't think of anything better. My cousin is going to France to stay with a French family for a year and that is where I am supposed to be going. To keep her company.'

'Why France?' Annie asked, curious to know why it should be so far away and for a whole year. Fancy her sitting here and asking Miss Emily questions and her not minding one little bit.

'I'm just supposed to be going there. My clever cousin is anxious to improve her French and living with a French family is the best way to do that.'

'It's not going to improve yours though, is it?' Annie couldn't resist saying.

Emily threw her head back and laughed. 'Good for you, Annie. Maybe I'll have to get out my old school books. That's a thought. How on earth are we going to occupy ourselves?'

Annie wondered what her duties would be but had no doubt that she would be fully occupied. 'We'll find something,' she said cheerfully.

'Do you like reading, Annie?'

'Never had much time for it.'

'Then here is your chance. I'll take you in hand, Annie, that will give me something to do. I'm not being insulting but I don't imagine you've had much education.'

That annoyed Annie. Of course she hadn't had much of an education but she'd made the best of what she had been given.

'I'm not totally ignorant,' she said huffily.

'No one suggested you were. You are far too sensitive for your own good, Annie. Had I thought you ignorant we would not be talking like this.'

'I'm sorry.'

'And so you should be. Here I am wanting to help because I feel I owe it to you. It won't be school as you knew it. Rather I will give you books to read that will improve your mind and at the same time give you enjoyment.'

Annie nodded. Not many books came her way and if this was a way to improve herself she should take it.

'I seem unable to concentrate.' Emily closed her eyes for a moment. 'My mind keeps leap-frogging and you have to know what is to happen. Not that I know very much myself but we'll talk about – about the baby.' She paused and moistened her lips. 'It won't be real to me.'

'Not yet but it will,' Annie said gently.

'No, Annie, you are quite wrong. There will be no chance to form a bond and that is just as well. I shan't know it at all. My mother prepared me for what will happen. Immediately after the birth the baby will be taken away and I won't see it.'

Annie gave a gasp.

'It is for the best. The midwife or someone like that will look after it until the adoptive parents take charge. I just have to get myself well and return home.' She smiled ruefully. 'My Great-Aunt Anne, she's dead now, and strict though she was, I think I would have confided in her before anyone else. After it was over she would have said, and I can hear her saying it, "Well, my dear Emily, here you are a little older and a great deal wiser. You've been silly, paid the price, and now you must put it all to the back of your mind and get on with your life."'

'What about the baby?'

'What about it? Annie, don't you listen? It will be adopted, of course.'

Annie felt the stirrings of anger. 'Won't you mind?'

'I don't think so. I honestly don't think it will bother me

33

too much. When I give birth it will be like getting rid of a burden and don't look like that,' she said angrily, 'I am just being sensible. How can I love something I won't see? I'm not uncaring and neither is my father. He will pay whatever is necessary to see that the baby goes to a good home. Probably to a couple who cannot have a child of their own.'

Annie pursed her lips. It was all so neat and tidy. Like a parcel carefully wrapped up and sent off to its destination. Couldn't Miss Emily see how wrong it was? That tiny life would grow into a human being deserving of a mother's love. And that mother, in this case Miss Emily, would recover and put the whole sorry business behind her. It was so wrong. Annie felt a sour taste in her mouth.

The raw hurt of herself being an abandoned baby made it all the harder for Annie to accept Miss Emily's callous attitude to her unborn child. The baby might well go to a good home, be loved and want for nothing but there was no guarantee. Nothing in this world was certain. How, she wondered, had it been for her own mother? Had it been painful parting with her baby or just a relief? Poverty might have played its part. She would never know. Like all abandoned children she had dreamed of a reunion. Had wanted to believe that there had been no other way and when fortune smiled on her parents they would come back to claim her. Annie was ten when she stopped dreaming.

She wasn't the only foundling to be left on the doorstep of the orphanage. Some left a pathetic little note with the child's name pinned to its clothing and a request that it be treated kindly. At least, Annie thought bitterly, they had an identity. She didn't even have that. The note, if it had ever existed, had been lost. An unwanted baby without a name or an exact date of birth. The matron, a hard-faced woman, who could occasionally be kind, had suggested Annie for a Christian name and someone else had come up with the name Fullerton. She had become Annie Fullerton and the orphanage was to be her home until she started work in Denbrae House.

34

'Don't you approve of adoption?'

'That depends.'

'Depends on what?'

'Whether whoever gets it will be good to the child.'

'Don't be silly, Annie, of course they will. People don't adopt babies unless they want them.'

'Circumstances change,' Annie said stubbornly.

Emily's face softened. 'I'm sorry, you are thinking of yourself. But it won't be like that, Annie. You weren't adopted and what happened to you couldn't happen to my baby.'

'You can't know that. How do you know what happened to me?'

'I don't, how could I? Probably your mother was very poor and maybe she already had children and didn't want any more.'

Annie winced. It was very likely the truth but she didn't want it put in words. 'Money makes everything all right, does it?'

'It certainly helps,' Emily said coldly. 'You are just trying to upset me and don't you think I have enough to worry about without you trying to make things worse.'

'I wasn't but I'm sorry if you think I was.' Annie knew she had gone too far. 'I had no right to say what I did.'

'No, you didn't. However, we'll say no more about it. Perhaps you had better return to your duties,' she said stiffly.

Annie got up and hurried away. Perhaps after all that, Miss Emily might have second thoughts and get someone else to accompany her to wherever she was being sent.

Emily hadn't changed her mind, far from it. Better to have someone who didn't agree with her all the time and who was dependable. In any case there was no one else.

One monotonous day followed another. The morning sickness was less troublesome now and Emily was eating better. Occasionally there were shopping trips with her mother but never to the shops where they were known.

Maud was looking ahead to a time when Emily's clothes would no longer fit her. They bought loose-fitting gowns and skirts that could be altered at the waistband. Emily had been proud of her small waist and she hated the clothes she would be forced to wear in the later stages of her pregnancy.

Unless she was accompanied by her mother, Emily wasn't allowed out other than into the garden. Maud was careful to keep as much as possible to her usual routine. She visited friends and attended the occasional meeting but no invitations came from Denbrae House. The excuse given was that Emily was suffering from a very bad cold and had to get herself well before going off with her cousin Lily to spend a year in France. Such a thrill for a young girl. Maud said it all smilingly, adding that she thought she might be coming down with the cold herself. The ladies fully understood and kept their distance.

Breakfast was over and Emily was about to make her escape. Her father's cold, disapproving face made her want to spend as little time as possible in his company.

'No,' he said sharply, when she made to excuse herself. 'You will come upstairs to the sitting-room.'

'Yes, Father,' she said meekly and sat down again. He went ahead and Emily waited for her mother who seemed to be deliberately prolonging her stay at the breakfast table.

'Emily, do whatever your father asks and show a willingness.'

'A willingness to do what? I'd have to know what it is first.'

Maud's face flushed angrily. 'There are times when I wonder if you have ever given thought to the position you have put us in. The strain on me is terrible. It is like acting a lie and I don't find that easy.'

'What more can I say except that I am sorry?'

'It isn't enough. We ought to know this man's identity.'

'No.'

'It is a pity that we can't force it out of you but since we

36

cannot, at least show some humility. Your father is a proud man and he is finding it repugnant to make these arrangements for you.'

'I know and I really am very, very sorry.'

'Come along then, he'll be wondering what is delaying us.'

Emily's head was beginning to ache. If only her mother would stop going on and on and repeating herself. There were times, she thought, when it was worse than her father's silence.

Alfred Cunningham-Brown dropped his newspaper to the floor when they entered and waited until they were both seated before speaking.

'This is to do with the arrangements—'

'Was it very difficult?' his wife said timidly.

'Humiliating would be how I would describe it.' He cleared his throat. 'You will be comfortable, Emily, but it won't be a bed of roses, but then you could hardly expect it to be.'

'Where am I being sent, Father?' Emily said quietly. She looked demure with her hands in her lap and Maud nodded approvingly. Perhaps she looked and sounded composed but her hands told another story. They were clasped tightly and the knuckles showed white.

'Dundrinnen.'

'Where might that be, Alfred?'

'In the north-east. From what I gather it is a village some miles from Stonehaven.'

'Isn't that near Aberdeen?'

'Not very far away.'

Maud turned to her daughter. 'Aberdeen is a lovely city,' she smiled as though Emily was going off on holiday. 'Your father and I were there, oh it is a few years ago, but I do remember the shops. Your aunt and I met up and we spent most of our time in Union Street. Do you remember, Alfred, how—'

'Stop your twittering, Maud, Emily won't be anywhere

near Aberdeen and I don't imagine she will be doing much shopping.'

'She isn't going to be a prisoner is she?' Maud said tartly. She didn't often talk back to her husband, just when he was being impossible like now.

'She will not be a prisoner and neither will she stray – she appears to have done that already,' he said sarcastically.

'Unnecessary.'

'Quite. She will be looked after.'

'Of course she will be looked after. Isn't that what you are paying for?'

'Paying sweetly for that, my dear.'

'I had hoped, indeed expected, you would have found some place nearer for Emily but since you haven't I shall have to make it an overnight stay.'

'Overnight stay? What are you talking about, woman?'

'Surely I can visit my daughter to satisfy myself that she is well and getting proper care.'

'There will be no visiting, Maud, I thought that much would have been clear even to you.'

Emily looked at them both. They did have the occasional disagreement but she had never seen them like this.

'Mother, it is all right,' she said gently.

Maud ignored her and looked at her husband. Her face had an ugly flush. 'That remark of yours was uncalled for. I am not a fool and I accept that one would have to go about it discreetly.'

'I'm sorry, dear, we shouldn't be quarrelling but I must make it absolutely clear to you that visiting Emily is completely out of the question. Emily has got herself into this mess and she must just make the best of things.'

'Which I am prepared to do.'

'I'm glad to hear it and now if you would both let me continue. Dundrinnen, I am told, is off the beaten track—'

'Primitive,' Maud said aghast.

'Not in the least primitive, just off the beaten track as I said. The house is well furnished and comfortable and there is a large garden to the back and very secluded. The woman who owns it is a Mrs Beatrice McIntyre, a widow with nursing experience. She did, however, make it very clear to my contact that she is not prepared to put up a maid.'

'Then I don't go.'

'You, my girl, will do as you are told if you know what is good for you.'

'I will not,' Emily said loudly and firmly. 'Unless Annie is to accompany me I make my own arrangements.'

'You wouldn't know where to begin or how to go about it,' he sneered.

'Then I'll have to learn.'

Maud, the peacemaker spoke gently but with a pleading note. 'Perhaps if we gave more thought to it we might find a solution.'

'Oh, I have a solution but I fancy Emily won't find it to her liking.'

'Let me hear it, Father, then I'll decide.'

'Very well. This woman, this Mrs McIntyre also owns a cottage close by which is furnished and let out to summer visitors or others in need of a longer let. Going there would mean you would have to look after yourself.'

'Not with Annie there, she will look after me. Yes, Father, the cottage,' she smiled.

'Don't be too impetuous, dear, it might be quite impossible.'

'If I'm in the cottage will this woman still look after me? I mean when I have need of her services.'

'Yes,' her father said tersely.

Maud was looking alarmed. 'Don't be too hasty, Emily, the cottage may be damp and I think I have a better idea. How would it be for you to stay in the house and Annie in the cottage?'

'Out of the question and an unnecessary extravagance. I am prepared to pay the maid her wages since she is entitled to them but I am most certainly not forking out money to have her stay in the cottage.'

'We will both live in the cottage, Father, I have made up my mind.'

'Very well,' he said heavily, 'just remember it was your decision.'

'If it fails to please me I have the money to improve it or look for accommodation elsewhere.'

'That might not be so easily come by.'

'Money talks, it is something you are always saying yourself.'

She would use her own money and willingly. In fact she would see to withdrawing a sizeable sum. Better to be prepared.

'Your Great-Aunt Anne did you no favours leaving you that money.'

'On the contrary, Father, her generosity to me means I can take care of myself.'

'Which quite clearly you have not managed to do.'

Emily chose to ignore that. 'She wanted me to have the means to be independent and I shall always be grateful to her.' Emily's eyes grew moist. 'I loved her very much and she knew that. The others only pretended and she knew that too.'

Maud's face had taken on its familiar worried look. 'If this village is at the back of beyond, will there be a doctor in case of complications? Not that that is likely,' she said hastily. 'You are a healthy girl, Emily, it is just it would give me peace of mind to know a doctor was nearby if required. As for this Mrs McIntyre, what do we know about her? Nursing experience could mean anything.'

'Maud, don't go looking for trouble. God knows we have enough of it. There is a doctor in Dundrinnen and a midwife who lives locally and as for the woman McIntyre she may or she may not have written qualifications but she does have a great deal of experience.'

Maud nodded unhappily.

Emily wasn't as brave as she was pretending to be. The mention of complications had unnerved her. It must be a possibility or why bring it up. No, she was not going to be worried. Thousands and thousands of women from all over the world brought children into it. Why should it be any different for her? She knew next to nothing of what to expect and her mother hadn't been any help.

'The midwife will tell you all you need to know.'

Emily imagined it to be a few hours' discomfort before the baby put in its appearance and then a few weeks for her to regain her strength.

Even so she gave a shiver. Everything didn't always go as planned.

'When do I leave for Dundrinnen?' Emily said in a small voice.

'You leave a week on Friday, the arrangements are in hand and only have to be confirmed. Your trunk will be sent in advance so you will have to see to that right away.'

'Won't you both come and see me even once?'

Her father's face softened and there was real regret in his voice. 'No, my dear, it is better that we don't. You are supposed to be in France, remember?'

Emily couldn't see what difference that made.

'What will you tell Michael and Robert?'

'That you are with Lily.'

'They would expect a postcard or something.'

'I'll deal with their questions but I don't foresee any problems with those two. Too busy with their own pursuits.'

Emily didn't see any problems either. Even when her brothers were home from school she didn't see much of them.

'Shall I write and tell you how I am getting on?'

'No. No correspondence at all. I shall hear if there is anything to report.'

She swallowed painfully. She was beginning to feel like an outcast.

'Alfred, what harm can a letter do?'

'We can't risk it,' he said shortly. 'Emily,' he turned to his daughter. 'This is the best part of a year out of your life, think of it that way. Take great care of yourself, live quietly—'

Emily suppressed her laughter. Live quietly, how else could she live stuck in the back of beyond.

'You look amused,' he said, 'and for the life of me I can't think what could be amusing.'

Maud collapsed in tears and sobbed into her handkerchief.

Alfred Cunningham-Brown got to his feet, picked up his newspaper from the floor, glanced at his wife, shook his head and left the room.

It was left to Emily to comfort her mother the best she could.

Chapter Four

The evening before her departure for Dundrinnen Emily's father said goodbye to his daughter. He had come into the room where Maud was busy with her embroidery and Emily pretending to read a book. Going over to the fire he stood stiffly with his back to it.

He cleared his throat. 'Tomorrow morning will see you on your way.'

'Yes, Father.' Emily raised her eyes and looked at the man who had turned into a stranger.

'Take care of yourself,' he said gruffly, 'and once this unfortunate business is over you will be welcome to return home.' He paused and cleared his throat again. 'I do not intend seeing you again before you go, I think it better that way, so this is goodbye.' He made no attempt to kiss her, nor did he touch her. She hadn't really expected he would, only there had been a tiny hope in her heart that he might. Still she supposed she should be grateful that he had at least said she would be welcome to come back. She wondered when that would be. If she was supposed to be with her cousin in France then she could be away for the best part of a year. Or would there be another fabricated story that she had cut short her stay for some reason or other? Once on that slippery slope it was one lie after another until the whole thing became a nightmare. Her poor mother would get herself tied in knots.

'Thank you, Father,' she said quietly.

He nodded, opened his mouth as if to say something, changed his mind, and left the room. With the closing of the door mother and daughter looked at each other.

'You heard your father, Emily. You will be welcome to come home when all this is over and in time it will be forgotten.'

'Don't be stupid, Mother, it will never be forgotten. I won't be allowed to forget.'

'It won't be like that, I'm sure it won't. Time is a great healer and if you—'

'If I what?' Wariness had crept into her voice.

Maud closed her eyes tightly and prayed for control. The girl was impossible and she had to fight a desire to shake her. Maud would have welcomed floods of tears and implorings for forgiveness. After all didn't she have a mother's loving heart and it would have gone out to her child. Admittedly there had been some tears and regret shown for the trouble she had brought on the family. Who was the stupid girl protecting and why? Maud's brow puckered in perplexity. She had asked herself a thousand times and was no nearer an answer. What angered her most was Emily's composure and the total absence of shame.

Maud was wrong, she should have known her daughter better. Emily was very far from being composed and a keen observer would have seen by her strained expression that she was dangerously close to breaking-point. It was agonising for her to realise that Jonathan's face, once so dear and familiar, was beginning to fade. He had warned her it would be this way but she hadn't believed him, hadn't thought it possible. How could it be? How could love, and she had been desperately in love, fade away and be lost? A tear fell down her cheek followed by another and she brushed them away with the tip of her finger. She didn't want her mother to see.

Emily blamed herself. She had been at fault, brought this on herself. Jonathan hadn't encouraged her, not once. He had been honest telling her straight out that she should stay away from the cottage. There was no future for her with him, he wasn't the settling down type. He was an artist he told her and his work would always come first. He had to be free to go where he pleased and a wife had no place in his life.

'No woman in your life,' she had said lightly and not believing him. 'Is that the way your life is going to be, Jonathan?'

He had thrown back his head and given that deep-throated laugh that she loved to hear. 'I didn't say that, little one. I said no wife.'

That had dismayed Emily for a moment or two then she decided that Jonathan was just being protective. He always called her 'little one' as though she were still a child. Well, she wasn't a child, she was a warm-hearted young woman and an attractive one at that. Everyone told her that she was lovely and though not conceited, Emily was well aware of her charms. Perhaps it was time she used them more provocatively on Jonathan. A mischievous smile played around her mouth.

Emily had flirted before but never seriously, just girl and boy nonsense. The difference was that Jonathan wasn't a boy. He hadn't told her his age but she thought him to be in his late twenties or early thirties. He was tall and broad-shouldered with thick jet black hair worn longer than fashion dictated. He had the bluest eyes Emily had ever seen. His clothes were good but shabby and he looked well in them. There was an elegant carelessness about him that marked him as a man who cared nothing for appearance or for what anyone thought of him. For Emily the twinkle in his startlingly blue eyes had been the initial attraction.

That first kiss had been no more than the brushing of lips and immediately after it Jonathan had put her firmly from him. She hadn't heeded the warning, how could she when she was completely and gloriously in love and the hours without Jonathan were just empty hours to be got through.

Any time she could get away from home and her mother
would see Emily flying across the fields that separated the
farm from Denbrae House. Farmer Briggs was careless
about the dry-stone wall and much of it was in a state of
disrepair. Emily had no difficulty finding her way to the
cottage Jonathan had rented from the farmer. Sometimes the
door would be wide open and she would go in tremulous
and excited, calling his name and at times getting no
response. On these occasions he would be nearby sketching
or painting. Interruptions, she was to find out, made his face
darken with annoyance. He needed silence to work, he told
her and Emily, obsessed with this man, was content to sit
near him, keeping quiet and happy just to be there.

The cottage was damp and sparsely furnished with no
home comforts but Emily barely noticed. As long as
Jonathan was there it was a little bit of heaven.

'Do you love me, Jonathan?' she whispered as they sat on
an old sofa that sagged with their weight.

'Perhaps I do, little one.'

A lovely flush deepened her skin. 'I love you, Jonathan,
and no perhaps about it.' She saw no reason to act coy. She
loved him and she wanted him to know it.

In spite of finding her a trial at times and a bit of a
nuisance, he was amused and touched. 'You mustn't,' he said
gently, 'I'll soon be off on my travels. You knew the way it
would be, I told you.'

'You can't go off, not yet, you haven't finished the work
you intended doing,' Emily said desperately. She would die
if he went away.

'Nevertheless I'll be on my way very shortly.' He got up.
'You, my dearest one, are a distraction I can do without.'

She was on her feet her eyes bright with unshed tears. 'I
can't do without you, Jonathan,' Emily said brokenly.

Seeing her standing there looking lovely and tragic,
Jonathan was torn between shaking her or taking her in
his arms. He did neither; instead he spoke severely.

'Don't be silly, of course you can do without me. In a few

months you won't remember what I look like. Emily, this has been nice, nice for both of us. You are sweet, and you are also a very pretty girl.' And one he thought who has been thoroughly spoilt and denied nothing in her whole life.

'Don't treat me like a child, Jonathan.'

'That is what you are to me and it is time you went home before you are missed.'

'I don't care if I am missed.'

'Yes, you do. You don't want to upset your parents and it would more than upset them if they knew what you were up to. Emily you are a little minx.'

She grinned. That was better, she didn't mind being called that. Her eyes were laughing and he kissed her upturned face. It was to be a goodbye kiss and one to hurry her on her way. Only it didn't. Suddenly she was clinging to him and burning with a longing she didn't understand. Vaguely at the back of her mind was the danger of losing control and with it the certain knowledge that she couldn't help herself. She was drowning in a sea of longing.

It would take a strong man to resist that soft and so willing body and Jonathan found he couldn't.

Appalled at what she had allowed to happen but trembling with happiness, Emily tidied her clothes and tried to dim her shining eyes. Neither of them spoke but words were not necessary. Jonathan loved her, she knew he did. Nothing else mattered. He wouldn't think of her as a child now, not after what had happened. Even so she was nervous. Somehow she had to get herself home and act as though nothing had taken place. How that could be managed with her heart doing somersaults she just didn't know. Poor Jonathan, the darling man looked dazed but that was what love did.

Blowing him a kiss she left the cottage and felt she had wings on her feet. Her heart was singing as she raced home. Life was wonderful, Jonathan loved her. And one day soon they would be together for always. He had described for her his nomadic life and the novelty, romance and freedom of it appealed to her. Wherever Jonathan's travels took him she would be there by his side. As for her parents they couldn't fail to love Jonathan and give their blessing. For a moment she felt a flicker of doubt; it was, she knew, far from what they had in mind for their only daughter. Then she dismissed it, this was her life and with or without their approval she would go with her beloved.

Next day it had been impossible to get away to the cottage. Emily had begged and fumed to be let off but Maud was adamant. The invitation was for both of them to attend a fashion show with the proceeds going to one of Maud's charities. It would be the height of bad manners not to turn up and hadn't she always been interested in the latest fashions? What was wrong with her, Maud wanted to know. In the end Emily smiled her way through the display and the tea that followed, and resigned herself to waiting another day to see Jonathan.

Next morning and in a fever of impatience she waited until her mother was occupied with Mrs Martin concerning the menus for the following week. Maud invariably agreed with what was suggested but as mistress of the house she had to be consulted.

Even before she reached the cottage, Emily thought it had the appearance of a deserted house. Her heart hammered wildly and she flew the last few yards. Everything was still and quiet. Deathly still. The door was locked, the cottage deserted. To make absolutely sure she looked in the window and saw the unnatural tidiness. There was none of Jonathan's clutter. He had gone and he wouldn't be coming back. Emily knew that with certainty. Her joy drained away and with a sob she turned to retrace her steps.

The pain gripped her unbearably, the awful emptiness her constant companion. Honest with herself as always, Emily knew she was to blame. Thinking back she burned with shame. How could she have acted the way she did? Jonathan had not been at fault, she had thrown herself at him. Worse she had chased him away. He could have stayed but he hadn't wanted to. In the weeks that followed Emily slowly began to recover. She saw it now as a painful experience and one that filled her with shame. It had taught her a lesson. Never again would she be so foolish as to throw herself at a man.

When did the terror take over? For two months she had refused to believe that anything was wrong. Then in desperation she had asked one of her friends for a loan of a book. It was a slim volume bought by the girl's mother to explain what lay ahead for her daughter and save her the embarrassment of having to explain the facts herself. Emily had read every word of it in the privacy of her bedroom and what she read had her trembling with fear and horror. Telling lies about being with a friend, she had a consultation with a Perth doctor and he had confirmed what she dreaded. She was pregnant.

Alfred Cunningham-Brown made sure that he was away from the house before the carriage took Emily and her maid to the station. Maud was to see them off but at the last minute she went to pieces and had to make her tearful farewell in the hallway. Annie had said her goodbye to Mrs Martin and the others. There had been some awkwardness since it hadn't been made clear why Annie was accompanying Miss Emily when that young lady was going to France with her cousin. It was all very confusing but it did give them something to gossip about. The cook, who knew the true situation and had been sworn to secrecy, told her staff only what she thought they required to hear. No one believed Miss Emily was going to France. They weren't daft and had worked out the real reason for her departure from Denbrae House.

A trunk and a large leather suitcase containing Emily's clothes, shoes, books and other items had gone ahead and should have reached Dundrinnen. No one had thought to send Annie's belongings with them. Mrs Martin, upset at losing Annie and anxious to be helpful, had unearthed an old battered case. Into this went Annie's entire wardrobe including a pair of heavy boots. They didn't fill the case but it was heavy to lift since the case itself was quite a weight. Not too sure that the catches would hold, she wound a strong piece of cord round the suitcase. Taking it on herself, Mrs Martin prepared a basket of food which if not required on the journey could be eaten at a later time.

Emily was determined to be calm and she was. Her mother wasn't, she was distraught, her face ugly with weeping.

'Emily! Emily! oh my darling child this is so dreadful,' she sobbed, 'I can't bear it, I just can't.'

'Don't, Mother, please. You mustn't upset yourself,' Emily said unsteadily. They clung together, then Emily eased herself away.

'How can I help it? Nothing will ever be the same again and we were such a happy family,' Maud wailed.

'You are still a happy family without me.' Emily was very thankful that her mother wasn't going to the station. It would have been just too awful if she had made an exhibition of herself in front of the other passengers.

Maud shook her head sadly and Emily swallowed the lump in her throat. 'I'm so sorry I've caused you and Father so much pain.'

'You have and I don't think you realise how much.'

'I must go.' They exchanged one last despairing look then Emily was gone, down the steps and out to the waiting carriage.

Annie thought Miss Emily looked pale but lovely in a hyacinth-blue cloak and matching pert little hat. She had a rose-pink cloak as well and Annie could never make up her mind which she preferred.

Annie was already in the carriage, sitting on the edge of her seat and looking and feeling ill-at-ease. She hadn't been at all happy about entering the carriage before Miss Emily arrived but Dundas, showing some impatience had indicated she should get in. She didn't like the pompous Dundas who thought himself above the rest. She thought about refusing but decided it was better to obey.

Emily and Annie exchanged a smile and the carriage moved off. Only when they reached the end of the drive and were going through the gate did Emily turn back for that last look at Denbrae House. How lovely it looked and sad, as if it knew she was leaving in disgrace and was sympathetic. The uncertain sun disappeared behind a cloud and the sky darkened. In her highly nervous state Emily saw it as a bad omen and she shivered.

Annie saw the shiver. 'Are you cold, Miss Emily?'

'No, Annie, I'm not cold.' Emily made a determined effort to be cheerful. Annie must be feeling apprehensive and wondering what was ahead for her. She, herself, thought it strange and sad that a maid should look on her employer's house as her home. Emily had never been in the servants' wing but knew there would be few comforts. Servants didn't expect any. For a few moments her eyes rested on Annie. How drab her clothes were and why did she pull her hair back that way? Then she forgot about Annie. She had her own plight to think about and her mouth drooped in the familiar despair.

On reaching the station Emily was given a helping hand out of the carriage and Annie was pointedly ignored. Her suitcase was dumped at her feet and she picked it up.

'What a disgusting looking object, Annie, and tell me why wasn't your luggage sent on ahead with mine?'

'No one suggested it, Miss Emily.'

'Then you should have.'

Annie didn't think that worthy of an answer. Maids didn't make suggestions and if they did they were ignored. 'I didn't have a suitcase of my own and Mrs Martin found me this.'

'We can't make a better of it now.' Emily moved away. 'Come along, follow me. We do have some time before the train leaves but for all that we had better get a move on.'

The station noises were bewildering and the babble of voices alarmed Annie and made her nervous. She had never been on a train in her life nor had she been inside a station.

Everyone appeared to be hurrying and to know where they were going which was more than she did. How awful if she lost sight of Miss Emily and for a few panic-stricken minutes she did. The suitcase and the basket were weighing her down and hampering her progress. A family with a push-chair had forced themselves between causing her more delay. Beads of perspiration were on her brow and she had an urgent need to get out her handkerchief and blow her nose only she couldn't. Instead she made do with several sniffs. Annie was on the verge of tears when she spied Miss Emily's hat. Smiling foolishly with relief she started to hurry and someone got a bang on the legs.

'Ouch! Can't you watch where you are going with that thing?'

'I'm so sorry.' She bit her lip and looked at the man apologetically. He was a smartly dressed businessman and his anger melted when he heard the genuine concern in her voice. 'Did I hurt you?'

'Crippled for life I'd say.' He laughed. 'Not as bad as that, young woman, but go easy.' He hurried away.

Annie saw that Miss Emily was in conversation with a railway porter and sighing with relief she joined them.

'There you are, Annie, what a slowcoach you are. Our train is in the platform so do try and keep up,' she said impatiently.

'I am trying, Miss Emily.' Annie wondered how quickly her young mistress would move with a heavy suitcase in one hand and a well-filled basket in the other. Not that she was ever likely to find out. The Miss Emilys of this world were not expected to carry anything. That was what servants were for.

'Here, lass, let me have that.' The porter had a kindly, careworn face and he smiled to Annie as she gladly handed over the case. His lips twitched. 'It's to be hoped that piece of string holds.'

'It will, it's a good strong piece of cord and I put a double knot in it.'

'Safe enough then.' It was like a conspiracy between two of the world's workers and that exchange helped to calm Annie.

With only the basket to carry she had no difficulty keeping up. The train was busy but their seats were booked and as there weren't many first class passengers, they had the compartment to themselves. The porter came in and put Annie's case on the luggage rack.

Emily smiled and handed him a coin.

'Much obliged, miss.' He went out whistling. Not many good tips came his way, only an occasional copper or threepenny bit. Not like the old days. The well-to-do didn't take the train so often unless on long journeys. Them new motorcars were to blame and how any right-minded person could prefer one of those contraptions to the speed and comfort of the train was beyond him. A novelty that was all they were. They would never take the place of the train.

Uncomfortably hot after all the hurrying, Annie took off her felt hat and shabby grey coat. It was her one and only coat and had to do for all the seasons. In a few weeks the weather should be warmer and a cardigan would be enough. Her old but well-polished boots peeped below the grey skirt. With the skirt she wore a blouse that had started life a bright pink but after countless washings had faded until only a suggestion of colour remained.

'Miss Emily, do you want to take your cloak off?'

'No, I'm quite comfortable as I am. Do keep sitting, Annie, the train is about to move and it very often does so with a jerk.'

Annie didn't have to be told twice, she didn't want the embarrassment of losing her balance and making a fool of herself. She sat well back in the seat and prepared herself for a jolt. Looking out of the window she heard doors up and down the train being banged shut. There was a whistle then a green flag waved and the train moved off with only a slight jerk.

Emily smiled. 'It isn't always like that and stopping can be worse.'

'I'll bear that in mind.' Annie couldn't tear her eyes away from the window. She was as excited as a child bound for the seaside.

Emily was amused and was surprised to find herself a little envious. Nothing was quite the same as that first experience and it reminded her of her childhood and the happy times. Poor Annie had been deprived of so much.

In a cloud of steam the train puffed its way out of the station and Annie watched the grimy buildings and ugly walls give way to green field after green field. Cattle grazed peacefully, seemingly undisturbed by the noise of the train. In time and just like people they had become used to it. Trees and farmhouses sped by and then a row of houses. Washing hung on clothes lines and danced merrily in the breeze. The sun, slow to make up its mind, came out in fits and starts. Annie thought the washing would dry very quickly but wondered about the soot. Would some of it get on to the clothes and an overworked woman have to wash them again? Children stopped their play to watch the approach of the train and began to wave excitedly. Annie couldn't stop herself waving back.

'What on earth are you doing?'

'Just waving to some wee ones. Didn't you see them?'

'I wasn't looking and in any case they wouldn't be able to see you. You are too far away.'

That didn't make sense to Annie. If she could see them then surely they could see her. She didn't answer but a little of the light had gone from her face.

Emily noticed and felt angry with herself. 'You are enjoying this, aren't you?' she said gently.

'Yes, but then I've never been on a train before.'

'You told me that and I should have remembered the excitement of my first train journey. I was quite small and Nanny was looking after my two brothers. Being the eldest I was getting more attention from my parents. To me the engine looked like a huge monster and I was terrified. My father thought it best to face my fears and he took me to see the engine driver. Whatever was said must have been reassuring because from all accounts I was all smiles when we returned to the compartment.' Her voice faltered and she turned quickly to the window to hide her face.

Poor Miss Emily thinking back to happier times. She must be feeling dreadful but being the lady she was she couldn't show it. Maids didn't have that problem, they could howl themselves silly and no one would bother. They might get some sympathy from their own kind but that would be all. It was well known that crying your eyes out was the best way of getting over something. Annie turned back to the window and caught a glimpse of a church spire that was quickly lost as the train hurtled past. Then it was a bridge over a stream and in the fields she saw farmhands and working horses. Most surprising of all were the wild flowers that grew in profusion on the banks beside the railway line. Delicate pinks and blues and a deep shade of purple were bravely showing despite the smoke and grime.

'I would like to travel abroad,' Emily said.

'Would you, Miss Emily?' Reluctantly Annie took her eyes away from the window and gave her attention to her young mistress.

'In different circumstances France would be rather nice. Not with my cousin Lily though, that would have been far from my liking. We have absolutely nothing in common. Even so I do envy her.'

'One day you'll go there.'

'I don't think so, I can't see it happening. My parents wouldn't trust me. This one mistake will follow me for the rest of my life. It may not be spoken of, indeed I'm sure it won't, but it will be remembered. I won't be allowed to forget.' She paused. 'That is the way of life.'

'Can be the very devil.'

'What can?'

'Life, like you said.'

'You had a wretched start. You don't mind me saying that do you?'

'No, I don't mind. It is true I had a rotten start but then so did many others. I try to remember that, Miss Emily. However bad things are somebody is getting it worse.'

'Meaning I should remember that.'

Annie bit her lip. 'No, of course not, I just spoke without thinking.'

Emily gave a peal of laughter. 'If we all had to think before we spoke there would be very little said.'

Annie grinned. Miss Emily could be quite funny when she wanted.

'Don't answer this if you don't want to but have you ever reached the stage when you wondered if life was worth living?'

Annie was shocked. 'Thinking that way is dangerous. We are all put on this earth for some purpose or so the Bible thumpers who came to the orphanage used to tell us.'

'Did you believe them?'

Annie shrugged. 'Didn't give much thought to the matter but I expect there is some truth in it. We have to believe in something if it is just to survive.'

Emily looked at her maid curiously and with some respect. There was a lot of good sense in what she said and it showed she was a thinker. It could be that they would be good for each other.

As for Annie she was thinking that Miss Emily and her kind would always survive. She had money and family behind her and no matter her sin she would never be destitute. No one got off scotfree in this world but for all that there was a lot of unfairness. The troubles and disappointments of the rich were as nothing when compared to what the poor had to suffer. Miss Emily had never gone hungry or felt the bitter cold of an unheated room in the depth of winter, or slept in a bed with only a thin blanket for covering and the only heat to come from cuddling up to another body. There had been times in her own life when she had been so miserable that she hadn't cared what happened to her. Not making friends had been her own fault but she had preferred to be alone. Once she had made a friend and life had been a lot happier. They had been close like sisters then a couple had come to the orphanage and taken Martha away. Even yet she could recall the pain of loss and she had vowed then never to form a close friendship again. She despaired of ever getting away, no one had chosen her, but she prayed and her prayers had been answered. Mr Alfred Cunningham-Brown had taken her into his home as a scullery-maid. The lowest of the low but it hadn't seemed that to Annie. She had been shown kindness by Mrs Martin, given a comfortable bed, better food than she had ever tasted before and best of all no one had been cruel. The house-mother had been quick to box ears for the smallest misdemeanour.

She marvelled at the change in her fortunes. Here she was on a train, travelling with Miss Emily. In her wildest dreams she could not have imagined such a thing. In the midst of her enjoyment was guilt. Miss Emily was in the worst kind of trouble and here she was benefiting from another's mis‐fortune.

Under the eagle eye of Mrs Martin she had eaten a good breakfast.

'You get that into you, you don't know when you will get your next meal.'

'What about all the food in the basket?'

'Miss Emily, the way she is, may not feel like eating and if she doesn't you can't.'

Annie knew that. The lower orders had to wait.

'Annie, I'm not hungry but I am thirsty.'

'I'll get the flask of tea out.' It wasn't so easy pouring tea from a flask into a cup with the train rolling.

'Wait until we are on a straight stretch, Annie, then only half fill the cups.'

Annie recognised the wisdom of that.

'Pour it now.'

Annie did. She poured it quickly and without spilling.

Miss Emily sipped her tea with obvious pleasure. 'That was welcome, I was quite parched.'

'Something to eat?' Annie suggested hopefully.

'No, thank you. That needn't stop you, have what you want.'

Out of good manners she ought to decline then she rebelled. Why should she? The offer had been made. 'Thank you, I wouldn't mind.' She opened the greaseproof paper and took out a dainty sandwich. It was only a bite and if anything it made her hungrier. She couldn't bring herself to take another one and instead rewrapped the sandwiches.

'Won't be long now, Annie. I'm not quite sure what to expect when we get there, but that is maybe just as well,' she added with an attempt at humour.

'Better if you had been going to the house to be looked after properly.'

'That may well be, but I made my decision. Could be I made a wise decision, the woman might be quite impossible and would have driven me mad. A talkative creature and I can't stand that. That is what I like about you, Annie, you know when to be quiet and that is a compliment. My father warned me that staying in the cottage would mean looking after ourselves.' She gave a tinkle of a laugh. 'As if I could, but you are there to look after me.'

'I'll do my best.' Annie wondered if her best would be good enough.

'The food will be provided but you will have to cook it. You can cook?'

'Bit late in asking, Miss Emily, but yes I can but only plain fare.'

'That will do for a start and you'll improve with practice.'

'Yes, I hope so.'

'As for tonight we can eat up what is in the basket. Then get ourselves organised,' she added.

Annie wondered what Miss Emily was going to do to get herself organised.

'Is someone meeting us?'

'Of course, how else can we get to this place at the back of beyond.' She glanced at her timepiece. 'You should get down your case in readiness, Annie.'

'Yes.' She looked at the suitcase nestling in the rack and wondered how she was going to get it down. Her arms didn't quite reach it even standing on her toes.

'I can't reach without standing on the seat.'

'Then stand on the seat,' she said glancing up briefly from examining her face in the small mirror she had taken from her bag.

A hard wooden seat would have made it easier. The soft cover gave her no hold. If only the train would stop rolling. Gritting her teeth she pulled the handle with all her might, thought she had wrenched it off and she had certainly slackened it, but happily she got the case down.

'There you are, you managed it quite easily.'

Annie wondered if she had dislocated her shoulder in the process. After rubbing her shoulder she put on her coat and hat and sat down until the train stopped. There was a squeal of brakes before they came to a shuddering halt. The carriage door opened and they both got out. Annie with a struggle, but eventually she was on the platform with case and basket.

'Come along and this time try and keep up with me. There isn't a porter in sight so you'll have to manage.'

Annie thought if Miss Emily had been carrying even the lightest of luggage a porter would have materialised. By the time they were outside, the main rush of passengers had gone and they saw a small shabby carriage waiting with an elderly man holding the reins. The horse moved restlessly but became still at the sharp command.

'This I rather fear might be for us.'

'Are you by any chance waiting for us?' Emily said haughtily.

He studied them gravely. 'Now that I couldnae say for sure unless you be the young leddies for Dundrinnen.' He had a soft lilting voice.

'We are.'

'In you go then and I'll tak' that,' he said taking the case from Annie. He examined it. 'Seen better days that one,' he chuckled.

Annie grinned back. She didn't take offence and knew that none had been intended. All the same she wouldn't mind a better-looking suitcase on her next journey whenever that might be. So many remarks became a bit wearing as well as embarrassing.

Leaving the town and the busyness behind them they were soon clip-clopping along the country roads. Annie was charmed, it was all so pleasant and peaceful.

'This is lovely, Miss Emily. Like home only different if you know what I mean.'

'I confess I don't. How can it be the same if it is different?'

'What I meant was that Greenhill is beautiful but so is this.'

'All right, I think I know what you are getting at. Frankly I really don't care if it is beautiful or not. I'm only here because I have to be and that applies to you as well.'

'You do care, you are just tired that is all.'

'Me tired at my age? Dear heavens I shouldn't be but I am. If I'm tired now, what on earth will I be like nearer the – oh, God, Annie, I don't know how I am going to get through it.'

'You will and I'll help you in every way I can.'

'I know and thank you.' She smiled though her lips were quivering. 'Do you remember, Annie, it was only a short time ago, and I asked if you were my friend and you said no that you were my maid.'

'I remember,' Annie smiled.

'Well, I was right and you were wrong. I do need a maid but I also need a friend.'

'I'll be whatever you want me to be.'

'That doesn't answer my question. Do you want to be my friend or do you find that impossible?'

'Not impossible just – just unusual.'

'An unusual situation but here we are—'.

'And we will make the best of it.'

'If we find it impossible, or if I find it impossible, we will find somewhere else. I have the money with me to do it.' She closed her eyes and put her head back and Annie looked at her worriedly. Miss Emily was talking wildly, not a bit like herself. Maybe she needed a doctor to give her something to calm her nerves or maybe a good night's sleep would do that.

Chapter Five

Dundrinnen was not the back of beyond after all. If not exactly lively, it was far from being dead. At one end of the Main Street was a church with a tall spire and the manse was next to it. At the far end was the Tally-Ho, the popular public house run by the pleasant and well-liked Murdoch Dryden. Being an easy-going man it fell to his wife, Matty, to keep order. Only when the noise exceeded a certain level did she enter that male bastion. She was big and buxom and her presence was enough to silence even the bravest. No one argued. For those unfortunate enough to have been at the receiving end of her tongue it was an experience none wished to have repeated.

Since there was such a fine variety of shops few of the villagers found it necessary to make the journey to town. Should an item be required that was not in stock, it could be ordered and for this service only a very little was added to the cost. All the shops were close together. The general store was also the post office, next to it the butcher's and then the baker's. The butcher made steak pies and bowls of potted hough – the bowls had to be returned – and the sisters, Mabel and Jean Ogilvy, were up at the crack of dawn to produce soda scones, treacle scones, fruit scones and cakes large and small for those who hadn't the time, expertise or inclination to bake their own.

A lane separated the women's outfitters and a department

for children. The men's outfitters occupied smaller premises and part of it was given over to gents' tailoring. Sixty-one-year-old Fergus Gordon had only recently taken over the business from his eighty-five-year-old father who had collapsed and died in the shop, some said with a tape measure in his hand though that was highly unlikely since all he did was to supervise from a chair. Very little was made from tailoring. The menfolk of Dundrinnen had no need of more than one good suit. Made from dark, hardwearing material, it would last a lifetime since the suit only came out of the wardrobe and the mothballs for wearing at weddings and funerals.

Directly opposite the outfitters was the hardware store and then the village sweet shop where the children of Dundrinnen pressed their little noses against the window and wondered in delicious anticipation how they would spend their Saturday penny or halfpenny for those children less fortunate. Bottles lined the shelves with all kinds of boiled sweets and also on display were packets of sherbert, liquorice sticks, home-made toffee and lucky bags. The lucky bags were made up from the dregs of the jars before they were refilled and a few toffee caramels were added for good measure. The attraction was the chance of finding a silver threepenny bit wrapped in paper and hidden among the sweets. Only once in a blue moon did that happen, but occasionally there would be a halfpenny. For the little ones of Dundrinnen it was a difficult choice and not one to be made in a hurry.

Most villages are centres of gossip and Dundrinnen was no exception. The big house, never called anything else though it was thought to have had a name at one time, was a never-ending topic of conversation as was its owner. Beatrice McIntyre, believed to be a widow and who had once let slip that she had nursing experience, kept herself to herself and no wonder. Live and let live was all very well, they all agreed about that, but this sort of thing put her beyond the pale. On the woman's arrival the hand of friendship had been offered and though she hadn't been rude, it had been made clear to the good ladies of Dundrinnen that she had no interest in the social life of the village and wanted no part in it. Her day, she said, was fully taken up with looking after a large house and the old gentleman who owned it.

This was no more than the truth and particularly so when the old man became bedridden. Rather than have a trained nurse come in and perform those unpleasant though necessary tasks, Mrs McIntyre had taken it upon herself to keep her employer as clean and as comfortable as possible. When the old gentleman died and left the big house to his housekeeper there was much talk and plenty of conjectures. Some were very wide of the mark and others remarkably close to the truth. The truth was that the frail old man had been encouraged to change his Will and leave Beatrice McIntyre the house. The bulk of his money was still to go to a niece and nephew who lived abroad. The house, the cottage nearby and a small sum of money were left to Beatrice McIntyre in return for her devotion to duty.

It was generally agreed that the woman had done well for herself and that she would sell the house and cottage and return from whence she came. They were wrong. Beatrice McIntyre loved that house and the thought of being its mistress gave her immense satisfaction. Sadly the money wasn't enough to keep it going. She would have to earn some. But how? Taking in paying guests was given consideration but not many holidaymakers came to Dundrinnen. The occasional family did rent the cottage for a few weeks in the summer but there wasn't a lot to be made from that.

When an old friend first put forward the suggestion, Mrs McIntyre had been affronted but even so she hadn't dismissed it out of hand. The money was very, very good and her friend had the contacts. It became very tempting and slowly but surely, Beatrice was allowing herself to be persuaded. As her friend kept pointing out she was ideal for the job. The house was large and secluded and it belonged to her. She had nursing experience, admittedly not much, but even a little was an advantage and most important of all she was discreet.

These girls came from wealthy families who to hide their disgrace required to be housed and looked after for several months. Since they were already in trouble it was unlikely they would cause more. It was equally unlikely they would stray far from the house and the garden. In other words it would be easily earned money.

The more Mrs McIntyre thought about it the better she liked the idea. There was a midwife in the village and a doctor in the event of one being needed. Dr Thomas Rutherford served Dundrinnen and beyond and had the good sense to have his home in Dundrinnen.

Talk there would be, no question about that. Some of it would come directly from those employed in the house. Mrs McIntyre was not greatly perturbed. For the kind of return she would be receiving it would be worth it. What she was contemplating was not illegal. Had it been she would not have considered it, no matter the reward. All she was doing was providing a hiding place for young ladies forced to leave their own home. Arrangements would be made to have the babies adopted and once that was all taken care of and the young ladies fully recovered they would return to the bosom of their families, themselves wiser and their parents poorer.

It was late afternoon when the carriage reached Dundrinnen. Not all of the villagers did their shopping in the morning as the well-filled baskets bore witness. Women chatted at the shop doors but tongues stopped wagging and necks craned to see the passengers bound for the big house. Unaware of the interest shown in them, Emily and Annie glanced at the shops and remarked to each other that there were a surprising number. About a quarter of a mile beyond the Main Street the carriage came to a halt.

'This must be the house,' Emily said, 'and presumably we

have to report our arrival before going on to the cottage. Ah, here comes someone.' A woman was hurrying down the path and before she reached them they had a few moments to study the house. Solid and stone-built it was plain but graceful in its simplicity. A house built to withstand the worst of the winter storms. The windows had small square panes and there were shutters painted green that gave a touch of colour and softened the severity of the greystone.

The woman arrived slightly out of breath and leaning into the carriage, she said, 'Good afternoon, Miss Cunningham-Brown, I am Mrs McIntyre.'

Emily nodded and murmured, 'Good afternoon.'

'I trust you had a pleasant journey?'

'Very pleasant, thank you.'

'A cup of tea would be very welcome, I'm sure. Your maid can go straight on to the cottage. That's it just ahead.' She pointed.

'Thank you, Mrs McIntyre, but I won't accept your invitation. I would prefer for both of us to go to the cottage and get settled.' She paused and said rather haughtily, 'I take it that everything is in order for our arrival?'

'Of course,' the woman said stiffly and was unable to hide her annoyance.

Emily saw that she had angered the woman and sought to make amends.

'If I may I could call tomorrow afternoon?'

'That would suit me. Shall we say three thirty?'

Emily nodded and Annie spoke softly.

'The key, Miss Emily.'

Mrs McIntyre had a keyring in her hand with two keys on it. 'I have the key of the cottage here, Miss Cunningham-Brown and a duplicate in case it should be required.' She smiled to Emily and ignored Annie. 'None of us trouble to lock our doors in the daytime but it is advisable to do so at night.' She turned, nodded to the driver and walked smartly back up the path. Beatrice McIntyre was a good-looking woman in her early fifties. She was heavily built but with the height to carry it. Her iron-grey hair was piled high on her head and secured with two tortoiseshell combs and numerous hairpins.

The carriage moved off and Emily sighed. 'I didn't make a very good impression refusing her invitation.'

'You made it all right in the end by saying you would go tomorrow.'

'I really will have to think before I speak because I am likely to need her more than she will need me. Not a very comfortable thought. What did you think of her? No, tell me later. This is us, this is the cottage.'

The driver opened the carriage door then left them to it. He wasn't going to give them any assistance. Annie had expected an outburst from Miss Emily but she hadn't said a word. Annie helped her down and was about to deplore the man's bad manners when she saw him carrying her suitcase along the path and depositing it on the step.

'That was kind of you, thank you very much,' Annie said and gave him a smile as they passed each other.

He grunted and walked away his head bent.

'Not the most talkative of individuals,' Emily remarked.

'No, he isn't, but I'll forgive him a lot since he carried my case.'

Emily laughed and handed the key to Annie. Annie unlocked the door and pushed it open. She was very conscious of her mistress's changing moods and could hear the strain in her laughter. Poor Miss Emily, it was the stiff upper-lip for her kind. Tears were not for them, only for the lower orders.

'You go ahead, Annie. Leave your case where it is just now – no one is likely to run away with it.'

Very true, but it still held all her worldly possessions. Annie had thought the cottage charming from the outside but Miss Emily may not be of the same opinion, not after what she was used to.

Annie went in and along a narrow passageway that would

have been quite dark had the doors not been left open. Emily followed Annie into the kitchen. There was a fire burning and a big black kettle was half on the heat. A chair was beside the fire and it looked comfortable. Maybe Miss Emily would sit there until she got things sorted out.

'I feel a bit chilled, Annie.' Emily's lips were quivering.

'Then why don't you sit here beside the fire.'

'I think I will.' She forced a smile. 'I don't have to pretend to you, Annie. This poky little cottage is quite awful but I'm stuck here for the present.'

'A cup of tea and something to eat will make you feel a lot better.' There was a hook on the back of the kitchen door and Annie took off her coat and hung it up. Her felt hat went on the top and promptly fell to the floor. She put it on the dresser to be removed later. Dashing to the front door she brought her case indoors. Returning she put the kettle to boil, it hadn't been far from it and almost immediately the lid began to rattle. A brown teapot and tea caddy were to hand and she made the tea. The tablecloth was in one of the drawers of the dresser and Annie spread it over the scrubbed kitchen table. It was white with yellow stripes and had been freshly laundered. Without difficulty she found the crockery and other essentials and very soon she had the table set. There was food ready to eat: Annie gave a silent prayer for Mrs Martin's foresight. As she gave the tea time to infuse she had a quick look in the pantry and it was a cheering sight. There was a blue and white jug with milk, a bowl of eggs, bacon and butter on the cold slab. The covered dishes she would examine later.

Emily got up to take off her cloak and hand it to Annie. Annie took it and her hat along to the larger of the two bedrooms and placed them on the bed. She was relieved to see that Miss Emily's luggage had arrived.

'There you are, pour the tea, please. I am both hungry and thirsty.'

'I'm sure you are, you've had nothing since breakfast,' Annie spoke as though to a child. There were four wooden kitchen chairs round the table and Annie drew one out for Miss Emily and once she was seated pulled out one for herself. They ate in silence for a few minutes.

'These are rather nice these sandwiches but everything tastes nice when one is hungry.'

Annie felt irritated. Maybe she didn't mean it but it sounded like small thanks to Mrs Martin.

'Mrs Martin put herself to a great deal of trouble and I think they are delicious.'

'Yes, they are and I feel better for having eaten something. I shouldn't go so long without.' She looked about her. 'Never in my whole life have I eaten in a kitchen but there is a first time for everything.'

'I had a quick look. There is a sitting-room or maybe I should call it a living-room,' she said uncertainly. 'No dining-room.'

'Something else I will have to get used to doing without. Not like you, you must feel quite at home here.'

'Yes, I like it, I think it is very nice.'

They finished the meal and Miss Emily went back to her chair at the fireside. Annie cleared the table and took everything through to the scullery. She was relieved to see a tap over the deep sink. Thank heaven Dundrinnen was up with the times. There was running water and she wouldn't have to carry bucketfuls from some central source of supply.

'I forgot to ask Mrs McIntyre if my luggage had arrived.'

'It has. The chest and suitcase are in your bedroom.'

'We must unpack. The keys are in my purse.'

'Don't you want to see the rest of the cottage first?'

'That won't take long,' Emily said drily, 'very well, lead the way.'

There were three rooms, a kitchen, scullery and a bathroom which must have been added fairly recently. The second bedroom must have been intended for a child and certainly was no bigger than the cupboards in Denbrae House. She wasn't complaining, it would do her very well. The narrow iron bed was hard up against the wall. There was a single wardrobe with a deep drawer at the bottom, the only drawer. A mirror hung on a hook on the door. There was no chair and no space for one. There was, however, a shabby cabinet beside the bed with a lamp on it. The floral curtains at the small window were fresh looking but faded from the sun.

The other bedroom was in stark contrast. Thought had gone into making it comfortable and attractive. There was a fireplace and a marble-topped table with a jug inside a matching basin. Pretty curtains hung at the window which was quite big and had a deep windowsill that would take some of Miss Emily's little ornaments. There was a very large, heavy-looking wardrobe and a dressing-table with a triple mirror and drawers down each side. The crocheted cover on the dressing-table was ochre-brown. A patchwork quilt covered the bed and beside it was a cabinet with a lamp on top. There was an embroidered stool and two comfortable chairs, one with a donkey brown velvet cushion on it. Annie thought it delightful and hoped Miss Emily wouldn't find fault with this.

'You should be comfortable here, Miss Emily, it's very nice.'

'You think it comfortable, do you?' She made a face. 'It could be worse I suppose.'

Emily saw Annie's mouth purse as though she were annoyed and it angered her. She was only a maid, what right had she to air her opinion.

'Acceptable by your standards, mine are much higher. However, I grant you it is habitable.'

Annie was silent. She would have to watch not just her tongue but the expression on her face. Miss Emily was like, what was that word? A chameleon. She could be haughty, Miss High and Mighty one minute then charmingly friendly the next.

The trunk was open and Annie was kneeling before it. She had expected to be left alone to do the unpacking and then find a place for everything, but here was Miss Emily going to give a hand.

'Let me have the dresses and skirts and I'll put them on the bed. You can sort them out before hanging them in the wardrobe.'

'Yes.'

'Why on earth did I bring so many? How stupid, it isn't as though I will be attending any social occasions.' She gave a harsh laugh. 'In hiding that's me.'

'Still it will be nice to have a change of outfit and there is plenty of room in the wardrobe.'

'Not plenty of room in the gowns though. I'm getting bigger every day, I'm sure of it. Soon I'll be reduced to wearing those awful tents my mother would have me buy. At least no one will see me – I'll keep to the cottage and the garden,' she said resignedly.

Annie looked up, her face serious. 'You have to look after your health, that's important and that means a walk every day.'

'I suppose you're right, you usually are.'

'Oh, Miss Emily, these are beautiful,' Annie said holding up the exquisite baby clothes and the gossamer fine shawl.

'My mother just buys and buys I had to stop her. The assistant, of course, was encouraging her and asked when the baby was due. When I told her it was October she enthused about it being such a lovely month, just after the heat of the summer and before the cold weather. I kept my gloves on the whole time,' she added.

Annie just smiled and folded the shawl to wrap it in tissue paper.

'Mother was only being practical,' she said. 'The baby will, after all, require clothes and a shawl before it is handed over.'

'Where shall I put them?' Annie asked quietly.

'Obviously they can't take up drawer space, I'll need all that. Once you've emptied my case put them in there. And speaking of cases get rid of that monstrosity of yours.'

'I can't do that, it isn't mine. It belongs to Mrs Martin.'

'I doubt it, it would be some old thing lying around that's all. I'll buy you a new one. And now, Annie, where do we put these books?'

'They could go in the sitting-room.'

'Is there a bookcase?'

'No, but there are shelves.'

'Empty?'

'I think so, I haven't had time to look properly.'

'Go and take a look now.'

Annie came back. 'Empty apart from a Bible.'

Emily picked up the books one by one and then put them down again. 'This is to be your reading matter.'

'And when, tell me, am I supposed to have time for that?'

'Make time.'

'I'll have the cleaning and the cooking and very likely the shopping as well unless Mrs McIntyre has already made arrangements for that.'

Emily creased her brow. 'I think my father made mention that the food situation would be taken care of but we'll find out about that later. As regards work you won't have it all to do. If there is no help provided then the woman can engage someone from the village. Don't worry, my father will meet any extra expense and I should have mentioned this. He has arranged for your wages to be sent on at the end of each month or maybe it is the beginning but don't worry, you'll get them anyway.'

That was a relief to Annie who hadn't wanted to bring up the subject. She was saved that embarrassment.

'Come along. I want another look at this sitting-room, then we'll go into the kitchen and you can make another cup of tea. Unpacking is thirsty work.'

Annie had a silent laugh. How much of the unpacking had her ladyship done? Still she wouldn't say no to a cup of tea herself and one of the sponge cakes, the last of the food from the basket.

'Pleasant enough,' Emily nodded her approval. There was

a sofa with an antimacassar thrown over it and matching covers over the two armchairs. There was no clutter and Annie was pleased about that. The work was doubled when things had to be moved. The small table could be used for afternoon tea or just for holding bits and pieces. In the corner was a basket chair which could be carried out to the garden, Annie thought. And on the wall was a picture of Highland cattle. 'Go and get the books and we'll get them in place.'

Annie returned with them in her arms and Emily took one at a time and examined it. '*Jane Eyre* is my favourite, I think she is everybody's favourite and I've read it at least three times. *Little Women* that's lovely too and *Sense and Sensibility*. Oh, silly me, I haven't brought *Pride and Prejudice* and you simply must read that. Never mind perhaps I'll be able to buy a copy here.'

'Don't do that,' Annie said horrified at the amount of reading that lay ahead. 'I won't get through half of it. I've read *David Copperfield*,' she said with a touch of pride and glad she could lay claim to that.

'I should hope so. This is very refreshing this tea, I'm getting as bad as my mother. And Annie—'

'Yes, Miss Emily?'

'I have rather a lot of money with me. Where would be a safe place to keep it? One of the drawers in the bedroom perhaps?'

'When you say a lot—'

'I mean precisely that.' She smiled. 'I don't mind you knowing that I am quite wealthy in my own right. I did tell you that I withdrew a large sum. No doubt most of it will go back with me but I feel better knowing I have money of my own should I need it.'

'For safe-keeping it would be better on you.'

Emily frowned. 'I certainly don't want to carry it with me and the way my mind is just now I could very easily lose it. Surely you can come up with something more sensible than that?'

'I didn't mean what you think I meant. Someone told Mrs Martin and she told us that long ago when wealthy ladies had to travel they used to carry their money and jewels in a pocket stitched to the inside of their skirt.'

Emily clapped her hands. 'That would be crinolines, of course, but what a splendid idea. Could you make me one of those pockets or perhaps two?'

'If I had a strong piece of material I could.'

'Surely we can get that in the village along with thread and needles and whatever else is needed?'

'I should think so.'

'Two of my dresses are already a bit tight. Sew a pocket in each and they can go to the back of the wardrobe. No one would dream of looking there.'

'No, they wouldn't and your money should be safe enough.'

'Nowhere is completely safe, Annie, as you should know. There are rogues and thieves in every walk of life. My father used to say that the worst kind of rogue is a gentleman rogue because no one would believe bad of him.' She yawned. 'I'm tired.'

'You want to go to bed, Miss Emily?'

'Yes, I do. See to my bedroom and I'll follow in a few minutes.'

Annie pushed the trunk and the suitcase against one wall. Tomorrow she would have to find another place for them. Folding back the quilt she put the snowy white nightdress on the pillow, put on the lamp and drew the curtains making sure they were completely closed.

'That's everything ready for you, Miss Emily. Sorry about the trunk and the case—'

'Can't they go in your bedroom?'

'Not an inch to spare, there isn't room to swing a cat. Not that I am complaining,' she said hastily, 'I like a small room – it is what I'm used to.'

She nodded. 'Help me with these fastenings then you can go.'

Annie's unpacking didn't take long and after it she went on a proper inspection of the cottage. She was quiet about it so as not to disturb Miss Emily. The pantry was her first stop. There was a small steak pie to heat up and that would take care of tomorrow's main meal. Sliced ham and a round of cheese were on the cold slab and on the bottom shelf potatoes and a selection of garden vegetables in a creel. The creel was a large wicker basket used by anglers but used now for vegetables. All very satisfactory. Investigating further she opened a cupboard and found a pail, a scrubbing brush, some old rags for cleaning cloths and a brush and shovel. There was coal, sticks and a pile of newspapers some of which had been made into curls for the lighting of the fire. There would be a coal cellar outside which could wait until tomorrow.

Looking after her young mistress was going to be quite a big responsibility. She liked her own way but it would be a mistake to give in to her too much. She would get a cup of tea in bed but Annie would encourage her to get up for breakfast and take a little exercise even if it was just a walk in the garden and round the cottage. Annie yawned and since there was nobody about she didn't bother to cover her mouth. Undressing she put her clothes over the foot of the bed and almost before her head touched the pillow she was asleep.

Next door Emily was wide awake, sleep far away even though she felt wearied to death. Lying there she felt so lonely and abandoned. This was to be her home, her prison with only Annie for company. Intelligent but with little education there was no chance of stimulating talks. A short time ago her life had been full of laughter and she had enjoyed popularity. What would her friends think if they could see her now stuck in this frightful cottage? After meeting Jonathan she had treated them shabbily and they wouldn't forget that in a hurry. If only she could turn the clock back. What a silly fool she had been.

And her brothers, what would they make of her absence?

Her eyes filled with scalding tears. Her father didn't see that as a problem but her parents were so naïve. Michael and Robert knew what she thought of her cousin Lily and to believe she was prepared to put up with her for a whole year was laughable. They might pretend to believe it but they wouldn't. Did her parents really believe she would get away with it? What if Lily were to hear that they were supposed to be together? Not very likely but again not impossible. More likely to reach the ears of her aunt and uncle and then the cat would be out of the bag. Emily, the pretty one, now Emily the wicked girl. How they would gloat and enjoy her downfall while pretending otherwise. Was it human nature to enjoy another's misfortune? No, she didn't believe that. The vast majority were good and kind. She only wished her relatives were among them. Great-Aunt Anne had been different. Her generosity to Emily had upset the others but they hadn't loved her and hadn't deserved to benefit. Whatever the future held Great-Aunt Anne's money would help smooth the way.

Chapter Six

As though she had her own inner clock, Annie awoke at her usual time of five thirty. For a few moments she lay quite still wondering if she could be dreaming. Nothing was familiar, the window was in the wrong place, the bed softer, the ceiling lower and the furniture different. It took her a few more moments to realise where she was and to recall the events of the previous day. Once she did, Annie decided there was no call for her to get up this early. She could easily snuggle down for another half hour. After twenty minutes she couldn't lie any longer and throwing back the covers got herself out of bed. She yawned and stretched and then on bare feet went over to the window to draw back the curtains. Daylight flooded in.

Studying the view from the window Annie thought it different from Perthshire but would have been hard pressed to say in what way. The sky was a pale washed-out blue and the hills in the distance a dark contrast. Bracing was how she had heard the weather described and she was prepared for it being colder with the chill wind coming from the North Sea.

It was rather pleasant and certainly a change not to be hurrying to begin her tasks in Denbrae House. Her bedroom was at the back of the cottage and the window looked out on an area of short grass with part of it used as a drying-green. Four metal poles held a washing line and Annie expected to make good use of it. It was tidy and that was about all that could be said for it. The border where once flowers had grown was neglected and only a few tired plants remained. She had an urge to do something about it herself and would if there were garden tools to hand. Miss Emily might want to sit out.

Her eyes went beyond her immediate surroundings to the undulating fields where cattle grazed. The grass was a lush green that came from soft rain and bursts of sunshine. A sombre dark brown marked those fields that had been prepared for the new season's plantings. In the winter with a thick covering of snow it would be very beautiful.

Annie felt her spirits rise and excitement bubbled up inside her. Then she was immediately ashamed. She wasn't here to enjoy herself, she was here to make life easier for Miss Emily. The poor lass was going to need a lot of looking after and it could be that she was awake at this very moment and pondering on her misfortune. More likely she was still asleep and she would have to be quiet as she went about her household duties. Putting on her working clothes Annie took time to study her appearance which was something she seldom did.

This morning she really looked at herself and her own description would have been that her face was nothing to write home about. Miss Emily would stand out in any crowd whereas she, Annie Fullerton, would go unnoticed. That didn't bother her but she got to wondering why God made some women beautiful and others plain. Was it fair of Him? The same could be said about folk getting an unequal start in life. Who could blame them if just occasionally they showed some resentment. Of course it wasn't only looks, some were clever, some were not. The very lucky had a special gift. Musicians and artists gave so much pleasure to others as well as satisfaction to themselves.

She had another look at herself. Light brown hair, some would call it mousy, a thin nose and brown eyes. It didn't add up to very much. Other eyes would see more. A small slim girl with a neat figure and soft brown eyes that spoke of kindness and caring.

Being neither beautiful nor clever and with no special gift, Annie decided she was no worse off than many others. Perhaps in the next world the scales would be tipped in their favour. It was a nice thought to be going on with, she thought, and carrying her shoes Annie hurried along to the kitchen.

A proper wash would come later, meantime she would make do with splashing her face with cold water and drying herself briskly with the towel.

The fire had to be lit and that was the first job. Picking up the poker she gave the ashes a good rake out leaving a covering of cinders. The screwed up paper went on top followed by sticks arranged crosswise. Annie got off her knees to reach for the box of matches and striking one set a light to the paper. The sticks caught and once they were crackling she added small pieces of coal. It would be a good going fire in no time. She half filled the kettle at the sink for the first cup of tea of the day. Miss Emily might be ready for one.

On tiptoes in case her mistress was still asleep she went along to the bedroom, opened the door a fraction and looked in.

'I'm awake and have been for a long time.'

'Good morning, Miss Emily, I didn't want to knock and disturb you. Are you ready for a cup of tea?'

'I am. Before you go open the curtains, I don't imagine anyone will come looking in the window.'

'No, I shouldn't think so.' She opened the curtains. 'Another lovely morning.'

'How do you know it was lovely here?'

'No, that's right how could I?' Annie wished her mistress wouldn't pick her up on every small mistake. 'I'll get the tea.'

'Thank you,' she said a few minutes later. 'Put it a little nearer. That's better.'

Annie stood back. 'Did you sleep well, Miss Emily?'

'No, but then I didn't expect to. You did I suppose?' She said it a little waspishly.

'Yes, I did.'

'You have no worries and that makes the difference.'

Annie almost smiled. Much of her life had been one long worry but Miss Emily would never understand that.

'Should I get up for breakfast or have you bring it to me in bed?'

Annie would have preferred Miss Emily to stay in bed, it would let her get on but that was selfish.

'Better to get up for it. Sitting at the table would let you enjoy it more.'

'I can't think why but I'll take your advice.'

'You can take a little walk to yourself, it looks like being a nice day.'

'I'll think about that. Meantime tell me what there is.'

'For breakfast? Bacon and egg and I'll make fried bread if you would like that?'

'Perhaps I would and I do have the excuse that I am eating for two. You see, Annie, I can make a joke of it.'

'That's good.'

'Don't encourage me to eat too much,' Emily added anxiously, 'or I may have difficulty getting my figure back.'

'Not you, Miss Emily, you'll be as slim and lovely as ever and now if you will excuse me I must get on.'

'Take the cup with you,' she said draining the last of the tea then slipping under the bedclothes, 'come back in half an hour and put out what I am to wear and that's another thing I am not going to strain my vocal chords to get your attention. We must see about purchasing a handbell.'

'Yes, one of the shops in the village may be able to oblige.' Annie was looking forward to a walk to the village shops.

'Annie, before you go—'

She half turned, her hand on the doorknob.

'We'll have our breakfast together, no, correct that, we'll have all our meals together. I'm going to find it very strange eating in the kitchen but then I'm going to find a lot of things strange.'

Annie hurried to put the kitchen to rights then set the table. She was a bit apprehensive about taking her meals with Miss Emily. Having them on her own would be much more enjoyable. Certainly more relaxing not having to watch her table manners. In the event it turned out not to be the ordeal she expected. Perhaps it was the humble kitchen table but before long Annie was completely at ease. They didn't speak out of politeness but only when one of them had something of interest to say. The silences let them think their own thoughts and were not awkward.

'Annie, what time did I arrange to go and see this woman?'

'Mrs McIntyre?' Surely the woman was entitled to her name, Annie thought crossly. She had done all that was expected and more. 'You were to call on her about half past three.'

Emily sighed. 'I must go, of course, but I am not looking forward to it. She is going to try and organise me, I just know it.'

'No, she won't, she's only trying to be helpful.'

'You don't know anything and I am going to be bored, bored, bored. How can you be expected to understand when you've led such a simple life.' She shouted her frustration and banged the table with her hand setting the china rattling. 'Well, why don't you say something?'

'There is nothing for me to say.'

She closed her eyes as though in pain. 'Forgive me, Annie, I don't mean to take it out on you.'

'I don't mind. You've got to yell at someone and I'm here.' She smiled. 'In your condition you are allowed to be moody.'

'Thank you for making excuses for me. You shouldn't, you should give as good as you get.'

'And lose my job?'

'No fear of that. You might leave me if I became impossible.'

'Where would I go?'

'Back to Denbrae House, you would be welcome there. My mother wanted to keep you, so you see I had to fight for you.' She smiled her old enchanting smile that would melt even the coldest heart.

Annie wasn't sure of anything. Miss Emily might get tired of the cottage and decide after all to take up residence in the big house. She hoped not. Annie loved the cottage and knew she could be happy just pottering about. Already she was pretending it was her own.

'That's me then, I'm off to the lion's den, Annie.'

'Oh, Miss Emily,' Annie giggled, 'you shouldn't be saying that.'

'Why not, she might be an old dragon, we haven't had time to find out.'

'She isn't that. She knew you had a maid and she could have left a lot of the work for me only she didn't.'

'You seem to forget my father is paying for all this. Still maybe you have a point.' Emily wore a gown of sprigged muslin and looked delightfully summery. Her face was pale but her hair shone as hair often does during pregnancy. The gown felt tight and she tried to draw herself in. Why did having a baby have to be like this? She who loved her body now hated it.

Mrs McIntyre answered the door herself. She knew how to dress and looked well in a fine-knit two-piece in a pale shade of mauve. With her height, her regal bearing, she looked every inch the lady of the manor.

'Good afternoon, Miss Cunningham-Brown, do come in.'

Emily smiled and stepped into the vestibule. Beatrice McIntyre closed the door and led the way through the spacious hall and into the sitting-room. A small fire burned and she waved a hand in its direction.

'We don't get many days even in the middle of summer

when we can do without a fire completely. Usually I put a match to it at night but I thought you might feel the cold. Perthshire, I imagine, is warmer than here.'

'You may be right. Thank you,' she said when the woman invited her to sit in one of the easy chairs. Emily had taken a quick glance round and liked what she saw. The room was restful, the colours of the carpet and the curtains muted. It reminded her a little of the family sitting-room in Denbrae House though the furniture here was darker and probably more old-fashioned. Everything looked cared for, the furniture gleamed, the mirror above the fireplace sparkled and there were ornaments but not too many.

'I'll ring for Molly and we can have our tea and discuss the arrangements,' she said, suddenly businesslike.

Emily raised delicate eyebrows.

'Arrangements for the birth I should have said.'

At the mention of the birth Emily felt her stomach knot. It was her reason for being in Dundrinnen yet her mind was still distancing itself as though she could still wish it away.

'Here is Molly.' The door opened and a knee pushed it wider. She was dark-haired, plump, with a lovely skin and she came in carrying a tray.

'Put it down on the table, Molly, and napkins you've forgotten them.'

'No, I didn't, I just forgot to pick them up.' She hurried away and returned with two dainty embroidered linen napkins. 'Do you want me to pour the tea, Mrs McIntyre?'

'No, I'll do that. You just get back to your work.' Molly left after taking a good look at Emily. 'My previous maid left to be married and Molly, willing though she is, has a lot to learn. Milk and sugar?'

'Yes, please.' Milk went into the cups then the woman poured the tea through a strainer. 'Is that sufficient?' She was showing Emily a level teaspoon of sugar.

'Yes, thank you.' Emily had to hold back her mirth. She had an insane desire to laugh. The woman was trying too hard and it reminded her of when as children she and her friends used to play at pretend tea parties and overdo the politeness. She accepted a piece of buttered fruit loaf and bit into it.

'This is lovely,' she said truthfully.

'Most people like it. An old recipe and one that has been in the family for many years.' They ate in silence for a few moments then Beatrice put down her cup and spoke. 'Your time, I am led to believe, is the beginning of October.'

'Yes, the first week. I think the doctor said the fifth of October but apparently some first babies take their time about arriving and a week late is nothing out of the ordinary.'

'That's very true and it applies the other way as well. Sometimes they come early.'

'Has my father been in touch with you?' It upset Emily to have to ask the question of Mrs McIntyre but she had been told the very minimum.

'No, Mr Cunningham-Brown has not been in touch with me.'

'You mean someone else, not my father, has been making these arrangements on my – on my behalf?'

'That would appear to be the case.'

'I see,' Emily said slowly, 'and regarding the cottage, how am I placed? When do I have to vacate it?' Emily moistened her lips. 'I'm not putting this very well. I suppose what I am trying to say is how long after the birth . . .' she trailed off.

'The cottage is at your disposal until the end of the year.' Really the young woman knew very little, but obviously her parents had thought it enough.

'But why? Why the end of the year? I have no intention of prolonging my stay and surely two or three weeks should see me fully recovered.'

The woman nodded. 'Perhaps I should explain that I had a party who showed an interest in occupying the cottage for several months and I make no bones about it, Miss Cunningham-Brown, I am not prepared to lose money because you are not willing to stay in the house.'

'I understand and, of course, I would not wish you to be

out of pocket through me. My father agreed to this?'

'Yes, there were no problems. The let was extended to the end of the year. Whether you remain until then will be your decision. Do help yourself.'

'Thank you, I'll have another piece of fruit loaf if I may?'

'Please do.'

Emily put the dainty triangle on her plate. 'Forgive me but I do need to be fully in the picture and regarding the actual birth I have to confess complete ignorance.'

'Don't worry about that but before we go on, tell me whether you wish to give birth in the cottage or here in the house?'

Emily hesitated. 'The cottage I think or would I get better attention—'

'My dear, you will be well taken care of wherever you choose to be.'

'The cottage then.'

'You spoke of your ignorance regarding childbirth and that isn't necessarily a disadvantage. I'm not a mother so I can't talk from experience but believe me you have nothing to worry about. The midwife will answer all your questions when the time comes. You look to be a healthy young woman who will come through it without much trouble. Mrs Drummond, she is the midwife, is very experienced and most of the village children you see running about were brought into the world with her help.'

'Thank you for being so understanding.'

'The baby will go to a good home where it will be loved and cared for.' She paused to take a drink of her tea. 'There are many childless couples desperate for a baby and to be able to adopt one is for them like a very special gift from heaven.'

The woman was leading her to the door. 'If you have any health worries even minor ones come to me at once. Nearer the time I shall introduce you to Mrs Drummond in whom you can have every confidence.'

★　　★　　★

'Annie, I hope you made yourself a cup of tea.'

'Yes, Miss Emily, I did and if you want another cup the kettle's on the boil.'

'No, I had a very nice afternoon tea and I was wrong, she really is a very kind and understanding woman. By the way she had home-made fruit loaf which was quite delicious. I wish now I had asked her for the recipe. Never mind I have no doubt I can get it another time.'

Annie nodded without much enthusiasm. She considered herself a reasonably good cook but had little experience of baking. Watching Mrs Martin throw ingredients into a bowl and then beat furiously was one thing, doing it herself was quite another. She wouldn't mind having a go but only if there was something in the tin in case her effort didn't rise to the occasion.

'You feel happier, your mind more at rest,' Annie said sympathetically. They were sitting together and each occupying a comfortable chair.

'I think so. I thought the woman straightforward and honest and I didn't know this until she told me – no, don't light the fire just yet, I am not in the least cold.'

Annie returned the matches to the mantelshelf and sat down again. She didn't feel at ease sitting down in the afternoon, always felt she should be doing something.

'I am at liberty to remain in the cottage until the end of the year if I have a mind to. That surprised me I must say.'

It was surprising Annie too.

'My father had little choice in the matter. Apparently she had the offer from someone who wanted to occupy the cottage for several months or perhaps longer. A long let was how she described it I think.'

'She didn't want to lose out?'

'Exactly and who could blame her. She has her own interests to look after.'

'Would you stay on in the cottage?'

Emily looked at her as if she had taken leave of her senses. 'Of course not, what a ridiculous thing to say. The end of October should see us finished with this place.' She gave a deep sigh. 'Tomorrow, Annie, we'll take a walk down to the village shops and see what they have to offer. The provisions are supplied by Mrs McIntyre but we may see something we fancy.'

'That would be nice.' Annie cheered up at the thought. Better to get out and shorten the day for Miss Emily.

'Apart from clothes I've never shopped in my life. Do you like shopping, Annie?'

'That depends. Shopping is a pleasure if you don't have to count the pennies.'

'Well, we don't.'

The morning was pleasantly warm, the kind of morning you wanted to be out and about. Annie had done a washing in the early morning and it was hanging on the clothes line. She didn't want them to be too dry and before they left the cottage to go shopping Annie dashed out with her clothes basket to test what was ready. Most were dry enough for ironing and she let those fall into the basket after unpegging them. She would have liked to roll them up but there was no time. Miss Emily was short of patience and the tapping of a small foot had Annie reaching for the shopping bag.

'I'm ready.'

'And about time. Do I show in this?'

'No.'

'Don't lie to me.'

'I'm not, you hardly show at all.'

'Which means I do. Help me on with my cloak. I'll melt but it can't be helped.'

'There is a breeze,' Annie said trying to say the right thing. She was going to have her work cut out dealing with her mistress's many moods.

'Annie, in the eyes of everyone I'm a sinner.'

'That's not true,' she said gently as she locked the door. Poor lass her moods fluctuated between black despair and forced cheerfulness, both difficult to deal with. Just now she sounded frightened.

'Your little one will be a love-child.'

'A love-child for someone else to love. Yes, I could look at it that way. My misfortune for want of a better word, is to be another person's joy.'

Chapter Seven

In the bright sunshine and with a faint breeze blowing the walk to the village was pleasant and they were taking it leisurely. There was nothing to hurry them and they took time to admire what would soon become familiar. The meandering burn gurgled its way round Dundrinnen with the water flowing over smooth stones and broken-off branches from the trees. For those unwise enough to have overindulged in the village pub there was hidden danger where long grasses and vegetation covered the water. Though it was not deep he who lost his footing would arrive home with wet feet and dripping trouser legs or worse if he were to fall flat on his face.

Soon they were in the Main Street where women laughed and chatted among themselves but as the young women, one with a shopping bag over her arm, drew near they stopped their conversation and made no secret of their curiosity. Annie was quick to sense the atmosphere and the bristle of disapproval. It was clear by the shaking of heads and the pursing of lips that they were not welcome in Dundrinnen. Annie was angered and glanced at Miss Emily. She should have known that the well brought-up had this special armour. They could ignore, or seem to ignore, what they didn't want to see. Miss Emily might feel scorned and diminished in the eyes of these women who stared so rudely, but it wouldn't show. She stared straight through them and they were the first to look away. Brazen was how they would describe her but her complete indifference would win a reluctant admiration which they wouldn't voice.

Going first to the baker's shop they studied the well-filled window.

'Quite a selection,' Emily said.

'Yes, but remember we have food in the cottage.'

'What have we?'

'Bread, a jam sponge and shortbread.'

'Not very much and hardly exciting. Those apple tarts and the fruit scones look tempting. Come along, Annie, we'll go in and choose what we want.'

Misses Jean and Mabel Ogilvy were behind the counter and had exchanged looks when Annie and Emily entered the shop. One of them began arranging cakes on a glass shelf. No one could doubt that the women were sisters. Mabel was taller by about two inches but they had the same features. The nose was flared at the nostrils, the mouth too small and the eyes green with flecks of yellow not unlike a cat's eyes. Both had grey hair parted at the side and kept in place by a long slide.

Jean Ogilvy came to offer her assistance. 'Yes, can I help you?' The smile didn't quite reach her eyes but business came before scruples. The very lovely young woman was expensively dressed and since she had her maid with her that spoke of wealth.

'Annie?'

'Two fruit scones,' Annie said pointing to them, 'and two small apple tarts.'

'Just two Annie?'

'That's enough, it is always best to buy fresh.'

Miss Ogilvy put two fruit scones into one bag and the apple tarts in another.

'Annie, sultana cake, I just love sultana cake.'

'Far too big, Miss Emily, that's a family size.'

The woman brought it down from the shelf. 'Usually we have the one-pound size but the lady who came in before you got the last one. I can cut this in two.'

'Yes, do that,' Emily said ignoring Annie's frown. 'What about a gingerbread and a piece of cherry cake for a change. We want a bit of variety.'

'No, Miss Emily,' Annie said firmly. 'What we have is more than enough.'

'Oh, very well then,' Emily said losing interest.

The woman wrapped up the sultana cake in case that wretched maid decided it wasn't necessary and they had enough without it.

'Annie, you really are mean and it is my money or had you forgotten that?' said Emily outside the shop.

'If I hadn't stepped in you would have bought the shop,' Annie said tartly.

'Don't exaggerate.'

'I'm right though. Who would be the first to complain if I served her a piece of stale cake?'

'Very well, now what else do we need?'

'Material.'

'For the pockets? Good thing you remembered.'

'Half a yard of strong linen should do, cotton wouldn't take the weight of coins.'

'Half a yard is that enough?'

'How many pockets do you want?'

'Annie, you are getting very cheeky.'

'I'm sorry.' She knew she was taking liberties and Miss Emily was right to remind her that she was only a humble maid.

The bell tinged as they entered the shop. The girl behind the counter had sad eyes but she was extremely helpful and Annie got what she wanted. The assistant knew who the lady was and her reason for being in Dundrinnen. She wasn't narrow-minded like some of those old biddies. Had they ever been young and known what it was like to love someone? By the sour look of a few she would say they had never had a kind look from the opposite sex, so who were they to judge others? As for herself she had a lot of sympathy for the young woman. Wasn't it a true saying that bad girls didn't have babies, they made sure of that. The boy in her life was threatening to leave her if she refused to be a bit more understanding of his needs. Life could be the very devil.

'Good luck,' she said as Emily and Annie prepared to leave.

Emily looked startled then gave her lovely smile. 'Thank you.'

'They aren't all horrors after all, Annie. Wasn't she sweet?'

'Yes, she was and she didn't look too happy.'

'Crossed in love? I hope whatever the trouble, it works out for her.'

Annie looked at her mistress approvingly. Miss Emily had changed. A few short weeks ago and she would never have said that.

'A handbell, that was the other thing you wanted.'

'Where are we likely to get that?'

'We could try the hardware shop.'

Mr Prentice, the owner, scratched his head and looked at the conglomeration of goods on the wooden shelves. Judging by the layers of dust many of the articles must have been there from the time the shop opened and that wasn't a day less than thirty years.

'A handbell you say. Now what kind of bell would that be?'

'One that rings.'

Annie choked into her handkerchief.

'Well, it would be a strange one that didn't,' he said with dignity, 'and I confess I haven't come across one.'

'I'm sorry.' Emily looked and sounded apologetic. 'I shouldn't have said that but honestly I couldn't resist it.'

He smiled, completely disarmed by her smiling apology. 'No harm in finding amusement, the world would be a cheerier place if more folk would see the funny side. And now back to this bell. For what purpose would it be used?'

'To summon my maid if she should happen to be at the other side of the house.'

'A good loud ring.' He winked at Annie. 'There's the deaf and then there is those who don't want to hear.'

Annie thought she would put a word in. 'I'm not stone deaf but a little tinkle wouldn't be heard if I was busy in the kitchen. Do you have anything in stock that might suit us?'

'I doubt it. A handbell isn't something folk ask for every day. I doubt if I have had a request for one before.'

'You could order one,' Emily suggested.

'I daresay I could. Wait there and I'll get the order pad.' He disappeared into the back shop.

'Annie, he's an absolute scream.'

'A droll customer as Mrs Martin would say.'

'Here we are leddies.' Licking the pencil before starting he began to write slowly and carefully. It was copperplate writing and a joy to watch, 'One handbell with a loud ring. That should be clear enough for anyone. And now if you'll let me have your name.'

'Miss Cunningham-Brown. It's hyphenated,' she added.

'It's what?'

'Never mind,' she said quickly. 'The address is—'

'Care of Mrs McIntyre of the big house.'

Emily frowned showing her annoyance and he saw it.

'No secrets in a village, lass, more's the pity. Although I don't know, it can have its advantages too.'

'I've yet to find them.'

'Give yourself time, you've only been here five minutes. Now you'll understand I can't be saying how long this order will take but I'll say it's urgent. Not that they'll take a blind bit of notice but it keeps me right.'

'My maid will call to see if it has arrived.'

'No need for that. Molly or someone else working at the big house will hand it in and you can come in and pay for it first time you are passing. You'll appreciate there'll be a wee bit added for the extra work involved?'

'Of course and many thanks for your help.'

'You're welcome. Good day to you both.'
'He looked such a dour little man, Annie.'
'No, he didn't, not with that twinkle in his eye.'

Ten days later Molly arrived at the cottage carrying a parcel.
'Mr Prentice asked me to hand it in.'
'Thank you, Molly.'
Annie saw that the package was addressed to Miss Brown c/o Mistress McIntyre and watched Miss Emily's face when she saw it. It was a study.
'I have never been addressed that way in my life.' Then she grinned. 'You know I'm sure this was deliberate. He was anything but stupid and he knew perfectly well that my name is hyphenated but he didn't approve. Probably thought it a bit of swank.'
'Why is your name hyphenated?'
'How should I know? I haven't the faintest idea. It is my name and I just accept it.' She was examining the parcel. 'A lot of wrapping for one small article. I'll open it if you get me the scissors to cut this string.'
Annie got the scissors from the kitchen drawer and handed them to Emily. She cut the string and removed the wrapping, then Emily gave a peal of laughter and when Annie saw what was there she began to laugh too. It was certainly a handbell but the kind used by teachers to hurry the children into lines ready to march into school.
'What are you going to do with it?' Annie said holding it aloft.
'Keep it, of course. I couldn't possibly take it back.'
'I could and explain that it is too big.'
'No, he went to all that trouble and we keep it. I'll keep it on the floor beside the bed and give it a light ring. Should you be slow to answer then I shall really ring it and they'll hear it in the big house.'
'You wouldn't, it would deafen you first. Joking apart it should be possible to get a smaller one.'
'And end up with a pathetic little cow-bell one wouldn't

hear ringing behind a newspaper. We had a cow-bell at home, I think someone brought it back from Switzerland. I remember it had a lovely little tinkle and I used to imagine a huge herd of cows with each one of them having a bell round its neck and the delightful sound that would make.'

'Why did the cows have a bell round their neck?'

'Think about it, Annie,' Emily said in a schoolmistressy voice, 'try and work it out for yourself.'

Annie shot her mistress a sharp look, she hated to be made to look a fool. 'In case they strayed?'

'Exactly. You see you had no need to ask. The cow-bell is in case one strays away from the herd and so endeth the lesson for today.'

'The school-bell stays?'

'It does.'

The pattern of their life together had been set. The weeks went by and though Emily still had fits of depression when she refused to set foot outside the cottage door, they didn't last long. Annie was to learn that it was better to leave her alone, it saved tempers and was less wearing. For days a battle of wills waged over the question of employing a girl to assist with the work in the cottage. Annie had been adamant that she wanted no assistance and in the end it was Miss Emily who had to give in.

'You misunderstand me, I am well aware that you are capable, that was never in dispute.'

Annie's colour was high. 'I would think shame of myself if I couldn't look after a small cottage on my own.'

'You are entitled to some free time and another thing, when are you ever to read those books I brought especially for you?'

'I daresay I'll manage a page or two in an evening.'

'That is less than useless. A chapter or two would be more like it. Once you are really interested in a book, Annie, it is very difficult to put it down.'

'There you are then.' Annie smiled. 'I might keep on reading and forget the jobs I'm paid to do.'

Emily looked exasperated. 'You are becoming impossible, Annie Fullerton, you have an answer to everything, haven't you?'

'I'm learning Miss Emily, you are a very good teacher.'

'And I'm wasting my breath.'

'The garden needs a bit done to it – not the front, it is quite nice – but the back needs attention,' Annie said in an attempt to change the subject.

'Does it matter?' Emily said wearily, 'This is a temporary home, remember.'

'I know but you don't want to sit in the front garden do you or go round to the garden at the big house?'

'You know I don't.'

'Then we must see about the back so you can sit there.'

'And watch our unmentionables drying on the line? That would be a pretty sight.'

'I'll have the washing in before you are ready to sit out.'

Emily smiled. 'You look after me very well, Annie, and as it happens I had a word with Mrs McIntyre about tidying the border and putting in a few plants. She's going to see to it since she can't persuade me to make use of her garden.'

Emily was in the garden sitting in the wicker chair and Annie was struck by the radiance in her face.

'Annie, I've had the strangest feeling.' She touched her swollen stomach. 'Like a fluttering. My baby moved, I felt it.'

Annie dropped down on the grass beside the chair.

'That's your little one making its presence known to you,' Annie said softly.

'It was wonderful, I don't know any other word to describe it.'

'I know.'

'You can't, how can you?'

'Not the feeling, that is special to you, but I've heard it said that it was only then that some of them realised the – the wonder of it.'

Emily seemed lost in a world of her own and didn't notice when Annie got up and walked into the cottage. For the next few days Emily was broodingly silent.

'Annie, when you finish tidying up I want to talk to you. We'll go into the sitting-room.'

'Yes, all right, I'll be as quick as I can.' She washed and dried the dishes and put them away in the cupboard then she tidied the kitchen. The rest could wait.

'Shut the door and sit down. Don't look so worried, there is nothing wrong.'

'What is it then?'

'I've been doing a lot of thinking and a lot of soul-searching and I have decided to keep my baby.'

'Keep your baby?'

'Yes. Aren't you pleased? I thought you would be.'

'Pleased, Miss Emily, I couldn't be more pleased. I'm just that surprised, that's all.'

'I've rather surprised myself.'

'What—'

'What brought this on? What made me change my mind?'

'Yes.'

Her eyes softened and a lovely smile played round her mouth. 'I felt it again, my baby moved. Annie, it's mine, my own little baby. How could I ever have thought that I could give it away? It was the baby's way of telling me that I have responsibilities.'

'Yes, Miss Emily, your baby has a right to your love but what are you going to do about your parents? Maybe they will come round to your keeping it after all.'

'No, they won't, I know them too well. They don't want a grandchild born out of wedlock, they couldn't stand the shame. Keeping my baby will mean cutting myself off completely.'

'That's sad.'

'Yes, Annie it is sad, but they have each other and the boys, they'll survive without me. I have to be practical and look to my own welfare. I shan't tell them yet. It is better that my father is kept in ignorance so that he continues to pay for all this. He might not if he knew that I had had a change of heart. I shall, however, tell Mrs McIntyre so that she can inform those involved with the adoption that I am to keep my baby.'

Annie was looking at her wonderingly. Miss Emily was very pale but determined. She wasn't going into this lightly, it had all been well thought out. 'Will Mrs McIntyre go along with your wishes or will she make problems?'

'I don't know that, Annie, that's something I'll have to find out and the sooner she knows the better.'

'She could be pleased, you know.'

'If she is so much the better, but it won't make any difference. It is what I want that is important. More to the point is what about you, Annie, I can't stop you going back to Denbrae House if that is what you want.'

'Do you want me, Miss Emily?'

Emily's eyes swam with tears. 'More than you'll ever know, but even if you are not prepared to be with me I would still do this on my own.'

Annie was openly crying. 'As if I would leave you, what do you take me for?'

'I should have known, shouldn't I? Annie, will you stay with me for always?'

'For as long as you want me.'

'Bless you. That will be for always.' She paused to hand Annie a handkerchief since she didn't seem to be able to find her own. 'Are you all right now?'

Annie gave a sniff that at another time would have earned a rebuke.

'Sorry, yes, I'm fine now.' She sounded sheepish at her lack of control, it wasn't like her to break down.

'You need to know what I plan to do and fortunately there is enough money hidden away in those pockets to see us through until the baby arrives. The cottage, how fortuitous that we can occupy it until the end of the year.'

'That will give you the chance to get back your strength before having to move.'

'Exactly, though I'll be fighting fit before then. I'm thinking about the baby and that he or she will be that bit older. It'll be winter and we must be careful of the weather.'

'How will you go about finding another place to live, Miss Emily?'

'As soon as the birth is over I'll write to my solicitor and explain the position. They are sworn to secrecy, Annie. They will deal with the purchase of a house and all I have to do is tell them my requirements and that I want to live in the Aberdeenshire area.'

'Won't you have to go and look at the houses?'

'Of course, silly, but those they suggest I inspect will meet most of the requirements.'

'You wouldn't want to return to Perthshire?'

'Yes, I would, but it is out of the question. I would like to put a lot of miles between us and Denbrac House.'

'And Dundrinnen, I don't suppose you want to be too near it either?'

'No, I don't. This should be a fresh start and Aberdeen, according to my mother, is a lovely city. A house on the outskirts shouldn't be too difficult to get. It won't be a mansion you know, I haven't that kind of money.'

'Then we'll have to be careful and not be extravagant.'

Emily gave a peal of laughter. 'Extravagant – you? Annie, you don't know the meaning of the word. No, no, we'll be very comfortably off but I see myself buying a house something like the one my Great-Aunt Anne had in Newport. She had a nice garden, not too big, and suitable for a child to play in. This is beginning to sound quite exciting.' She gave a happy laugh.

Annie didn't want to spoil these moments. She was both surprised and delighted to know the baby wouldn't be going to strangers but Miss Emily would only see what she wanted to see. She knew nothing about babies and young children and how demanding they could be.

'You will have to start thinking about a name for the baby.'

Emily looked smug. 'I already have. If I have a daughter she shall be called Tina.'

'Short for Clementina?'

'No, certainly not, I hate that name but I do like Tina. Tina Cunningham-Brown.'

'And if it is a boy?'

'I am almost sure I am going to have a daughter but should it be a boy then I should call him after his father I think. I told you he is an artist and that is more than my parents know. They tried but they got nothing out of me.'

Annie felt some sympathy for Mr and Mrs Cunningham-Brown; they would believe they had a right to know about the man who had ruined their daughter and want to make him answer in some way.

'I'm thirsty,' Emily said abruptly. They were in the sitting-room where a small fire burned.

'I'll go and make tea and then I must do some ironing.'

'No, it can wait. Make the tea and bring it through. I haven't finished what I want to say.' She sounded weary.

'Can't the rest wait until tomorrow, you sound tired?'

'I am tired, I always seem to be tired and I'm tired of being tired,' she said petulantly. 'I feel like talking about this and I may not by tomorrow.'

Annie made the tea and brought it through.

'I can't tell you much about the baby's father because I know so little. That must sound quite dreadful since I am carrying his child. You can't begin to understand because you have never been in love, have you?'

Annie felt irritated. Why should it be taken for granted that she hadn't been in love? That she had never experienced what it was like. It was true, of course, that she hadn't, but she had her dreams like most girls. Unlike other girls she wanted it kept that way. The reality could prove disappointing whereas nothing could spoil the dream.

'No, I haven't been in love.'

'That could be a mixed blessing. I've flirted as you very well know but this was different. He was a man not a boy and I made the mistake of forgetting that.'

'You weren't to blame for what happened, it was your sheltered life.'

'You would have had more sense.'

'I like to think so but then I've never been tempted,' she grinned.

'Annie, you are becoming frivolous.'

'No, I'm not, I'm being truthful.'

'People like you always learn the facts of life early on and there you have the advantage. My mother, and so many like her, couldn't bring herself to discuss such personal matters. We, my friends and I, picked up little bits here and there and pooled our knowledge which didn't add up to a lot and most of it was nonsense. It all seems so long ago, in another life almost and when I look back I find it humiliating that one man could have had such an effect on me. I was so besotted, Annie, that the days I didn't see him were just days to be got through.' She looked sad. 'Would you believe it if I told you that I can no longer recall the face of the man I loved so dearly.'

'Maybe it was infatuation and not love.'

'It makes no difference now and I have to say this in all honesty that he, I'm not going to say his name, was in no way to blame for what happened.'

'It takes two.'

'I threw myself at him.'

'I can't see you doing that.'

'Nevertheless I did. I wouldn't leave him alone and I know he found me a pest. In the end I chased him away. My poor frantic mother couldn't understand why I was protective of him.'

'Neither can I.'

'He never knew about – about the baby. He had long gone before I discovered I was pregnant. Isn't that a strange word – pregnant – my mother doesn't like to use it. You aren't saying much, Annie, don't you want to ask me anything?'

'Did he have a job, Miss Emily?'

'I told you what he did.'

'No, you didn't. Maybe you thought you did but you didn't.'

'He was an artist and someone who couldn't settle in one place. Let me show you something and again you are the first to see it.' She went inside her bag and brought out an envelope. The slip of paper inside she handed to Annie.

'Oh, Miss Emily, it is good and you to a T. Caught you real natural like.'

'I wasn't aware he was sketching me and I had to plead before he would let me have it. He didn't specialise in portraits but he said that was where the money was. He was very, very talented,' she said wistfully, 'and I especially liked the paintings he did in Italy. He loved Florence, it had a special place in his heart.'

'What would you do if you saw him again?'

'I haven't the faintest idea but there is no chance of that happening.'

'You never know. Life can play strange tricks.'

'If it were to happen he would have to make the first move. If he didn't recognise me I would not introduce myself.'

'Some would say he had a right to know about his child.'

'Some undoubtedly would but I wouldn't be one of them.' She paused and looked searchingly at Annie. 'You think I haven't given this enough thought.'

'No, I don't think that at all. What I am afraid of is that you don't realise the difficulties ahead.'

'I do, but I am not dwelling on them. I'll be a social outcast, an unmarried woman with a child. No one will want to know me. That has all occurred to me and I had it pressed home when, to my mother's distress, I didn't seem to be going along with the adoption.'

'True friends accept a person for what she is, faults and all.'

'I fear I have very few friends.'

'You'll make more, the right kind,' Annie said loyally.

'I could pretend to be a widow, that would make life easier.'

'Would you?'

'I don't think so but I can't be absolutely sure. Enough about me, we are going to talk about you. Your status must improve. Instead of my maid you will be my housekeeper and employ your own staff. I will take on a nursemaid to look after the baby.'

'Won't you want to do that yourself?'

Emily couldn't have looked more shocked. 'I'll cuddle my baby and play with it but as to the unpleasant tasks those will be done by the nursemaid.'

Beatrice McIntyre was more than surprised to see Miss Cunningham-Brown on the doorstep.

'Miss Cunningham-Brown, do come in. I trust you are well?'

Emily followed the woman into the sitting-room and took the chair offered.

'I am well enough apart from being tired, thank you.'

'They say the last month is very trying.'

'Whoever they are are absolutely right. Only to be expected with the weight getting heavier every day.'

'Would you like a word with the midwife?'

'No, I came to see you to tell you that I have decided to keep my baby.'

'Really! This is surely a very sudden decision?'

'No, for some time I have been giving the matter a good deal of thought and with the decision made I wanted you to know so that you can cancel the arrangements made for adoption.'

Beatrice McIntyre remained silent.

'You can do that, can't you?'

'Of course, it is the mother's privilege to change her mind. Some do when they see their baby.'

'You are not going to try and dissuade me?'

'Why should I?'

'I just thought you might, that's all.'

'I happen to approve,' she smiled. 'Perhaps it is because I have seen too many broken-hearted girls forced to give away their baby because of parental pressure.'

'I'm so glad to have you on my side and it will make it easier to say what I have to. I want my parents kept in ignorance as long as possible. If they were to learn of this they would do everything in their power to stop me keeping my baby and that scares me.'

'It shouldn't. You sound very brave to me.'

'I'm not, this is just an act.' Her voice faltered. 'Will you promise?'

'What are you asking of me?'

'Don't let my parents or anyone else force me to give my baby away. I might weaken and that would be dreadful. Just promise me that it won't be adopted?'

'What happens to your baby is for you to say.'

'They'll say, I know they will, that I am in no position to know what is best.'

'Rest assured that not even your parents have the power to go against your wishes.' Even as she said it Beatrice McIntyre wondered if she was making a false promise. There were always ways and means and wealthy families with the right connections very often got what they wanted.

Chapter Eight

When she returned to the cottage and let herself in, Emily was feeling quietly happy and hearing Annie in the kitchen she went straight there.

Annie was humming to herself and looked up briefly from where she was standing at the sink peeling potatoes.

'How did you get on, Miss Emily?' she said plunging her hand into the cold water and feeling in it for another potato.

'Let me sit down first then I'll tell you. Goodness don't I sound like an old woman,' she said as she sat down in the one comfortable chair.

'Just be glad you don't look like one.'

'Don't I?'

Annie smiled at her fondly. 'You look even more beautiful than usual.'

'My skin and my hair, yes I have to agree with you there. Just as well I don't look as I feel. No, Annie, get that worried frown away. I am not unwell, just bloated for want of a better word. And now let me tell you about Mrs McIntyre, she isn't at all the ogre I was making her out to be. Actually she couldn't have been nicer and according to her the final decision regarding my baby is mine. If I choose to keep it then no one can stop me. Some girls, she told me, change their mind at the very last minute. They find that they cannot go through with it, the parting I mean.'

Annie was delighted that it had all gone so well and she

was smiling as she drained the water away leaving the potato peelings in the basin. Later they would be thrown into the bucket.

'Your worries are over then, Miss Emily.'

'They are just beginning,' Emily said as her face took on a worried look. 'Mrs McIntyre had me very nearly convinced but thinking about it and knowing my father, Annie, I cannot help being afraid.'

'Don't be, Miss Emily,' Annie said seriously and drying her hands sat down herself. 'If you need to fight to keep your baby then fight.'

'And if I lose the fight – and I'm very much afraid that is what will happen?'

'It won't. The baby is yours, you have to remember that and if the worst comes to the worst I'll hide it myself.'

'I do believe you would,' she smiled.

Annie had made the remark half in jest. She knew that she would do anything to keep the infant from being adopted.

'I'd have a good try.'

'Bless you. You are on my side and so is Mrs McIntyre and most important of all I am not penniless. I must keep reminding myself of that. It didn't trouble me before but suddenly looking after my own child and loving it has become very important to me.'

'You are growing up, Miss Emily.'

'Perhaps I am. Thank you, Annie, for always being there when I need you. I do take you for granted but, believe me, without you I would feel very lost.'

'Your parents may come round when they see how much it means to you.'

'They will never come round. Well mother perhaps, she might, but that wouldn't do any good. She wouldn't go against my father and he has the final say in everything.'

Annie imagined that to be true.

'I won't tell them and neither will Mrs McIntyre.'

'Are you sure about Mrs McIntyre?'

'Reasonably sure. In any case she isn't in direct communication with my father. All this,' she waved a hand round the room, 'is done through someone else.'

'And yet you aren't sure, are you?'

'Not completely. It isn't as easy as you would like to make out.'

'I wasn't,' Annie protested.

'You don't know just how difficult it is for me. You only know my father as an employer. I love him and he loves me even though I have disappointed him. He has his faults, don't we all, but we are family and you cannot understand that.'

'Oh, yes, I can understand it,' Annie said bitterly. 'I may not have a family but that doesn't mean I lack understanding.'

'Sorry, I always seem to say the wrong thing to you. Let us get back to my father. Do his bidding and he is kindness itself, cross him and you'll regret it. He has a ruthless streak and he has friends in high places. It would be a mistake to underestimate him.' She gave a small shiver. 'This is wrong of me and I shouldn't be talking like this and certainly not to you.'

'Because I am a maid?'

'That is what you are, Annie. A very, very good maid but still a maid.'

'And one, I hope, who can be trusted to keep her mouth shut,' Annie said, hurt and angry to be spoken to like that.

'That was rather vulgar of you but I shall ignore it. It is tiresome always having to remember how sensitive you are.'

Annie went back to the sink to get on with the work and nothing was said for a while then Emily spoke, 'You are in a pique.'

'I am not.'

'Yes, you are and all I can say is sorry for whatever I said that offended you. Am I forgiven?'

'Yes. Just don't go on about me being sensitive. How am I to know what to do when one time you are treating me like a friend and the next as a maid who hasn't the sense to know when to keep quiet.'

'That was quite a speech.' She giggled and Annie couldn't keep the smile from her face.

'Yes, I'm learning fast, wouldn't you say?'

'No comment. To be serious again, Annie, I worry what he might do.'

'What could Mr Cunningham-Brown do?'

'If all else failed he could have me declared an unfit person to be in charge of an infant.'

'All new mothers have to learn. No one could declare you unfit.'

Emily gave a wry smile. 'I wouldn't have the faintest idea where to begin.'

'That wouldn't matter since you have the money as you said yourself—'

'To employ a nursemaid?'

That wasn't what Annie was about to say but she nodded her head.

'Dear, dear Great-Aunt Anne, she was all for women having independence. She said it was power and, of course, it is. Thinking about her is giving me strength and you'll be pleased to know my brain is beginning to work. I do see a way forward. There is no correspondence between here and Denbrae House. That hurt me terribly at the time, Annie, but I see it as an advantage in the circumstances. Not hearing to the contrary they will just assume that the adoption will go ahead as arranged.'

'They won't know you have instructed Mrs McIntyre that the adoption will not go ahead.'

'Exactly and by the time they do I shall have been in touch with my solicitor to release me some money and to go ahead with finding us a house.'

'And you can stay in the cottage until the end of the year?'

'Yes, though I do see one problem.' She stopped and Annie looked at her. 'What if my parents suddenly take it into their head to come and see me?'

'Is that likely?'

'No, it is very unlikely, but it is not impossible. My

mother's pleading to be allowed to visit me might eventually wear him down. You have to help me.'

'You know I will, I'll do anything.'

'I could be feeling weak and be at my most vulnerable. Or I could be afraid and I am afraid of pain and what is before me.'

'Don't be, just remember how many babies are born every minute of the day.'

'That doesn't help me. If they work on me just to get peace I might, just might, give in and let them have their way.'

'You might have done so at first but not now. I won't let you weaken, Miss Emily.'

'I don't want to but I know myself. Standing up to my father was difficult enough at the best of times——' She closed her eyes and left the rest unsaid.

'If you give your baby away you will never forgive yourself.'

'I know that, you don't have to tell me. Oh, why does everything have to be so difficult,' she said petulantly.

'It needn't be.'

'Anyone hearing you, Annie, would think this is as important for you as it is for me.'

'They wouldn't be far wrong. Rather than see it going to strangers I would run away with the baby myself.'

'I hardly think you would do that but you are a strong person, Annie. Your hard life would make you that, so some good came out of it.'

'It taught me what matters and what doesn't. Belonging is——' she broke off. When she got emotional she was inclined to say too much. Once she had bottled it all up and now she had a great need to talk about it. Not to anyone, but to someone who would understand. Miss Emily was not that person.

'Belonging, what were you going to say?'

'It doesn't matter.'

'It does to me. We are educating each other, Annie.

You know about my world and I want to learn about yours.'

'I'm not asking for sympathy, you asked. I never belonged to anyone. If I had disappeared there would have been a half-hearted search, no more than that, then I would have been forgotten.'

'Surely not?' Miss Emily was shocked. 'Surely someone . . .'

'No, I would have been missed less than the others because I kept myself to myself.'

'How sad.' She moved herself to a more comfortable position in the chair. 'You do belong now, you belong to me. If I were to lose you I would be heartbroken. You are part of my life now whether you like it or not.'

'That is the nicest thing anyone has ever said to me,' Annie sniffed.

'I am being ridiculous but I'm curious. How would you manage with a baby if this had happened to you?'

'Where there is a will there is a way.'

'You would manage somehow.' She yawned. 'I'm so wearied and I wonder to myself how women can bear to go through all this time and time again. Once is more than enough for me.'

'The decision isn't always in their hands,' Annie said drily.

'Annie, there are some things better left unsaid,' Emily said primly.

'Soon be over, you haven't long to go.'

'Every day seems like a week. I dread what is ahead but I want it over.'

'You could be one of the lucky ones and get it over very quickly.'

'No, I don't think so, my mother had a difficult time with me.'

'Doesn't mean it will be the same for you.'

'No and she did have an easier time with my two brothers. All this baby talk reminds me I'll need a crib, a pram and masses of other things.'

'Not right away apart from the crib.'

'Thank heaven for Mrs McIntyre, she will know what to get and she can order them on my behalf.' She began to laugh.

'What is so funny?'

'We are cramped enough, where on earth are we going to put a pram?'

Annie wouldn't have said they were cramped. She loved the cottage and if she could have her wish it would be her dream home.

'We'll find a place and the shop will keep it until it is required.'

Emily didn't tell Annie everything. She couldn't know how much Emily was missing her mother and how desperately she longed to be back in Denbrae House. The thought of cutting herself off for ever was going to be far more difficult than she had imagined. Denbrae House had been home to her all her life. She missed it and she missed her family and longed to be back in her parents' good books.

Annie saw the fleeting expressions, the sadness in those lovely eyes and wondered what thoughts were going through her head.

'The fire is lit in the sitting-room,' she said gently, 'you would be more comfortable there.'

'I doubt it, I don't seem to be comfortable anywhere and surely I shouldn't be this tired? Even the thought of getting up and going through is an effort.'

'The last wee while is the worst. You think about it, Miss Emily, it is like carrying a heavy parcel with you all the time. You cannot put it down and take a rest.'

Emily looked down at her bulging figure. 'What bliss it will be to have my body my own again.'

One monotonous day followed another. September had been very mild with less than average rainfall. The farmers were showing concern and the gardens looked tired and dried up. All that changed on the first day of October when the heavens opened. Fortunately after forty-eight hours of constant rain it stopped, thus avoiding the flooding which could have become a major disaster. Prayers had been answered. Dundrinnen breathed a sigh of relief when the skies cleared, a drying wind got up and the countryside got back to normal.

The midwife had called in to see Emily on several occasions and declared herself satisfied. Mrs Drummond was stout and motherly-looking with a quietly confident manner that helped to reassure Emily. Annie had been given her instructions and knew exactly what to do. First babies, they were both told, were seldom in a hurry to put in an appearance but for all that it was better to be prepared and not wander too far away. There was no chance of Emily straying, she seldom ventured over the door.

Sleeping was becoming a problem with no position comfortable. She welcomed the morning when she could sit up, have a cup of tea and let Annie fuss over her. Annie had to help her to dress and brush her hair. The handbell that had caused so much hilarity when it was bought was being put to good use. Poor Annie was back and forward until even her patience was being sorely tried.

When Annie got to bed she slept the sleep of sheer exhaustion. Somewhere a bell was ringing, disturbing the silence and irritating her with its insistence. If only it would stop, but instead it was getting louder. As if through a haze Annie became aware that the sound was coming from Miss Emily's room. How long had it been ringing? Throwing the bedclothes back and on bare feet Annie hurried along to see to her mistress.

She was sitting up in bed looking angry and frightened. 'I thought you were never coming. I've been ringing and ringing.'

'I'm sorry, I was sound asleep.' She turned up the lamp and saw by the clock that it was a few minutes after four o'clock.

'It's started, Annie, I'm sure of it.'

Annie forced herself to be calm. She knew exactly what was expected of her.

'Miss Emily, I am going to dress myself then I am going to the big house to waken Mrs McIntyre and have her come over,' she said it quietly and clearly as though to a child.

'What about Mrs Drummond?'

'Too early for her. Mrs McIntyre will know when.'

'You can't leave me on my own,' her voice was rising dangerously.

'Calm down, Miss Emily, it will be only for a few minutes,' Annie called back as she reached her bedroom and began throwing on some clothes. Snatching a coat from the peg she hurried to Miss Emily. 'Don't worry, you'll be fine and I'll run all the way.'

Emily tried to smile but the sudden unexpected pain changed it into a grimace. She bit her lip and tears slid weakly from the corner of her eyes, down her cheek and into her mouth where she tasted the salt. 'Mother, I want my mother,' she shouted to the empty house and knowing her mother was far away.

Mrs McIntyre in a warm coat over her dressing-gown, asked some questions and nodded at the answers.

'A false alarm. You rest, my dear, the baby won't be putting in its appearance for some time yet.'

'Are you sure?'

'Quite sure. Believe me you will get more warning than that.'

'What about the midwife, shouldn't she be here?'

'Mrs Drummond is attending another birth, she will call in when she can.'

'What happens if I need her before then?' Emily's eyes widened and a little of the old haughtiness appeared.

'I can assure you, Miss Cunningham-Brown, Mrs Drummond will be here when she is required.'

Emily had the grace to look ashamed. 'I am so sorry, but I am a terrible coward.'

'Aren't we all? No more pains just that one?'

'It was two, one more severe than the other and I did think—'

'No need to apologise. We'll get busy when the pains become regular and we'll time them. You just relax and get some sleep. That applies to you as well, Annie, and myself for that matter.' She yawned.

'I'm sorry, it seems I was fussing for nothing.'

The woman and Annie exchanged looks and smiled. They couldn't have agreed more.

Another day dragged on. Pale and anxious, Emily wandered about the cottage, going from the sitting-room to the bedroom then the bedroom to the kitchen. Most of her time was spent in the kitchen since she needed to be with someone and that was where Annie was usually to be found. The weather had turned colder and the fires were on all day and into the night which made for more work for Annie. She didn't mind, she preferred to be kept busy. Emily carried a book with her but was finding it hard to concentrate. She said she could read a whole page without having taken in a word of it.

Everyone agreed the young woman was making an unnecessary fuss but then, as they said, that was the way with some spoilt young ladies. No one would think anyone had had a baby before. She had brought the trouble on herself, irresponsible behaviour and this was the result. It would do her good to see how other women coped. How many worked until the last minute and when the baby was born they were lucky if they got a full day to recover.

Annie was more sympathetic, she understood her mistress, knew her strengths and weaknesses. She might call herself a coward but she wasn't.

Night came and Miss Emily was in bed and asleep. Annie had drossed up the fire in the kitchen to keep it burning until morning. The big black kettle was never far from the boil and as well as it, there was a large pot filled with water on the range ready for the time when it would be needed. Annie felt on edge and didn't undress. She lay on her bed and willed herself to stay awake. Something told her it would be tonight and she was proved right. Hearing the bell

Annie was up and on her feet and hurrying through to Miss Emily. She turned up the lamp until it lit up the whole room.

'I don't think this is a false alarm.' Emily smiled and looked surprisingly calm, a lot calmer than Annie who had dashed to the big house and then back. Mrs McIntyre followed in ten minutes and ordered Annie to get her skates on and dash the half mile to the house where Mrs Drummond lived with her husband. The man was on regular nightshift and used to doing for himself when he got in from work. He didn't mind or perhaps he did and just didn't say. Mrs Drummond said he never complained. Not so their two daughters who were now working and in service in Aberdeen. They had been glad to get away from home and were thoroughly enjoying life. Both had been well placed so their mother said and she had no worries. They had received a good Christian upbringing and knew right from wrong. They weren't likely to stray from the straight and narrow. Perhaps it secretly worried her that they hardly ever visited Dundrinnen but she made the excuse that they led busy lives. The truth was that the girls had not been happy at home. With their father on night duty and sleeping through the day they always had to tiptoe about. And having a midwife for a mother meant she could be called out at any time. They liked what the extra money provided but still felt it didn't compensate for an absent mother.

Mrs Drummond was already with Emily and before Mrs McIntyre went in she called to Annie over her shoulder.

'The time will go faster if you keep yourself busy, I don't see much happening for a while yet.' She smiled. 'A cup of tea would be welcome, would you see to that?'

'Right away. The kettle is just on the boil and I'll bring the tray along in a few minutes.'

'Just knock, don't come in. Mrs Drummond wouldn't like it and she is in charge.'

Annie infused the tea and felt hurt and left out. What

harm was there in speaking to Miss Emily for a minute or two? None that she could see and who, she wondered, was fussing now? She would keep herself busy, anything was better than twirling her thumbs and listening. There was always washing to be done and after filling the sink she got out the scrubbing board and the hard green soap and set to with a will. Three rinses, the last one cold, made sure that no soap remained to darken the whites. With the basket on her hip she went outside and began pegging the washing on the line. In that wind it wouldn't be long before they were ready for ironing.

She was back indoors and polishing the furniture when her heart almost stopped. The screams, blood-chilling, filled the house and Annie went white with shock. Instinctively she made to rush to Miss Emily but good sense prevailed and she forced herself to remain calm. What was happening was normal, she told herself. Childbirth was no picnic but the pain, so they said, was quickly forgotten else there would be fewer children in the world. The joy of motherhood was the gift at the end. The bedroom door opened and Mrs McIntyre came out looking agitated.

She closed the door behind her and said in an urgent whisper, 'She's having a difficult time, Annie, and Mrs Drummond feels the doctor should be called. Go quickly and tell Dr Rutherford to come at once.'

'Is Miss Emily very bad?' Annie asked fearfully.

'This isn't the time for questions. Just hurry if we are to save the baby.'

It was late afternoon, people were about their business and some looked in surprise at the flying figure of a young woman. Her hair had come loose and hung untidily and when she reached the doctor's house there was a painful stitch in her side. Her breathing was ragged as she rapped the knocker repeatedly. It was answered by a middle-aged woman who looked distinctly annoyed.

'No need for that, I haven't wings on my feet and I happened to be upstairs. What is it you want?'

'The doctor,' Annie said breathlessly. 'It's an emergency. Mrs Drummond and Mrs McIntyre—'

'The baby is coming, is that it?'

Annie nodded her head and then shook it. 'Yes, no, I mean something is wrong.' Why didn't the stupid woman get the doctor instead of standing there wasting time?

'Dr Rutherford is out on a call but I'll tell him when he gets in.'

Annie's heart sank. 'Please! It's very urgent.'

Seeing the young woman's distress the face softened. 'The minute he gets in I'll tell him. I'll tell my husband it's an emergency. Try to remember that babies are tough little things and they can stand a lot. You'll be from the big house?'

'No, the cottage.'

'As I say I'll tell him.' She was closing the door.

'He won't be long will he? If she just had that assurance.'

Mrs Rutherford had no idea how long her husband would be, but it would do no good telling the girl that.

'I shouldn't think so.' The door closed and Annie turned away.

When she got back an anxious Mrs McIntyre was waiting for her.

'The doctor wasn't there but his wife said she would tell him to come the minute he got in.'

'She knows it is an emergency?'

'Yes, I made sure she did.'

'Then all we can do is wait.'

'How is Miss Emily?'

'Very tired as is only to be expected.'

Dr Rutherford arrived within the hour. He was a stout man with a florid complexion and a small neat moustache. He took in the situation, removed Mrs McIntyre, then recalled her fifteen minutes later.

Annie walked the floor biting her nails to the quick and wondered how much longer it would take. Then it came, the first cry of the newborn that sounded remarkably like outrage but to Annie it was the sweetest of sounds. Tears of joy and relief were pouring down her face and she sat and rocked herself in the chair. Any moment now someone would come and tell her whether it was a boy or a girl. No one came, not for a very long time. Then the door opened and a drawn-faced Beatrice McIntyre appeared with the precious bundle in her arms. Annie got up quickly for that first peep at the baby.

'What is it?' she asked.

'A girl.'

'Is she all right?' The woman wasn't smiling and Annie became anxious.

'A perfect little girl,' she said and stopped as Dr Rutherford came out of the bedroom followed by the midwife. The doctor was grim-faced and Mrs Drummond looked completely exhausted. They were all looking at Annie.

'What is it?' She had a creeping sense of dread as she looked from one face to the other. None of them seemed in a hurry to speak and after clearing his throat it was the doctor who spoke.

'Miss—?'

'Annie Fullerton,' she whispered, 'that's my name.'

'I am so very, very sorry, Miss Fullerton, but I have to tell you that Miss Cunningham-Brown is dead,' he said quietly. 'We did everything possible but she just didn't have the strength left.' He shook his head, clearly upset.

Annie, who had never fainted in her life crumpled to the floor. When she came to the doctor had gone and she was stretched out on the sofa and two pairs of anxious eyes were watching her. As she struggled to a sitting position she was remembering and a look of horror crossed her face. A nightmare; she hadn't had one for a very long time. Not like this one though, this was worse. And then she knew it hadn't been a nightmare. Miss Emily was dead and she would never see her beloved mistress again. Or, and she clung to this, could there have been a mistake? Annie tried to move her lips to form a question but she couldn't – she was too afraid of the answer.

'She's in shock,' Mrs McIntyre said.

'And she's not the only one,' the midwife said brokenly. 'I can't believe it, she seemed such a healthy young woman—'

'You heard the doctor, Mrs Drummond, you heard what he said. There was nothing more you or anyone else could have done. The poor lass had no more strength left and it is a miracle the baby survived.'

'I'm not blaming myself. I did what I could and no one can do more than that. Telling myself that doesn't make it any easier. In all my time as a midwife I've had two stillbirths and that was upsetting enough but I've never lost a mother until today.'

Annie heard voices but couldn't make sense of what she was hearing.

Mrs Drummond got to her feet and passed a hand over her brow. 'I've some tidying up to do,' she said heavily.

'Let me help.'

'Kind of you but I'm better on my own. I take it it will fall to you to inform the parents?'

'Yes, word will have to be sent to them and then there are all the arrangements to be made.' She nodded to the still figure. 'One thing is for sure, she can't remain here.'

'Where will she go?'

'I'll have to take her. She looks as though she might go to pieces, there appeared to be a very strong bond between mistress and maid.'

'Strange that, it isn't usually the way, but then again in the circumstances she would need someone and the family were keeping their distance.' She paused. 'Or that was what I gathered.' She didn't want to be accused of listening to gossip.

'Protecting their name, that is so very important for people in their position. There will be plenty of talk now. The poor lass is going to cause more trouble in death than she did in life. There is no way they can hide the truth.'

The midwife gave a deep sigh, went into the bedroom and closed the door.

Annie moved and made to sit up. 'Feeling a little better now?' Mrs McIntyre said kindly.

Annie nodded. How could she be feeling better? It was as though a part of herself had gone with Miss Emily.

'You can't stay in the cottage, Annie, you must know that?'

Where would she go? 'I can, I'm not afraid.' What was there to be afraid of?

'No, Annie, until you are more like yourself I am taking charge. You will pack a few things and stay with me for a day or two.'

She didn't want that and neither, she thought, did Mrs McIntyre. She was doing it out of kindness. 'No, really . . .'

'You cannot stay in the cottage and that is final.'

Annie knew when she was beaten and nodded. In spite of her reluctance to go to the big house Annie was glad to have someone take charge. There was a roaring in her ears making it difficult to think. Something was troubling her, there was something important she had to do. Just as she was despairing of remembering, it came to her in a flash. The baby. Miss Emily's baby. How could she have forgotten it. What if it was already too late and it had been spirited away? What about her promise to look after the baby and to make sure it didn't go to strangers? Her eyes dilated and she clutched at Mrs McIntyre's arm making that woman wince.

'The baby, what have you done with it?' she almost shouted.

'Stop it, Annie. Stop it at once. The baby is being looked after—'

'No, I don't believe you, you've given her away.'

'Mrs Drummond has taken the baby to a wet nurse and there she will remain until suitable arrangements can be made,' the woman said coldly. The girl was just a maid and Mrs McIntyre was not prepared to be spoken to like that.

Annie was just realising that. 'I'm sorry but you just don't understand. Yes, you do, you must, you gave your promise.'

'Annie, calm down you are not making sense.'

'Yes, I am. Miss Emily told me herself that you were in favour of her keeping her baby and there would be no fear of it being adopted.'

'All perfectly true,' she said soothingly, 'but sadly Miss Cunningham-Brown is not here to look after her child.'

'I'm here. She trusted me to see that her baby wasn't adopted.'

'Yes, I'm sure she did.' The girl was raving but she would come to her senses later. It would be laughable if it weren't so tragic. A single woman, a humble maid, daring to believe she could take this baby. The dead woman wouldn't have wanted her child brought up by someone like that. Mr and Mrs Cunningham-Brown weren't prepared to accept the child when their daughter was alive. They would be less willing now.

Annie packed some clothes and walked to the house. She should have been embarrassed going to the front door but she was too numb to feel anything. Molly already knew of the tragedy and being a kind-hearted girl she wasn't going to show any resentment at being asked to prepare a room for Annie. As well as making up the bed she had prepared tea and sandwiches. Annie couldn't eat, the lump in her throat wouldn't let her but she appreciated the kindness and tried to say so. Mrs McIntyre told Molly to put a couple of sandwiches on a plate and put them in Annie's bedroom, she might eat them later.

She was looking agitated and was wringing her hands.

'Is there something the matter?'

'Tina. I must talk about Tina.'

'And who is Tina?' The girl was worse than she thought.

'The baby, Miss Emily chose that name.'

'Clementina?'

'No, definitely no, just Tina. Tina Cunningham-Brown.'

Mrs McIntyre smiled to humour the girl. Whoever adopted the infant would want to choose a name.

'Tina is my responsibility and tomorrow I'll go and see this wet nurse. I know she is needed for the first week or two but she can teach me how to look after a baby. I know it is just common sense but I want to do everything right.'

'Annie, you haven't thought this through. Where are you going to get the money?'

'I'll manage.' She smiled to herself as she remembered the two pockets she had made for Miss Emily's money. Miss Emily had called it a sizeable sum and a sizeable amount to her would be a very large sum to Annie. Even counting what she had spent there would still be plenty left and the cottage was paid for until the end of the year. That would give her time to make plans.

'How can you manage? You have to earn your living and not many employers would be prepared to engage a single woman with a baby.'

Annie knew all that. 'Plenty of women would be pleased to look after a baby with their own children. They would think it easily earned money. I'd take her in the morning and collect her when I finished work.'

'Would you trust the baby with just anyone?'

'Of course I wouldn't,' Annie said indignantly, 'I'd make sure Tina was being well cared for.'

'You seem to have it all worked out.'

'We talked about it a lot. Miss Emily had plans made and I was always part of those,' she said proudly. 'You don't believe me, do you?' she said accusingly.

'I do believe you. My worry is that you don't know what you are taking on.'

'I know all right. And you have to remember this, Mrs McIntyre, I am the one person who can tell Tina about her mother. When she is old enough to understand I'll be able to tell her about Miss Emily,' she said unsteadily. 'She'll learn from me that her mother was the loveliest and kindest person I have ever known. Don't try and make me change my mind because nothing will. This is the one way I can repay Miss Emily for all she did for me.'

'You seem to forget the grandparents—'

'They don't want her.'

'That's probably true but they will want some say in what happens.'

'They won't. I bet they won't even ask about it.'

'We are both exhausted and I suggest you go to bed and try and sleep. Tomorrow is another day.' What she meant was that after a night's sleep she would rid herself of the silly notion that someone like her could be put in charge of that poor motherless mite. Adoption was the only sensible course.

Chapter Nine

It was all over and in an almost indecent haste, Annie thought. She was more than shocked, she was outraged since she had fully expected Miss Emily's body to be taken home and laid to rest in the cemetery close to her beloved Denbrae House. But no, she had been buried in the graveyard behind Dundrinnen Church in a steady drizzle that quickly soaked the few people gathered there. No one had thought to ask Annie to attend the short service and she hadn't known whether to be glad or sorry. Upon reflection she thought she should be glad since it saved her an ordeal. Miss Emily was dead. Annie had loved her, respected her and she was deeply mourned. It was still almost impossible to believe that she would never see that lovely face again or hear her voice. How could she have borne it? The women would hear the short service and then the men would go to the graveside to see the coffin lowered, a handful of earth sprinkled on it by her father and then they would turn away while the grave-diggers got busy to complete their job.

Staying at the big house had been a mistake, she ought to have stood her ground and refused to move. No one could have forced her but, to be honest, at that time she had been incapable of making decisions. It was a time charged with emotion and Mrs McIntyre had spoken impulsively probably regretting her words almost immediately. Since it had been more of an order than an invitation the woman could hardly have withdrawn it without losing face. Annie had felt uncomfortable and unwanted. She wasn't a guest and her offer to help Molly had been refused. There was relief all round when Miss Emily's body was removed from the cottage and Annie was able to return there. In the cottage she could be herself. No need to put on a brave face, she was free to do her weeping.

The wet nurse who went by the name of Mamie Reid lived in one of the narrow sidestreets in a small but spotlessly clean house. Annie liked her on sight. She was small, stout and heavy breasted and a natural with babies. Annie watched the gentle but firm way she handled Tina and breathed more easily. Mamie Reid didn't have much to say for herself and Annie imagined her to be more at ease with babies than with adults. Tina was in safe and capable hands. She would come to no harm.

Molly came to the cottage door the next morning to say that Mrs McIntyre wished to see her and to come over when she was ready. Anxious to learn what this was all about Annie got her coat and accompanied Molly to the big house.

'Thank you for coming so quickly. Sit down, Annie.'

Annie sat down and waited. She was alarmed but tried not to show it. The woman's first words didn't help, they made matters worse.

'I want to talk about the baby—'

'Tina is fine,' Annie said hastily. 'I've been to see her and Mrs Reid is marvellous with babies.'

'Mamie Reid is very experienced and I didn't ask you here to discuss the wet nurse. What I want to say to you concerns the adoption arrangements which were cancelled on the instructions of Miss Cunningham-Brown.'

Annie nodded. She knew all about that.

'At the time I was in total agreement but not now, not in the changed circumstances. Then I believed that the young woman was to take full responsibility for her baby.'

'That's right, so she was. We had it all arranged,' Annie said eagerly. 'Miss Emily was to buy a house and—'

'Which can't happen now,' Beatrice McIntyre interrupted impatiently. She had some sympathy for the girl but she was being impossible.

'Would you go against the wishes of a dead woman, Mrs McIntyre?' Annie said harshly. 'We both promised her that the baby wouldn't go to strangers and I won't break my promise.'

'What happened alters everything.'

'No it doesn't. She said whatever happened.'

'You mean – surely you don't mean that Miss Cunningham-Brown thought she might die?'

'No, I don't mean that at all. She was just afraid—'

'Afraid of what?'

'That someone might try and take her baby without her consent and when she couldn't do anything about it.' Annie moistened her lips. 'She was afraid that her parents might come through and her not being able to hold out against them.'

'She said something of the sort to me.'

'You can't go back on your promise, Mrs McIntyre,' Annie pleaded.

'I like to keep my word and I don't break a promise without good reason. This may sound unkind but it has to be said. Miss Cunningham-Brown did not want her child adopted, I accept that, but neither would she have wanted her baby brought up by a humble maid. Illegitimate babies of good families are always carefully placed. The authorities see to that.'

'What about love? Is there any guarantee that Tina would receive any? More than likely she would just be given over to a nursemaid.'

'That is to be expected. Miss Cunningham-Brown would have been the same when she was tiny. There would be a nursemaid then later a nanny. Parents in their class see little of their children until they are older. You should know that yourself.'

Annie did, it was all very true. That didn't mean she was going to give up.

'I do have some savings, I'm strong and I can work.'

'Annie, can't I get it into your head that this attitude of yours is not only foolish but cruel. One day Tina will have to know the truth about her birth and she may be bitter to think that she might have been the adopted daughter of doting parents who could have given her anything.'

'I'll have to take that chance, won't I?' Annie's heart was beating wildly, it was like fighting for her own life.

Beatrice McIntyre was wearied of it all and wanted nothing more than to be finished with the whole unhappy business. She no longer saw it as any concern of hers. She had done all that she had been paid to do and more.

'The final say will be with Mr Cunningham-Brown.'

'He won't want Tina. Just promise me, please, that you will say nothing?'

'I won't say anything unless he asks.'

Annie had to be content with that. 'Thank you.' All she could do now was hope and pray.

Mrs McIntyre had told her that Mr Cunningham-Brown was staying in a hotel in Stonehaven and that his wife had not accompanied him. She was said to be distraught and quite unable to make the journey. The day before Emily's father was to return home Molly brought her a note, written by Mrs McIntyre to say that her employer would call in at the cottage in the morning.

Annie was mystified as to why he would want to see her. Perhaps it was to make arrangements for her return to Denbrae House though she thought that unlikely and dismissed it from her mind. Why would he take the trouble to do that when a letter and her train fare was all that was necessary? If things went as she hoped, and pray God they would, then she wouldn't be returning to Denbrae House. If on the other hand all her efforts failed then she would need her job back. She wouldn't stay long, it would be too painful. Just long enough to find herself another position.

She was up early in the morning cleaning an already spotless house. That done she changed into her dark grey skirt and a black blouse. The black robbed her face of any colour it had. Getting more keyed up by the minute, Annie went back and forward between the window, looking out to the road, and the chair, forcing herself each time to be seated for five minutes. What should she do when he arrived? Should she offer to make a cup of tea or would that be out of place for someone in her position? Maybe it was, but making a cup of tea for herself wouldn't be a bad idea. It might help to calm her. She made it and was sitting at the kitchen table about to take her first sip when she heard the knock. Putting down the cup her hand jerked and tea spilled into the saucer. Nervously she smoothed her skirt and hurried to answer the door.

Opening it wide she stood back to let him in. Nothing was said, he merely nodded and she gave an uncertain smile. The door to the sitting-room was open and he went ahead and into it. What should she do? Ask him to be seated? No, no, that would make her sound like the lady of the house. She felt the beginning of hysterical laughter and pressed her lips together. After a look around the room he went over to the chair that had been favoured by his daughter and sat down. Annie stood until he gestured impatiently that she should find herself a chair. She did and sat on the edge of it, her hands folded in her lap. Soon she would learn the purpose of this visit.

'A sad business, Annie.' There was a catch in his voice and despite herself she felt her heart go out to him. How must he be feeling? When it was too late did he now regret the harsh way he had treated his daughter? Or, and she thought this quite possible, was all his anger directed towards that unknown man who had brought pain and tragedy to his family?

Annie nodded and bit her lip feeling the familiar lump come into her throat.

'You helped my daughter and for that I am grateful.'

'Miss Emily was the kindest, the best—' She couldn't go on and covering her face with her hands Annie wept.

Alfred Cunningham-Brown looked at the heaving shoulders feeling surprised at such a show of grief and there was annoyance too. A maid had no right to subject him to this display. Heaven knows it was all quite dreadful enough without Annie carrying on in this fashion. He gave her time to recover then cleared his throat.

'I'm sorry,' she said quietly and raised a tear-stained face. She thought he looked uncomfortable and wondered if that was caused by her tears or what he was about to say.

He cleared his throat again. 'I'm sorry, Annie, that it has come to this but I am afraid it will not be possible for you to return to Denbrae House.'

She stared at him.

'You must see that having you there would be a constant reminder.' He was frowning as though she was making it particularly difficult for him or perhaps he was thinking that she should know how it would be without having it spelt out. Across his waistcoat hung a gold watch, the chain strained by a stomach paunch. For a moment he studied the timepiece then put it back in his pocket. He would be allotting her so much time and already some of it was used.

Having her at Denbrae House would be a constant reminder? Did she see that? No, she did not. There was a growing anger inside her and a sense of outrage. Hadn't he just said he was grateful to her? Strange way to show gratitude by dispensing with her services. Was that the reason for this visit? Was she supposed to be honoured that he had taken the trouble to tell her himself? Face to face.

Alfred Cunningham-Brown misunderstood the silence. 'This has come as a shock to you I can see that.' He smiled. 'Needless to say, Annie, you will be given an excellent reference which is only your due. It should, however, enable you to obtain another position without much difficulty.' He paused. 'Regarding your wages and taking into account your loyalty to my family, I am going to continue paying them until the end of the year.' He looked over at her as though waiting for some acknowledgement of his generosity.

Maybe it was generous, he would certainly think so, but Annie didn't feel any gratitude. 'Thank you,' she said deliberately withholding the 'sir' which Annie decided was no longer his due.

About to get up she surprised him with a question. 'The cottage, Mr Cunningham-Brown, when do I have to vacate it?'

'Glad you reminded me. The cottage is let to me until the end of the year and I see no reason why you cannot occupy it until then.'

'Would you please make sure that Mrs McIntyre understands that?'

He almost blinked with surprise or was it shock? This was a very self-possessed young woman and a far cry from the quiet, mouselike creature he remembered. Her speech was much improved too although he reminded himself that she had never been as rough-spoken as the other domestic staff. He began to wonder if Emily, bored with nothing to do, had decided to take her maid in hand and improve her speech and manners. That could only be it and the result must have pleased Emily as much as it was surprising himself.

'I'll do that. Mrs McIntyre will be informed that the arrangements are to be the same as before.'

'Thank you.' That was a big relief to Annie and was more than she had dared hope. There would be no immediate problem about a roof over her head and not having to buy food or coal would mean her wages could be saved. Every penny was going to be important. He was still there and she knew there was something else she needed to ask, but what was it? Then it came back to her.

'About Miss Emily's belongings, Mr Cunningham-Brown, what would you like me to do with them?'

His hand had been ready to grasp the doorknob and she saw a spasm of pain cross his face.

'Do with them as you wish, Annie, but on no account is anything to be sent to Denbrae House. It would be too upsetting for my wife.'

Shutting the cottage door behind him, Alfred Cunningham-Brown gave a huge sigh. This whole shocking business had been a nightmare. In the end there had been no hiding the truth and in a strange way it had been a relief to have it out in the open. There is only so much pain one can stand and after that it becomes a dull ache that goes on and on.

Close friends had been sympathetic and understanding, brushing aside the disgrace as something that could have happened to anyone's daughter though thank God not to theirs. The gossips would have plenty to say but the hurtful words would be unlikely to reach the ears of those at Denbrae House. He and Maud had gone beyond that, nothing touched them any more. Maud had gone to pieces and there was that terrible look in her eyes, the silent accusation. Until her health improved she would need plenty of rest and quiet, the doctor had told him, and Alfred had moved out of their bedroom and into one of the guest rooms. He didn't see himself ever returning.

There were times when he felt that he might have been to blame then wondered what else he could have done. Others in his position and desperate to save the family name, would have done precisely what he had. As for that damned doctor, what was his name? Rutherford, he had gone into every unnecessary detail to make sure he knew that everything possible had been done to save his daughter. If he had stopped there but no, the fool had to go on about the baby surviving against all the odds. Couldn't he see that it would have been better if it hadn't survived. If they had concentrated all their efforts on saving his daughter instead of the baby, then Emily might be alive today.

There was no baby as far as he was concerned and he would make no mention of it. If Maud should ask he would have to tell her it was a girl, but he didn't see her asking. She was in a world of her own and didn't seem to know or care what was going on.

Annoying though that the maid hadn't shown the gratitude she should. Not many employers would have been so generous. His generosity had been to make him feel less guilty. Dispensing with Annie's services had been his carefully considered decision. Maud knew nothing of it and when she did it might mean more conflict. Still that could be dealt with if and when it arose, he thought, and in the meantime he had enough to worry about. He was far-seeing and knew it would be better for everyone, the staff of Denbrae House included, if they never set eyes on Annie Fullerton again.

Once the door was shut and she heard the gate click, Annie sat hunched in the chair with her mind going over all that had been said. No mention had been made of the baby but that was hardly surprising. Dr Rutherford would have told Miss Emily's father that she had given birth to a girl but what he wouldn't know was his daughter's decision to keep her baby. He would expect the adoption to go ahead as arranged.

Or that was what Annie was hoping and praying would be the case. Her anxiety for the baby mustn't get in the way of good sense. It was very important that she exercised restraint and showed herself to be a calm and responsible person. Be patient, don't rush it, she told herself, wait another day before going to the big house.

Annie was standing at the front door and had knocked before it occurred to her that perhaps she should have gone round to the back. Molly must have had the same thought if her face was anything to go by.

'Is Mrs McIntyre in, Molly? I need to ask her something important,' Annie said by way of explanation.

'I'll see if she can see you. Wait there.' She half closed the door. Annie heard voices and Molly returned.

'You can come in,' she said ungraciously, and led the way into the sitting-room where Mrs McIntyre was sitting writing at her bureau. She finished what she was writing, folded the sheet of notepaper and put it in the envelope before looking up. Annie wasn't asked to sit down and clearly she wasn't welcome.

'As you can see, Annie, I am busy so whatever you have to say kindly be quick about it.'

It was strange, Annie thought, how tragedy seemed to bring out the best in people but only for a short time. Very quickly the barriers went up again to remind her that she was a mere maid. Annie didn't need to be reminded and she had better be quick about asking her question.

'I just wanted to know if Mr Cunningham-Brown made any mention of the baby.'

'No, he did not.'

'Thank you, he didn't mention the baby to me either.'

'I hardly expected he would,' Mrs McIntyre said drily. Really the girl was quite forgetting her place.

'Nor did I. He probably thinks the baby has been adopted.'

'Very likely since that was the arrangement.' The woman was in two minds. It had been stupid to get herself in this awkward position and perhaps it wasn't too late to save that poor wee soul. What kind of life would she have with a maid and one without a job. At best it would be a hand-to-mouth existence. 'Annie?'

'Yes, Mrs McIntyre?'

'You won't find it easy to get a job with an infant to look after.'

'I know, I've thought of all that.' She smiled. 'I'll manage – there is always a way.' Mrs Martin used to say that. Where there is a will there is a way.

'I'll say this for you, you are determined.'

'Very determined, I've never been more determined in my life.'

'Then don't blame anyone but yourself if you find, as you surely will, that you have bitten off more than you can chew.'

'I won't blame anyone.' She paused thinking she had better get the cottage settled too. 'You do know that I am being permitted to stay in the cottage until the end of the year?'

'Yes, so I understand,' Mrs McIntyre said coldly. 'The same arrangements will continue until then.'

'Thank you.'

'Molly is busy but you can see yourself out?'

'Yes.'

Before bringing Tina to the cottage Annie wanted everything done and that meant clearing out Miss Emily's bedroom. She would take her time over it. For two hours each day she would be out of the cottage, that was when she was in Mamie Reid's house nursing Tina and getting to know her. Annie loved to hold the baby in her arms and feel its endearing warmth. She longed to have her in the cottage but she was afraid too. There was far more to looking after a baby than she would have believed.

She had been walking back from Mamie's when a young woman pushing a shabby pram caught up with her and spoke.

'Excuse me but I just wanted a word with you.'

Surprised, Annie stopped and looked into the pram.

'He's asleep, the only way to get him over was to bring him out in the pram. I really just wanted to say how very sorry we all are about your mistress. It was a dreadful tragedy.'

'Yes, it was, it was dreadful,' Annie said carefully.

'You are thinking this is just curiosity and I wouldn't blame you for thinking that. Folk weren't very kind. In the town it wouldn't matter so much, people aren't so narrow-minded there. Here it is something to gossip about. Sorry I'm not saying this very well.'

'It's all right I do understand and I don't imagine they are all narrow-minded.'

'I'm not and there are a few like me. I'm Madge Niven by the way.'

'Annie Fullerton.'

Madge Niven was of medium height, quite heavily built and with gorgeous thick red–gold hair tied back with a black ribbon. She was untidy, a button was missing from her blouse and the coat she wore open had one hanging by a thread. Annie longed to pull it off in case she lost it on the way home.

'I don't suppose you have many friends here about?'

'None,' Annie smiled. She was warming to this friendly young woman.

The baby gave a whimper and immediately got their attention. Madge made cooing noises and adjusted the cover.

'He's lovely. It is a boy?' Annie said suddenly unsure.

'Yes, this is Duncan and he doesn't like it when I stop the pram for a blether so I had better go and get my bits of shopping. Come and see us, we live in Pennycook Lane off Church Street, Number 3, you can't miss it. Bob painted the door a hideous shade of blue, it's all streaks and I'll have to live with it for heaven knows how long. He's a builder by the way.' She stopped for breath. 'Morning or afternoon best for you?'

'Afternoon if that is all right with you.' Mamie didn't mind what time she came but Annie had been going in the mornings and didn't want that to change.

'Fine. Any day but Thursday, my mother-in-law expects me then.' She made a face. 'It would be easier if she came to me but she doesn't see it that way. Could be the untidy house puts her off,' she grinned.

'I don't believe that.'

'Perfectly true, I'm usually in a muddle and poor Duncan here gets blamed for it, don't you my little lamb?' There was no reply from the little lamb, he had fallen asleep. 'Cheerio for now.' She waved and set off at a brisk pace.

Annie was delighted to have made her first friend in Dundrinnen and as well as being pleasant it could be useful. Madge Niven was local and it might come to her notice if a room and kitchen became vacant. And as for a job she might be able to help there too.

In the early afternoon of Wednesday, Annie set out to visit her new friend. The morning mist had lifted to give another warmish day with a fitful sunshine and a light breeze pushed the thin wispy clouds across a pale blue sky. Her worries forgotten for the moment she enjoyed the walk by the side of the burn that gurgled and wound its way over tangled and sodden overgrowth.

Pennycook Lane turned out to be a row of farm cottages that had been renovated by Madge's husband Bob. The farmer had been unwilling to spend more money on them, believing it to be a waste. Labourers expected too much these days, there was no pleasing them. The pub was the place to air grievances and by luck Bob Niven was having a drink and listening in on the conversation. Thinking about it Bob decided he might have a solution that would benefit them both. He was a builder by trade, newly married and living in cramped conditions. In exchange for making the cottages habitable he and his wife would be able to occupy one rent free for as long as they wished. The others would be available to whoever was prepared to pay the farmer a fair rent. After careful consideration the farmer agreed to Bob's suggestion.

Annie had to agree about the door. The bright blue wouldn't have been her choice but it would have been acceptable had it been well done. Bob Niven might be a good builder but he should have left the painting to some-one else.

Madge answered the knock almost immediately.

'Come in. Come in. I wondered if you would come.'

'I was looking forward to it,' Annie said as she stepped inside. There was a small passageway then the living-room door on the left. Madge went ahead and Annie followed. The low ceiling made the room look smaller than it was. There was a fire burning in the grate and the pram was to one side of it. Duncan was sitting on the sofa gurgling contentedly.

'He's lovely, Madge.'

'Yes, I have to agree we made a good job of him,' she said proudly.

Annie was short of small talk and wondered what she should say next. Soon she was to discover that Madge had enough to say for both of them.

'Take off your coat. Has it got a loop?'

'Yes.'

'Good, I'll hang it on the nag in the lobby.' She took the coat.

'Make yourself at home, take a chair. No, not Bob's, he's almost through it,' she giggled.

Annie took the one indicated and found it perfectly comfortable.

'Keep an eye on Duncan will you while I make the tea? He isn't likely to fall off but I never take chances.'

Annie liked that, she would never take chances with Tina.

A few minutes later Madge was back. 'There you are, hope it isn't too strong.' She put the tray on the footstool which was to act as a table.

Annie took the cup. 'Thank you, this is just the way I like it.'

'Shortbread from the baker's. I can recommend it, try a piece.'

Annie knew it was good. She and Miss Emily had enjoyed it on several occasions.

Madge took a bit of the shortbread and gave a small piece to Duncan. 'When do you get the baby?'

'At the end of the week. Mamie Reid has Tina just now.'

'Then she is all yours?'

'Yes.'

'Not scared are you?' She smiled as she said it.

'I am I'm ashamed to say. Most girls would have some experience of looking after babies, especially if they come from a large family. I've had none.'

'Poor you, an only child.'

'You could say that,' Annie said carefully and was about to tell the truth when Madge spoke again.

'You'll manage, I did.'

'You have your husband for support.'

'You must be joking. I've only got to mention a job needing done and he is out that door at the double. His mother's fault, she ruined him as well as his brother and her husband. She did everything, they never had to lift a finger. Help yourself,' she said offering the plate.

'No, thank you but I enjoyed that.'

'More tea?'

'Just half fill it, please.'

'Where was I? Oh, yes, talking about my useless husband, useless about the house I mean. Duncan isn't going to be brought up like that. I won't make a cissy of him but he'll learn to bring in the coal and chop the sticks and generally make himself useful. One day his wife will thank me.'

'That's a long way ahead.'

'I know but start them young. Enough about me and my family, tell me about yours unless, of course, you'd rather not.'

She would rather not but it would be rude to say so. In any case why should she feel shame in confessing to having no family or at least none known to her.

'My early years were spent in an orphanage,' Annie said quietly.

'How early? I mean how old were you?'

'A baby, I was a foundling.'

'Tough,' she said sympathetically and Annie was relieved that she hadn't said any more.

'Tough, yes I suppose it was but I survived.'

'You would, you quiet kind do. You won't want to talk about it so instead we'll discuss this baby of yours. First let me say that it takes a lot of guts to do what you are doing.'

'It is what I want, Madge.'

'Yes, I can see that. The grandparents want nothing to do with the poor wee mite I take it?'

'That was made clear from the start.'

'Who chose the name if I may ask?'

'Miss Emily. She seemed very sure she was going to have a daughter.'

'I saw her once, your Miss Emily. Very lovely but haughty too I thought.'

'They are taught from an early age to behave like that, Madge.'

'Huh! To make them believe they are superior.' She said it with a laugh but Annie heard the resentment in her voice. 'Doesn't that madden you, I know it does me, folk thinking they are better purely by the accident of birth?'

'Not really, Madge. That's the way of life. There will always be the master and the servant and by the same token the mistress and her maid.'

'You don't talk like a maid,' Madge said abruptly.

'If I don't it is because Miss Emily took the trouble to help me and encourage me to read books. It helped to pass the time for her I suppose,' Annie added.

Duncan was nodding and Madge put him in the pram. 'How long will you be staying in the cottage?'

'Until the end of the year.'

'What happens then?'

'I don't know but I must find some place. If you hear of a room and kitchen becoming vacant would you let me know? I would be very grateful if you would.'

'Don't build up your hopes, in fact you have no chance. If you were given one ahead of a local I wouldn't like to be in your shoes. Only fair when you think about it, Annie.'

Annie nodded. Madge was right. 'What about a job or is that out of the question too?'

'Depends what you are looking for.'

'Housework is all I am trained to do but I would be prepared to turn my hand to anything.'

'I'll keep my ears open.'

Annie got to her feet. 'Thank you, Madge, I must go

now. This has been lovely and I'm so pleased to have made a friend.'

'Don't wait for an invitation, just come – I'll be glad of your company. Most of the folk around here are old or if not old, middle-aged. Oh, I'd better know if you are looking for full-time employment or part-time.'

'Part-time to begin with. I would have to get someone reliable to look after Tina while I was working.'

'Would you consider me reliable?'

'Very reliable but are you serious?'

'Why not? I have the time.'

Annie tried to ignore the untidiness of the house. Madge wasn't an organised person but she was kind and she was careful with Duncan.

'Once I get a job we'll discuss the matter of payment.'

'I won't take much, I'm not doing it for the money.'

'I know that but I don't want to take advantage and as I say we'll discuss that later.' Annie thought about the amount of food coming into the cottage. Mrs McIntyre would expect her to ask for less to be sent only she wouldn't. She had a home for the extra food. With a hungry man to feed Madge might be glad of it. She would have to be careful how she offered it so as not to cause offence. Somehow she didn't see Madge refusing it.

Madge was thinking the little extra money for looking after a baby for a few hours would come in very useful. She must ask around to see if anyone wanted domestic help.

Chapter Ten

After leaving Madge Niven's house, Annie returned to the cottage fully intending to make a start on Miss Emily's bedroom and pack away her clothes in the trunk. Only she didn't, the task was put off once again. Annie was well aware that she couldn't go on doing this. When she had Tina with her they would require the larger bedroom. The crib would go alongside her own bed and if the baby awoke she would be there to see to her needs.

If only she could rid herself of this feeling of guilt. It was silly, it was ridiculous, and there was no reason for it. Hadn't Mr Cunningham-Brown said, indeed he had been emphatic about it, that nothing belonging to his dead daughter should be returned to Denbrae House? Of course when he said it he hadn't known about the money hidden away in those pouches and she had omitted on purpose to tell him. What did that make her? A thief? Hardly! She hadn't stolen anything. The money, and she had no idea how much was there, was for Miss Emily's child and no one had a better claim. Even so the uneasy feeling persisted that she had done wrong.

Whatever the rights and wrongs no one could pass judgement since no one but herself knew about the money. Annie just hoped and prayed that it was enough to keep them until she found herself a job. It wouldn't be easy but then nothing in her life had been. There was the strong possibility that she would have to look further afield than Dundrinnen but, if she did, who would look after Tina?

That night as she lay in bed with the curtains parted and the moon shining in, Miss Emily seemed very near and Annie had the warm feeling that what she was doing was meeting with approval. When sleep eventually claimed her there was a tender smile on her face and when she awoke at six o'clock she felt refreshed and ready for the new day. She got up, washed and dressed and for the first time in days felt hungry. Getting out the frying pan she cooked herself bacon and egg with a slice of fried bread and sat down to enjoy it with a cup of strong tea.

She could face what had to be faced now and once the dishes were washed and put away, the table cleared and a quick tidy to the kitchen she went through to the bedroom and dragged the trunk to the middle of the floor. She opened it ready for the clothes. The sensible thing to do, Annie decided, would be to put everything on the bed, fold the dresses carefully and put them in the trunk.

As she folded each garment tears slid down her face. They were all so lovely and heartbreakingly familiar. She had only to close her eyes to see Miss Emily looking at herself in the mirror and herself doing up the hooks or fastening the tiny buttons. For a little while it was too much for Annie. Her grief turned to anger and she wanted to scream and stamp her foot at the cruelty of life. Why did it have to happen to Miss Emily? Why was her life cut short? They could have had such a lovely life the three of them. Miss Emily would have bought her house with its garden where Tina could have played. The father figure would have been missing but you don't miss what you have never known. Or was that true? She hadn't known her parents and had felt an emptiness in her life but Tina would know love and that made the difference. Annie began to wonder if she would have been a different person with different values if she had had a normal upbringing. Probably. Certainly less sensitive, she thought.

How sad but true that being an orphan brought its own stigma. It was as though in some way the child was responsible.

The outburst over, Annie dried her eyes and began again on the task she had set herself but her thoughts kept straying to what might have been had Miss Emily been spared. She would have wanted to protect Tina as much as possible, maybe even considering passing herself off as a widow. Annie hardly thought so, she was more likely to have brazened it out. A governess would have been engaged for Tina thus saving the child from the cruel jibes of classmates. Children, as Annie well knew, could be incredibly cruel. She smiled thinking of the improvement in her own status. From maid to housekeeper. That would have suited her very well. She was more qualified for that job than to be a substitute mother.

The gowns made a delightful splash of colour on the bed and one by one Annie folded them and placed them carefully in the trunk. Only the gown at the back of the wardrobe remained. She brought it out and slipped it out of the coat-hanger. Her fingers felt the thickness at the waist and taking the gown with her sat on a chair and opened first one pouch then the other. The money went on the bedside table and looking at it Annie thought it a huge amount. Getting out pencil and paper she counted the money and jotted down the total. Going to the other side of the page she listed the expenses that would have to come out of it. Not so very much when there was accommodation to find before they had to leave the cottage. The rent for a modest room and kitchen would be a constant drain on the money and there was no guarantee a landlord would see her as a suitable tenant. He would be suspicious of a woman and a baby and no sign of a husband. Annie decided not to dwell on that else she would become thoroughly disheartened.

Was she doing the right thing for Tina? A tiny thread of doubt began to trouble her and all of a sudden Annie was frightened of the responsibility. Mrs McIntyre was a wise woman and she could be right. Was she being foolhardy rushing into something she might live to regret? Her own life was unimportant and she could gamble with it but what right had she to gamble with the child's? It was dreadful to feel this way but there was no going back. Tina was hers, she had fought for the baby and won and now it was up to her to prove that she could give Tina the kind of upbringing she deserved. Money might be short but never love, there would be an abundance of that.

The money position kept raising its ugly head but Annie was feeling a little more optimistic. She most certainly wasn't penniless and many a woman with a family would envy her. As well as Miss Emily's money there was her own savings. She had spent very little since coming to the cottage and she had her wages from Mr Cunningham-Brown until the end of the year.

Annie finished the clearing out and decided to return the gown with its money pouches to its former place at the back of the wardrobe. The money would be safe there until she had to give up the cottage. Everything did not go into the trunk. Annie decided it would be plain daft not to make use of what she could. The gowns were much too fancy but looking ahead a good dressmaker would be able to use the material to make dresses for Tina. The skirts and high-necked, long-sleeved blouses she would be able to wear herself. The skirts would need to be shortened a little but though no needlewoman, Annie thought the task wasn't beyond her.

She could have had new clothes, Miss Emily had suggested it time and time again but Annie had kept putting it off. She picked up the velvet cloak and felt its softness. That shade of pink had suited Miss Emily's colouring and it had been one of her favourites. Annie fingered it then gave into temptation. She would try it on, there was no one to stop her and where was the harm? Slipping it on and relishing the rich softness, Annie felt like a princess. To look in the mirror would be to bring her down to earth and she was reluctant to spoil the dream. The ugly duckling wasn't going to turn into a swan. When she did at last gaze at her reflection she was pleasantly surprised. The dark colours she habitually wore did nothing for her pale skin whereas the pink did wonders. For a fleeting moment she thought she looked almost pretty. What was that saying about clothes not making the person? Perhaps they didn't but they certainly helped. Attractive and well-chosen clothes could make even the plainest woman look nice.

Annie took off the cloak, laid her cheek against the velvet, then placed it on top of the gowns. One day Tina would wear it. She would grow up to be beautiful like her mother and like her mother, come in for a lot of admiration. The main part was done, just the drawers left. Annie drew out the dressing-table drawer where Miss Emily had kept her jewellery. She hadn't brought much with her knowing she would have little need of them. There was a pearl necklace, an assortment of strings of beads and three pretty brooches. All to be Tina's one day. The elegant comb and brush set on the dressing-table with a few tiny ornaments would remain where they were. The other drawers held gloves, stockings, underwear and nightwear. Enough to do Annie a lifetime she thought. The footwear was too big, Annie had a small narrow foot. Much as she disliked the idea of just anyone wearing Miss Emily's boots and shoes she had to be practical. There was a second-hand shop tucked away in a lane not far from Madge's house and one day she would take them, hidden in the pram, and see what they would fetch.

Annie knocked and entered as Madge had instructed her to do.

'It's just me,' she said popping her head round the door.

'Come in.' Madge was sitting on what she liked to call the nursing chair which was an ordinary chair with the legs shortened.

Annie fussed over Duncan who was clearly delighted at the attention then went over to a chair.

'I'm getting Tina home tomorrow.'

'Great!' Madge finished changing Duncan and put him on the sofa wedged between two cushions. 'What is she to call you when she gets that length?'

Annie looked blank. 'Call me?'

'She'll have to call you something.'

'I hadn't given that a thought.'

'Time you did.'

'What do you suggest?'

'Not for me to say.'

'Why not?'

'Tricky that's why.' She paused. 'Do you want her to call you Mummy and if so—'

'Sorry, I'm a bit slow but I do see what you mean now.'

'Folk in Dundrinnen know the situation but if you were to leave then you could very easily be classed as an unmarried mother. Would that bother you? It would certainly bother me. Bad enough if you deserve it but hard lines when you don't.'

'It wouldn't upset me, not especially. What is important is that Tina thinks of me as her real mother.'

'Until she is a little older you mean?'

'I wouldn't tell her, not before she is twelve.'

'Some would say that was a mistake and it is better to let the child know the truth from the beginning.'

Annie shook her head. 'In some cases I would agree but not in Tina's.'

'Your decision, so Tina will call you Mummy.'

'Miss Emily called her mother Mama when she was little.'

Madge looked sceptical. 'I don't see that going down well around here.'

'Neither do I. Mummy it will have to be.'

'With that settled would you do me a favour, Annie?'

'Of course, that's to say if I can.'

'Would you sew a button on Bob's jacket? He was complaining the other day that his precious mother would never have allowed him out of the house with a button

missing from his jacket. I meant to see to it but here I am.'
She gave Annie a pleading look.

'No trouble, give me thread and needle and I'll get it done.'

Annie sewed on the button and strengthened the others.

'Bless you, Annie, I hate sewing on buttons and I hate darning.'

'Buttons I'll sew on for you but the darning you can do yourself or try and get another soft mark,' she grinned.

'Little chance of that but here is my news. You asked me to keep my ears to the ground about a job—'

'You've heard of something?' Annie said eagerly.

'Don't get too excited, I don't see it coming to anything.'

'That's encouraging, I must say.'

'It is housework but for an old man and you know how set in their ways some old folk can be.'

'No first-hand experience, Madge, but I would make allowances so I don't see a problem.'

Madge went closer to the fire. Her feet were in shabby carpet slippers with absolutely no support for her feet.

'Forgive me, Madge, but if you want to ruin your feet you are going about it the right way.'

Her reply was typical. 'Since they are ruined already I might as well have some comfort. We were discussing a job for you, not my feet.'

'A job I'm not likely to get.' She smiled. 'Tell me about it anyway.'

'A Mr Hamish Brown is looking for a woman to do a bit of cleaning and prepare him a meal. The rest of the time he likes to scutter about and do for himself.'

'A few hours a day is what he is looking for?'

'I imagine so.'

'And what is wrong with me?'

'Too young. The woman who has been doing for him since his wife died some years ago was old and she suited him. The house is probably in a bit of a mess since the woman wasn't able to do much more than make a meal.

Stubborn too, and she would have carried on until she dropped if her family hadn't persuaded her to give up her house and make her home with a daughter in Aberdeen.'

Annie jumped at the mention of a house.

'I know what you are thinking but you haven't an earthly.'

'Meaning it is already spoken for?'

'I wouldn't know but I do know you haven't a hope. A local will get it and that is only fair. I might call you my friend but I would hate to see any incomer getting a house over the head of a local.'

'I suppose I have to agree,' Annie said but sounded disappointed. 'No job, no house.'

'Give it time, the job I mean. Mr Brown will want a middle-aged woman.'

'And if no one applies?'

'Then he might consider you. No harm in trying your luck.'

'Where does this Mr Brown live?'

'Hillside House. If I tell you the house looks on to Powrie's farm would you know where I mean?'

Annie nodded. 'Miss Emily and I used to take walks out that way.'

'It's a good house, well-built so Bob says and he should know. All the joinery work Mr Brown did himself, that was his trade. At one time or so I am told, he had a small but thriving business.'

'Thanks, Madge, I am grateful. By the way how big a house?'

'From the look of the outside and the number of chimney pots I would say two rooms, kitchen and scullery downstairs and a couple of bedrooms upstairs although that could be three. All bedrooms don't have fireplaces.'

'When would be the best time to call?'

'Morning and not too early I imagine. I'll keep Tina.'

'I was going to ask you if you could look after Tina if I were to get the job.'

'Of course – I thought we had already agreed on that.'

'Thanks and Madge, would you be offended if I brought some food?'

'No, but you don't have to.'

Annie explained about the food coming to the cottage.

Madge beamed. She was better off than many but she still had to watch the pennies. In the building trade a spell of bad weather could mean short-time or even lengthy unemployment.

'I would have murdered you if you'd returned it to Mrs What's-her-name.'

Annie reached Hillside House and was frowning at the state of the brasses. They hadn't seen Brasso for a very long time. Apart from that she liked the look of the house, plain with no embellishments. Fancy adornments were for the really big houses and Annie thought they looked ridiculous on smaller homes. The brasses had been neglected but not the small front garden. Surrounded by a thick hedge it obviously received attention and she supposed Mr Brown must have a handyman or retired gardener employed for the job. She looked for a bell or a knocker but there was neither. Just a brass doorknob and a brass name-plate with the name Brown and no initials.

Annie used her knuckles and rapped on the door. She waited and waited. Time for another knock she thought and louder this time. She rapped again with bruising persistency and was rewarded by a sound of shuffling feet then the key turned and the door opened.

'You'll have that door in if you're not careful,' he glared.

'Sorry, I didn't know if you had heard my first knock.'

'Young woman, my hearing may not be what it once was but I am not stone deaf, not yet.'

Annie bit her lip and waited on the doorstep.

'Come in if you've a mind to or are you going to stand there all day?' He turned and shuffled away.

Annie hid a smile. She had met his kind before and usually

their bark was worse than their bite. Closing the door she followed him into what she saw was the kitchen. It was very hot. He was old and without the stoop Annie thought the man would be about average height and his age she put somewhere in the seventies. His face was gaunt, his cheeks clapped-in and his nose looked pinched and had faint blue threads showing. The eyes, pale blue, were rheumy but alert and challenging. Old he may be but no one would pull a fast one on him.

'Age doesn't come itself,' he said and she winced as the springs of the chair protested as his body all but fell into it. He saw the wince. 'Your day will come so don't look so smug.'

'I wasn't,' but she was smiling.

'Standing, sitting it's all the same price.'

She went over and sat in one of the chairs. 'I'm Annie Fullerton, Mr Brown, and I believe you are looking for someone to do domestic work.'

'Domestic work? Is that what they're calling it these days?' The eyebrows, grey and surprisingly bushy shot up. 'I would describe it as a wee bit house cleaning and a wee bit cooking.'

'I could do that for you, Mr Brown.'

'I daresay. Not from these parts, are you?'

'I'm not local but I've lived in Dundrinnen for quite a while,' she answered carefully.

'I take it you've been working in Dundrinnen?'

'Yes.'

'Lost your job and looking for another,' he said suspiciously.

'That, I suppose, is true. The lady I worked for died.'

The bantering tone had gone. 'I'm sorry, lass, I can hear the sadness in your voice but don't be too upset. It's just life and when a body gets old it is only to be expected and in some cases welcomed.'

She nodded. There was no need to say that her employer had been a young girl.

'A lass like you would be better looking for a position in one of the big houses.'

'It's not what I'm looking for.'

'And looking after an old man is?'

Annie burst out laughing, she couldn't help it. 'I've never looked after an old gentleman but I'm sure I could.'

For a long time he gazed into the fire and she began to think he had forgotten she was there. She took the chance to look around. The kitchen was square-shaped, high-ceilinged and a good size. There was a door half open and Annie could see a sink and taps, that would be the scullery. The table in the centre of the kitchen had four chairs round it. There was a handsome dresser with a wally dog on either end and it took up most of one wall. A chest of drawers was opposite and on it was a collection of ornaments placed just anyhow. A fire burned in the range and there was a black kettle to the side. Annie felt an urge to get her sleeves up and give the range a good clean and a black lead. What a difference it would make. Hamish Brown sat in the large, shabby armchair and at the other side of the range was another armchair but this one was smaller and in much better condition. She thought his wife must have sat there. Annie was occupying a high-backed chair that looked out of place in a kitchen and she thought it had probably been brought through from the parlour for some occasion and forgotten to be returned. Judging by the furniture in the kitchen, Annie imagined that this was a nicely furnished house but one crying out for attention and a bit of loving care. The windows were dirty, the curtains grimy and they were hanging uneven. What troubled Annie most of all was the clutter of dirty dishes on the table and unaware of it she had given an expression of distaste. For the last few moments the old man had been watching her.

'Seen everything now?' he rasped.

Annie started and coloured uncomfortably. 'I *am* sorry, I didn't mean to be rude.'

'Everything's in a mess that's what you were thinking.'

'What I was thinking was that your house, if I can judge it from the kitchen, could do with a good clean,' Annie said honestly.

'It wasn't always that way. Jessie looked after me after my wife died and I won't hear a word against her. Like me age has caught up with her but she did her best. She was in tears before she left and I can tell you I wasn't far off them myself. Her daughter is to look after her but I doubt that she'll settle. Old folk are better to bide where they are and that's what I'm doing. The only way they'll get me out of here is in a box and feet first.'

'You shouldn't talk like that.'

'Why not? We all come into the world with nothing and we all go out of it with nothing. Why am I telling you this?'

'I haven't the faintest idea.'

'An old man's ravings.'

'Would you let me do something?'

'Like what?' he said suspiciously.

'Like clearing the table and washing the dishes.'

'Think it will help your chances of getting the job?'

'Not at all. I'd like to do it, that's all.'

'What did you say your name was?'

'Annie Fullerton.'

'Miss Fullerton?'

'I'm more comfortable with Annie, Mr Brown.'

'Who told you I was looking for someone?'

'A friend.'

'Who shall be nameless?'

'That's right.'

'You're unusual I'll say that for you.'

'I'm not forward, Mr Brown. I know my place, I learned that when I was very young.'

'Do I detect a note of bitterness?'

'I try not to show it.' She stood up. 'May I clear your table?'

'If you want. It would be silly to object since you offered and it will save me.'

Annie removed her coat and placed it over the back of the chair.

'Annie?'

She turned to look at him as she rolled up her sleeves.

'When you finish that how about making a cup of tea. I could do with one and I daresay you could too. Not dishwater mind, I like a good strong cup.'

'So do I.'

Before carrying anything through to the scullery Annie went to have a look and find out if there was space for the dishes. She found the scullery to be tiny but well fitted and with sensibly placed shelves. The sink had a thick rim of grease but the basin was reasonably clean. Pots and pans sat haphazardly on the bottom shelf with some below on the floor. Using the hot water from the kettle she poured some into the basin, found washing-up powder and added some. Then she refilled the kettle and put it back on the heat for the tea. Collecting the dishes she carried them through and began on the job she had set herself. Annie worked swiftly. She found a clean tea towel in a drawer in the dresser after asking where she could get one. The tablecloth was badly stained and she longed to take it off but thought she had better not.

'That's the kettle on the boil,' he said helpfully.

The teapot was to hand and so was the tea caddy. Annie poured a little of the boiling water into the teapot and went to the sink to empty it. She spooned in two heaped caddy spoons of tea then added a little more for good measure; he had said he liked a strong cup. Two of the cups and saucers Annie had washed she brought back to the table. The sugar bowl was already there and she went to the cold slab in the pantry for the milk.

'Do you take sugar and milk?'

'I do. Two half decent spoons of sugar and a fair drop of milk.'

When it came to pouring the tea Annie was careful not to fill the cup too full, she had noticed that his hands were not quite steady.

'Bring it over here, lass.' There was a small table beside him on which were his pipe and tobacco pouch. 'Thanks, that's just grand. If you look in the tins you might find a bit of gingerbread. I'm not for any but you take what you want.'

'Just the tea, this is fine, thank you.'

They were both silent with the only noise the slight gulping sound he made when he was drinking.

'You'll do.'

'Pardon?'

'I said you'll do, Annie Fullerton. You want the job, don't you?'

'Very much.'

'By my way of it a lass who can make a good cup of tea can't be too bad.' He paused and gave her a searching look. 'Something tells me that you are holding back, not being completely open. That's your business just so long as it is nothing bad.'

By not telling him about Tina she was holding back. Whether she did that later or not would depend. Madge would be looking after the baby and it didn't affect anyone else. Annie took a deep breath.

'There is nothing in my life that I am ashamed of. Why you should think there might be I don't know,' she said stiffly.

'No need to get on your high horse with me, missie. I'll take your word for it that you haven't robbed a bank.'

Annie laughed at that. He was an old devil but she thought she was going to like him. 'If I had I wouldn't be looking for a job, Mr Brown.'

'The job is yours but I'll ask you one more question. Do you have anyone or are you alone in the world?'

It was a strange question to ask her but she would answer it.

'I have no relatives if that is what you mean.'

'That puts us in the same boat. I lost everyone who was dear to me. Oh, I believe there might be cousins and the like,

I wouldn't know nor care for that matter. I didn't seek them out and they didn't bother about me. Good friends are better than some relatives, but when you reach your three score years and ten you begin to lose them. Some have gone to meet their Maker and others, like me, are more or less housebound.'

She smiled. He had talked because he was lonely and Annie had always been a good listener.

'I'm keeping you back so we'll talk about arrangements, then you can get away home. I'll want you for four hours a day except Sunday. The Sabbath day was meant for resting and I see no reason to change that. Nine to one would suit best but I'll make no difficulties if you need to fit it in with something else. You would have preferred a full day?'

He was fishing and she couldn't blame him. A single woman with no ties would be looking for full employment. 'Nine to one would suit me very well, Mr Brown.'

'You haven't asked what I'm prepared to pay you.'

'I was waiting for you to tell me.'

'You'll get what I consider to be a fair wage and you can be the judge of that when you get it.' He grinned wickedly. 'I have my faults, young woman, but I have never knowingly cheated anyone in my life. Now as to the washing—'

'I will consider that part of my duties.'

'You may have to. There's a wifie been collecting it one week and delivering it the next, but the last time the woman was here she was muttering about a bad back and having to give up taking in washing. A right moaning Minnie if there ever was one,' he said disgustedly.

'Tell her she won't be required.'

'That'll be a pleasure. As to the garden—'

'What about the garden?'

'Don't look so alarmed. I'm not expecting you to do it. I like my money's worth but I am not a slave driver.'

'I noticed the front garden was well kept.'

'So is the back. I'm lucky there. The Powries—'

'The farm folk?'

'One and the same. We've been friendly for years and they send one of the laddies to tidy up the place. Mind you I think it is just their way of finding out if I am still in the land of the living.'

'Handy for milk and eggs,' she smiled.

'Milk delivered to the door every morning and eggs when I need them. Now, lass, when do you want to start?'

'Monday?'

'Monday will do fine, now get yourself away home. I'm tired and I need a rest. All women are great talkers.'

Annie thought she had done very little. He had closed his eyes and after slipping on her coat she went out quietly without saying another word.

Chapter Eleven

Tina's first night in the cottage would not be easily forgotten. She had screamed and screamed and screamed until Annie was almost a nervous wreck. Picking her up she had walked the floor and for a little while peace had been restored. Then the minute she tried to put Tina in her crib it started up again. By this time Annie was so afraid the baby would damage herself with all this crying that she even thought of going to the big house to waken Mrs McIntyre. That was a last resort and would, she knew, only serve to convince that woman she had been right all along and Annie was quite unfit to care for a child.

It was the thought of this that brought Annie to her senses. There was nothing seriously wrong with Tina. She was out of her usual routine and in strange surroundings that was all. They were both new to this and both had a lot to learn. She tried telling that to a scarlet-faced screaming infant and miraculously it worked. Or perhaps the wee soul had just exhausted herself. Either way the heartbreaking sobs stopped. Tina managed a smile that was like sunshine through the rain, her eyes closed and she slept.

Bathtime proved to be another ordeal. Watching Mamie it had all looked so easy and even when she had bathed Tina under supervision Annie had felt reasonably confident. On her own it was very different. The water was at the right temperature, she had tested it with her elbow and she was carefully following Mamie's instructions. But with Tina wriggling about like an eel Annie's fear was that the tiny body would slip through her hands. What had Mamie said, to hold her firmly, that babies needed that. Once she did and got the knack of holding Tina firmly all was well. She soaped the little body then washed away the soapy suds and, putting a large warm towel over her knees, gently dried her. Powdering came next then a playful poke in the tummy that had Tina gurgling in delight. From then on bathtime was a sheer delight.

It was a completely new way of life for Annie. The alarm went off at six o'clock and she got up immediately. Not to do so could have been disastrous, she might have slept in. She prepared what she could the night before and when the fire was going she had her breakfast. Tina was no trouble, she had settled into her new home. When Annie went to fetch her sometimes she would be wide awake and looking about her with the curiosity of the very young. At other times Annie hated having to disturb her but it was necessary. The baby and pram had to be wheeled over to Madge's house for the time Annie was in Mr Brown's house.

The women of Dundrinnen no longer turned their eyes the other way. Instead they made a point of stopping in the street to look in the pram and admire the baby. Annie had mixed feelings though anger was uppermost when she remembered how these same women had treated Miss Emily. Nevertheless she was pleased to have them admire little Tina. Sometimes she wondered what her late mistress would have made of it. Probably Miss Emily would have been amused.

Tina was a gorgeous baby. Annie watched the faces soften as they bent over the pram and some showed their envy. Seeing it Annie felt all the pride and satisfaction of a new mother showing off her first-born. Her baby was as good as gold and seldom cried though what was there to cry about when her every need was anticipated. Like a tiny princess she lay in her expensive pram, under an expensive cover and gurgled contentedly as she charmed everyone.

The once houseproud young woman was less so now. It wasn't that Annie neglected anything, it was rather that she didn't do the unnecessary. Polishing was done when there was a need for it and not just because it was the day for that particular job. What gave Annie a great deal of satisfaction was pegging out the baby washing and watching it flap in the wind. The beginning of November had been remarkably mild but that could change very quickly. Wintry weather could arrive in the space of one day. When it happened the washing would have to be dried indoors. Not that it would be a problem, there was a pulley in the kitchen and plenty of heat. What would be missing would be the sweet smell and the softness that only fresh air could provide.

With each passing day Annie's fears were growing. In less than six weeks she would have to leave the cottage and so far she had failed to find alternative accommodation. Only one room had been offered and Annie thought she would prefer to sleep in the open rather than take it. The woman, slovenly and greedy-eyed, had invited her in. There was the smell of dampness together with that of boiled cabbage. The room she was shown into was sparsely furnished and what was there was cheap and some of it broken. There was a fireplace with cold ashes from the last fire. The window was shut tight to make sure no fresh air could get in. Had it been cleaned more light would have got through and it might have looked less depressing. Or perhaps it helped hide more neglect. Annie couldn't bring herself to go over and examine the bed.

The woman saw the barely disguised disgust and spoke angrily, 'You can't expect a palace for the pittance I'm asking,' she spat out. 'There's others will be glad of it.'

Annie thought the amount asked was more than a pittance and only someone very desperate would take it. She hadn't come to that.

'Thank you for showing me the room,' Annie said politely as she moved to the door, 'but it is not what I am looking for.' The door banged shut and outside again Annie breathed in the fresh air. She was glad she had left Tina with Madge. How could people live like that? Soap and water were cheap enough.

Walking away Annie thought it ironic that she could afford the rent of a modest room and kitchen but none was available. It was difficult to know what to do for the best. The money wouldn't last long if she had to keep digging into it. Mr Brown paid a fair wage but once away from the cottage it wouldn't keep them. Annie's brow was almost permanently furrowed. She needed more work, another cleaning job.

Hamish Brown sat in his chair and looked about him with satisfaction. What a difference that lass had made. The house gleamed, the windows sparkled and everything shone like a new pin. It had been a lucky day for him when Annie Fullerton had come to his door. The lass was worth her weight in gold. Not since his wife died had he felt so well cared for. Didn't talk too much either though she could be a bossy wee besom at times. He smiled thinking about it. Without as much as a by your leave she had taken another pair of trousers from the wardrobe and ordered him, yes, ordered him in that I-am-not-taking-any-nonsense voice to put them on and let her try and remove the tobacco and other stains which, she told him, were of very long standing. Another thing, he didn't dare to forget to change his underwear not with clean ones put on the chair beside his bed. Though he grumbled as a man had every right to do, he was secretly pleased. To lose her was unthinkable, the very thought of it filled him with dread. Life had suddenly become pleasant and worth living. He tapped the bowl of his pipe against the grate, blew into the stem to clear the passage, then reached for his leather tobacco pouch. Filling his pipe the old man was thoughtful. There was no doubt in his mind that the lass was deeply worried about something. This very day he was going to get her to sit down and talk about it. Her worry had become his.

'Sit down, Annie.'

'Me sit down with all I have to do!'

'The house will be none the worse to be left. I'll warrant there isn't a speck of dust anywhere. This is an order so for once sit down and do what you are told,' he shouted.

Annie sat down abruptly and looked at him questioningly. 'Is there something wrong, Mr Brown?'

'I would say so. Not with me, with you. You are worried and don't try denying it. I have the evidence of my own eyes.'

'I'm sorry, I didn't know it was so obvious. I *am* worried but, honestly, it needn't concern you. I'll still be coming here or I hope to be anyway.'

'It does concern me,' Hamish Brown said, his voice quiet now. 'I don't want to lose you but it is more than that. A young lass like you shouldn't have worries, wee ones mebbe, but not serious and something tells me this is serious.'

What a nice old soul he was, Annie thought, fighting back the lump in her throat. How much should she tell him?

'Is it a man?' he asked suddenly deciding it could be that. Although he wondered why that should be a worry. Not unless it was some awkward so-and-so. Could be but he rather thought Annie would be able to handle that.

'A man?' she said sounding very surprised. 'What made you think that?'

'You'd make a fine wife for some lad.'

She laughed. 'Nothing to do with a man.'

'You're not seeking a husband?'

'No, I am not.'

He wondered why she was so emphatic. Not exactly a bonny lass but not plain either. Still if there was no man on the horizon he could breathe again. Marriage wasn't on the cards.

'I have to get out of the cottage by the end of the month.'

'Is that all?'

'I'll be homeless.'

'Nonsense. A single young woman shouldn't have any difficulty in finding accommodation.'

'It might be simple for a single girl, Mr Brown, but I have a baby.'

'Oh!'

'You'll agree it makes a difference?'

'Indeed it does. Comes as a surprise to me I have to say. And you no' married? I gave you credit for more sense.' He sounded shocked and disappointed.

'Tina is mine, Mr Brown, but I didn't give birth to her,' Annie said quietly.

'You've saddled yourself with someone else's bairn.'

'Not saddled. I wanted to do it. The mother died giving birth.'

'I'm sorry, Annie, I spoke out of turn.'

'It's all right.'

'No, don't get up,' he said as she made to rise. 'Maybe you should start at the beginning. I'm a good listener, Annie.'

'It's a very long story if you want it all.'

'I want it all.'

'Just remember you brought it on yourself.' She tried to smile.

'Telling it could help you.'

'Yes, you could be right but first let me make a cup of tea. It'll help the telling.' She half rose.

'You do that, make a good strong pot. Forget the housework, it'll do no harm to be left for a day.'

She made the tea, took it through and told Hamish Brown everything. She left nothing out, going back to her life in the orphanage right to the time she came to work for him. She told it in a flat voice as though it were someone else's story. Hamish Brown didn't interrupt, not once. So engrossed were they, one in the telling and the other listening that the cups of tea remained untouched.

She stopped and raised her eyes. 'That's it, Mr Brown, now you know all there is to know about me.' She brought the cup to her mouth, drank some and shuddered. 'It's stone cold, don't touch yours. I'll make fresh.'

'That can wait. You are a remarkable woman, Annie Fullerton. Not many would have your courage.' He shook his head in admiration.

'Do you think I did the right thing for Tina?'

He didn't answer straight away. 'That's a difficult question. The bairn, as you know yourself, could have gone to a good home and wanted for nothing. Or there again she might not. We have no means of telling. What we can be sure about and I have to say this, is that the wee lass could be in for a rough time once she is the length of school.'

'Not here surely? I mean folk know the circumstances.'

'They know you aren't the natural mother so that spares you. They also know that Tina is illegitimate.'

Annie got up to rinse out the cups and make another pot of tea. She found that she was shaking.

'Drink that before it gets cold,' she said putting a cup beside him. 'Do you think Tina would be pointed out, made to feel different?'

'I'm afraid so, not by all but it only needs one to start something. I don't like using the word sin, Annie, because I don't know the ins and outs of it. Folk can be very narrow-minded and holier than thou.' He grinned wickedly. 'Are those that get away with it less sinful than the likes of Tina's mother who wasn't so lucky? Not many think on that.'

Annie was close to tears. 'Miss Emily was a good and kind-hearted lady. A real lady and you are not to say a word against her.'

'You're loyal but the fact remains she was thoughtless and the wee soul she brought into the world is the one who has to suffer.'

'Let anyone say anything to hurt Tina and they'll have me to deal with,' Annie said harshly. 'Tina is going to be proud of Miss Emily and one day I am going to tell her what a wonderful person she was.'

Annie's hand was unsteady as she lifted the cup and

drained it. The other one was already empty and she took them through to the scullery leaving Hamish Brown deep in thought. He could ease her burden very easily. There was room enough for her and the bairn but would it work? At his time of life and the way he was some days, could he cope with a bairn crying? All bairns cried, some had screaming fits. Would it get on his nerves? On the other hand what would he do if Annie left him? Find someone else, a voice inside him said. Not so easy, he was used to Annie. She put up with his bad temper and she knew when to be quiet. He couldn't be doing with a woman who spoke non-stop and there were plenty of those around.

Well, Hamish Brown, he asked himself. What is it to be? Are you going to ask her to bide here or not?

'Annie?'

She came hurrying through. 'Sit down.'

'Again? This is getting to be a habit.' He looked very serious and it made her feel apprehensive. What was he about to say? Mr Brown was an old man and he had told her quite bluntly when she had come about the job that he was looking for someone older and more mature.

'What happens to the bairn when you are here?'

'Madge, my friend, keeps her. Mrs Niven has a young child of her own.'

'You make her a payment or does she do it out of the goodness of her heart?'

'I pay her but she doesn't take much,' Annie said shortly. She couldn't help thinking that it was none of his business.

He nodded and drew his breath in through his teeth, something she had noticed he did when he was thinking.

'I'm not sure if I am doing the right thing but I won't see you without a roof over your head,' he said slowly as if weighing up every word. 'You and the bairn can sleep upstairs and make use of the sitting-room during the day.' He raised his watery eyes to look into her face. 'You'll mind though at my time of life I need a bit of peace and quiet so leave the kitchen to me as much as possible.'

'Yes, of course.' Annie was looking as though she couldn't believe her ears. 'I'm very grateful, Mr Brown.'

'We'll give it a try and see how it works, that's all I'm saying.'

Annie knew what it must have cost him to make the offer. No baby was good all the time and in any case crying was their only way of gaining attention. He would expect his peace to be shattered on occasion and it was up to her to keep the occasions to the minimum.

'Tina doesn't have to be here all day. Madge will be quite happy to keep on looking after her.'

'Is that what you would prefer?'

'No, it isn't, I was thinking of you.'

'Then stop thinking of me and think of the bairn. It's a piece of nonsense moving the wee lass from here to there. She'll not rightly know where she belongs.'

'I'm deeply grateful and in the meantime I'll keep looking out for a room and kitchen to rent.'

'I wouldn't do that. If I want you to go I'll give you fair warning, until then you are welcome here.'

'Thank you.'

'I'm tired,' he said fretfully, 'all that talking has tired me, I'm just not used to it.' His head dropped and in a little while she heard his laboured breathing made worse by his mouth being open. Very gently Annie bent over him to remove the pipe from his hand and put it down beside his tobacco pouch. Her heart felt lighter than it had done for weeks and all thanks to this wonderful old man. Smiling to herself she began to make out a shopping list. She did the shopping in her own time telling Mr Brown that it wasn't work, it was something she enjoyed doing. Money was put in a jug on the shelf beside the cake tins and Annie had been told to take what she needed. He hadn't asked for a detailed statement but he got one. Annie accounted for every penny she spent.

Hamish slept for about forty minutes and like many old people he experienced that small disorientation when awakening from a nap. He looked around vaguely then his eyes settled on Annie.

'There you are, I must have dropped off for a few minutes.'

'You had a good forty minutes, Mr Brown, and you'll feel the better for it.'

'I've kept you over your time?'

'No, you haven't.'

The rest had done him good and helped to clear his mind. Shame on him for thinking he couldn't be bothered with a bairn about the house. Might be nice, like being a grandpa and give him a new interest in life.

'Off you go, Annie.'

'You have all you need?'

'Don't fuss, woman, what would I be wanting. Oh, there is something. You can bring that bairn to see me. Better to break her in gently and let her get used to this face of mine.'

'I'd love to.' Tina had a sniffle so had Duncan. Duncan had the cold first so he must have given it to Tina. She would wait until Tina was over her cold and back to her sunny best for the first meeting.

Hamish was seldom over the door but he still managed to wear a hole in his knitted socks. Annie found darning wool, threaded a needle and began on the job. Should she ask him? Was it a good time? She didn't think he would mind since he knew all there was to know about her. All she did know was that he had been a master joiner with his own business.

'If you don't mind me asking, Mr Brown, did you and your wife have any children?'

'Why should I mind? Yes, Annie,' he said heavily, 'we had two bairns and lost them both.'

She was immediately sorry to have brought up the subject. 'I'm so sorry, that must have been quite awful for you both.'

'It was, it was awful. The wee lass, we called her Hannah after the wife's mother, had something wrong with her when she was born. We knew we wouldn't have her long and I suppose we were prepared, or as prepared as you can be. It was different with Matthew, he was a big bouncing baby. Oh, as a wee lad he could be a holy terror and a little devil at times. He was twelve, Annie, only twelve when the fever took him. We weren't the only family, it was a terrible time for everybody. Right to the very end we thought our bairn would come through it. He was a strong, healthy lad, never a day's illness in his life and we were so sure he could be saved. But it wasn't to be. Matthew was taken like the others, his own best friend among them.'

Annie shook her head in sympathy.

'They all tell you that time is the great healer and granted it dulls the pain. Not the wound though, it never heals. Remembering something opens it up and for a little while you are dragged back into that pain-filled time.'

'I think I can understand that,' Annie said quietly.

'Can you? I doubt if anyone can. All my grand plans for my boy were gone. He was good with his hands and I saw the day when he would come in with me. In my mind's eye I could see the sign, HAMISH BROWN & SON.' A faraway look came into his eyes and when next he spoke she heard the sadness. 'Poor Marian was never the same after Matthew died. It was as though a light had gone out. In her own way she had come to terms with Hannah being taken knowing in her heart that it was for the best. You see, Annie, the wee lass would have needed looking after all her life and who but a mother would be prepared to do that?' He gave a deep sigh. 'God works in mysterious ways and it is hard for us to understand. My faith was sorely tried I can tell you and what I felt most was anger. It all seemed such a waste.'

'Most people would have felt as you did.'

He smiled to lighten the moment. 'One day it will all be made clear to us, not in this world but in the next.'

'You haven't had an easy life.'

'Better than some, worse than others.' He reached for his pipe but made no attempt to smoke it. She had noticed that holding it in his hand seemed to give him comfort. 'It was so much worse for Marian, I had my work to help keep my mind off it. Marian didn't have that. She couldn't sleep, though she pretended to and during the day she couldn't keep still. Always busy, if it wasn't cleaning it was polishing. She was wearing herself out and me too.'

'Couldn't the doctor have helped her?'

'He couldn't have done more. Dr Sturrock tried everything, even going as far as telling her she was selfish. That she wasn't only harming herself but driving us both into an early grave.'

'That was cruel but sometimes it is necessary. Did it help?'

'Maybe for a little while it did.' He shook his head. 'Then her health seemed to go and she hadn't the will to live. Whatever was put on the death certificate and I can't recall what that was, Marian died of a broken heart. She's buried beside her bairns and there is a place beside them for me when my turn comes.'

Annie wanted to weep. The world was full of pain and suffering but there was great happiness too. Perhaps it did us good to hear about the heartbreak suffered by other folk and to make us dwell less on our own tragedies.

'Since then you've been on your own?'

'No, I was never that. Folk were kind and no one more than Jessie. She and Marian had always been close. Jessie lost her man and we were a comfort to each other. She was my friend and helper all those years and now here I am with you, Annie. Maybe I should be counting my blessings.'

On her arrival in Dundrinnen, Annie had gone about largely unnoticed, just a maid accompanying her young mistress. Now she was being pointed out as the young woman who was going to bring up her dead mistress's baby since nobody else wanted it. With so much attention being paid to her, Annie was becoming self-conscious about her shabby clothes. Maybe it was time to pay some attention to her appearance. Nothing drastic, not to be too noticeable, she didn't want a complete transformation. It would have to be gradual. In the evenings she busied herself altering a few of Miss Emily's skirts to fit her. The blouses hung loosely but for all that they looked well on her. Annie had small, firm breasts while Miss Emily had been better endowed.

The gradual transformation took the form of wearing one of Miss Emily's blouses and teaming it with a skirt of her own. Then it was the other way. An expensive skirt with a cheap, faded blouse. This halfway measure made Annie feel more comfortable. It was as though she wanted to hold on to part of herself while trying to improve the other.

She had never been one for walking unless it was for a purpose. There had been those short walks with Miss Emily but now she was walking miles without feeling tired. She wondered why pushing a pram made it easier when surely the opposite should be the case. No one had been able to give her a sensible explanation or one that made sense to her.

How quickly babies outgrew their first pram and what a wrench it was going to be to part with it. Nevertheless it would have to go and a push-chair be bought.

Chapter Twelve

Annie had made up her mind to remain in the cottage until the very last day, and why not, she was entitled to do so. Before then she would make arrangements to have her few possessions taken to Hillside House which shouldn't pose any problems.

When she set out from the cottage that afternoon the weather was cold with a chill wind blowing. Annie found it colder than Perthshire which was more sheltered. The real winter didn't set in until after the new year but there were sharp reminders like today, of what was in store. Annie didn't bother about how she looked, she dressed for the weather. An old felt hat was crammed on her head and a woollen scarf wrapped round her neck. The scarf had been one of Miss Emily's and Annie delighted in its soft warmth. Her own shabby coat was poor protection against that cold wind but she thought she would get this year out of it before it went to the ragman in exchange for a few coppers.

She didn't like her thoughts, was uncomfortable with them. Madge was a good friend and she shouldn't be finding fault. In her real need she had turned a blind eye to her friend's carelessness but now it was beginning to worry her. It was unfair to be judging others by her own high standards which were, after all, thanks to her training at Denbrae House. Had Madge always been like this or was she getting worse? Mamie had been particular about covering food whereas Madge wasn't. The table was only cleared when she eventually got round to it. The grease in the frying pan did again and again and though the dishes got a proper wash the pots didn't come off so well. Particles of food, difficult to move, were just left. No one appeared to suffer, Annie had to admit that to herself, but even so she knew how relieved she would be to have Tina with her at Hillside House.

They had been seen from the window and Madge had the door open. Her smile was welcoming but Annie thought she looked tired. Annie got the pram in the doorway and to the usual place in the narrow lobby. Madge stopped her as she was about to take Tina out of the pram.

'Don't disturb her, bring the pram in.'

'Is there room?'

'No, but bring it in just the same. Duncan's pram can go in the bedroom for the time being.'

'How is he?'

'Girny,' she answered as she manoeuvred the big, ugly pram out of the door and signalled to Annie to put Tina's in the space. Duncan was sitting on the sofa positioned between the usual two cushions and looking miserable. Annie, fussing over him, didn't help and she couldn't raise a smile. The poor wee lad was dribbling down his chin which looked red and sore.

'Madge, have you any cream to put on that?'

'It's finished,' she said shortly. They both looked at Duncan, watched his face pucker then the howls began. The noise had both wakened and alarmed Tina who screamed in protest. Madge began laughing and putting a hand to her forehead, grimaced in pain before taking Duncan into her arms and cuddling him. Annie did the same with Tina and both children, now getting the attention they wanted fell silent.

'Tina seems to have got over her cold.'

'Yes, she's much better. Poor Duncan is a lot worse.'

'He has a bad cold right enough but that isn't the trouble. He has a tooth coming through and his gums are tender.'

'I hate to see children suffering,' Annie said giving Duncan a little pat.

'My mother used to say that teeth were a bother to come and a bother to go and the only good thing to say about false ones was that you never got toothache.'

'Suppose she had a point,' Annie laughed.

Madge yawned. 'No wonder I feel washed out, I'm up half the night just now.'

Annie nodded in sympathy. 'You do look tired. I didn't want to say because that often makes you feel worse.'

'This will pass and there isn't a lot I can do except cuddle him and walk the floor.'

'I have this ahead of me.'

'Not necessarily, some babies are lucky and don't have much trouble.' She paused. 'Any luck with accommodation?'

Annie shook her head. 'I did look at a house in Henderson's Lane, the woman had a room to let but it was quite awful.' She shuddered at the memory.

'So what now? Any chance of Mrs McIntyre letting you stay on in the cottage?'

'Not a hope and I couldn't afford to anyway. Actually, Madge, Mr Brown has come to my rescue. It's a temporary arrangement until we see how it works.'

Madge looked taken aback. 'That was decent of the old man, he is quite ancient isn't he?'

'Elderly.'

Madge seemed to be doing some thinking. 'If you are going to be there all the time what does that make you?'

'What do you mean?' she said putting Tina back in her pram.

'That makes you a sort of housekeeper.'

'I hadn't thought of that but I suppose I'll be doing the work so I could call myself that.'

'Had he been a bit younger there might have been gossip.'

Annie was annoyed but tried not to show it. 'Had he been younger it is unlikely that I would be there in the first place. In any case I am still looking for a place of my own.'

'This will mean you are going to look after Tina yourself?'

'Yes, Madge. You've been marvellous and I'm grateful but it will be lovely to have Tina with me.'

Madge was thinking about the money. Not a lot but she had got used to it. They were both silent, less at ease with each other and Annie, anxious to end the silence, spoke about a push-chair.

'Any word about the push-chair for Duncan?'

'No, and I'm getting very annoyed I can tell you. Duncan is too big for his pram and screams blue murder when I try to put him in it. Honestly if I had known it would take this long before Jean McKenzie was prepared to part with hers I would have looked elsewhere.'

'Not an immediate problem for me but when Tina gets that length how do I go about selling the pram and getting a push-chair?'

Madge looked across at the expensive pram. She had been very envious and curious too. Annie was friendly but not very forthcoming. Even when questioned she gave little away.

'You'll need to advertise but before we go into that how about a cup of tea? I'd make it but if I move Duncan is liable to start screaming again.'

'I'll make it,' Annie said getting up quickly. She had done this before and soon the tea was ready and the cups set on the wooden stool.

'Bring the biscuit tin.'

Annie brought the tin with its faded picture of Balmoral Castle on the lid.

Madge drank some of her tea then put the cup down on the saucer.

'About this advertisement – putting a card in a shop window doesn't cost much. That's a lovely pram so don't be daft enough to let it go ridiculously cheap.'

'What makes you think I would?'

'I just do.' She smiled. 'Maybe it is because you never seem too worried about money.'

'I do worry about money or rather the lack of it,' Annie said drily. Madge was fishing, she knew that.

Madge was fishing. She wondered if money had changed hands when Annie took over the care of Tina. It didn't look as though she was going to find out. Duncan had fallen asleep and Madge gently eased him back on the cushion and Annie handed her a cot blanket to put over him.

'Hopefully he'll sleep for an hour,' she said rubbing her arm where it had taken Duncan's weight. 'Harry the newsagent would be best,' she said going back to the advertisement. 'Everybody looks at the notices whether they want something or not.'

'Idle curiosity.'

'Probably. Harmless though and I must confess to reading them myself. Some are a hoot. Honestly, Annie, you wouldn't credit what some folk try to sell. Here, help yourself,' she said pushing the biscuit tin nearer to Annie.

'No thanks, I've had one and that's fine.'

'Have another.' It was an order.

Annie took one knowing Madge would be annoyed if she refused. She could be prickly at times. The surplus food still found its way to Madge and would continue to do so until Annie left the cottage.

Bob Niven had been enjoying the best beef and would take bad when the supply stopped and they were reduced once again to the cheaper cuts. Madge kept reminding him that the end was in sight and he would nod as though he was taking it in though she knew he wasn't. Though grateful to Annie for bringing the food there were times when Madge saw it as a mixed blessing. Bob had been well enough pleased with what she had served him but now he would be more choosy. Her cooking would be to blame. She sighed and shrugged. She would just have to try and keep her temper under control. Madge wasn't as contented with her life as people, including Annie, believed her to be. She had her dreams where there was no one else to consider but herself. There was a restlessness, a feeling that life was passing her by and soon it would be too late even for dreams. It wasn't that she hankered after great wealth, she didn't. Enough to keep her comfortable would do very nicely. When they were first married Madge had tried to share her dreams with Bob. Didn't he want to travel, to see far-away places? He didn't and thought it plain daft to dream about something that would never happen. Bob had no imagination yet given the chance would she change her lot? She knew she wouldn't. He worked hard to keep them, they had a much loved son and she had no big worries. He could take a drink but she had never seen him drunk. He wasn't a gambling man though he liked a small flutter. She thought if he had a wish it would be that his horse would come in and put a few pounds in his pocket.

Dreams were just for breaking the monotony.

'Madge, you dozed off.'

'Never!' she said sitting up straight.

'You did and don't apologise, even a small nap helps after a lost night's sleep.'

'Had we finished whatever it was we were talking about?'

'Just about.'

'Use a postcard and make your writing big so that folk can read it.'

'I'll manage that. How's this? Pram for sale, very good condition.'

'Needs more. Superior pram for sale, perfect condition – and Annie, state a price well above what you expect to get.'

'What's the point of that?'

'To get the best price. Everybody likes to haggle, Annie.'

'In the hope of getting a bargain?'

'Exactly, it is human nature. By haggling the seller is likely to get less than the asking price but as much as she expected. The buyer will consider herself very clever to have knocked down the price and—'

'Everybody is happy.'

*　　*　　*

Friday was the day for washing the kitchen floor and Annie was down on her knees. Her sleeves were rolled up and a coarse apron covered her skirt. By her side was a bucket of hot soapy water, a scrubbing brush and two cloths. Most of the floor was already washed and patches of it were beginning to dry. What was left to be done was under Mr Brown's chair. He gave no sign of moving though he knew perfectly well that she was waiting for him to do so. Annie sighed. She didn't like it when it came to this. Two options were open to her. She could ask him to get up and risk his wrath or leave that part of the floor unwashed. The latter was unthinkable. How could she leave it undone, she who prided herself on doing a job properly?

'Mr Brown,' Annie said timidly. 'I'm sorry to have to trouble you but could I ask you to get up so that I can move your chair and wash under it. It will only take a few minutes.'

'Leave it, how can the bit under the chair be dirty when nobody has walked over it?'

'It still gets dusty and it needs to be done especially where you put your feet,' she persisted.

'I can see there will be no peace for me until I move,' he grumbled. Rising from the chair was always a slow process but he was making the most of it. Annie hid a smile, men were just like children. Hamish Brown, grimacing as though in great pain, shuffled to another chair and held on to the back of it. Standing just as long as he had support was better than sitting down and having to get himself up again.

Quick as a flash Annie had the chair moved and the floor given a quick scrub and then dried. That done she hauled the chair back.

'Thank you, Mr Brown, that's it all over, you can sit down now.'

'That chair is not back where it was.'

'Isn't it? I thought it was. How do you know?'

'By the pattern on the linoleum that's how. The leg of the

'chair should be there and I mean exactly there,' he said pointing with a tobacco-stained finger.

Annie thought it better to pacify him, after all he was old and allowances had to be made.

'Will that do?'

'It might but I'll tell you in a minute.' He sat down. 'Aye, that'll do fine. You see, young woman, I'm not as daft as you think. With the chair where it is I can stretch easily to anything I need without having to get up.'

Annie laughed. 'Top marks to you, Mr Brown, I would never have thought of that.'

'You don't when you are young but your day will come. What have you done with the bairn?'

'What I always do, I left Tina with my friend Madge.'

'Is she happy enough to be left?'

'Quite happy. Madge is like a second mother.'

Hamish Brown took a bit of getting to know but Annie was beginning to understand him. If he was irritable and short with her it was because he was in pain or discomfort. At other times he had her laughing at his droll sense of humour.

Annie had the bucket emptied and the scrubbing brush drying on the scullery window sill. The cloths were wrung out and draped over the bucket and she was untying the strings of the coarse apron when she heard the door. Mr Brown had heard it too and shouted to her in the scullery.

'See who that is, Annie and if it's anyone selling things shut the door.'

It wasn't a salesman, it was Dr Sturrock, a stocky little man with a round face and a beaming smile who delighted his small patients by always having a sweetie somewhere in his pockets. Sometimes it took a very long time to find but that time was well spent. It let the doctor examine the child while its attention was on finding that sweetie.

'Good morning, Annie,' he said stepping inside, 'is the man of the house up and about?'

'Of course I'm up and about. When have I ever been one for lying in bed?'

The doctor winked to Annie and carrying his black bag went into the kitchen to see his patient. The two were good friends and went back a long way. They could exchange insults without danger of hurt feelings or anything being taken amiss. Annie was always highly amused at the pair of them and pleased too because the exchange seemed to do her employer good.

Both Dr Sturrock and Dr Rutherford had patients in Dundrinnen and the neighbouring villages. The older people preferring to consult Dr Sturrock. He understood his elderly patients and the value of a friendly chat. Often just that wee talk did more good than the medicine. That was where the young ones failed, Dr Sturrock thought, they didn't take the time. It wasn't a waste, it was when the real worries came to the surface. His nephew, also Dr Sturrock, was a case in point. Recently qualified and a clever lad who in time would take over his uncle's practice, he was always in too much of a hurry. Over-confident too and that was dangerous. In his uncle's estimation he wasn't yet ready to be in complete charge.

'Watch your feet on that wet floor unless you want to go all your length.'

'It's dry,' Annie announced, 'apart that is, for the bit under the chair.' She left them together and set about polishing the furniture in the sitting-room. It was a pleasant room with a big window that let in plenty of light. The furniture was good, heavy and had been well cared for. And this was where Mr Brown had said she and Tina could spend their time during the day. How very kind he was and somehow she would try and repay that kindness.

Back in the kitchen Dr Sturrock was examining his patient.

'This would be a lot easier to do if you were in bed.'

'Well I'm not and I had no intention of biding there until you decided to show up.'

'You're no worse and you're no better,' he said putting his instruments back in the bag.

'Is that all you can say?'

'That's all, Hamish. Take it easy.'

'I'm not likely to be doing the Highland fling,' he said waspishly. 'You'll take a dram before you go?'

'Thanks but I'd better not. The good ladies of Dundrinnen would have something to say if they were to smell whisky on my breath.'

'I'll no' force it down your throat. How's the young doctor shaping?'

'Knows it all. You can't tell the young ones anything these days. I keep telling him that all that learning from the text books is just the beginning, that it's experience that counts.'

Hamish nodded as he fastened his shirt buttons.

'He doesn't exactly call me an old fool, you understand, but I can tell that is what he is thinking.'

'Don't be too hard on the lad, you might well have been the same in your young day.'

'Never. I had more respect for my elders.'

'So you say. Away and give Annie a shout.'

Annie was waiting for the summons and had the door ajar.

'You're wanted, lass.'

Annie put the lid on the tin of polish and went through to the kitchen.

'Dr Sturrock here is in need of a strong cup of tea, Annie, could you see to that?'

'Of course, but don't you want one yourself?' Annie said innocently.

'I'll need to keep the man company, won't I?'

Annie made the tea and set it on a small table between them. She put some ginger snaps on a plate knowing that both men were partial to them. Neither had the teeth to cope with a hard biscuit and that gave them an excellent excuse for dunking.

She left them, only returning to see Dr Sturrock to the door. Before taking his leave the doctor spoke softly.

'How has he been?'

'Some days he's fine, quite jokey, then other days he'll snap at me for nothing.'

'He won't mean it.'

'I know.'

'Pain makes us all irritable.'

'What are you two whispering about?'

'We're not whispering. I was just telling Annie that she has the place looking like a wee palace.'

'It's taken you a fair while to say that.'

Dr Sturrock went away chuckling.

Chapter Thirteen

A pair of startlingly blue eyes and a pair of pale blue watery eyes met. The very young and the very old were taking stock of each other. Annie had left the pram in the hallway and had Tina in her arms for that all important first meeting. So much depended on how Tina behaved and Annie was nervous. The whiskery face, kindly though it was, might frighten her and if she cried it would be a poor beginning. Mr Brown might, just might, have a change of heart about them sharing his house.

Tina, as it happened, didn't seem in the least afraid. She was giving Hamish Brown the unblinking stare that some adults find so uncomfortable. Hamish wasn't among them; he was delighted as well as being amused. Annie watched them both and saw Mr Brown winking and being rewarded with a smile that quite bowled him over.

'My but she's a bonny bairn, Annie, and I'll warrant when she grows up she's going to break a few hearts.'

'Her mother was beautiful,' Annie said softly, 'and Tina is very like her except for the eyes. Miss Emily's were grey.'

'Little bright eyes, that's what I'd call this one.'

'She's taken to you, do you want—?'

'No, no, it's too early. We won't rush it, she'll come to me in her own time.' He paused. 'Between us we'll need to take great care of her.'

Annie was touched by the 'we'. 'I can see Tina being thoroughly spoilt.'

'Where's the harm in a wee bit spoiling? Bairns are precious and you don't know just how precious until you lose one.'

Annie nodded. She knew he was thinking of his own loss.

'This is going to work out grand,' he continued. 'In fact, come to think of it, there is nothing to hinder you coming here now instead of staying where you are until the end of the month.'

'That's very kind of you, Mr Brown, but I had better keep to the arrangements since I was the one who made a fuss about staying on for the full time.'

'Ah well, you know your own business best and I won't interfere. And since we are on the subject we'd better discuss this flitting. What are you going to do about that?'

'Not much of a flitting, Mr Brown,' Annie laughed. 'All my worldly possessions will go in one trunk and one suitcase. Both belonged to Miss Emily.'

'And the bairn's things, what about them?'

'There is the cot and the blankets to come over. The rest will go in the pram and I'll bring a few of our belongings with me each time I come.'

'Fair enough and tell me how this trunk and the cot—'

'I'll need to hire someone but my friend Madge will know—'

'No need for that. I'll have a word with the Powrie lads. Real obliging pair they are. It'll be no bother to them to use the pony and trap to transport your bits and pieces across.'

'Are you sure?' Annie said anxiously, 'I don't want to put anyone about.'

'You wouldn't be.'

'I'll pay them, of course.'

'That you won't, not the Powrie lads. They wouldn't hear of it. Their grandparents and the wife and I were good neighbours. I obliged them when they wanted a shelf or the like put up and we were never short of a rabbit or a fresh egg. No money was ever exchanged.' He leaned over. 'Bless her, she's fallen asleep. My it must be grand to be able to go off like that.'

'Not so grand if she won't sleep at night.'

'Can't have it both ways.'

Annie got up. 'I'll get her back in the pram.'

'Is this you away then?' He sounded disappointed.

'I must.'

'If you must you must and I can tell you I'm looking forward to having you both living here. It'll be like the house coming alive again.' He paused and gave a sad smile. 'Loneliness is something I wouldn't wish on anyone,' he said quietly.

Christmas made little difference to Annie, it was just another day. Tina was too young to take any interest and it seemed pointless to put up decorations in the cottage. Next year it would be different. Tina would have a Christmas tree with baubles and silver tinsel and maybe a fairy or an angel for the top of the tree.

Not being an official holiday in Scotland, Christmas wasn't given the importance and the significance it deserved. Those with money to spare lavished presents on their families but most of the children did not have high expectations. They would be thrilled and happy to receive an apple and an orange and a penny. If it was a shiny new penny that was a mixed blessing. An old one could be spent but it was difficult to part with a shiny new one.

Dundrinnen followed the Scottish tradition and celebrated the new year. Housewives saved up for this night of all nights. They had huge bakings and their homes got a special Hogmanay clean. The more superstitious if unable to finish a piece of knitting before the stroke of twelve would unravel it rather than risk bad luck with unfinished work. Excitement would ripple through the village and intensify as midnight drew near. A small crowd always gathered at a central point and as the clock ticked away the minutes they would fall silent. A strange silence that affected all and brought tears to the eyes of some. The old year gone, what would the new year bring? Then as the church bells rang out hands would be shaken, quarrels and differences forgotten as they wished each other a happy new year. Lights shone in windows and tables could be seen with traditional fare and a selection of drink. Dressed in their best the housewives would patiently await the arrival of their first foot. A dark-haired person was preferred but that wasn't always possible. No one came empty-handed, even if it was just to bring a lump of coal. Coal was considered lucky and everyone wanted luck. Come the wee sma' hours and after several houses where they had enjoyed hospitality, some were none too steady on their feet and had difficulty finding their way home. They were convinced the house had moved!

Aware that Hogmanay was not the best day to move house, Annie brought the removal forward to the thirtieth. The Powrie boys said they would be over about two o'clock or as soon after as they could manage. Annie had met them briefly. Henry Powrie was a gangling seventeen-year-old who looked as though he didn't get enough to eat whereas, in fact, he had a huge appetite. He was painfully thin with a shock of dark brown hair which kept flopping over his brow. Malcolm, two years younger, was of a sturdier build. He had the red-gold hair that went with freckles which he hated. In the summer months he had a liberal sprinkling but come the winter they all but faded to a pale brown. They were nice, polite lads with not a great deal to say for themselves. When Annie tried to thank them they blushed furiously.

On the day of the move the weather was dull, depressing and cold but thankfully there was no sign of rain. The previous day there had been a hint of snow in the wind but nothing had come of it. Annie was ready and waiting with everything packed. She had kept the case open for the last-minute things and now they were in and the suitcase shut.

Annie had loved this cottage but now that she knew she was leaving she was anxious to get away.

In her outdoor clothes she did another inspection of the cottage to reassure herself that everything was as it should be. Everything was. When Miss Emily had taken possession of the cottage it had been clean and tidy but not polished and shining as it was now.

The knock when it came took Annie by surprise and a glance out of the window told her it wasn't the boys arriving early. There was no pony and trap to be seen. Going to the door she opened it to find Mrs McIntyre standing there and looking none too pleased.

'Come in, Mrs McIntyre,' Annie said standing aside.

She sailed in, going straight to the sitting-room. Annie with a puzzled frown followed. They stood facing each other in the middle of the room.

'I was under the impression you were vacating the cottage tomorrow,' she said icily.

'A change of plan, Mrs McIntyre, that's all,' Annie said quietly. 'With tomorrow being Hogmanay I thought it more convenient for everyone concerned if I made the move a day earlier.'

'Without telling me?'

Annie was taken aback. 'I didn't think that was necessary and once I'd locked up I was to hand in the keys.'

'You thought that was all that was necessary?'

'Yes, I did.'

'Then you thought wrong. The condition of the cottage is very much my concern. I need to satisfy myself that you have left it as you got it. I'll make my inspection now.'

'Do that.'

Annie felt a spurt of anger but controlled it. The cottage had been lovingly cared for and looked it. She felt like pointing that out but bit her tongue and remained quiet. Mrs McIntyre could be awkward, the way she was being now, but she mustn't forget that the woman had been very supportive during that dreadful time.

When she returned Mrs McIntyre gave a satisfied nod. 'Yes, all in order, which was what I expected but I had to make sure.'

'I quite understand.' Annie waited for her to go but Beatrice McIntyre appeared in no hurry to leave and Annie decided the visit had been as much to find out her future plans as to check on the condition of the cottage. Her next question proved her to be right.

'Is it true what I hear that the widower for whom you do some cleaning has offered you and the baby accommodation.'

'Yes.'

'For how long if I may ask?'

'I can't answer that, I don't know.'

'Be warned, my dear, that it may not last very long. Old folk, and I'm told Mr Brown is elderly, do not take kindly to having their peace shattered. Babies, even the best behaved, have their difficult days.' She smiled as though she'd had first-hand experience.

She must not show impatience or irritability; after all it could be kindly meant. 'We'll just have to see how it goes.'

'Talking of the little one, where is she?'

'A friend of mine is looking after Tina.'

'Well, Annie, I hope things work out for you, although I fear otherwise. I thought, and I still think, that you made a big mistake taking that poor infant.'

'I know you do but I happen to disagree.'

'You are a very stubborn young woman.'

'I'm also optimistic and I have a feeling things will work out,' she said while making a move to the door. The woman could do nothing else but follow.

Before the door closed Mrs McIntyre spoke about the keys. 'You have two sets so kindly remember to hand in both.'

'You can have one set of keys now.' Annie darted back for the spare set.

With the door shut, Annie leaned against it for a moment.

She was glad that was over. It wasn't that she disliked the woman, it was just her unfortunate manner that got Annie's back up. Still their paths weren't likely to cross, not even in the village. The woman had Molly to do the shopping or rather to hand in the orders to the various shops for the message boy to deliver the food the next day.

Annie couldn't believe just how easy it had been to settle in at Hillside House. The three of them were getting along splendidly. Tina, like all children, liked attention and she was getting plenty from Hamish. He had great patience and hadn't forgotten a few tricks he could do with his hands. Once upon a time they had amused his young son and now it was Tina who was chortling. It didn't take much to keep a child happy, just love and patience.

Mr Brown's comfort was Annie's first consideration and she fitted her housework to suit. Living in the house she could wash the kitchen floor and have it dry before Hamish was up out of bed.

'I never see you washing that floor, Annie.'

'Does it look dirty, Mr Brown?'

'No, I couldn't say it does, it's just I never see you on your knees scrubbing it.'

'That's because it is done before you are up out of bed.'

'Would that be a hint for me to get up earlier?'

'You know it isn't. I like you in bed until I have the house back to rights.'

'Just my wee joke, lass. You're a grand worker and in fact I don't think you ever stop.'

'I'm not overworked, far from it.'

'Somebody missed the boat when they didn't marry you and as for that bairn you keep her looking a treat.'

That made them both look at Tina. At six months she was as bright as a bee and interested in everything that went on around her.

'While I mind, Annie, go to yon cupboard on the stair landing. Jessie kept it locked for some reason known only to herself. Maybe she told me but if she did I don't remember. The key should be in that jug on the dresser.'

It was. Annie knew there was a key there. She had washed the jug several times and replaced the key.

'You'll find a doll's house on the shelf. Tina is too young for it yet but the day will come when she will enjoy playing with it.'

Annie climbed the stair the key in her hand. A doll's house, she thought wonderingly, there had been one, fully furnished, in the nursery at Denbrae House.

The key was stiff to turn but after a short struggle she managed it. The cupboard had broad shelves and on the middle one was the handsome toy. Lifting it very carefully she put the doll's house on the floor, shut the cupboard door and then picking it up made her slow and careful way down the stairs.

'Can you manage?' he shouted.

'Yes, I'm just coming.' She came in the door and set the house on the table. Hamish got up slowly from his chair and looked lovingly at what he secretly thought of as his masterpiece.

'Nice piece of work, wouldn't you say?'

She stared at him. 'You didn't—'

'I did. A labour of love it was. Marian did the curtains and the wee cushions, she was good at the sewing.' She watched him undo the catch and open the front of the doll's house. Each room was furnished with tiny, exquisite pieces of furniture and so beautiful that Annie felt the tears come to her eyes.

She was shaking her head. 'I don't think I have ever seen anything so lovely,' she breathed. 'Mr Brown, you are a genius.'

'I'm certainly not that, but I'll say it for myself, it isn't bad for a joiner.'

'You were a lot more than a joiner, you were a cabinet-maker and a very good one.'

'A joiner to trade, Annie, the rest was just a hobby. Mind

you, I wouldn't like to say how many hours went into making it and in the end it was wasted,' he said sadly. 'Hannah, our poor damaged bairn, was very destructive, she broke everything she got her hands on. We couldn't let her have it but here we are, the saying is keep a thing for seven years and you'll get a use for it. Tina is to have it, Annie.'

She felt like crying. 'Tina will cherish the doll's house and so shall I,' Annie said unsteadily.

'No need to upset yourself, it is all in the past.'

'But it is just so sad.'

'Life can be the very devil as you know yourself and we are hard put to make sense of it.' He paused. 'With them both taken from us we wanted the toys away and they went to those who would appreciate them. Not the doll's house though, we couldn't part with that.'

'No, you couldn't.'

'I put it in that cupboard and I know Marian used to look at it sometimes. Jessie didn't approve, she was of the opinion that there was a time for grief and after that life had to go on. Which would be the reason the cupboard was locked, she hadn't wanted Marian upset. Put it back again, lass, and when Tina is a bit older let her play with it.' He closed the front of the house, careful to get the hinge in place then shuffled back to his chair.

'It's just so — perfect,' Annie could hardly tear her eyes away.

'Not many toys where you were brought up, Annie?'

'No, we had to make our own amusement. Tina isn't the only one who is going to enjoy playing with it.'

'A belated childhood,' he said gently.

'You could say that,' she smiled.

It was as though he was fading before her eyes. There was never a word of complaint from him but she could see how frail he was becoming. Even his voice was getting weaker. She took endless trouble to cook meals that would appeal to him but he only picked at what was on his plate. Dr

Sturrock paid a twice weekly visit and always had a word with Annie at the door.

'He won't eat,' she said worriedly.

'He has no appetite, but just carry on as you are doing. The little he does take is helping—'

'Not much and he seems to have so little strength.'

'Yes, my old friend is getting weaker by the day and there is nothing we can do about it. What we have to be thankful for is that he is in no pain, some discomfort, but no pain.'

'I'm glad, I don't think I could bear to see him in pain.'

'Hamish is contented, Annie. You and the bairn have given him a lot of joy and he thinks the world of the pair of you,' he said gruffly.

'I do worry about the noise. She isn't really a noisy child but she gets excited.'

'And why not, she's a bairn. Could be Hamish likes to hear her.'

'Sometimes I take her out to give him peace but then he frets if he thinks I'm away too long.'

'He needs you, Annie, and you've grown fond of him haven't you?'

'Very fond. He's the kindest person I have ever known.'

He smiled. 'Be your usual cheerful self and give him as much of your company as you can and Annie—' She looked up. 'We could have him with us for a long while yet.'

'I hope so and I promise you I'll stay with him as much as possible.' And she would. For how ever long he was spared she would make that time as happy as possible.

Chapter Fourteen

No one could have accused Hamish Brown of being an impetuous man. Before committing himself to anything important he would first give the matter his serious attention. What he was contemplating at this moment and, provided a certain party agreed, would most certainly set the tongues wagging in Dundrinnen. In the whole of his long life he had done nothing that would have merited gossip yet here he was in his seventies and about to give them a field day. No wonder he had a nervous feeling in the pit of his stomach.

In the afternoon Annie had wheeled the pram to the shops and put a loaf of bread and other bits of shopping under the pram cover and safe from little kicking feet. The main shopping was delivered and for his trouble the message boy got threepence. Not many tipped other than at Christmas, and the boy considered himself well rewarded. Some excused themselves by saying that the boy was paid for the job he did. Only when one of their own bairns took on the job did they sing another tune.

March, that unpredictable month, had been wet and windy for several days but today it was dry with a nip in the air. Annie found it exhilarating and pleasant just as long as she kept on the move. The sky was blue with racing clouds and there was a playful wind that at times became boisterous. Tina was happy, her eyes were shining and there was a delicate flush on her cheeks. She loved to be out of doors and made a pretty picture in her warm pink jacket and matching knitted bonnet. She was entranced with the birds, her eyes darting here and there as she tried to follow their flight. Annie laughed at her as she twisted about in the pram and pointed excitedly.

Life was good and Annie felt contented. Hamish seemed a little stronger and was eating better. She would have been the first to agree that she was lucky but it more than annoyed her, it angered her, to have Madge tell her she had landed on her feet. She had, but others had no right to say so. Madge's voice had held a mixture of resentment and envy. Why envy for heaven's sake? It didn't make sense. Hillside House was a comfortable home and Mr Brown was liberal, there was no scrimping on food. Even so she was his housekeeper and nothing was hers except her savings from the housekeeping which Hamish said belonged to her. Madge had a great deal for which to be thankful. Admittedly the house was modest but it was her own home and she could make improvements if she had a mind to. She shared it with a good husband and a much loved child. Surely what Madge had was more desirable. She had security whereas Annie's position was uncertain and always at the back of her mind was the worrying thought that life as it was couldn't go on for ever. The doctor had warned her that Hamish could slip away at any time even when he appeared to be improving. Where would she be then? Exactly where she had been before going to Hillside House. She would be looking for a job and a place to live.

Annie had no idea that her employer was deeply concerned about her future welfare and the child's. It had taken a lot of soul-searching before coming to a decision but he was sure it was the right one. Whether Annie agreed remained to be seen. There was no use approaching the matter until Tina was in bed and asleep. He had to have a smile to himself when he remembered how fearful he had been about having his peace protected. He had told Annie to make use of the sitting-room and leave him the kitchen other than at mealtimes. That didn't work out, how could it? The kitchen was the hub where everything happened. Annie tried her best but it was he who called a halt.

'This won't do, Annie.'

He saw she was alarmed. 'What won't do, Mr Brown?'

'Leaving me so much on my own, it just isn't good enough.'

'But you wanted it that way,' she protested.

'And can't a man change his mind?'

She smiled. 'You want us beside you?'

'Seems like that, doesn't it?' he grunted.

'I'm glad. I'd prefer it if we were together and so would Tina.'

From then on Hamish enjoyed a little of family life. Annie would bring the tin bath to the fire and he loved to see Tina splashing about. After being dried and in her nightdress Hamish would take her on his knee until Annie cleared up.

Anxious to get it over and done with Hamish was becoming exasperated as Annie began on a pile of ironing. The waiting had to go on until that job was completed and the clothes neatly hung over the drying horse until they were put away. With rising impatience he watched her turn the iron on its end and put it down by the side of the range. After that the blanket and sheet were taken off the table and folded. They went into the cupboard below the stairs. When she reached for the basket to do some darning his patience ran out.

'Sit down, Annie and allow your hands to be idle for five minutes,' he said tetchily.

'I can sit and darn can't I?'

'Not just now you can't. I want to talk to you and I don't want to share your attention with a pair of my socks.'

'Sorry.' She put the basket away and sat with her hands in her lap. 'I was always made to feel guilty if my hands weren't occupied.'

'I've never made you feel that way?'

'No you haven't, you've been kindness itself.'

'Then marry me, Annie.'

Her ears were playing tricks, what had he just said? 'Mr Brown, I don't think you could have said what I thought you said.'

'I don't need to repeat it, you heard me well enough. Well, what do you say?'

'I'm speechless.'

'Then you'd better find your tongue and give me your answer.'

'Mr Brown, I am your housekeeper and my job is to keep your house clean and tidy and look after you.'

'Which you do to my complete satisfaction and more.'

'Then why—?'

'Why have I proposed marriage?'

'Yes, why have you?'

He didn't answer. Instead he said, 'I can see by the expression on your face that the idea has no appeal. You are thinking it ridiculous that an old man on his last legs should be proposing marriage to a young lass like you. Well, looked on that way it is ridiculous.'

'Is there another way of looking at it?'

'I would say so.' He put a light to the tobacco in his pipe and puffed away for a few moments. Then very carefully he put the pipe aside and looked at her gravely. 'It could be for our mutual benefit.'

She shook her head.

'Don't reject me out of hand, not before you hear what I have to say. There are advantages in a union between us. Marriage to me, Annie, would give you respectability—'

'I can't think why.' Her colour had risen and she sounded angry.

'Of course you can't, I haven't explained myself properly. You see, lass, folk hereabout respect you as they should, but you may not always be in Dundrinnen.'

'Why not? I like this part of the country.'

'So you should. I've never lived out of the Mearns myself

and never wanted to. For me there is no place like it but that doesn't have to apply to you. What I am saying is that there is nothing tying you, no family links.'

'No,' she said slowly, 'you are right and if it came to the bit I suppose I could settle anywhere.'

'That is all to the good.'

'Mr Brown, I've lost you completely.'

'I don't blame you, we seem to have strayed.' He paused as though to gather his thoughts together. 'Tina's welfare and happiness should be our main concern.'

'Tina's happiness *is* my concern and that will always be the case.'

'I do know that, Annie, and I have given this a great deal of thought. My advice to you is to leave Dundrinnen before Tina is the length of school.'

'That may not be easy.'

'It could be extremely difficult which is why I am offering you a way out. My name would protect you both, don't you see that?'

She smiled.

'You are amused?'

'No, of course not,' she said hastily, 'but I was just thinking that Tina has your name already. On her birth certificate she is Tina Cunningham Brown without a hyphen. Cunningham is taken to be a middle name.'

'Fancy that! That's fate taking a hand.'

'No, the problem is still there.'

'Meaning no father's name and there is nothing we can do about that. However, it needn't be such a drawback, certificates go missing, get lost and only on marriage has it or a copy to be produced.'

'Which is a long time away.'

'Exactly. Tina will grow up to be a lovely lass and he'll not be the right one for her if the circumstances of her birth upset him.'

She nodded.

'Take heart, each new generation shows more tolerance

than the previous one. It will take a long time but the day could come when born out of wedlock hardly raises an eyebrow.'

'You don't really think that?'

'Just wishful thinking for Tina's sake.'

'How would you feel if it wasn't for Tina?'

'Saddened. If we lose sight of what is right and wrong we will be the poorer for it. Children need stability, Annie, and that means the love of parents.'

'In an ideal world,' Annie said drily.

'True and we don't have an ideal world. It is the weak and the blameless who suffer and no child should have to bear the stigma of another's guilt. I look at Tina, at that lovely innocent little face and I feel a terrible rage at what might be ahead for her' – he paused and looked at her – 'if—'

'If what, Mr Brown?' Annie was very still.

'If you don't give serious thought to my offer.'

'I am giving it serious thought,' she said quietly. 'The advantages to myself and Tina are obvious but I fail to see what you are getting out of it.'

'Oh, there are advantages for me.'

'Name them.'

He was quiet for a moment. 'You wouldn't be tied to me for very long, Annie, my life is—'

'No,' she said sharply, 'I won't listen to talk like that. You are improving, Dr Sturrock said so.'

'Don't upset yourself, Annie, I'm old, my health is deteriorating as I and the good doctor well know and we all have to go sometime.'

Annie wanted to weep. Miss Emily had been a dear and much loved friend but Mr Brown had taken the place of family. To her he was the father she had never known and to Tina he was a loving grandfather.

'I want to be prepared and have my affairs in order before I go and I don't want you leaving me.'

'I would never leave you, Mr Brown, and whatever care

you need you'll get from me and that willingly. There is no need to offer marriage to keep me.'

'I think I know that.' He leaned over and patted her knee. 'Now just you keep quiet and let me explain what I have to before I get too tired.'

She nodded, wiped a tear away and sat forward. Sometimes his voice dropped and she had to strain to hear.

'When I'm gone I want to know you won't be penniless and marriage to me would make it very much simpler. There isn't a great deal of money but then you aren't extravagant. Sell the house, Annie—'

'You would want that?'

'I would. It should fetch a fair bit but as I said before, get away from Dundrinnen and though it is hard to give up friends you should do it. One word to the wrong person is all that is needed to spoil Tina's life. Folk don't necessarily mean to be unkind but some can't resist spreading gossip.'

'Do you want your answer now?' Annie said quietly.

'That would be expecting too much but don't keep me waiting long. Time is what I don't have a lot of and don't look like that, I am not afraid of dying but I would rather not be alone when my time comes.'

She took his hands in hers feeling their dryness. 'I'll be with you when you need me and that means with or without a gold band on my finger.'

'The ring, glad you brought that up. We've a fair bit to see to once you make up your mind.'

'I have made up my mind and the answer is yes. Yes, thank you.'

'Bless you.' She heard the relief. 'The minister will come to the house to marry us and we'll need two witnesses but the Powries will do the necessary.'

'You have everything arranged in your mind,' she said accusingly.

'Plenty of time to think when all you do is sit around the house.'

'May I ask you something, Mr Brown?'

'Mr Brown won't do, you'll need to train yourself to say Hamish.'

'I won't find that easy.'

'It'll come and now what was it you wanted to ask?'

'Did you ever think of remarrying after your wife died?'

'Never. Marian was my first love and there was never anyone else.' He smiled. 'If she is looking down and hearing all this she would approve. This isn't a marriage, just a way of making sure that all I leave goes to the right person. Independence for a woman, especially one with a child to support, is a grand thing. You can make a new life for yourself and not as someone's servant. I don't want you ever to be a servant, Annie. My hope for you is that you will meet someone and have a happy marriage.'

'I don't see that ever happening and truly it doesn't bother me, I have Tina.' Marriage was too big a risk perhaps not for herself but for Tina. The stepchild didn't always fit in and there could be resentment on both sides. Annie could see herself torn in two, trying to please both and ending up pleasing neither. She couldn't afford to get in that position and Tina must come first. She owed it to Miss Emily's memory and to her own love for the child who was so dear.

'You're exhausted,' Annie said anxiously.

'I am, Annie, it's a long time since I talked so much but I'm glad it is all settled.'

'Will any of your relatives feel . . .' She searched for a word and he supplied it.

'Cheated. Let them, my dear. Needless to say the odd cousin would be delighted to benefit but I have no wish to let any of them get their hands on my hard-earned money.'

'Not another word,' she said, 'I'll make tea and you rest with your feet up.'

'That sounded like a real wife.' He closed his eyes and she smiled.

Next morning his first words were, 'You haven't changed your mind have you?'

'No, I haven't, but I can't help wondering what folk will say.'

'Don't let that bother you.'

'Probably say I've led you on and I'm a little gold-digger.'

He didn't smile. 'Annie,' he said seriously, 'there will be talk, nothing surer and you must ignore it. Just remember these are people who are not important to you and never will be.'

She nodded. He was right, of course, but it was going to be very uncomfortable knowing she was being talked about. She would have to tell Madge, warn her if that was the right word, before it became common knowledge. She wasn't even sure of Madge and what she would have to say.

'Take your tea,' Annie said putting the cup near him, 'and how about a biscuit, Mr Brown?'

'There is no Mr Brown here.'

'Would you like a biscuit, Hamish?' she said and blushed.

'No, thank you, but that wasn't so very difficult was it?'

'It was but I'll get used to it.'

'A wedding ring — that has to be purchased.'

'That's true. I'll need something to show I'm a married woman.' She tried to smile but her lower lip quivered. Had she given enough thought to this? Marriage was a big step and should not be treated lightly. It was the joining of two people, a commitment, the sharing of a life. Only it wasn't that at all. It could be said and with some truth that she was marrying this old man for what she could get out of it. That was how others would see it and if she had their respect now she would quickly lose it. It wasn't too late to have a change of heart and he would understand. He wouldn't lose out, she would nurse him devotedly for however long that might be. But what about Tina? In her short life she had lost out badly. Miss Emily's money from her great-aunt should have gone to her daughter but that was out of the question. Hamish Brown wasn't wealthy, he had made that clear, but there would be enough to keep them in reasonable comfort. She would be a fool, would have failed Tina if she didn't agree to this marriage. Folk shouldn't judge when they didn't know the full facts. She would hold her head high.

'Lass, that's the second time I've spoken about this ring.'

'Sorry, I was thinking and I didn't hear you.'

'That's all right, I was doing some thinking too and I want you to buy a wedding ring but not here in Dundrinnen.' He laughed. 'That would set the cat among the pigeons. No, Annie, you go further afield.'

'That would be best,' she said quietly.

'Now what I'm about to say or rather ask of you might not meet with your approval and if it doesn't then that is the end of the matter.' He paused. 'There is a ring, if I mind right it is in one of the bedroom drawers—'

'Was it your wife's ring?'

'Yes, her engagement ring. We went together to buy it.' A faraway look came into his eyes. 'She was right proud of it, Annie, and for that matter so was I. Mind I thought I needed my head examined paying that kind of money when there was a house to furnish. To give Marian her due she was for taking a cheaper one but I knew her heart was set on that one.'

'You can't want me to wear it?'

'I'd like nothing better. If you don't want it the ring will go to the auction room and end up on the finger of a stranger. Marian would agree with me I am in no doubt. You don't need to wear it, just keep it.'

'But you would rather I wore it?'

'It would give me a lot of pleasure.'

'Then I'll wear it but only when I am in my Sunday best. Of course it might not fit, we hadn't thought of that.'

'I had. We would get the jeweller to alter it to fit your finger.'

In bed that night Annie went over in her mind all that had happened. It wouldn't really alter her life, the days would follow the same pattern. There would be one change. Hamish Brown would cease to be her employer, she would be his wife and she must remember to call her husband Hamish. She closed her eyes and fell into a dreamless sleep.

In the downstairs bedroom Hamish was lying awake. The marriage must take place soon, very soon. He knew he was getting weaker and just prayed that he would be spared long enough to give Annie his name and provide for her and the child. For some time he had thought of making a Will and leaving his house and money to Annie. That would have been better for Annie. She had an expressive face and he knew she was entering this marriage not for any gain for herself but for Tina's sake. Perhaps this marriage wouldn't have been necessary but he couldn't risk it. Relatives of his or Marian's might have contested the Will saying he wasn't of sound mind when he made it. Marriage was the only sure way.

The arrangements were made in a remarkably short time. The marriage was to take place in Hillside House on the last Friday of March. The Reverend Alexander Gray had reluctantly agreed to perform the ceremony but he was far from happy. Annie paled under his searching look which spoke volumes. What he thought of her was clear and Annie thought if that was his opinion, a minister's, what could she expect from the ordinary folk of Dundrinnen. Dr Sturrock like the Powries knew the true reason for the marriage and approved. The couple had their blessing. Cissie Powrie had been very impressed with the way Annie looked after Hamish and kept the house spick and span. Being such old friends they felt some responsibility for Hamish and were relieved that he had Annie. They had a busy life, the farm was large and even with their son, his wife and the two grandsons to assist there was still plenty of work for the older couple.

Madge was in her usual muddle but seemed pleased to see Annie and Tina. She came to the door in a pink, flowered overall that could have done with a wash and iron. Duncan's woollen jumper had been washed without due care and looked tatty. Annie decided the water had been too hot or the soap hadn't all been taken out in the rinsing water. That didn't trouble the child, he was perfectly happy, the tooth had come through and he was back to his sunny self. He had a pot and a large spoon and was making as much noise as he possibly could.

'Sorry for the racket but if I take it from him he'll howl and that will be as bad if not worse. If we ignore it he'll soon tire and look for something else to amuse him. Still got the pram, thought you would have had a push-chair by now?'

'I intend getting one shortly.' She had mentioned to Hamish that she was to sell the pram and buy a second-hand push-chair.

'There is no second-hand push-chair coming into this house, I can tell you that straight,' Hamish had said and looked real put out.

'A good second-hand one, not just any old thing.'

'Not good enough. You will buy a new one and I shall pay for it.'

'No you won't. I should get a good price for the pram and more than enough to buy a new push-chair.'

'Then why this talk about a second-hand one?'

'To save money.'

'Save on other things, not on that.'

'Yes, Hamish,' she said meekly.

'You're learning.'

'Have you got your advertisement in?' Madge was asking as silence was restored. Duncan was tearing up a newspaper and Tina an interested spectator.

'I've something to tell you, Madge.'

'Oh, and what would that be? I'm all ears.'

'I'm getting married.' She almost choked getting the words out.

'You are what?' Madge screeched.

'I'm getting married,' Annie repeated.

'This is very sudden. Is this to someone you knew before you came to Dundrinnen?'

'No.'

'Then who is it? I didn't know you were seeing anyone,' Madge said accusingly.

'Mr Brown has asked me to marry him.'

'Your employer, that old, old man?'

'Yes.'

'I can't believe what I'm hearing. Heavens, he must be in his seventies.'

'He is.'

'One foot in the grave.'

'Don't say that,' Annie said angrily.

'Why not when it is the truth. He can't have long when he's already had his three score years and ten.' She paused and looked long and hard at Annie. 'How could you even think about it?' she shuddered.

'What do you mean?'

'Don't come the innocent, you must have thought about it.'

'If you are thinking what I think you are then you ought to be ashamed of yourself.'

'That's rich, me being ashamed. If he hasn't designs on you why is he marrying you?'

'Because he is fond of me and he loves Tina. All he wants, Madge, is to provide for us and give Tina a better chance. I thought that would have been obvious to you.'

'A marriage in name only? Is that what this marriage is to be?'

'Of course it is,' Annie said quietly.

'You're a dark horse, Annie Fullerton, and I have to hand it to you. You've played your cards very well. All that loving care for the old boy is paying off. You are going to be handsomely rewarded. Once he's six feet under you'll be laughing. I'd be filled with admiration if I wasn't so disgusted.'

Annie said nothing but she felt sick.

'Don't go through with it, Annie, and I speak as a friend.'

'A friend?' Annie said sarcastically. 'Some friend you are.'

'I have your best interests at heart.'

'Have you? Then thank you for your concern but it won't alter anything.'

'I can see that. When is the big day to be?'

'It won't be.'

'A quiet affair?'

'Very.'

'No invitation for me then?'

'No, Madge, no invitation.'

'You've fixed the date?'

She didn't have to say, but what was the point of keeping it a secret? 'The last Friday of the month.'

'Apart from the minister who else is to be there?'

'Close friends of—' she stopped and Madge gave a peal of laughter.

'You were about to say Mr Brown. Aren't you on Christian name terms yet?'

Annie had had enough. 'Come on, Tina, we're going home.'

'Aren't you staying for a cup of tea?'

'No, thank you.'

'You are offended, but if you think what I said was hurtful it is only a small taste of what to expect. Frankly, Annie, I wouldn't be in your shoes for all the tea in China.'

Tina appeared to notice something was wrong but she made no demur when Annie put her in the pram. She manoeuvred it through the door and into the lobby and Madge held the outside door open. The door closed without another word having been spoken.

She had only gone a few yards when Annie was blinded by tears. She had to stop to find her handkerchief and wipe them away. Her lips were quivering but she managed a brave smile for Tina.

'Mummy has a cold coming on.'

Chapter Fifteen

The wedding was over. She was Mrs Hamish Brown. Annie had bought herself a dress and shoes as instructed. Get something nice and not cheap rubbish was what Hamish had said. Dundrinnen had little to offer in the way of fashion and for this purchase she would go elsewhere. She was maybe being hard on the villagers but she had a sneaking suspicion that the cost of the dress and its description would be circulated if she was to give the local store her custom. Cissie Powrie, the farmer's wife, had come to her assistance. Stonehaven, she told Annie, had some fine shops and that was where she should go. Go on your own, I'll take Tina and don't worry about the child, there is plenty on the farm to keep her happy.

Getting away on her own had been a pleasant change for Annie and she enjoyed her afternoon shopping. Wandering from shop to shop she had studied the windows and then gone into one. The assistant had been especially helpful, probably because she saw a very uncertain young woman, the kind who would leave with something unsuitable rather than demand to see what else was in stock. There were plenty of those who tried on everything and in the end bought nothing.

'Good afternoon, can I help you?' she said pleasantly.

'I'm looking for a dress.'

'May I ask if it is for a special occasion?'

Annie wasn't going to say what special occasion, pictur-
ing if she did the totally unsuitable dresses that would be
brought for her inspection.

'Not – not really—'

'Something smart, not too dressy and can be worn at any
time?'

Annie brightened. 'Yes, that is exactly what I am looking
for.' How lucky to have an assistant who understood her
requirements.

'About colour, do you have a preference?'

'I thought of blue.' She knew it was Hamish's favourite
colour.

The woman looked at her and nodded. 'Blue would suit
your colouring provided it wasn't a deep blue. Then again
you could wear the paler pinks or peach. Indeed you could
wear red which is a favourite colour this year.'

'Not red, too bright for me,' Annie said quickly.

'Not at all but if you are happier with the blues and pinks
I'll go and see what I have in your size. Meantime if you
would just go into the cubicle and take off your skirt and
blouse.' She drew the curtain and left Annie. Annie hung her
coat on the hook and after removing her skirt and blouse put
them over the back of the chair. She didn't have to feel self-
conscious about her underskirt, it was one of Miss Emily's
and hung beautifully.

In a few minutes the woman arrived with several dresses
over her arm.

'What a lovely selection,' Annie smiled.

'Yes, you came at the right time, our new stock has just
arrived.' The assistant was slim and Annie's height but much
older.

She had tried on four dresses and liked them all. Looking
at herself in the long mirror she twisted this way and that to
get a better view. The excitement had put colour into her
cheeks and the woman thought it such a pity the young
woman wore her hair in that severe style. She suited it but it
made her look older.

'Which one do you think I suit best?'

'Don't you want to try on the other two?'

'No, I wouldn't suit the neckline in either of them. I feel better with a collar. I'll choose between these four but I would be grateful for your opinion.'

'I would be inclined to go for the blue with the lace collar.'

'Yes, I do like it. I love the soft pleats and the full sleeves.'

'Try it on again just to make sure.'

'I don't need to but I will,' Annie said happily.

'Yes,' she said after another look in the mirror, 'this is my dress and thank you very much for being so helpful.'

'My pleasure. I'll go and get a box for it.'

Before she took it off Annie had another look at herself. Hamish was an old man but not too old to take an interest in her appearance. If he liked something he would say so and if he didn't he would make a comment such as, you must have bought that with your eyes shut or worse, someone saw you coming.

She was less fortunate in the shoe shop. The girl was bored and looked it.

'Is that all you can show me?' she said looking at the two pairs of shoes.

'You have a narrow foot and that makes it difficult.' She yawned without taking the trouble to cover her mouth.

Annie got to her feet. 'Perhaps if you got enough sleep you might be able to attend to your customers in a satisfactory manner. I'll take my custom elsewhere.' She left the shop and a deeply shocked assistant. Annie was just as shocked at herself. Fancy her daring to say that? Where had she got the courage? That was the sort of remark Miss Emily might have made and here she was acting in the same way. She was changing, no doubt about that.

The shoe shop at the other end of the street was busy but one very efficient assistant was coping and coping well with two customers, an elderly woman and Annie. She disappeared and came back with a pile of boxes that all but hid her from sight. One lot she placed in the front of the elderly lady and the others beside Annie. Annie tried on quite a number and selected two pairs. It might be a long time before she was back in Stonehaven. In a small café she had a quick cup of tea then headed for the bus.

Hamish hadn't needed any persuasion to wear a formal suit. He had a few in the wardrobe and left the choice to Annie. She thought the dark grey worn with a white shirt and a stiff collar would be best. It came out of the wardrobe with a strong smell of mothballs about it but after hanging it at the open window for a couple of hours the smell had gone. The trousers could do with a press was Annie's thought and she quickly got out the iron and a damp cloth.

After it she wondered if it had been the shortest marriage ceremony on record. The minister said no more than was absolutely necessary and once he had pronounced Hamish and Annie husband and wife he took his departure. His excuse was that he had another appointment. Annie didn't believe him but she was glad to see him go and she wasn't the only one.

John and Cissie Powrie gave them a lovely tall crystal vase and from Dr Sturrock was a set of six whisky glasses.

Tina, solemn for the occasion she didn't understand, behaved beautifully. She looked as pretty as a picture in a pale yellow dress with little rosebuds edging the skirt. By the time they were drinking a toast the child obliged by falling asleep on the sofa. Annie had provided cake and shortbread and the farmer, red-faced and beaming, declared it was just like the new year.

While Hamish was deep in conversation at the other side of the room, Cissie took Annie aside and spoke softly.

'Hamish is right, Annie, this is the best thing that could have happened for the three of you. In the fullness of time and when he is no longer here you will be in a position to make a whole new life for you and Tina.'

Annie nodded, too choked to answer.

'There could be some awkwardness—'

'I'm prepared for that.'

'I'm glad. All folk see, all folk allow themselves to see, is an old man marrying a young woman. They will see Hamish as an old fool who has been taken in by a scheming young woman. They will be angry, Annie, because he is one of them and they have always known him. You will be blamed.'

'I know,' Annie said resignedly, 'I'll be the villain.' Her voice faltered, 'Even my friend, Madge, has turned against me.'

'Not much of a friend and if it is the end for you two it will be her loss not yours. Hold your head high, Annie, and try to feel sorry for those who would bring you down. They lead such empty lives and this gives them something to talk about. And Annie—'

'Yes?'

'If they give you a hard time try and keep it from Hamish, it would only upset him.'

'I know. But don't worry, I won't let them upset me. I have done nothing to be ashamed of and they can think what they like.'

'That's the spirit.'

'No, don't go yet, let me say this first. I didn't want marriage because it didn't seem right to me and I knew he would get himself talked about.'

'He insisted because it was the only way he could be sure that what he left would go to you and Tina.'

'I wish I could do more for him,' Annie said sounding distressed.

'You have given him the best gift of all, you have given him peace of mind. And another thing and I want to emphasise this, if you need us, day or night, don't hesitate. Come over, we are always there for you.'

'How very kind of you and it has relieved me of one big worry. If Hamish was to fall ill during the night I wondered what I would do, I mean about getting the doctor. I couldn't leave Tina—'

'Of course not. You must bring her over to us and we'll do what is necessary.' She looked at the sleeping child on the sofa. 'Don't they look like little angels when they are asleep? Hamish dotes on her you know. We, John and I, think she has taken the place of the grandchild he never had.'

'Yes, I think you are right,' Annie said softly.

'We'll go before Tina wakens.' She caught her husband's eye and he nodded. They had perfect understanding, Annie thought.

When they had gone she followed Hamish out of the sitting-room and into the kitchen. Sinking into the soft leather he heaved a huge sigh.

'Fine to be back in my own chair.'

'Are you tired?'

'Yes, Annie, I am. That's enough excitement for one day, wouldn't you say, Mrs Brown?'

'Yes, quite enough.' She was feeling awkward and shy and beginning to bite on her lip.

'Don't do that, lass,' he said gently. 'You made a fine-looking bride in that bonny dress.'

'Thank you, I chose the colour because I know you like blue.'

'Fancy you remembering that!' She saw how pleased he was. 'Marian wore a lot of blue and just the once, I mind, she bought a yellow dress, canary yellow and I must have gone on a bit about it because she hardly ever wore it.'

'You don't like yellow then?'

'On Tina it looks lovely, but then that is a bonny pale shade. You know what they say about yellow on grown-ups?'

'No.'

'Yellow is forsaken.'

'I'll remember that. And now I'll go up and change out of this dress.'

'Don't, I like to see you in it. It would be a shame to spoil the day by changing into your everyday things.'

'Tina has to be bathed and put to bed.'

'She'll manage one night without a bath. Come and sit down, time enough to get up when we hear the bairn wanting attention.'

He was loosening his collar. 'You'll be wanting to change though?' she smiled.

'Uncomfortable things these hard collars and I wouldn't like to say when last I wore one. You'll have to excuse an old man and help me off with this jacket.'

She did and then helped him on with his cardigan. 'That better?'

'Champion.'

Annie was not looking forward to her first visit to the shops after her marriage to Hamish. They would all know with the banns being read out in the church and Madge may well have spread the word.

'I'm going to the shops, Hamish, anything special you want?'

'No, I've all I need but mind and get sweeties for the bairn.'

'Too many are bad for her.'

'Nonsense.'

'I thought about steak and onions; how does that appeal to you?'

'It does. Get the best steak, it takes less chewing.'

Annie had ordered a new push-chair but it was taking longer than expected to arrive. Hamish's advice had been sound. She had been for advertising the pram and ordering a push-chair at the same time.

'No, Annie, the push-chair arrives first then it will be time to get rid of the pram. There is plenty of space in the hall.'

Hamish said to take her time, there was no hurry, and she was going to take him at his word. The fresh air would do them good. Wheeling the pram she followed the winding road until the turn-off for the big house and was tempted to go further and have a look at the cottage. She didn't give in to temptation lest she meet Mrs McIntyre. They had passed each other in the village with the woman giving an incline of the head and a weak smile. This time on the lonely road she might decide to stop and ask questions Annie didn't want to answer.

'This is far enough, Tina, we'll get back now and buy a piece of frying steak in the butcher's for Grandad's dinner.' Annie was finding it easier to call her husband Grandad than use his Christian name.

The drapery and baby linen shop was the first she came to and Annie stopped to look in the window. There were cardigans and jumpers, scarves and Fair Isle gloves plus the usual selection of knitted tea-cosies. Most of the goods were knitted locally by those women who did the work at home. The return for their efforts was very small but they seldom grumbled. They enjoyed knitting, finding it soothing, and with the leftover wool they knitted something for their own family. The baby clothes were in another window but there wasn't a big demand. They were too expensive and most of them could knit their own or if not they would know someone who would do it for them.

Leaving the shop windows her heart sank. A few women were gossiping at the door of the grocer's and she would have to pass them. As she drew near she recognised two of them as well-known gossips and their gossip was usually malicious. She began to recite into herself, sticks and stones may break my bones but names will never harm me. Whatever insults they hurled she would ignore and keep a dignified silence.

She couldn't control her colour and she could feel it flood her face. Miss Emily would have dealt with a similar situation with amusement but Annie knew she couldn't. Leaving the pram where it could be seen from inside the shop, Annie went in with her shopping list. A few women were waiting to be served and she saw from the corner of her eye one woman nudge another and whisper. The message boy was behind the counter and gave her a cheery smile. He had heard the talk about her marrying an old man to get his money, but she could do what she liked as far as he was concerned. That was threepence he could depend upon.

'May I leave the list with you, Tim?' Annie said as she stepped forward to the counter.

'Sure, Missus, I'll do that.' Missus Brown, that was what he should have said.

Tim gave the list to the assistant who was busy serving but not too busy to study Annie. She wondered if she had grown two heads.

'Bold as brass, did you see that?' It wasn't said in a loud voice but was clear enough for Annie to hear.

Annie moved to the door. 'Would you excuse me, you're blocking the entrance?'

'Ladies, it's the new bride, make way for her. Ina move your body.'

'In a minute when I've had my say.' She puffed out her chest and moved her bulk a fraction. 'I knew old Mistress Brown and a finer woman you couldn't hope to meet. The poor woman would turn in her grave if she knew what was going on.' Her thick finger pointed to Annie. 'There is a name for your kind but I'm too polite to use it.'

'You astonish me,' Annie said unable to resist it and a few folk tittered.

Another said, 'I knew Marian Brown and Hamish too. I gave him credit for more sense but you know the saying there is no fool like an old fool.'

Annie would stand insults to herself but not to Hamish.

'Now that you have had your say would you kindly get out of my way,' Annie said angrily, as she pushed her way through.

'Here you, just be careful who you're shoving.'

For a moment Annie closed her eyes. She had wanted to carry this off in a dignified manner but her temper had got the better of her. She pushed the pram to the butcher's, glad to see the shop empty.

'What can I do for you Miss Fullerton, begging your pardon, Mrs Brown?'

'A piece of steak for frying.'

'I have a fine bit here just let me give it a wee trim.' He weighed it. 'Just short of a pound would that do?'

'Nicely, thank you. A pound of beef sausages and I think that will do today.'

'My congratulations, Mrs Brown,' he said kindly, 'you and the bairn will be all right with Hamish Brown and—' He stopped.

'Ignore what others are saying?'

'Do that and remember this, lass, the vast majority of folk hereabout think you have done a grand job with that poor bairn. Not many would have taken on that responsibility.'

'Thank you for telling me, I thought I was the village outcast.' Annie managed to smile as she said it.

'Far from it. There's your steak and sausages and I'll guarantee that's as fine a piece of steak as you'd get anywhere.'

At home Hamish was wondering about Annie. She was a brave lass but too sensitive at times. He hoped the unchari-table ones were not giving her too hard a time. His own name would be bandied about and if he was honest he didn't like to be the butt of jokes. An old fool is what they would be calling him or it might be worse. His face worked with annoyance then he was angry with himself for bothering. No one would say it to his face though the minister, that dried-up bag of old bones, had come close to it. That had been a mistake choosing him but there had been only two applicants for the vacancy or the calling as he supposed was the correct way of describing it. He wondered how the Rev Alexander Gray had got it, perhaps the other one had withdrawn his application. Whatever, the man wasn't a patch on his predecessor. Now there was a man you could take to. Michael Craig had owned a sense of humour and could take a joke against himself. And another point in his favour, he wouldn't say no to a dram and a crack round the fire. The talk would seldom touch the church, instead it might be a heated discussion on politics or the milder topic of what the weather was doing to the crops.

They were back, he had heard the door opening and for him it was like the sun coming out to see Annie and Tina appearing. He studied Annie's face for signs of distress but none were visible. For a few moments he gave Tina his full attention then he spoke to Annie.

'How did it go with the women of Dundrinnen?' He would keep it light and jovial. 'Did they shower you with their congratulations?'

She would answer in the same vein. 'Hamish, if the ladies of Dundrinnen were of a mind to shower me with anything you can rest assured it wouldn't be with congratulations.'

He was serious. 'Was it very unpleasant?'

'No, not at all.' Why worry him. 'Jimmy in the butcher's used my married name and offered his good wishes. None of the others had much to say,' she lied.

'Don't treat me like a fool, young woman, someone had a go at you.'

'All right, if you must know one woman did have her say. I don't know her name but she looked like the side of a house and I had a job squeezing passed her to get in the door. She said she was speaking as an old friend of your wife's, that Marian would turn in her grave if she knew and was generally nasty. But don't you worry, Hamish, I think I gave as good as I got. Actually I intended being terribly dignified but needless to say I couldn't carry that off.'

'She would be no friend of Marian's, she was careful whom she had for friends and as for—'

'Hamish, we won't talk about it. Instead congratulate me on getting a choice piece of steak for your dinner.'

'Away and get on with what you want to do and I'll watch the bairn. Put up that fireguard so she can't come to any harm.'

'You don't get the same heat when it's up.'

'Don't mollycoddle me, Annie. Maybe it does keep a little of the heat away but what is that compared to a bairn's safety. You'll remember I'm not so fleet on my feet to take action.'

He was so careful of Tina and Annie would have had no hesitation in leaving them together while she went out for an errand if it hadn't been for Dr Sturrock's warning.

'I'm not being an alarmist but you have to prepare yourself for Hamish going at any time even when he appears better than usual. What I'm really saying is that it wouldn't be safe to leave the wee lass with him if you were to go out.'

'I wouldn't do that, Dr Sturrock. Hamish is wonderful with Tina but she is getting to the stage of being a handful.' She laughed, 'Even for me.'

'A good sign when a bairn's active.'

Few, including Dr Sturrock, had expected to see Hamish lasting a year yet here he was frail but cheerful. Tina was eighteen months, quick on her feet and into everything. Annie had her work cut out looking after a bundle of mischief and a husband getting weaker. Dr Sturrock had retired and handed over to his nephew who was eager to be given full responsibility. He had found it frustrating to accept advice he considered old-fashioned and sometimes totally wrong. The recently retired Dr Sturrock would continue to visit Hamish as a friend. It was over a whisky that the two of them had decided that Hamish would be more comfortable with the old-fashioned Dr Rutherford than under the care of the young doctor with all his modern ideas.

The previous week the doctor and his former patient had enjoyed a dram and a chat. Hamish had seemed well and Annie had made tea to follow the dram and had joined them. At the door she and the doctor had spoken briefly.

'Hamish is looking a lot better, don't you agree?'

'I do, indeed, and it is thanks to all the attention you give him.'

That was why it had come as such a shock. Certainly Annie had no premonition when she went in with his early morning cup of tea.

'Good morning, Hamish, shall I draw back the curtains a little?'

There was no reply and she supposed he was sleeping. Thinking he might waken in a minute or two she put the cup down on the bedside table. If he appeared to be sound asleep which was unusual she would take it away and slip out without disturbing him.

She couldn't have said when the first fear took hold or when it dawned on her that Hamish would never waken again. Lying there he looked so peaceful with just the hint of a smile on his face as though he were having pleasant dreams. It was when she touched his cold hand that she knew. She covered her mouth to stop the scream she felt in her throat. He couldn't be dead, not Hamish. She had come to depend on him so much and she had a terrible urge to shake him until he came back to life. First Miss Emily and now Hamish. The only two people in the world who had genuinely cared for her. Then she was backing away to the door as if afraid to turn round. She must get a grip on herself and face what had to be done. The farm, she must get word to Cissie and John Powrie and they would get someone to bring the doctor although she wondered what a doctor could do. Then she remembered the death certificate that had to be made out. Why had the house become deathly quiet? This wasn't the usual early morning quietness; it was different, it pressed down.

Slipping on her coat she went through to Tina. She was asleep, her breathing regular, and she hardly stirred as Annie lifted her bedcover and all and went downstairs. Without bothering to close the outside door she hurried across the field, Tina's weight heavy in her arms, to where the Powries had their house. A much smaller and more attractive one than the sprawling farmhouse where their son, Dick, his wife Sarah and the two boys lived. Already there was activity, farming folk were very early risers.

Cissie Powrie had been on her way to feed the hens but seeing the hurrying figure and recognising at that distance that it was Annie, she put down the basin she had been carrying and went to meet her.

'Mrs Powrie, it's Hamish,' Annie said breathlessly and tearfully, 'he won't waken and I'm sure he's—' She couldn't say the word but Cissie immediately had taken control. John and she had been prepared for this knowing it could come at any time.

'Give me Tina, you're almost dropping,' she said taking the child in her arms. 'Come along inside, Annie, and be seated—'

'I can't, there's so much—' she protested.

'Nothing that can't wait a few minutes,' she said gently. 'You sit there and I'll go and find John. One of the lads will go and get Dr—' She hesitated.

'Not the young Dr Sturrock, Hamish was seeing Dr Rutherford.'

Mrs Powrie nodded as she settled the sleeping Tina on the sofa with a pillow for her head which she had taken from their own bedroom. 'I won't be long.' She hurried away. When she came back John was just behind and Annie felt an overwhelming sense of relief. Mr and Mrs Powrie would take over and do all that was necessary.

'Give me the keys of the house,' John said gently.

She stared at him. 'Keys?' she said stupidly.

'I'll go over there but I'll need the keys to get in.'

'Sorry! Sorry! My brain isn't functioning. It's open, the door I mean, I should have locked it, I don't know why I didn't—'

'Make tea and lace it with brandy,' he said to his wife.

'No, I don't need, I'll come with you—'

'No, Annie, you stay here. Tina will need you when she wakens up.'

As if she had heard, Tina opened her eyes and gave a whimper.

'It's all right, darling,' Annie said cuddling her, 'Mummy's here and remember this is Aunt Cissie and Uncle John's house.' She turned to Cissie, 'I didn't bring her clothes.'

'Not to worry, I'll go with John and collect them.'

'On the chair beside the cot.'

'I'll soon find them, don't worry.'

'Want home, Mummy.' She set up a piteous cry as though somehow she sensed there was something wrong.

'All right, Tina. Mummy will drink a cup of tea and then we'll go back to Hillside House.'

Annie was grateful. She wanted to be home, it was her place to be beside Hamish.

John Powrie came through from the bedroom and nodded to his wife. 'He's gone but peacefully I'd say. Probably just slept away.'

'The blinds, John?'

'I'll see to them,' Annie said, glad to have something to do. Then she looked uncertainly in the direction of Hamish's bedroom.

'I pulled the blinds down in there, Annie.'

They were sitting together talking quietly when the doctor arrived.

He wasn't long and when he came out of the bedroom he pronounced the cause of death as heart failure.

'Would he have suffered at all?' Annie asked him and he shook his head.

'Likely as not went in his sleep and wouldn't have known a thing about it. Best way to go.' He remembered Annie and the earlier tragedy in her life. Annie didn't think he had, he had given no sign of recognition. 'Try to remember that the man had a good innings and death is only a tragedy when folk die young.' It sounded callous when death had just visited the house but they knew, too, that he spoke the truth.

When he went Cissie was putting on Tina's clothes and judging by the giggles was no expert.

'Funny how quickly one forgets,' she laughed as at last the task was completed and Tina had hauled out her toy box and emptied it on the floor.

The drop of brandy in the tea had helped and Annie felt calmer.

'Sorry I went to pieces,' she said apologetically.

'You didn't. You had a dreadful shock and shock takes us all in different ways. As it happens, you did the right thing.' She paused. 'Perhaps you should both come and stay at the farm until the funeral is over?'

Annie shook her head. 'You are very kind but I won't. The worst of the shock is over and I will be able to cope.'

'You wouldn't be afraid?'

'No.'

'That is brave, I'm not so sure I could do it, but if that is what you want I'll respect your wishes. I will, however, see to the food situation and save you thinking about that.'

'Thank you, that would be a great help.'

Annie had very little to do, the Powries saw to everything including the announcement in the newspaper. A number of the villagers attended the funeral and Dr Sturrock and a few others came back to the house for a refreshment. Annie wondered about relatives, but if any had been present they didn't make themselves known to Hamish's widow.

Tina was being tearful and difficult. Where was her Ganda, she wanted her Ganda? Annie had the difficult task of explaining to a very young child that he had gone to live with the angels in heaven. Tina hadn't been satisfied, she didn't know about heaven and the angels, she only knew she wanted her Ganda to play with her and he'd gone away without telling her.

Annie's eyes went again and again to the empty chair and a feeling of intense loneliness swept over her. It was even worse than when Miss Emily had died. Hamish had represented the family she had never known. He had given her his name, his loving care and now all his worldly possessions.

For a week after the funeral Hamish's bedroom had remained shut and at the end of the week it had needed a lot of willpower to open the door and go in. But she did.

She opened the window wide then she stripped the bed and took everything through to the scullery for washing. Weather permitting she would get it all done and dried and the sheets mangled. Life, she knew, had to go on.

Chapter Sixteen

Annie had no visitors apart from Cissie Powrie. The boy who brought the messages was a bright happy laddie and gave a huge smile when he departed with threepence in his pocket. There was a small change taking place in the village with some of the women having a gradual change of heart. Perhaps they thought she had suffered enough. Whatever the reason they were beginning to smile, albeit a stiff smile, which made life for Annie more pleasant. She didn't feel the same need to hurry with her shopping. Madge, she thought, must do hers at a different time of day since not once had they come face-to-face. She remembered the one occasion when they had caught sight of one another and Annie had been all ready with a smile. She had wanted the coolness to end but apparently Madge didn't. She had deliberately turned away to give her whole attention to a window displaying fishing tackle. Annie knew that Madge's husband, Bob, had no interest in the sport and it was unlikely that would have changed. It was a pity to carry on that way when they had once been good friends, but she wouldn't lose any sleep over it.

If it didn't bother Annie that she had no friends of her own age, it bothered Cissie and she tried to do something about it.

'It isn't good being so much on your own, Annie.'

'I have Tina.'

'Yes, you have Tina but you know what I mean. Children are wonderful company but it is hardly the same as having an adult conversation. I do know that Sarah would be only too pleased—'

'Mrs Powrie,' Annie interrupted, she was alarmed. Sarah was kindly but a bit intimidating. 'I am grateful and I know what you are trying to do but your son's wife is very different from me. She is outgoing and popular and I am neither. Honestly I'm perfectly happy at home.'

'Oh, the lass is a live wire and there are times I'm exhausted just listening to her, but she means well and she would introduce you to those young women with children about Tina's age.'

'I know and as I said I'm grateful but please—'

'Leave me alone is what you are trying to tell me and I'm wasting my breath.'

'I'm afraid so.' They were at ease with each other and able to be plain-spoken without giving offence.

'We'll leave it at that.'

'If you haven't to rush off I could do with some advice.'

'I don't, and no one will come looking for me.'

'It's about Hamish's clothes and what I should do with them. Those the worse for wear will go to the ragman but he has a good overcoat that looks almost new and there are suits and shirts—' She spread out her hands.

'With Hamish being so seldom over the door he didn't need to be dressed. I think he almost lived in cardigans,' Cissie smiled.

Annie smiled too. 'An old pair of trousers and a cardigan that was what he felt comfortable in.'

Cissie gave Annie a sympathetic look. 'I always think it is the worst job after somebody dies. I mean knowing how to dispose of everything. Which friend should get this and which one that. People do cherish getting a little gift, a reminder from one they once held dear but not clothes, even those never worn. Somehow it is too intimate, too personal.'

Annie nodded in agreement.

'It is for that very reason that they can only accept them being worn by strangers. I would suggest bundling up the old clothes including boots and shoes ready for the ragman. He hasn't been round for a while so we must be due a visit. And if you cannot think of anything better I do know someone who would be glad of the coat and suits. The woman I have in mind does a lot of work for the poor and does it in a quiet way. Dundrinnen has its share of the needy but most are too proud to seek help.'

'By all means let her have them, Cissie,' Annie said then touched the other woman's shoulder. 'Come and have a look if you will.' Annie led the way into the sitting-room where the low round table had Marian's jewellery spread over it. 'Hamish wanted you to have something.'

'No, Annie,' Cissie said sounding flustered, 'truly I have a drawer full of jewellery. John knows or should know that I haven't much interest in brooches and the like yet each birthday and Christmas another piece appears.'

'You don't have to wear it but you must take something.' She paused. 'These are Hamish's instructions I am carrying out. Jessie, the woman who looked after him before—'

'Before you came on the scene.'

'Yes. She is to be remembered and since you knew her you'll know what she would like.'

Cissie pressed her lips together and took a careful look at the selection. 'I seem to recall she liked blues and purples so perhaps the amethyst brooch,' she said picking it up and holding it to the light where it sparkled. 'Yes, Annie, I'm sure she would love this.'

'Good, I'm glad that's settled, I have her address so I can get that away. Now your own choice and take your time.'

'This is embarrassing, I feel I have no right.'

'Every right. Hamish made his wishes very clear.'

'Very well but I don't want to choose something you may want for yourself.'

'Don't argue, Mrs Powrie. If not for yourself choose something for your daughter-in-law.'

'Sarah got a loan of my amber beads, it must be months ago, and hasn't returned them. Perhaps she thought I meant her to keep them but I didn't. If you don't mind I'll take the amber beads.'

Annie smiled and took the beads from her. She had the boxes put aside. The brooch for Jessie went into a velvet case lined with silk and the amber beads into a shabby, very worn, black box which made Annie think the beads must have been left to Marian by her mother or a relative. Cissie had the same thought when she saw the box.

'You know, Annie, I have a horrible feeling that this might be an heirloom.'

'Whether it is or not you were a good friend to Marian and I'm sure she would be pleased to know you had it.'

'You are a very persuasive young woman. Thank you, I'll treasure these and take great care of them.' They went back to the living-room where Tina was just where they had left her. 'What a good wee soul she is.'

'Not always,' Annie smiled as she looked at the rapt little face. The doll's house fascinated her and she could amuse herself for long spells. She loved to take out the furniture and rearrange it. Annie could trust her, the child had never been destructive and it was a joy to see how careful she was with the tiny pieces of furniture.

Cissie got down on the floor to watch Tina at play.

'Annie, can you imagine the patience and skill that went into making these, each one quite perfect. Poor Hannah, it was to be hers you know but sadly she was never allowed to play with it. Their little daughter was born damaged and she was terribly destructive. If she'd got her hands on this' – she pointed to the house – 'it wouldn't have lasted five minutes. For such a young child she was very strong.'

'I know, Hamish told me about his children. It was so sad, so terribly sad.'

Cissie got up from the floor but not without a struggle. 'Old age doesn't come itself, as I am discovering.'

With Mrs Powrie gone, Annie began clearing away the

rest of the jewellery. She fingered the silver locket and chain, it was very dainty and Tina would have it when she was older. The single string of pearls with the diamond clasp she would have for herself. Life was strange. A few short years ago she had owned nothing of value and here she was with Marian's cherished possessions and the jewellery Miss Emily had left.

How quickly the days were passing and not one went by when she didn't think of Hamish. She owed him so much. Every Sunday afternoon, unless the weather was particularly bad, she and Tina, hand-in-hand would visit the grave. The granite headstone was already there. Three names were on it, Hamish's wife Marian and their two children Matthew and Hannah. Annie had contacted the stone-mason to have Hamish's name added.

'Mummy let me put the flowers in.'

'All right, dear, but first I'll have to fill this vase with water.' There was a tap near the gate of the cemetery and Annie put water in the container, carried it back and stuck it firmly in the black soil just below the headstone.

Tina, her little pink tongue protruding as she concentrated, carefully put in the flowers gathered that morning from the garden. Annie rearranged them until she was satisfied.

'Is Grandad in heaven?' the little voice piped.

'Yes, Tina, I told you that Grandad is safe in heaven.'

'But how can he be when he is here?'

Questions, always questions and some not easy to answer.

'Grandad's soul is in heaven and his body buried here.'

'What is a soul?'

'A spirit and don't ask me what a spirit is because it is too difficult for me to explain and for you to understand.'

Tina frowned. She didn't like to be told she wouldn't understand. But she knew from past experience she would get no more out of her mother.

As the child skipped along beside her, Hamish's words

kept coming back to Annie. He had been insistent that she should sell Hillside House and move on. In Dundrinnen the circumstances of Tina's birth were too well-known and, as he said, folk had long memories. There would be talk when the child was old enough to attend school. They would be unable to resist bringing up the past and children were quick to pick up what wasn't intended for their ears and make use of it. It was one of the mysteries of life, Annie thought, why some children should so delight in being cruel to their own age group. Some would say that they were too young to understand the harm they were doing but, of course, that was nonsense. They knew very well their words were wounding and could cause great distress.

It was now the month of June and on 5th October Tina would be four years of age with only another year to go before she started school. Annie was noticing, how could she not, that with each passing day the child was growing more like Miss Emily. She had the same golden fair hair that curled naturally. Those curls were the envy of mothers whose little daughters had straight hair that absolutely refused to curl no matter what was tried. Tina's eyes were different, they were a vivid blue whereas Miss Emily's had been a clear grey.

Dundrinnen held memories for Annie that were both good and bad. There had been sadness and despair as well as unexpected happiness. She had lost Miss Emily and then she had lost Hamish. But she had been left with a precious gift. Honesty forced her to correct that statement. She had not been given Tina, she had taken the infant and perhaps that was a punishable offence. True Miss Emily hadn't wanted her baby adopted but neither would she have wanted the child brought up by her maid. Given the choice in the tragic circumstances, it was more than likely Miss Emily would have preferred that Tina be adopted. It was too late and she couldn't change anything, even if she wanted to which she didn't.

The past kept intruding on the present and Annie was

deep in thought as she and Tina sat on the grass at the side of the burn. Annie wore a short-sleeved summer dress in green and white and her arms, where the sun had caught them, were turning a pale brown. Picking up a smooth pebble she tossed it into the water and watched the ripples until they grew less and less and finally disappeared. Tina glanced up briefly then turned her attention back to the doll that was getting a severe scolding for not doing what it was told.

It was a perfect June day when it felt good just to be alive. The summer breeze whispered among the trees and shading her eyes, Annie could see the moors yellow with broom and in between a powdering of purple from the heather not yet in full bloom. The Grampians were a hazy outline in the far distance. Annie had come to love this part of the country and it was going to be a wrench to leave Dundrinnen. Hamish had made no secret of his feelings. There had never been any desire on his part to see the world. All he had ever wanted was here. To see the sun set over the Mearns is to see a little bit of heaven, he had told Annie and she believed him.

Where did the time go? She appeared to be drifting from one day to the next but it couldn't go on. The house had to be sold and she had no idea how long that would take. And before vacating Hillside House she had to find somewhere else to live. The real problem was that she hadn't the faintest idea how to go about it. What she would have done without Mr and Mrs Powrie, Annie didn't know. She supposed she would have muddled through somehow and in the process she could have made expensive mistakes. Solicitors gave advice and willingly, but at a price.

The contents of the house would have to go. Hamish had strongly advised selling off completely and making a fresh start somewhere else. But where, that was the question that concerned her most. Where should she go? Had Miss Emily lived, she was to have bought a house in or near to Aberdeen. Thinking about that now, Annie realised how difficult that decision had been. Miss Emily had loved her native Perthshire in much the same way as Hamish had loved the Mearns. Maybe she should return to Perthshire, it was after all where she had lived before coming here. There was no need to worry about being recognised. After nearly five years no one would remember Annie Fullerton, the quiet, insignificant maid who had worked at Denbrae House, left it and never returned. Even if someone did recognise her it wouldn't matter. She was no longer Annie Fullerton, she was Mrs Brown, a widow with a small daughter. No one would suspect the truth, how could they? She and Tina would be quite safe. She wouldn't, however, make the mistake of living in Greenhill, better to put a safe distance between them and Denbrae House. There were pretty little villages not so many miles away.

Annie had another reason for not living too far from Denbrae House. One day Tina would have to learn the truth about her birth and who she really was. Annie would hold nothing back. Painful and difficult though it would be she wouldn't shirk what she considered to be her duty. Only by telling the truth in its entirety and that meant her own part in it, would she avoid misunderstandings.

How Tina would react was anyone's guess. She might not be too bothered but that was wishful thinking. More than likely she would be shocked and angry and might feel a sense of outrage that she had been brought up by her mother's maid when she might have had a good home with adoptive parents who would have been willing and able to give her all she wanted. Annie shivered at what might come next. What if she decided to contact her grandparents and their former maid's part in this was uncovered? Annie tried not to think about it.

'Get rid of the clutter, Annie, be ruthless. All the stuff you put aside because you couldn't bear to throw it away, has to go. Make up your mind and let it go.' She laughed. 'Listen to me, the world's greatest hoarder.'

'It's the thought of throwing away something that might come in useful but I'm going to take your advice and be hard on myself.'

'If I were in your place, Annie, I'd sort out the linen, cutlery, ornaments not forgetting the china and get them packed ready for your new home or to be put in store until such time as you need them. May I make another suggestion?'

'Please do, I need all the advice I can get.'

'Leave some of the furniture in the house until it is sold. A furnished or partly furnished house is easier to sell. And you never know, the purchaser may be interested in buying some of the furniture.'

'Is that likely?'

'It's a possibility. They may consider what is there suits the room and if they get what they consider a bargain—'

'I wouldn't ask too much,' Annie said hastily.

'I know that, but don't be silly and give it away for next to nothing.' She paused. 'We'll miss you and Tina when you go and, speaking of that, have you given any more thought to where you might decide to live?'

'Perthshire. It's where I come from after all.'

'Sounds sensible.'

'Does it? How do I go about finding a house there?'

'Not easy. In your place I would give myself a holiday. Apart from the change of air doing you both good it would give you a chance to look around and see what is available.'

'Have a holiday in Perthshire? Mrs Powrie, what a splendid idea and something that just hadn't occurred to me. You see how much I need you?'

'And you, Annie, need a rest, a complete rest.'

'A holiday with a purpose, I wouldn't feel so guilty about taking one in that case.'

Cissie Powrie almost spluttered. 'Annie, for heaven's sake, spoil yourself for a week or two. Have you ever had a holiday?'

'Never.' She bit her lip as she did some thinking. 'I can't

offer for a house until I know what Hillside House will fetch. Listen to me, I sound knowledgeable and the truth is I don't know the first thing about buying or selling. Maybe, of course, I could get a three-roomed house to rent and that would solve a lot of problems.'

'It isn't my business to say this but you won't be counting the pennies, not for a while anyway. Hillside is a desirable property and I imagine there will be a few after it.'

'I'm very fortunate I know that and once Tina is at school I'll find myself a job, one that works in with the school day.'

'What kind of job?'

'Anything, I'm not fussy though—' she stopped.

'Though what?'

'Hamish said I wasn't to be anyone's servant.'

'Quite right too, you've done your share of that.'

'Housework is all I know but I suppose I could serve behind the counter. Shop work shouldn't be beyond me.'

'Nothing is beyond you if you ask me,' Cissie laughed as she prepared to go.

On her own, Annie sat down to do some serious thinking. She felt excited at the thought of going on holiday with Tina. It wasn't an extravagance and she could afford it. Much as she had grown to love this part of Scotland, going back to Perthshire would be like returning home. She had read in one of her books that Sir Walter Scott had described the city of Perth as the most beautiful in Scotland and he would have known what he was talking about. She would be able to show Tina the 'fair city'. The child was growing at an alarming rate and Annie imagined she would be a lot taller than Miss Emily. Perhaps her father had been very tall. Annie gave a passing thought to him and tried to recall the little Miss Emily had told her. Not much, no name, just that he had been an artist, a very talented painter, who had made no secret of the fact that everything, no matter what, would take second place to his painting. Where was he and what would he think if he were to know that he was the father of a very beautiful child?

The dresses that had once belonged to Miss Emily were still carefully wrapped in tissue paper but the time was just ahead when she must find a good dressmaker who would use the material to make dresses for Tina.

They were on their way and Annie was almost as excited as Tina. She was remembering that first train journey with Miss Emily, the fear of losing sight of her mistress in the station then the wonder of the passing scenery from the carriage window. Miss Emily had been amused at the maid's excitement and Annie's inability to contain it. Those days were gone and now she could control her feelings. Tina was on her knees the better to see out of the window and Annie was holding her feet lest they come in contact with the seat. The child's voice was shrill as she exclaimed at the passing scenery to the delight of those sharing the compartment. Annie thought she ought to apologise but there was a general shaking of heads.

'Not at all,' the sweet-faced old lady said as she put the book she had intended reading back into her raffia bag and her spectacles into her handbag. 'We no longer look at the scenery, which is a great pity, and it takes a child to remind us of what we are missing.' Those others who usually maintained an aloof silence and avoided eye contact began to talk. A stout woman who had been sucking a sweet surprised herself and her companion by handing round the bag of assorted boilings.

'I always take them on a journey, saves getting thirsty,' she said offering them to a well-dressed gentleman in a dark business suit and spats.

'Kind of you, but I won't.'

'Please do.'

'All right then, I will and thank you.' He chose a striped ball and popped it into his mouth.

Tina took her time about choosing. 'I like them all, I don't know which one to take.'

'Take two, dear, that'll make the choice easier.'

'You shouldn't encourage her,' Annie protested.

'Didn't we as children all go through that stage?'

There was murmured assent and Annie felt a sadness that she couldn't join in and agree. She supposed it would always be like that. The early years were so important to those who had enjoyed them and such a source of pain to those who hadn't.

Tina was nodding, sleep was catching up with her and, losing interest with the scenery, she laid her head on Annie's shoulder and was soon asleep.

'All that excitement has been too much,' the old lady whispered.

'She was up very early.' Annie let her sleep for as long as possible and only when they were approaching Perth station did she give her a gentle shake to waken her.

'Come on, darling, we are just coming into the station.'

Tina made no protest as the train came to a shuddering stop and suddenly she was wide awake. The compartment emptied at Perth. The gentleman took charge of Annie's suitcase until they were on the platform, then he said goodbye. The others did the same then hurried away. Annie kept a firm grip of Tina's hand, the bustle of a busy station, she found, could still alarm her.

'Mummy, you're holding my hand too tight and hurting it.'

'Sorry, dear,' she said easing her grip, 'I don't want to lose you in the crowd.' At last they were out of the station and into the open. The fresh, cool air was very welcome.

'I'm hungry, Mummy.'

'So am I.' A little ahead Annie saw a sign for a tearoom and when they came to it she liked the look of it. They would go in. A smiling waitress took charge of the suitcase and showed them to a table with a clean white tablecloth. Cooked meals were not available she was told, only sandwiches, scones and cakes. Annie ordered egg and cress sandwiches which had to be made and were brought to the table in a few minutes. There was a three-tiered cake-stand on the table, the top plate held plain and fruit scones, the middle one pieces of jam sponge and below was a selection of small cakes. Tina had her eye on the one with cream but was told she had to finish her sandwich first.

Tina's red velvet coat was over the spare chair at their table. Annie had kept hers on but had it unbuttoned. The coat was a lightweight tweed in a heather mixture. It had turned out to be a good buy although at the time Annie had thought it an unnecessary extravagance. In the end she had allowed Mrs Powrie to persuade her. Always buy something good, Annie, she'd said and make sure you like what you are buying. A cheap coat is false economy since it quickly becomes shabby and you've had no pleasure from wearing it. That had been a lovely day, Annie recalled and so unexpected. The previous evening Cissie Powrie had dashed across to Hillside House to say that John had business in Stonehaven, she was going for the run and how about them coming too? Annie had been more than delighted to accept. It would be a treat for Tina and for her to travel in Mr Powrie's motorcar.

In the shop Annie was dithering.

'Perfect on you, Annie, go on spoil yourself you deserve it.'

'I could get two coats for the price of this one.'

'That I don't doubt for a moment.'

'Then you agree it is an extravagance?'

'I do not and I did not say that. A good quality tweed coat is an investment. Believe me it will look good for years and years and, another point in its favour, that style of coat never goes out of fashion.'

'It's just I feel guilty spending so much on myself.'

During this discourse the assistant had been patiently waiting for the lady to make up her mind or rather have the older one do it for her. Tina had wandered off with a warning not to touch anything.

'Annie, I can only advise, the decision has to be yours. Make it the right one.'

She took another look at herself in the mirror. It did

something for her, no doubt about that. Yes, she would have it.

Fearful that madam might have second thoughts the assistant hurried away with the coat over her arm.

Next stop was a shop specialising in children's wear. Tina, unlike most little girls of her age, was not very interested in new clothes and it was only when she tried on the red velvet with the black trimming round the collar and cuffs that she brightened.

'This one, Mummy.'

'There's another one to try on yet.'

'I don't want to, I like this one the bestest,' she said stubbornly.

'She's lovely in it, Annie.'

'Auntie Cissie likes it,' Tina said hopefully.

'I like it too, but there is hardly any hem to let down and you'll outgrow it in no time,' Annie protested and looking at Mrs Powrie.

'You can't let velvet down, it always shows and I've never believed in buying clothes too big. They don't look right to begin with and by the time they do fit the newness has gone.'

'It will have to be the red velvet then,' Annie said resignedly, 'but Tina—'

'What, Mummy?'

'You will have to be very careful not to get a mark on it.'

Cissie Powrie hadn't finished. 'She'll need the matching beret to complete the outfit.'

Annie nodded; she had no fight left in her. Shopping with Mrs Powrie was an expensive business and just as well it didn't happen too often. The woman had never had to count the pennies or make any economies. Her folk had been comfortably off and she and John had not long been married when John inherited the farm.

Annie's thoughts had been pleasantly drifting as they enjoyed the meal in the tearoom. A light meal which would do them until they were settled in a boarding house. Before leaving, Annie asked the waitress where they could get a bus to Woodside.

'Just out the door and to your left, that's the stop and you should get one in about five minutes if it is running to time.'

The bus was a few minutes late and by the time it arrived there were six people waiting.

'What did you say the place was called, Mummy?'

'Woodside.'

'Is it far?'

'No, not very far.'

'What are we going to do when we get there?'

'Look for a place to stay.'

'What if there isn't a place?' Tina said looking worried and on the verge of tears.

'Of course there will be a place, a very nice place.' What if she was wrong? Maybe it wouldn't be as easy as she had thought. She should have fixed up accommodation before she left, but the truth was she hadn't known how to go about it and she hadn't wanted to ask Mrs Powrie. The woman would think she was a dimwit and she wouldn't have been far wrong. Too late to make a better of it now, and surely at this time of the year it shouldn't be too difficult.

They got off the bus in the square and after glancing around Annie decided to try the newsagent, they might know about accommodation for visitors. As luck would have it the shop was empty and the woman behind the counter was taking the chance to read the newspaper. Only when Annie reached the counter did she look up.

'Yes?'

'Perhaps you could help me?' Annie smiled. 'I'm looking for somewhere to stay.'

She looked at the suitcase. 'Holiday accommodation?'

'Yes.'

'Always better to have that arranged before you come.'

'I know but I haven't.'

'Private house or boarding house?'

Annie thought quickly. A boarding house would be more impersonal and she didn't want anyone taking an interest in them.

'I would prefer a boarding house.' She looked at Tina who was looking tired and sucking her thumb. 'One not too far away.'

'The Beeches is the nearest. It calls itself a guest house not a boarding house and bairns might not be welcome.'

'If you could give me directions I could try.'

The woman came quite willingly from behind the counter and once outside she pointed to the road leading from the square. 'Halfway up that road you'll come to Elm Street. I'll tell you now that all the streets around here have names of trees. Go along Elm Street and first left is Sycamore Street and that's where you'll find the Beeches. Can't miss it, there's a big sign in the garden.'

'Thank you very much.'

'You're welcome. If the Beeches is full or they won't take you they'll suggest somewhere else for you to try.'

Annie's heart sank as she picked up her case, it didn't sound too hopeful.

'Be good, darling, it won't be long now.'

They found Sycamore Street very easily. There were a number of big houses with the Beeches the biggest. It was a three-storeyed building with an attractive frontage and from what Annie could see there was an extension built out the back. She pushed open the gate and once Tina was inside she made sure it was properly closed. Three wide marble steps led up to the oak door which was open and showed a vestibule made bright with colourful plants. There was a tug-bell and she pulled it.

'Mummy, it's ringing.'

'Yes.'

'Someone's coming.'

The someone was a tall, stately-looking woman in a calf-length black skirt and attractive floral blouse. Her hair was grey, very thick and worn short. She had a pleasant smile which embraced the child.

'I'm looking for accommodation and the lady in the newsagent's suggested I try the Beeches.'

She appeared to hesitate. 'For you and the child?'

'Yes.'

'I don't normally take children. Not that I have anything against them,' she said hastily, 'it is only that my elderly guests have to be considered.'

'Tina is well behaved and she isn't noisy.'

'Come in anyway. Yes, that will do, leave your case beside the umbrella stand.'

Annie did, noticing a selection of walking sticks and two umbrellas that had seen better days.

'Come in here, it is unoccupied at present.' She led the way.

Annie found herself in a large high-ceilinged room which looked as though it had once been very much larger and had been divided. It couldn't have been easy to do, rooms seldom were but this had been well done, Annie thought. Sympathetically was the word that sprang to her mind.

'How long would you be staying?' the woman asked once they were seated.

'A week.' Annie had hoped to stay for ten days but if she said so it might spoil their chances.

'I should manage that. I have two elderly resident guests who regard the Beeches as their home. Mostly I take businessmen who come for two or three nights every month and I always try to oblige them. You would require a room with two single beds?'

'Yes, though a double bed if that is what you have available would do very nicely.'

Tina had been silent all this time but she was listening. 'Mummy, I want to sleep with you.'

The woman laughed. 'The matter appears to have been decided for you.'

Annie laughed too, relieved that they were to be accommodated at the Beeches and not have to look further. 'The room with the double bed, yes, please.'

The woman stated her terms and Annie nodded. It was more than she had expected to pay but not by so very much.

'Let me introduce myself, I am Miss Galbraith.'

'And I am Mrs Brown and this is my daughter Tina.'

'There is a nice little park close by, Tina, where you can play.'

'We might go there tomorrow,' Annie said just as they heard the bell.

'Excuse me I shan't be long.' She left them.

'Mummy, this is nice, isn't it?' Tina whispered.

'Very nice.' She took the time they were alone to study the room. She liked the frescoed ceiling and the walls papered in a heavy embossed paper in cream with a gold leaf pattern. There were two sofas. They were sitting on one, Tina well back with her legs sticking straight out. Several comfortable armchairs were placed about the room and there were two low tables. The fireplace had a high mantelshelf and in the centre of it was a handsome marble clock. The curtains at both windows were floor-length and made of a heavy brocade in shades of soft greens and browns. The dull red carpet had touches of pale pink and the tapestry cushions and silk-shaded lamps gave the room a rich, old-fashioned look.

Miss Galbraith was back. 'Let me show you the bedroom.'

They followed her up. Looking very solemn Tina held on to the handrail and went up slowly step by step. Miss Galbraith opened one of the doors on the first landing. 'Will this be suitable?'

'Yes, thank you, this will suit us very nicely.' The window was open at the bottom and the breeze was moving the curtains.

'Perhaps you would like the window shut?'

'Oh, no, please leave it. I like the fresh air coming in.'

'That makes a change from our Miss Middleton. She's

old, of course, and old people do feel the cold even in the summer. I must confess to opening the window of her bedroom when she is out and hurrying to close it when I hear her coming in.' Coming out of the bedroom the woman pointed along the passage. 'That is the bathroom and there is a separate toilet. As for baths let me say this before I forget. I do need to be told beforehand.'

'I understand.'

'Good, you'll know then what a drain they are on the hot water. As long as I am told beforehand there is no problem.' They went downstairs. 'How does the child amuse herself?'

'Drawing,' Annie smiled. 'A box of crayons and sheets of paper and Tina will be perfectly happy. I have both with me I may add.'

'A quiet pastime.' She sounded relieved. 'Would you like a cup of tea?'

'That would be very welcome.'

'A cup of milk for the child?'

'Yes, please.'

Once they were served with tea and milk Miss Galbraith left them and went out, leaving the door slightly ajar. They heard the front door then voices.

'Is that you, Miss Middleton?'

'Yes, I'm back and feeling decidedly chilled. I met a friend and talked or rather she did. I hardly got a word in edgeways and I had to be almost rude to make my escape.'

Annie didn't have to strain to hear.

'A cup of tea will heat you up.'

'Only if you are making one anyway.'

'Just made. A young woman, a Mrs Brown and her little daughter have just arrived.'

'To stay?'

'Yes, for a week.'

'Not a noisy child, I hope?' The voice was anxious.

'No, I don't see her being any trouble at all. In fact a very well behaved child I would say.' It must suddenly have dawned on Miss Galbraith that their conversation could be overheard in the lounge. There was the sound of a door being shut. In a little while Miss Galbraith returned.

'You might have heard someone coming in, that was Miss Middleton. Our other permanent boarder is a gentleman by the name of Mr Cuthbert. You'll be together for the evening meal.'

Annie smiled, not knowing if she was required to say anything and in any case what was there to say.

'Miss Middleton sold her house, she was unable to manage on her own and rather than employ a housekeeper she came to us. At that time my sister was here and we ran the guest house between us. Sadly my sister died.'

'I'm sorry, you must miss her?'

'More than I can say but life must go on and I manage. If you are wondering why Miss Middleton isn't joining us it is just that she enjoys the warmth of the kitchen and,' she smiled, 'since this is her home I let her have as much freedom as possible. You'll find this out for yourself but one of the main attractions of the Beeches is the food. Mrs Archibald is a wonderful cook and I am just so very fortunate to have her.'

Tina yawned.

'Poor wee soul, this must be very dull for you, my dear.'

'If she gets a little sleep she'll be all right so if you will excuse us we'll go upstairs. I'll get my case—'

'Your case is already in your bedroom. Dinner is at six thirty.'

'Thank you.'

Chapter Seventeen

Annie didn't know if she should wait for the dinner gong or indeed if there was one. Better to wait in the bedroom until a minute or two before six thirty. They had just reached the hall and Annie saw that there was a dinner gong. A maid came out from the kitchen quarters and proceeded to give two ear-splitting raps that echoed then slowly died away. Tina had been hopping from one foot to the other but stopped to watch the girl disappear back into the kitchen.

'Mummy, why did she make that big noise?'

'That's the gong to tell everyone that dinner is ready.'

'Will I get to do it?' Tina asked hopefully.

'No, and don't ask. It will be the maid's duty to do that.'

Two people were coming slowly down the stairs. One was an elderly man and the other a woman who looked even older. When they reached the bottom step they smiled to the young woman and child waiting beside the door of the dining-room which was closed.

'Allow me,' the gentleman said opening the door and standing back to let the two ladies and the child enter. Tina was looking neat and pretty in a pleated navy skirt and a pale blue blouse with an embroidered Peter Pan collar. Annie was to have worn a dress but changed that to a fine woollen skirt in a small brown and cream check. With it she wore a long-sleeved cream silk blouse that had belonged to Miss Emily and which Annie still considered her best.

Miss Galbraith arrived and wished everyone good evening. She had on a black dress with a cherry-red bolero. After the introductions Miss Middleton sat down at her table and Mr Cuthbert went to his.

'Mrs Brown, if you and the child would like to sit here.' She indicated a table beside the window. Then she moved quickly to pick up a cushion and place it on the chair Tina was to occupy.

'That will be easier for the little lady.'

Annie smiled her thanks and tried to ignore Tina's scowls. Tina was offended. She wasn't a baby, she was a big girl and big girls didn't need a cushion to make them bigger. She didn't want the cushion.

Annie was relieved they had separate tables rather than being all round one big one. She saw that there were eight tables in the dining-room and each could seat four people. Annie thought it might be a full house at the height of the summer but not at any other time.

While waiting for the first course to be served Annie's eyes went to the old lady sitting bolt upright. Her face was a criss-cross of lines, her hair snowy white and her mouth a little drawn in but even so a faded prettiness remained. It was her clothes that immediately caught the eye and Annie thought with amusement that here was a woman who wore exactly what she pleased. Her long full skirt was bright orange with splashes of blue made all the more striking by the simplicity of the blouse which couldn't have been plainer. Coming down the stairs she had a Shetland shawl draped round her shoulders and that now lay over the back of her chair. Annie admired her with the admiration of someone who knew that never in a hundred years could she have appeared in those colours.

Tina's little bottom was moving the cushion and Annie looked at her warningly.

'Stop fidgeting, Tina,' Annie said softly but severely.

'It's the cushion, it's going to fall off.'

'It won't unless you make it and if you do I'll send you straight up to bed.'

Tina knew as well as Annie that the threat wouldn't be carried out but she didn't like her mummy to be cross.

'I won't do it any more,' she said giving Annie one of her sunniest smiles.

Annie's severe expression vanished. The little monkey made good use of that smile, she thought. It had been the same with Miss Emily, she had used her beguiling smile to get what she wanted.

'Put your napkin over your knees, dear.'

'No, lass, tuck it under your chin like me and you won't dirty your bonny dress.'

They both turned to where the voice came from. 'It isn't a dress it's a skirt and blouse,' Tina corrected him.

'Whatever it is.' He was high-coloured with a circle of grey hair showing lots of shiny pink scalp. The man was smiling broadly and Tina was wondering what to do. It couldn't be babyish if that man did it but the lady at the other table was shaking her head.

'Mr Cuthbert,' the woman spoke in a cultivated voice rather like the headmistress of a good school, 'just because you cannot be trusted to take your soup without spilling it doesn't follow that the child will do likewise. I'm sure she will manage perfectly well with the napkin on her lap.'

Annie wanted to keep the peace. 'Maybe not,' she said quickly, 'she is a little tired and this would make sure.' She got up to tuck the napkin into the collar of Tina's blouse. The maid arrived with the soup, four plates on the tray. Three were filled almost to the brim and the other, Tina's, was only half-filled.

'Too much for me, dear,' the old lady said. 'I do wish you would just give me a child's portion. I have mentioned it before.'

'Sorry, Miss Middleton, I'll tell cook.'

'You do that. Waste is sinful, I was brought up to believe that.'

Mr Cuthbert was making faces and shaking his head as though to let Annie know that this is what they had to put up with. Annie refused to be drawn into any more than a half smile. Her sympathies were entirely with Miss Middleton. If she had requested less, then that was what she should have been given.

The child had been taught table manners but Tina had little experience of eating out. Occasionally they were invited for a meal with the Powries but that was very relaxed and not very different from eating at home. The boys, Henry and Malcolm, spent a lot of time with their grandparents including having some of their meals. The painful shyness that had at one time afflicted them had gone and poor Tina came in for a lot of tormenting.

If Annie was to correct the child Mrs Powrie nearly always took Tina's side.

'Annie, she is doing very well and it is a mistake to expect too much of children when they are small.'

'You didn't say that to us when we were wee,' the boys grumbled, 'we were forever being told off.'

'No wonder, you were a couple of mucky pups,' their grandfather said with a wink for Tina.

There was no choice of menu at the Beeches which was only to be expected with so few guests but what was served would appeal to most. Miss Galbraith hadn't exaggerated when she said the Beeches had an excellent cook. The vegetable soup served with a warmed roll was very tasty and there was more for anyone who wanted it. No one did that night. When the businessmen were dining it was a different story and after a light lunch they were more than ready for a good meal in the evening. No one refused second helpings when they were offered. Lamb was the main dish and it was a favourite of Annie's. Cooked to perfection and served with a selection of vegetables and small even-sized potatoes everyone did justice to it. The pudding was a syrup sponge which was as light as a feather and the pouring custard smooth and creamy. It was no surprise that Miss

Galbraith had her regulars. And, thought Annie, it just showed that even the simplest meal properly cooked was hard to beat. Remembering how pleased the cook at Denbrae House had been when guests took the trouble to compliment her on the meal or on a particular dish, Annie thought she would show her appreciation.

'Miss Galbraith, that was a lovely meal, I really enjoyed it and so did Tina. You do have an excellent cook.'

'Thank you, Mrs Brown, I'll pass on the word to Mrs Archibald and like all cooks she likes to feel appreciated.' She bent down to Tina. 'I'm glad you enjoyed your meal, dear.'

'I liked the pudding best.'

'As good as your mother makes?' She raised her eyebrows and smiled to Annie.

'Better than Mummy makes but only a teeny weeny bit better.'

'Kind of you, darling,' Annie laughed, 'but I'm afraid I'm not in the same league.'

'This lucky young lady won't have to bother with curling tongs. How lovely to have naturally curly hair and if you will pardon me saying so, Mrs Brown, she hasn't you to thank for that.'

'No. My side of the family are all plain Janes.' Annie said it lightly and was amazed at how easily the words slipped out.

'Then it must be your husband or his side of the family.'

'My husband is dead, Miss Galbraith,' Annie said quietly and in a voice that clearly said she didn't want to talk about it.

Miss Galbraith was taken aback. 'I am so very sorry, that was clumsy of me and I do apologise.'

'It's all right, you couldn't possibly have known.'

'How sad it is when the young are taken.'

Tina yawned and her face had gone pale, the way it did when she was ready for bed. 'It's been a long day for her and I think we'll go up now.' Tina began climbing the stairs.

'Come down when she is asleep, Mrs Brown,' the woman said softly. 'I serve tea at half past nine and don't worry

246

about not hearing her if she wakens. Leave the bedroom door open.'

'Thank you, I'll do that another evening but I am quite tired myself and I think I'll have an early night.'

'Just as you please.' She smiled. 'I hope you'll be comfortable.'

'I'm sure I shall. Good night, Miss Galbraith.'

'Good night Mrs Brown.'

Tina was in her nightdress and had said her prayers.

'Into bed with you and snuggle down.'

'I'm not tired any more.'

'Yes, you are.'

'You won't go and leave me? That lady said to come downstairs.'

Annie marvelled at the acute hearing of small children. 'I'm not, I'm going to bed shortly.'

'Mummy?'

'Yes, dear?'

'Why don't I have a proper daddy?'

'You had a daddy but—'

'He's dead, but that's Grandad not my daddy,' she said sounding puzzled.

And no wonder, Annie thought. 'Your grandad died—'

'I know that, but was he my daddy as well?'

It was her own fault that she'd got herself tied in knots but it was so difficult to know what was best to say. 'Tina, do you remember your grandad?' she said gently.

She nodded. 'He had whiskers,' she giggled, 'they tickled and he made my doll's house.' Then she frowned. 'But you haven't told me if he was my daddy as well.'

'No, he wasn't your daddy.'

'Did Daddy die when I was a baby, is that why I don't remember him?'

Annie wanted to weep. 'Yes, darling, that's the reason. And now no more talking, close your eyes and go to sleep.'

Her eyes closed then opened. 'Will I go to heaven when I die?'

'Yes.'

'And you as well, Mummy?'

'I hope so.'

Tina gave a little smile, then she was asleep.

Annie waited until her breathing was regular then she unpacked the case. She hung up what would go on coat-hangers and the rest went into the drawers. That hadn't taken long and it was still ridiculously early to go to bed but she would, if not to sleep then to think.

How lucky for her that Miss Galbraith was so approach-able. She might well know about the housing position and be able to advise her as to how to go about finding a house. Three rooms would be ideal and if renting was impossible she would be in a position to buy once Hillside House was sold.

Staring up at the ceiling Annie wondered what the future would hold for them. She was no longer haunted by the fear of not having a roof over their head. Hamish had seen to that. Whatever was ahead she would never take anything for granted and they would live not frugally but carefully with something aside for a rainy day. Her orphanage years had been an early training ground and her memories of that time could never be completely blotted out. Perhaps it was better that she shouldn't forget the hard times and just be thankful they were behind her. No one could choose what they wanted to remember or what they would like to forget. Life wasn't that obliging.

A small house of their own would be bliss and hopefully it wouldn't be too far from a school. Starting school was a milestone in any child's life and Annie wanted Tina to be happy and make friends. Once she was settled then it would be time to look for a job and not only for the money but because Annie needed to be busy. She wasn't the sort of person to enjoy being idle. Housework was all she was trained to do but she was loath to go against Hamish's wishes.

When the idea came to her Annie wondered why she

hadn't thought of it before. It was perfect. She would buy a bigger house and take in lodgers. The more she thought about it the more excited she became. Sleep had completely gone and she was as fresh and wide awake as though it was morning. With the idea taking root, Annie was trying to get a complete picture in her mind of how it would be. There was bound to be a down side, there always was and it was better to face problems at the beginning. How, for instance, was she going to attract custom? And how did a newcomer do that? Did Woodside already have a sufficiency of boarding houses and bed and breakfast places? The answer could well be yes but not necessarily good accommodation. Breaking in would not be easy and folk tended to return to the same place. She wasn't, however, confined to Woodside, she could go further afield. Annie knew she would be happier in a village or small town, the thought of a large city scared her though no doubt in time she would get used to town life. Perth was busy and popular without being bustling and there would always be those looking for accommodation.

Sleep eventually claimed her and when she awoke she felt a surge of excitement and a great urge to be up and doing. Parting the curtains she checked on the weather and was relieved to see a clear blue sky with no trace of rain clouds. Lovely! They would have an hour in the park to let Tina run about and then see about the housing situation. There wouldn't be the same demand for the larger house.

'Keep still, dear, and let me button your coat.'

'Where are we going?'

'To the park. Miss Galbraith said it wasn't far, no more than five minutes' walk. In the event it took them double that with Tina's little legs and her frequent stops to look at something that had taken her attention. As they neared they could hear the shrill voices of children. It was a delightful little park with flowered borders leading from the gate and a good expanse of grass for the little ones. A few seats were provided where the mothers could sit and watch their little ones at play. Over to the far side were four swings, three of them occupied and Tina broke into a run to claim the unoccupied one. Annie was greeted with smiles from the young women.

'This is hard work,' one of them grinned as she pushed the swing. 'You're new here aren't you?'

'We're here for a short holiday.'

'Lucky you.'

Annie lifted Tina on to the swing and began to push.

'Higher, Mummy.'

'That's high enough.'

'No, it isn't.'

'Never pleased are they? Where are you staying if you don't mind me asking?'

'The Beeches.'

'Nice?'

'Very comfortable.'

'Thought it would be a bit staid. I mean, not much freedom for children unless yours is a little angel.'

'She's far from being an angel,' Annie laughed, 'but she isn't a noisy child.'

'Your one and only?' She was small and round-faced with bushy auburn hair.

'Yes.'

'One is easy to control, just wait until you have three. Mine are noisy wee so-and-sos but for all that I don't suppose I would change them.'

'I'm sure you wouldn't.' Tina had tired of the swing and with a smile and a wave they left the friendly young woman and walked away.

'Mummy, are we going to the shops?'

'Yes.'

'I want colouring pencils.'

'That isn't the way to ask.'

'Please, Mummy, I want colouring pencils and more paper.'

'That's better,' Annie said severely. Perhaps she was too

strict at times, more strict than she would have been if Tina was hers, but this was Miss Emily's child. Her mistress would have insisted on good manners and good behaviour.

Tina was as good as gold and kept opening the brown bag to have a peep at the selection of pencils and the small box of crayons. They had done a lot of walking but were now on their way back to the Beeches. As soon as she recognised where she was Tina ran ahead, opened the gate, ran along the path and into the house. At the door she stopped abruptly. Miss Galbraith wasn't alone, there were two tall gentlemen at the reception desk.

'Come away, Tina, don't be shy. This is our youngest guest,' she said by way of explanation.

They smiled and said hello and Tina dropped her eyes to the floor. Annie had just come in.

'I do apologise, Miss Galbraith, I couldn't stop her running ahead.'

'Why shouldn't she come in by herself, this is where she is living?' She turned to the gentlemen. 'Your usual rooms Mr McCormack and Mr Baxter.'

They nodded to Annie, one smiled and the other winked to Tina then they went upstairs.

'Both regulars and very nice gentlemen, Mrs Brown. Did you have a pleasant day?'

'Very nice. Miss Galbraith—' She hesitated.

'Was there something you wanted?'

'I'm really wanting to ask your advice, but only when you have the time to spare.'

'Then now is as good a time as any. No one is in the lounge so we could go there.'

'Miss Galbraith, look.' Tina was holding out the brown paper bag.

'And what is in here?'

'Coloured pencils.'

'You like to colour in pictures?'

'Sometimes but I like to make my own pictures, don't I, Mummy?'

'Yes. Off you go and get your drawing book from the bedroom and, Tina, leave your coat over the chair.'

'She loves to draw.'

'What does she draw?' Miss Galbraith sounded amused.

'Anything and everything,' Annie laughed.

'A nice quiet occupation. And now what is this advice you seek?'

'I'm seriously considering coming to live in the district.'

'Buying a house here?'

'I'm thinking of taking in lodgers – just in a small way,' she added quickly.

'Mrs Brown, may I be completely frank?'

'That is what I was hoping you'd be.'

'It is not an easy life and apart from keeping house for your late husband, is that the sum total of your experience?'

'Before I was married I was a maid in a large house and I was given a very good training.'

'Did that include cooking?'

'No, but I would call myself a good plain cook.'

'Which is probably all that would be required.'

'I do have some money. Perhaps I should explain that my late husband was a lot older than me. He had a good joinery business which was sold and I have our house to put on the market.'

'Thank you for being so frank, it is always easier to advise if one knows the true position. I can give you the names of two factors.'

'Thank you, that would be helpful. I'm aware that I am taking a risk but I don't want to be foolhardy.'

'And I don't want to raise your hopes too high. The demand for accommodation hereabout is limited but you could be lucky and if you give your guests what they want, which is a comfortable bed, good food and punctuality . . . I can't emphasise that enough, the punctuality I mean.'

'I'm an early riser.'

'Yes, you would be with your training. A rushed breakfast if the lodger has slept in is his own fault. If, however, you were to be the one sleeping in then it would be a different story and you wouldn't last long.'

'I wouldn't deserve to,' Annie laughed.

'It happens, believe me it does.'

'To be honest this idea has just come to me. I want to work but I also want to be at home for Tina and this way I would be.'

'Mrs Brown, I think you would be ideal. Remind me to give you the names and addresses of the two factors. Go and see them and see what they have to offer.' She got up and Annie did too.

'You've been very kind, thank you.'

'Do let me know how you get on and, who knows, I may have more advice to give you.'

Both factors were helpful but neither had the kind of property to interest Annie. The houses were either too big or would require too much to be spent on them. There was one three-roomed house that she might well have considered before she thought of taking in lodgers.

With the evening meal over there was a move to the lounge and Miss Galbraith approached Annie.

'Mrs Brown, when Tina is asleep please come down to my own sitting-room, it is in the extension at the back. There is something I would like to discuss with you.'

'Thank you, I'll be with you just as soon as I get Tina over.'

Tina had been going to sleep almost as soon as her head touched the pillow, but not tonight. She demanded a story, she wasn't sleepy, she wanted a drink and she wanted a biscuit. She got the drink of water but not the biscuit. Annie kept some in a tin but giving her one would mean getting her up to clean her teeth and then a struggle to get her back to bed. Her patience was being sorely tried and she was almost giving up hope of getting downstairs when Tina at last obliged by falling asleep. She waited five minutes then tiptoed out of the bedroom leaving the door half open.

'I'm so sorry,' Annie apologised as Miss Galbraith invited her in, 'this was just one of those nights when little madam was determined to stay awake.'

'Never mind, here you are now. You left the door open?'

'Yes.'

'We'll leave this one slightly ajar and then you can relax.'

Annie looked about her. It was a pleasant medium-sized room and not overcrowded with furniture. There was no sofa just four comfortable armchairs and two embroidered footstools. A china cabinet held figurines, crystal glasses, a silver tea service and upright at the back a colourful plate on each glass shelf. There was a handsome writing bureau and shelves the length of one wall held books.

'My personal sanctum,' she smiled.

'I love it,' Annie said softly, 'it's restful if I could describe it that way.'

'Thank you, that was just the way my sister described it.'

'Were you responsible for it or your sister?'

'Ethel mostly. She had excellent taste and I'm afraid I'm an impulsive buyer who forgets to consider if what I choose would go with what is there already.'

'I could make that mistake too.'

'And you are wondering what all this is about?'

'I must confess to being curious.'

'Are you quite comfortable there, remove the cushion if you don't want it.'

'This is just fine.'

'Let me start by asking if you had any luck with what you were looking for?'

'No luck but I half expected that I would have to look further afield.'

'Before you do that I wonder if what I am about to suggest might interest you.' She paused and Annie looked at her enquiringly. 'Would you consider taking over the Beeches?'

Annie stared, 'The Beeches? Me?'

'Why not?'

'I could give you numerous reasons.'

'Let me hear a few.'

'For a start I don't have that kind of money.'

'Neither my sister nor I had that kind of money either. We had to borrow just as you would be able to.'

'How can you know that?'

'I don't, of course, but I imagine you could. If you were without a penny piece to your name the bank would not be prepared to finance you. But then you are not in that unfortunate position. According to what you told me you have a good house that should realise a reasonable sum or am I speaking out of turn?'

'No, you aren't. I do have a little money as well as what I get for the sale of the house. It is a good house,' Annie said proudly, 'my husband had it built to his specifications and he did the joinery work himself.'

'What else is holding you back?'

'I just couldn't do it.'

'You are afraid you would be taking on too much?'

'I know I would.'

'You wouldn't want the Beeches?'

'I would love the Beeches, that isn't the point at all.' She paused and looked straight at the woman. 'May I ask why you are thinking of giving it up?'

'I wondered when you were going to ask that. The answer is that my heart is no longer in it. When Ethel was here we were a good team, we worked well together. She had the business head and made the decisions and I was happy to go along with that. Doing it all on my own is a strain.'

'Would you consider—' Annie stopped. She hadn't meant to say that and looked confused and embarrassed.

'You were thinking in terms of a partnership perhaps?' Miss Galbraith shook her head. 'No, it would be a clean break.'

'Wouldn't you miss the life?'

'Very likely for a while I would, but not for too long. The

Beeches has had a large part of my life and I would like to see it going to someone . . .' It was her turn to hesitate and Annie spoke.

'Who would keep it going much as you have?'

'No, not at all. Everyone has their own ideas which is as it should be. What I think I meant was that I wanted the new owner to be someone who would care for the Beeches and not just for the return it would bring.'

'I can understand that,' Annie said softly.

'Yes, I think you do understand. The Beeches is ideally situated and there is room to expand.' She smiled. 'It does need someone young and enthusiastic.'

'You make it sound very easy.'

'Then I am wrong to do that. It is hard work and long hours but on the other hand you are your own boss.'

'If, and this is a very big if, I did consider taking over the Beeches what would be the position with staff?'

'Sadly I can give no guarantees, but I imagine that given the same conditions the present staff would be prepared to stay on.'

Annie nodded. 'Really I was thinking about the cook.'

'Mrs Archibald.'

'She wouldn't be easy to replace should she decide not to stay.'

'No, she wouldn't. I can't say for sure but I don't think she would want to leave the Beeches. She lives nearby and I've always found her a very contented person. My sister and I believed in giving a fair wage and a little extra if we felt it was earned.'

'That would be my way too.'

'Excuse me,' Miss Galbraith said getting up, 'I'll just ask Gladys to bring in a cup of tea, I'm sure we could both do with one.' She went out leaving Annie struggling to believe that this talk was really taking place.

'Tea shouldn't be long,' Miss Galbraith said, coming back and sitting down. 'I popped upstairs and looked in on Tina. The wee soul is sound to the world.'

'Thank you. Miss Galbraith, another question. This is your home, what would you do?'

'Return to Edinburgh where I was brought up. I do still have friends there. Mrs Brown, I'm not pushing you in any way but I see no harm in making a few practical suggestions.' The tea arrived and nothing more was said until Gladys made her departure. 'Obviously you would need some guidance and I would stay on for a few weeks or until you were confident. You and Tina would take over the living quarters' – she waved a hand around the room – 'and I would occupy one of the guest rooms. Some of the time I would have to be in Edinburgh to look for a house for myself.'

Annie sipped her tea and was thoughtful.

'If the idea of having your own guest house doesn't appeal to you then say so and that will be an end to it. I shall wait a few months yet before putting the Beeches on the market.'

'I do need time to consider,' Annie said desperately. This was a chance that would never be repeated but dare she accept such a challenge? It would take every penny she could raise and then the repayment of the loan if indeed she could get one. If she were to fail and lose it all, what then?

Miss Galbraith looked at her kindly. 'You are very young for responsibility but it is when you are young that you have the energy and the drive necessary to make a success of it.'

Annie nodded and bit her lip.

'Don't be giving too much attention to the financial side, that will be worked out for you. Rest assured, my dear, that if you are considered too big a risk then the loan will not be forthcoming.'

'I'm glad you told me that. To have confidence in myself I need others to have confidence in me.'

'Have you someone at home to discuss this with, someone you trust to give you good advice?'

'Yes, I do.' Annie was thinking of the Powries. They would tell her if she was just chasing dreams.

'Good! Write to me when you have made up your mind.'

'You won't put the Beeches on the market until you hear from me?'

'Provided you don't take too long about it.'

'I won't, but is this fair to you?'

'What do you mean?'

'Other interested parties may be prepared to offer more.'

'It is quite possible but provided I get a reasonable offer from you I won't look elsewhere.'

'That is very good of you.'

'I am not being entirely unselfish. This way I am saved the expense of advertising and the wearisome job of showing people around. If at the end of the day they were serious one wouldn't mind, but for so many it is just curiosity and it makes them feel important.'

'Are there many like that?'

'Too many.'

Chapter Eighteen

John and Cissie Powrie were very surprised and a bit alarmed too, but once they got over the initial shock they began to like the idea.

'I believe you could do it, Annie.' They were sitting in the farmhouse kitchen and Tina had pestered the boys into letting her go with them.

'Do you, Mrs Powrie?'

'Yes, you have a good head on your shoulder and I don't see you doing anything stupid. You worked as a maid and presumably as a table-maid too?'

'Yes.'

'Then you know what is expected?'

'Oh, yes, I have no fears there. There was a very high standard at Denbrae House and I would make sure that standards didn't slip at the Beeches.'

'I'm a little concerned about this wonderful cook,' she turned to her husband, 'you are too, John?'

He nodded. 'From what I gather the guest house has a reputation for the food it serves and it is important that it continues. What if this woman leaves you in the lurch?'

'That worried me too, Mr Powrie, but Miss Galbraith says she is local and very dependable.'

'Even so, Annie, I would be inclined to get something in writing, something included in her contract.'

'She wouldn't have a contract, I'm sure she wouldn't.'

'Possibly not, but she might be happy to have one. It could be a safeguard for her as well as you and since she is such an important part of this venture I would suggest a small increase in her wages. I did say small, Annie, you can't afford to throw money away. Six months' notice either way would be ideal but unlikely. Hold out for three months though. It would let the woman know you expect loyalty and are prepared to show your appreciation in a way she understands.'

Annie laughed shakily. 'Until this moment I was talking about the Beeches and asking your advice but not for one moment believing that it could happen.'

'It may not,' John Powrie said, 'there are still a few hurdles. One we must tackle immediately and together. We'll make an appointment with the bank manager, Annie. As luck would have it, Hamish and I used the same bank and I don't foresee too many difficulties provided this Miss Galbraith is not asking too high a price.'

'She said as long as it was a reasonable offer—'

'Reasonable offer has a different meaning for different people,' John Powrie said drily.

'John don't bother Annie with that. It will be up to the solicitors to come up with something agreeable to both parties.'

'Fair enough, but Annie needs to be kept in the picture. And now the house, we must get that on the market without delay!'

'Do I tell Miss Galbraith I'm interested?'

'You are, aren't you?'

'Yes.' Annie was smiling happily. 'Yes, I am, I really am.'

'Then tell her right away. It doesn't bind you to anything.'

'I realise that, but do you really think the bank will lend me the money?'

'If I stand surety and I'm prepared to do that.'

'Oh, no, you mustn't,' Annie was horrified. 'I couldn't have you doing that and taking the risk.'

'Annie,' Cissie Powrie said severely, 'we know you and we trust you. This will be a success because you will give it your all.'

'Oh, I will, I can promise that. But what if something happened that I have no control over, what then? How could I meet my debts?'

'Nothing is without risk and none of us knows what lies ahead, which is just as well. For all I know we could wake up to flooding and if the waters couldn't be stopped everything we have worked for could be lost,' John Powrie said.

'A ray of sunshine isn't he?' his wife said. 'For myself I have a feeling that the Beeches is meant for you.'

'You know, Mrs Powrie, I have that feeling myself.'

'That's the spirit. You'll make a success of it and we will be very proud of the small part we played.'

'Anything but small.'

'Hold on, you two, it hasn't happened yet.'

'We know that.'

Everything went as hoped and if the bank manager seemed hesitant, his decision hanging in the balance, it was all an act, John Powrie assured her. They enjoyed their position and their importance and Bank Manager Frederick Foster was no exception. He took his time but in the end agreed to a loan.

Hillside House went on the market and there was a steady stream of people in the first week. Annie could tell the interested from the curious and was polite to them all. Only when the door was shut did she give way to her anger, muttering to herself as she went about her tasks.

'Why are all these people coming, Mummy?'

'To see the house and if they want to buy it.'

'Why can't we stay, I like it?'

'I do as well but we are going to the Beeches and you liked it, didn't you?'

'I think so,' she said uncertainly.

By the end of the third week two parties were genuinely

interested and both couples had returned for another much longer look. Two offers were made to the solicitor and a Mr and Mrs Allan were successful. They looked at the furniture and decided to buy the dining-room furniture if the price was right and Annie made sure that the price was right. Mrs Powrie had shaken her head saying she had practically given it away. Annie didn't mind, they were a nice couple.

With so much happening at once, Annie's head was buzzing with the speed of events. Deciding what to take to the Beeches and what to send to the sale-room was proving to be difficult, even impossible until she knew Miss Galbraith's plans and what she, in turn, was to take with her. The long letter that came made it all clear. The sale of the guest house had included everything apart from the furniture in the annexe or the owner's living area. The accommodation consisted of a sitting-room, two bedrooms, a small kitchen and a bathroom. Annie made her decision as to what she should take and that didn't at first include the handsome bureau. In the end she couldn't see it going to the sale-room, she wanted something that was 'Hamish' and apart from his chair which was in a sorry state, the bureau brought him to mind.

The Powries had insisted that Annie and Tina spend their final week in Dundrinnen at the farm and Annie was grateful. It had been a tremendous help just walking from the farm to Hillside House to organise the removal and once the house was empty Annie set to with a will. No one would say that Annie Brown had left a dirty house.

Leaving Dundrinnen was proving to be harder than she had expected and going from one empty room to another she wept a few tears. This was goodbye and she knew it was unlikely she would ever return to the Mearns. She would remember it though. The lovely countryside and those quietly happy days at Hillside House. The memories would be locked away in her heart. Hamish, that wise old man, had known how it would be. Much as he had liked and respected the villagers, he hadn't been blind to their faults. When it came to a juicy bit of gossip some folk had long memories. It had angered and distressed him that an innocent child like Tina should have to suffer for another's mistake and it further distressed him that folk had nothing better to do than dig up the past. Did they feel no shame? Were their own lives so spotless?

From the bedroom window Annie looked over to the back garden which had been given its final tidying up by the Powrie boys. Standing there she thought about the changes in her life which had all stemmed from Miss Emily's fall from grace as she had once described it herself. Poor, poor Miss Emily who died in such tragic circumstances. Who would have believed that such a healthy young woman would have lost her life giving birth? What happened after was even more difficult to believe and Annie marvelled at herself. Where had she got the courage or should that be nerve to take charge of that young life? It had worked out but what if there had been no Hamish? How would she have fared then? Annie didn't like to think about that.

The tongues were wagging first at the sale of the house and then the departure from Dundrinnen. They were curious to know her plans but Annie got a lot of satisfaction from keeping them guessing. Only the Powries knew and they would say nothing.

'There you are, Mrs Brown, and what is this I hear?'

'What did you hear Mrs Robb?' Annie said cheerfully.

'That you're leaving us, that's what.'

'Yes, I'm leaving Dundrinnen.' They were cutting off her path to the shop and she was forced to stop.

'And where is it you're going?' one of the other women asked.

'Back to where I came from.'

'And where might that be?'

'Perthshire,' Annie said shortly, 'and now if you would excuse me I am in rather a hurry.'

They didn't move, they weren't finished. 'All hoity-toity,' Ina Robb said with a sniff. 'You have to hand it to her she's been clever. Got what she wanted and didn't have to wait long either. Poor man I bet he came to rue the day he let her over the door.'

Annie was deathly pale, she had thought she could deal with the insults by ignoring them but she had a terrible urge to slap that face and had to keep her hands clenched at her side. Another woman had been standing apart but close enough to hear. She came nearer and Annie recognised her as someone who had always had a smile for her and Tina.

'Mrs Brown, let me apologise for these mean-minded folk. Thank God we don't have too many of them—'

'Here, just you watch—'

'Ina Robb you've said enough. With a tongue like yours it is no wonder that poor man of yours spends most of his time in the pub drowning his sorrows.' She paused and smiled to the others who were looking sheepish. 'I wish you and the child well, Mrs Brown. Hamish and Marian were a lovely couple and when he lost her a part of his world went. You and the bairn brought him a bit of happiness. I know that and so do quite a few others.'

'Thank you very much,' Annie said unsteadily as the others began to walk away.

'Good luck,' the woman said and hurried away.

Annie had recovered, got the shopping she needed, and returned to the farm where Tina was very much at home. Soon she would have another home but children were adaptable and the child would settle down.

As for herself this was a new chapter in her life. She had come up in the world and very shortly she would be the owner of the Beeches with its continuing success depending on her.

Chapter Nineteen

'Mrs Brown, if you could spare me a moment, please?'

'Of course, Miss Middleton.' Annie gave the woman a warm smile. The evening meal was over. Gladys had removed the cheese and biscuits and then returned for the last of the dishes. The guests had gone either to the residents' lounge or upstairs to their bedroom. Only Miss Middleton remained at her table and Annie, drawing out the other chair, sat down.

For all her advancing years Miss Middleton enjoyed raising eyebrows. She still dressed outrageously but it was so much a part of her that the remarks would have come if she had appeared in something dull and drab. Tonight she wore a long purple jacket with a huge embroidered peacock on the back and she smelled faintly of lavender. On one occasion when she had been particularly talkative, she told Annie about having relatives and friends abroad who, knowing her liking for the unusual, kept her supplied with eye-catching garments. Before she took up permanent residence at the Beeches and when she had her own home she said a chest of tea would arrive each Christmas which kept her going until the following Christmas. The tea boxes, she added with a smile, were much in demand for packing china and breakables for those moving house.

'I owe you an apology.'

'Why? What have you done?' Annie smiled.

'It's not so much what I have done, Mrs Brown, indeed I have done nothing, but do let me explain. I was, and I have to admit it, very apprehensive about the Beeches being run by someone so young and inexperienced. Miss Galbraith had looked after me very well and old people, my dear, do not welcome change. Frankly I didn't see how you could manage and you with a little child to look after.' She paused. 'You have shown me how very wrong I was to dare make such an assumption.'

'Thank you for telling me this, Miss Middleton. At the outset I was very nervous and it must have shown.'

'It didn't. The hand-over went very smoothly. Let me say you have passed all the tests with flying colours. Oh, and tell me about Miss Galbraith, how is she getting on and has she any regrets or is she just not saying?'

'No regrets. I had a letter a few weeks ago to say she was thoroughly enjoying what she called her new-found freedom.'

'Do give her my best regards when you write again.'

'I'll do that.'

She frowned. 'What was I going to say before I went off at a tangent? Oh, I remember now. The flowers on my dressing-table, how thoughtful of you, my dear, and very much appreciated.'

'I want you to be happy and if there is anything you wish please don't hesitate to ask.'

'Since you mention it, there is something. I hardly ever see that delightful child of yours.'

'Tina knows she hasn't to annoy the guests.'

'She most certainly doesn't annoy me.'

'Thank you, but I know Tina and she can be a little chatterbox and my guests are entitled to a bit of peace and quiet.'

'I get plenty of that,' Miss Middleton said tartly. 'I don't like noisy or cheeky children but Tina is neither, she is a well-behaved little girl. The very old, you know, and the very young have a lot in common. We have the time and we have the patience.'

'That is true and I am afraid I do not give as much attention to Tina as I would like.'

'How can you with the busy life you lead? Tell the little lass to come and see me when she feels like it and to bring some of her drawings.'

'She has shown you them?' Annie was surprised.

'Yes, she has and though I am no expert I would say for such a young child they show talent.'

Annie looked pleased. She liked to hear Tina being praised. 'A nice hobby,' she said a little dismissively.

'Sadly it may have to remain that. Women are not supposed to be gifted in that direction and those who are are not encouraged to take it up seriously.'

Annie didn't know much about it but supposed Miss Middleton spoke good sense. She would come from a middle-class family who would know about these things.

'Are there any artists in your family, Mrs Brown, or in your late husband's?'

'Not to my knowledge.' Annie felt a niggle of guilt as soon as she said it, Miss Emily had spoken that one time about Tina's father being an artist. And that he had never been able to settle for long in one place. Just as soon as he had completed what he had set himself he would be off on his travels. That small pencil sketch he had done of Miss Emily was all there was to show that he had ever existed. Annie had it carefully preserved between the pages of Jane Austen's *Sense and Sensibility*. The day would come when she would sit down with Tina and tell her everything she had a right to know.

'A gift or a talent is known to skip a generation and then again Tina could be the first in your family. Someone has to be,' she pointed out reasonably.

'Yes, I suppose that's true.'

'And now forgive an old woman's curiosity which is really a genuine interest. Tell me about the Beeches, are you doing well?'

'Can't complain,' Annie said carefully.

'Most of those who deserted you have returned?'

'Yes, I am glad to say.' Annie had been desperately worried when first one then another failed to make an advance booking and it had angered her that they had waited until Miss Galbraith's departure before deserting the ship.

'I would like to say shame on them but I wasn't much better myself. You see, my dear, I thought that standards were bound to drop but they haven't. Everything is just as it should be and you are doing splendidly. You work very hard.'

'I like to keep busy.' Annie didn't say that she had to keep going to stop herself brooding about the downturn in business, the beds cold waiting for the guests who never came. 'You will recall, Miss Middleton, that for a few weeks it was only Mr Cuthbert and yourself.'

'Oh, my dear, we both felt for you and those stupid little jokes of Mr Cuthbert's,' she shook her head as she spoke, 'was just his way of trying to cheer you up.'

'I know, he really is very kind.'

'Kind and very trying. Sadly I am not a very tolerant person but then again it takes all kinds doesn't it?'

Annie smiled. 'You both helped me over a difficult patch. I was becoming convinced that I had made a terrible mistake and it would only be a question of time before I was declared bankrupt.'

'And now things are looking up?'

'Improving.'

'Perhaps I can take a little of the credit.' She paused again to touch the corners of her mouth with a handkerchief. 'When I am out for my walk or coming back from the library, I do occasionally see Mr McCormack. Usually he just smiles and raises his hat but this particular time he stopped to enquire after my health but really to find out about the Beeches. I saw it as my chance to repay some of your kindness.'

'That was very good of you.'

'Not at all, the least I could do. I told him that everything was lovely and that you were looking after us every bit as well as Miss Galbraith had done.'

'Might I ask what he had to say to that?'

'Not very much. Just that he wished he hadn't been so hasty. Wherever he was staying, and I didn't enquire into that, the accommodation was acceptable but the food left a great deal to be desired. I told him there and then what he could do and he nodded, smiled and left me.'

Annie began to laugh. 'Poor man he did look rather shamefaced when he asked if I had a room.'

'Nice to see Mr Baxter back too.'

'Yes, he acted as though he had never been away.'

'Typical,' she said with the faintest of sneers.

'I am just happy they have returned and a few others with them.'

'Good, you won't be so worried and now I must stop, I have talked long enough, but before I hold my tongue let me say again how safe and protected I feel at the Beeches – much more so than when I was living alone and not as sprightly as I once was.'

Annie was touched. Lonely old people were very vulnerable, Hamish had been the same. 'Don't worry, we'll look after you,' Annie said gently.

'Thank you, my dear. I go on about my independence but there comes a time when we all need a little assistance.'

Annie lingered to see what assistance was required.

'If you would just help me out of the chair. I stiffen up, but once I am on my legs I am fine.'

Annie helped her up and an age-speckled hand reached for the stick hanging over the arm of the chair.

'I won't go into the lounge tonight.'

'Not even for half an hour?'

'No. I have promised myself to answer some long over-due letters and if I don't do it now my friends will think I am dead.' She chuckled. 'The old can joke about death and the young don't like to hear them do so.'

'No, we do not,' Annie said firmly. She waited until the old lady had reached the bottom of the stairs before turning away. Miss Middleton managed very well. Her bedroom was on the first floor and by using the banister and taking her time she got herself there. Annie came hurrying back to call up the stair, 'I'll bring a cup of tea for you about half past nine.'

'Bless you, that will be very welcome. By then I'll probably be in bed with my library book.'

There was a murmur of voices coming from the lounge and Annie had already checked that Tina was in the kitchen with Mrs Archibald. The two of them got on famously and the cook was adamant that Tina was not in her way. She enjoyed having a bairn about the place, she said and Annie knew that to be true. Mrs Archibald had a nice way with her and if she could keep the child happy then it let Mrs Brown get on.

Annie went behind the desk in the small reception area to make a start on the accounts. There had been no need to order stationery since there was a good supply. To get discount Miss Galbraith had bought in bulk.

'As it happened, false economy,' she had smiled. 'All it is good for now is scrap. Tina can make use of it.'

'That's a terrible waste, can't I use it up?'

'Don't you want your own name on the stationery?'

'Yes, in time,' she said slowly and fingered the good-quality, headed paper.

'If you were of a mind you could remove Galbraith as the proprietor and write or print in your own name. Or again you could leave it as it is.'

'What do you advise, apart from scrapping it all I mean?' Annie smiled.

'Score out Galbraith and put in A. Brown. It would avoid any confusion.'

Annie did so many each day but it would be a while yet

before she was through them all. The reception area was small but had been well planned. There were pigeonholes for headed stationery and another for envelopes, one for receipts and another for miscellaneous which meant anything that couldn't find a home elsewhere. There was a board for room keys, an inkstand, a blotter, a few sharp-pointed pencils and a rubber. The shabby leatherbound book was open showing the bookings for the week. There was a bell to press for attention if no one was about.

Looking after the rooms and keeping everything clean and tidy was second nature to Annie. Making out the bills was not and it was this part of the proceedings that had worried her so much at the beginning. In the event she needn't have worried since there were so few to make out at that time. When business did improve so had her book-keeping skills.

'How do I go about giving the guests their account or do they ask for it?' she had asked Miss Galbraith.

'Some might ask if they have an early start in the morning. I found it best to place the bill, folded, on the breakfast table where it could be seen.'

'Not under a plate?'

'Do that if you want but make sure it isn't hidden. As regards Miss Middleton, hers is sent monthly to her solicitor who settles within a few days.'

Annie let her mind drift to a small upset with a member of her staff and one she felt she had dealt with rather well. Gladys had been trying to see how much she could get away with unaware that she was under close scrutiny. Annie had plenty of experience, she knew that without good super-vision some maids would take short cuts, with the work being only half done. A quick look from the door would not have shown anything amiss but a closer inspection would. To begin with Annie said nothing just put everything to rights herself and waited her time. It came.

'Gladys?'

'Yes, Mrs Brown?'

'Finish what you are doing, then go along to my sitting-room.'

The girl looked startled and then worried. 'You did say your sitting-room?'

'I did.'

'Is something wrong, Mrs Brown?'

'You should know,' Annie said walking away. She went ahead to the self-contained part of the Beeches. This was her home, hers and Tina's, and it gave her a tremendous feeling of pride. She had brought with her the best pieces from Hillside House and how well they graced the sitting-room. The fitted bookshelves left by Miss Galbraith held a remarkable number of books. It had surprised Annie to discover just how many she had. The leatherbound ones that had belonged to Miss Emily were on the middle shelf in pride of place. The others had come from Hillside House and had been Marian's though a few, mainly Scottish books, bore Hamish's name.

The doll's house had a permanent place in the corner of the room and had immediately caught Miss Galbraith's eye.

'Where did you get that treasure?'

'My husband made it, it belongs to Tina.'

'Lucky little girl.' She had gone over to examine it. 'The house itself is wonderful and as for the tiny pieces of furniture they are quite exquisite, the detail is unbelievable. To be honest with you, this is far too good for a child to play with.'

'Hamish wouldn't have agreed with you. It wasn't to be an ornament but to give a child pleasure. Tina plays with it but she is very careful.'

'I would hope so. Unless I am very much mistaken the day will come when that doll's house is going to be worth a great deal of money.'

'Perhaps you are right, Miss Galbraith, but it will never be sold. Tina would never part with it and for that matter neither would I.'

The knock came.

'Come in.'

Gladys entered looking very apprehensive. She closed the door quietly and looked about her. She had never been in this room before. Her eyes widened as they settled on the doll's house.

'Is that Tina's?' She pointed.

'Yes.'

'It's lovely, I've never seen one as nice as that.'

'Probably not. Sit down.'

Gladys did, on the edge of the chair.

'This won't take long,' Annie said sitting down herself. She looked very smart in a black dress with a white lace collar and matching cuffs. It was both attractive and businesslike and Annie felt comfortable wearing it.

'Have I done something wrong?'

'I think you should be able to answer that yourself.'

'I – I don't know what you mean,' she faltered.

'I think you do but I'll explain.' She paused, there was no use hurrying this and when she spoke again it was slowly and deliberately. 'You, Gladys, are becoming lazy and careless. Your work, particularly in the bedrooms, is nothing short of a disgrace. The counterpane is just thrown on, the pillows are not as they should be and as for the dusting' – her eyebrows rose – 'in one bedroom I lifted the ornaments on the dressing-table only to find a circle of dust.'

'That must have been the day I was in a hurry.'

'It wasn't just one day or I may have been able to overlook it, it has gone on for far too long. You may not realise it but I have more to do than check on your work.'

Gladys was flushed and indignant. 'Miss Galbraith never found fault with my work.'

'No, she didn't because she had no occasion to. You did what was expected of you.' Annie looked directly at the girl. 'Have I reduced your wages?'

'No.'

'Have I increased your workload?'

'No.' A very quiet 'no'.

'Then you will agree, I think, that I am entitled to the same standard of work you gave to Miss Galbraith?'

'I thought I had given you that.'

'You thought nothing of the kind. I'll tell you what you did think, Gladys, you thought I would be a soft mark and that was your big mistake. The Beeches is mine and the comfort of my guests is very important to me. Unless you are prepared to mend your ways you will be looking for another position. Do I make myself clear?'

'Yes, Mrs Brown,' Gladys whispered. 'I'm sorry, it won't happen again.'

'It had better not. Just remember there are other girls just as capable and who are not in employment. You are not indispensable.'

The girl looked to be on the verge of tears and Annie softened her voice. The threat of dismissal still stood but Annie hoped it wouldn't come to that. Gladys was a good worker when she wanted.

'You can go now, Gladys, I think I have said all that I need to.'

She nodded and made her escape quickly.

Annie expected no further problems from that quarter and there were none.

Chapter Twenty

A solemn-faced little girl looking smart in her school clothes, shut the gate of the Beeches then took her mother's hand. This was to be Tina's first day at school and it was difficult to know which of them was the more apprehensive. Annie was dreading and at the same time welcoming, her child's first small step to independence.

The morning was pleasantly cool as they walked up the hill to where the road divided. The left fork led to farmland and beyond that to open country. The other and the one they turned into was Middlefield Road and on Middlefield Road was Middlefield Primary School. The building was fairly new and was a much needed replacement for the original two-classroom school with its mish-mash of bits added on. Woodside, once the size of a village, was now a thriving country town with a sizeable number of comfortably off folk. There were pockets where the less well off lived in badly maintained houses but these black spots were well hidden.

Children were already milling about the school gate and making as much noise as they possibly could. Tina began to drag her feet.

'Don't Tina, don't do that.'

'Mummy?' It was an urgent whisper.

'What is it, dear?'

'If I don't like school I won't have to go back, will I?'

Annie didn't know whether to laugh or cry. 'Tina, you know perfectly well that you must go to school. How else would you learn to be a clever girl?'

'You could tell me things and Miss Middleton knows a lot. She knows more than you, Mummy, because she always answers my questions.'

'Miss Middleton has more time,' Annie said feeling more hurt than she wanted to admit. Of course the woman was more knowledgeable.

'That's what she said, that you don't have the time because you are always working. Why do you have to work all the time, Mummy, is it because I haven't got a daddy to bring in the money?'

Annie was spared answering when a mother and child fell into step.

'I've been dreading this day,' the woman said. 'Are you having problems too?'

Annie nodded. 'Tina wanted everyone to know she was going to school but now that she is here it is a different story.'

'Is she your one and only?'

'Yes.'

'Ruth is an only child too.' Ruth was scraping her feet on the loose stones and Tina began to do the same.

'Let me introduce myself, I'm Phyllis Forbes and this woebegone wee soul is Ruth.'

'I'm Annie Brown and this is Tina.' They shook hands and went slowly into the playground. Phyllis Forbes was an attractive small woman with jet-black hair, dark eyes and neat features. Ruth resembled her mother except that she had light brown hair worn in a plait.

There were two doors, one marked GIRLS and the other BOYS. Once they were inside the girls' entrance a harassed looking woman directed them to a classroom. Coming from the classroom were screams which turned out to be a mother trying to separate herself from her clinging child. Miss Taylor, the infant teacher, got off her chair and went over to them.

'I really am sorry, Miss Taylor,' the woman was apologising profusely, 'I never expected her to be like this.'

'What is her name?'

'Euphemia.'

'Euphemia, stop that noise this instant.' And she did. The firm no-nonsense voice had done the trick and Annie and Phyllis Forbes exchanged smiles. 'Don't you want to come to school?'

'No.' A tear-stained face was raised.

'That's a pity because my little girls like school. Euphemia, that is a lovely name but quite a long one to say.'

'I'm Phemie,' the child said sullenly but she was coming round.

'Well, Phemie, go and sit down,' she said pointing to one of the seats.

After a small hesitation she did and was soon fascinated with the desk. There was a slit for the slate and she began to examine it. The teacher nodded to Phemie's mother to go and she did quickly and quietly.

Miss Taylor turned her attention to the other mothers hovering around the door. 'Ladies, once you have handed over your child please leave the classroom at once. Your little darlings will settle a lot easier once you are out of sight. Believe me, I am an old hand at this and I know. Now who is next?'

Phyllis Forbes and Ruth went forward and after a few minutes Ruth went, quite the thing, to sit at her desk.

Annie and Tina were next.

'Tina Brown,' she ticked off the name. 'Is Tina her name or is it shortened?'

'Tina is her name, not Clementina,' Annie added.

'For which she will one day be grateful. It was my mother's name and I was always thankful she didn't inflict it on me.'

Annie smiled and wondered what name had been inflicted on her.

'Welcome to school, Tina. You already have a friend I see, so go and sit beside Ruth.'

'Isn't she wonderful?' Phyllis said as Annie and she left the classroom.

'Firm but kind and children know where they are with a person like that.'

'I couldn't agree more. Ruth can be a little monkey, she gets far too much of her own way like a lot of only children. I do try to be firm and mean no when I say it, but I get no help from my husband. She can twist James round her little finger and when I complain to him all he says is that as a youngster he was spoilt rotten and look how well he has turned out.'

Annie laughed. 'I like the sound of your husband, he has a sense of humour.'

'He does and it isn't something you usually associate with a banker,' she grinned.

'Straight-faced and solemn is my experience, but then I've only met one.' Annie felt relaxed, she had been so keyed up and there had been no need. Miss Taylor understood children and Tina would be quite safe.

The teacher in question breathed a sigh of relief when the last of the mothers had departed. Some removed themselves at the first possible moment and these were supposed to be the uncaring ones. They weren't, they were just sensible. If the others just knew it, they made it hard for themselves and harder for their offspring. The longer they delayed the worse it was for all concerned.

'You are the lady, aren't you, who has taken over the Beeches from Miss Galbraith?' Phyllis Forbes asked Annie once they were out of the classroom and into the playground.

'Yes.'

'We live quite near in one of the semi-detached houses, number eighteen.'

'Then we are near neighbours,' Annie said. 'I know very few people, but the Beeches has taken up most of my time.'

'I'm sure, it is quite an undertaking. Folk hereabout are curious without being nosy and they thought you were running the guest house for someone. You are so young that's why.'

'I do own the Beeches but only after a substantial loan from the bank.'

'They do come in handy and especially so if you get on the right side of the manager. James always tries to be helpful I know, but sometimes he has to refuse when there is too big a risk.'

'The bank took a risk with me and I'm not sure that I would have been given the help I needed if it hadn't been for very good friends.'

'That's what friends are for.'

'I must go.'

'Before you do I just wanted to say that I would be happy to collect Tina for school.'

'Oh, no, I couldn't have you doing that.'

'Why not? I pass the door and it would be good for the two of them to go in together.'

It would be a great help, Annie knew that, but she didn't want to impose on Mrs Forbes, a young woman she had just met. 'I have to admit it would be a tremendous help, Mrs Forbes.'

'That's settled then and the name is Phyllis.'

'Mine is Annie.' They parted at the gate of the Beeches and both knew they had found a friend.

'Mrs Brown?' Gladys was leaning over the banister.

Annie, on her way to the kitchen looked up. 'Yes, Gladys, what is it?'

'Two women have been looking at the Beeches for ages.'

'No law against that,' Annie smiled. She knew that Gladys was anxious to get back into her good books and certainly her work couldn't be faulted.

'I know, but they seemed as though they couldn't make up their mind whether to come in or not.'

'More than likely they have just decided to do their chatting at the gate.'

'Maybe, but I don't think so.' Gladys turned away disappointed.

It was more to please Gladys than to satisfy her own curiosity that she went out of the door and down the front steps ostensibly to look at the garden. It was always tidy, the gardener and his assistant were conscientious workers and not many weeds would have been missed.

'Lovely afternoon,' Annie said when she was near enough to be heard.

'Yes, isn't it?' The two well-dressed matron ladies returned the smile and one said, 'My friend and I have been standing here wondering if by any chance you serve afternoon teas for non-residents?'

Annie had been about to say no but stopped herself. Why not? Why shouldn't the Beeches serve afternoon teas if there was a demand? She could see to that side herself and should it prove popular then it would be simple to engage extra staff. Annie's thoughts were rushing ahead.

'We haven't done so, but I'm sure we could oblige if you are prepared to wait a little while?'

'Of course, we are in no hurry.'

'You would be comfortable in the lounge.'

'How very kind of you.'

Annie opened the gate and they came in looking pleased.

'We meet every week and have done so for a long time. Usually we go to the Willow Restaurant for a cup of tea.' She made a face and her friend took over.

'It used to be such a nice clean place but since the change of ownership the restaurant has gone steadily downhill. I first noticed it with the stained tablecloths, quite put us off, and then to make it worse everything is bought in.'

'There is nothing to beat good homebaking,' her friend said. 'And if I were asked I wouldn't rate the Willow Restaurant any higher than a very ordinary café where the interest is in a quick turnover.'

Annie was taking it all in and nodding her agreement. How fortuitous that Mrs Archibald did a baking each day.

In Miss Galbraith's time it had been tea and a biscuit at nine thirty in the evening. That was still available for those who wanted it but in addition there would be a plate of buttered pancakes one evening and buttered scones another. Occasionally there would be a piece of sponge or gingerbread. Annie gave her cook a free hand knowing she could trust her. The woman wasn't extravagant and nothing went to waste. As well as the guests the staff had to be fed and that included Annie and Tina. Mrs Archibald liked to have the tins filled and as she was fond of saying it is always better to be prepared for like as not when you weren't that is when it would be needed.

The ladies admired the pots of geraniums on each side of the front steps then went inside. Annie got them settled in the lounge. Miss Middleton was visiting a friend and by the time she got back the ladies would have gone. This was the residents' lounge and it would remain that. This was a one-off. Should afternoon teas become a regular occurrence the ladies would go directly to the dining-room.

The ladies were impressed. 'This is very nice indeed,' they said.

Annie had everything just so and was thankful for her training at Denbrae House. She didn't strive for perfection, no one liked a too perfect house. Folk had to feel comfortable and Annie felt she had managed that. The room was spotlessly clean, the furniture shining and the tall vase of fresh flowers on the corner table caught the eye. The slightly shabby chairs were an invitation to sit down. Annie left the two ladies to their talk and hurried to the kitchen. Mrs Archibald and Gladys were off duty and it was only Bridget, the scullery-maid who was there. She was standing at the sink preparing vegetables and looked up.

'Bridget, leave what you are doing and give me a hand.'

'Yes, Mrs Brown.' The girl took her hands out of the water and quickly dried them on the roll-towel at the back of the pantry door.

The girl reminded Annie of herself when she had started

work as a scullery-maid at Denbrae House. She, too, had never questioned, just rushed to do whatever was asked.

'I have two ladies sitting in the lounge waiting to be served afternoon tea. While I set a table in the dining-room perhaps you could butter some pancakes – four should do – and split a few oven scones and butter those.' Annie was reaching for the cake tins and bringing them down while she was talking. Bridget wasted no time and without being told she put the kettle to boil then got out the butter dish, cleared a space on the kitchen table and began her task.

'I'm away to get a three-tiered cake-stand and you can see to filling it, can't you?'

'Easily, Mrs Brown. I'll cut the cake and make it all dainty,' she said, flushed at being given such an important job.

'Not too dainty, let them have a decent bite.'

'Yes.'

Bridget was very fond of Annie and would have done anything for her. The to-do with Gladys had been her own fault. She was lucky not to have got her books which only showed Mrs Brown was fair but not a soft mark. Bridget put a doily on each plate, then carefully arranged the food.

'Very nice indeed, Bridget.'

'Thank you. I'll make the tea now. Will I use the wee teapot and put boiling water in the jug?'

'Yes.'

Annie checked the table to see that everything was there. If the ladies were pleased they would very likely return and hopefully tell their friends. Advertising wasn't necessary, word of mouth was the best recommendation. She went through to tell the ladies that their table was ready.

'That was delicious, we both thoroughly enjoyed it,' one of the ladies said as they were getting ready to leave.

'I'm so glad that everything was to your satisfaction.'

Knowing what to charge was posing a problem. She didn't want to overcharge and perhaps chase them away nor to ask a ridiculously small sum. She was in business to make a profit. Bridget, surprisingly, came to the rescue. Jotting down numbers she added them up.

'Fine, Bridget, I'll charge that.'

'No, ask for more, this is a posh place.'

Annie burst out laughing but Bridget was serious.

'All right, I'll add a little on.'

If their faces were anything to go by she hadn't overcharged. They would be back they said.

Bridget was in for promotion if the afternoon teas took off. She would need a dark dress with a stiffly starched white apron. There was a shop in Perth where these could be bought and if alterations were necessary these could be done on the premises.

The Beeches became known for its delicious afternoon teas and the guest house became livelier than it had ever been before. It was lively without being noisy and it was confined to a few hours in the afternoon when few guests were about. No one was inconvenienced, the residents' lounge was available just as it always had been. Miss Middleton had been won over and she would occasionally invite her friends to the Beeches for afternoon tea.

'My way of returning hospitality,' she said, 'without having to take a step outside the door.'

Chapter Twenty-One

The loan from the bank was a constant worry for Annie who had a horror of debt. The Powries had tried their best to make her understand that it was normal practice for many firms to remain in the 'red'. That was the way they conducted their business. Annie wasn't convinced, for her it was still money owed, no matter how it was dressed up. Her greatest joy would come when she had paid back every penny and the profit was truly hers. Meantime she was seeing, albeit slowly, the debt getting smaller. There was a long way to go but she would get there.

Tina was happy and doing well at school. Ruth was her best friend and Annie encouraged Phyllis's daughter to spend some time at the Beeches. At other times Tina would be invited to Ruth's house.

'Ruth has a nice daddy, I like him and he likes me.'

'Mr Forbes is very nice, I like him too.' She had met James Forbes and liked his quiet good humour and the kindly way he treated Tina. It was seeing Tina with him and how she responded, that made Annie realise just how much the child missed a father.

Annie had been the owner of the Beeches for three years and in that time there had been a number of changes. The death of Miss Middleton had affected them all. The old lady had taken a bad fall when coming down the library steps and had never recovered. Annie regularly visited her in hospital but it was one of her friends who was with her when she died. Annie felt her loss keenly, she had grown very fond of Miss Middleton and Tina had been broken-hearted. There had been widespread grief in Woodside where she had lived all her life and had been a well-kent and colourful character.

Old Mr Cuthbert continued to crack his little jokes but he was getting very frail and his hands shook. Not so long ago he had held himself straight, like a soldier, but now he had the ungainly walk of an old man. Knowing he was unsteady on his feet, Annie tried to keep an eye on him and asked that others did the same.

Tina was eight years of age, growing tall and becoming prettier by the day as Mrs Archibald would have it. She was a bright, good-natured child but with a stubborn streak. Cook said there was nothing wrong with that, showed she had a mind of her own and Annie supposed she was right. Her school work was satisfactory and she now had a new teacher, Miss Etta Nicholson.

Life for Annie had never been better. Room bookings were up on the previous years and afternoon teas were more popular than ever. The Powries in Dundrinnen kept in touch and had driven through on one occasion to see Annie and Tina and to view the Beeches. They were delighted with everything and amazed at the difference in Tina. As Cissie Powrie said they had forgotten how quickly children grow up. The visit was too short, they all agreed, but an overnight stay was out of the question. There was no rest for a farmer.

There are days in everyone's life that stand out and become rooted in the memory. Annie would long remember the day Edward Galloway walked into the Beeches. It had been a little after three o'clock and she had just come through from the dining-room. Bridget had proved to be a treasure. Annie knew that she could be safely left to cope with the afternoon teas unless there was a rush, then Annie gave assistance.

She saw him standing at reception, a case at his feet and about to ring for attendance when Annie appeared. In that first glance she saw that he was tall and good-looking and probably in his forties. His hair was thick with traces of grey through the dark brown. His eyes were a peculiar golden brown.

'Good afternoon,' she said going behind the desk.

'A room for tonight, if that is possible?'

'I think so,' she drew the book towards her and picked up a pen.

'Edward Galloway,' he said before she could ask his name.

'I can let you have a room on the second floor, Mr Galloway.'

'Thank you, I don't mind where it is.'

She wrote in his name then called to Gladys who came over. 'Show this gentleman to his room,' she said and handed her a key.

'Yes, Mrs Brown.'

Edward Galloway picked up his case, hesitated, then spoke and Annie heard the surprise in his voice. 'You are Mrs Brown?'

'Yes, Mrs Annie Brown,' she smiled and wondered what had made her give her full name when it hadn't been necessary.

'Forgive me if I sounded rude. It is just I was here in Miss Galbraith's time and though I knew the Beeches was under new management I suppose I just expected someone very much older.'

'Did you?' she said stupidly. The way he was looking at her had her feeling breathless. 'Breakfast?' Annie began.

'Ah, yes, breakfast, what time is it?'

'We serve breakfast from seven thirty to nine but should you wish it before then it can be arranged.'

'Eight o'clock is about my usual time.'

She nodded and was glad when Gladys went ahead and he followed. She needed time to recover. No one had ever made her feel like this and all in the space of a few minutes. It was ridiculous, it was embarrassing and she just hoped that this Edward Galloway hadn't been aware of it.

Edward Galloway had noticed and was feeling the usual satisfaction. The plain ones didn't interest him but he was so used to exercising his charm that it had become second nature. Poor souls, it brought a little sunshine into their lives.

Gladys thought he was a bit of all right, but too old for her. She was amused that the charm had obviously worked for Mrs Brown, the woman had been all of a dither. She wasn't amused in a nasty way. Up to now it had been all work and no play for Mrs Brown and that wasn't good for anybody.

She opened the bedroom door and went in. 'Would you like the window shut, sir?'

'No, I don't think so and if I do I'll manage to do that myself.'

'Is the room to your satisfaction?'

'It will do nicely.' He didn't want her to go, not just yet. 'Tell me is business good these days?'

'Yes.'

He smiled into her eyes. 'Is Mrs Brown a good employer?'

What was it to him? Why was he asking? Gladys was edging to the door. 'She makes us work hard but she works hard herself.'

'What about her husband? Is he a tower of strength?' He laughed as he said it. 'No doubt Mr Brown sees to the financial side, we men are best at that.'

'There is no Mr Brown. Mrs Brown is a widow and now if you will excuse me,' Gladys said shortly.

'Certainly, don't let me hold you back from your work.' He gave her the full benefit of his smile and the irritation at the questioning disappeared. The man was friendly, that was all.

In the weeks that followed Edward Galloway became a well-known face. The one-night stay became two and on several occasions it was three. The man was always courteous but his presence was unsettling Annie and she avoided him when she could. Settling his bill was one of the times she couldn't.

'Thank you, Mr Galloway,' she said as he paid for bed and breakfast for two nights. As she handed him the receipted bill their fingers briefly touched and she felt her heart flutter.

'Will the weather keep fine today do you think?' he asked.

'The sky is clear which is a good sign.'

'I am surprised you have the time to notice, Mrs Brown. What a busy life you lead, never a moment to yourself.'

'That's the way I like it.'

'Shows business is brisk,' he said smilingly.

'Steady rather than brisk,' she corrected him.

'I do admire you.'

Annie looked startled.

'Forgive me, what I mean is it can't be easy looking after the Beeches and a young child as well.'

'I'm used to it.'

'Even so it can't be easy. Someone mentioned to me that you are a widow.' He was leaning on the desk and looking at her with sympathetic eyes.

'Yes, my husband died some years ago,' Annie said quietly. The catch in her voice wasn't for Hamish, she had done her mourning and now he was just a memory. A dear friend now gone. The sympathy had brought the unsteadiness.

'When the young die it is such a tragedy and one feels a sense of outrage that the person has been denied a full life.'

She nodded. What he said was true, Miss Emily had been cut off in her youth, cheated of life. Mr Galloway meant Hamish, of course, but she couldn't bring herself to tell him that her husband had been old. Very old.

'It is a great sadness that one never completely gets over but, my dear, life must go on. I do know something of what you must have gone through. You see I, too, am alone, more alone than you are, I imagine.'

'I'm sorry,' she murmured.

'You have a child, I was denied the joy of fatherhood. My

wife couldn't have children. Poor Estelle was very delicate and very lovely,' he said softly. 'For a whole year, Mrs Brown, I lived with the knowledge that she wouldn't get well. I watched her grow weaker and weaker—' He broke off. 'I'm sorry I don't usually talk this way.'

'It's all right,' Annie said gently, 'I do understand.'

'I know you do, we have both suffered and that brings us closer. You are very kind which is, I suppose, why I find myself drawn to you. You are a woman, I think, who all her life has responded to the needs of others without thought to herself.'

She loved his quiet, beautifully modulated speech and dropped her eyes in case he could read what was there. She had an urge to reach out to him, to smooth his brow and comfort him. And, dear God, so much more than that. She loved him, wanted to feel his arms around her and to fill this void in her life she had been unaware of until now. Miss Emily had tried to explain what it was like to love someone so much that everything else became unimportant. It stripped pride away leaving a raw longing. She hadn't understood then, she did now.

'Thank you for being such a good listener.' He glanced at his watch and seemed surprised at what he saw there. 'Time I was on my way, more than time.' He sketched a salute and went out.

Annie watched him go, watched the door close then heard the footsteps die away.

Edward Galloway was smiling broadly and just stopped himself whistling. It was all so easy, so incredibly easy, but even so, he told himself, don't rush it. She's an innocent, but she's not stupid. One small mistake could put paid to his plans. He would have to go carefully remembering what he had said and keeping to the same story.

Annie was beginning to recover. Time to rid herself of the notion that Edward Galloway was interested in her as a woman. His late wife had been lovely and he had loved her dearly. As he had pointed out she was a good listener and just then he had needed someone. Be your age, Annie Brown, she told herself sternly, what would a handsome man-of-the-world want with plain ordinary Annie Brown except as a sympathetic ear. She was being pathetic and what would he think if he knew the thoughts that had been going through her head? She felt herself flush with shame.

In the weeks that followed Annie learned that Edward Galloway was in the antiques business.

'I don't make a fortune, Mrs Brown, a living wage and not much more.' He gave a rueful smile. 'I would do better if I didn't have such a kind heart but I just can't bear to see someone disappointed. When I see that almost desperate look I'm afraid I pay out more than the article is worth.'

Annie nodded, she could well believe it.

The Beeches was quiet in the residents' lounge with the only other occupant, Mr Cuthbert, slumped in a chair with his eyes shut. They thought he was asleep and were taken aback when there was a snort and his eyes opened.

'Bunch of rogues, the lot of them as I know to my cost. Fool that I was to trust them. They made a pretty penny out of me I can tell you.'

Edward Galloway was seething but no one would have guessed it.

'In every trade and profession, Mr Cuthbert, there are a few rotten apples and I'm sorry if you were the victim of one of them. The decent, honourable ones such as myself, deplore dishonesty in others. It gives us all a bad name.'

Mr Cuthbert grunted something Annie couldn't make out but brought a glint of anger to Edward Galloway's eyes. Annie smiled and excused herself. Edward went up to his bedroom. Just of late Annie had been thinking that a live-in maid would make life easier for her. When the staff went home she was on her own with no one to call on in an emergency. Mrs Archibald had her own small cottage and would not be interested. Gladys might but Annie knew that she would prefer Bridget. The girl seldom spoke of her home life and Annie gathered it was none too happy. The parents were forever at loggerheads, her two brothers were bone idle and all of them expected Bridget to clean up after them when she got home from work.

'Bridget?'

'Yes, Mrs Brown.'

The afternoon teas were over and they were in the kitchen.

'Pour a cup of tea for both of us then sit down. I want to ask you something.'

Bridget busied herself with the tea and sat down.

'Bridget, would it upset you to leave your home, leave your parents?'

'No, it wouldn't, not unless I was going to some place worse.'

'Would you call the Beeches worse?'

The girl's eyes were shining. 'You mean – you can't mean—'

'I mean, Bridget, that I am asking you to be a live-in maid. That storeroom on the top floor, there isn't all that much in it and if it was given a good clean out and a coat of paint do you think it would do you?'

'Do me? I should just think it would. When – when would it be?'

'Just as soon as we get the room organised. There is plenty of spare furniture and we'll choose what would be best. You'll get to choose where possible since it is to be your home.'

'I don't know what to say.'

Annie smiled; it had been how she had felt leaving the orphanage for Denbrae House. 'We'll get pretty curtains and two rugs for the floor.'

'Thank you very much.'

'We'll arrange your working hours so that you can have a social life.'

Bridget giggled. 'Whatever that means I don't have one. I hardly ever go out except to the pictures with my friend Nellie. I like going on my own to look at the shop windows.'

'I want you to be happy and remember this, Bridget, any worries no matter how small, you bring them to me. There is nothing worse than worrying alone.'

She nodded happily.

'Now drink your tea and eat up some of the leftovers.'

Annie never sat down with her lodgers for the nine thirty cup of tea and it was Edward who had suggested that she should. He said the guests would like it and he was right there. He had taken to lingering until the others had said good night and gone to their rooms.

'Don't go,' he said urgently as Annie got up.

'I must, I have work to do.'

'Nonsense, whatever it is can wait.'

'Was there something you wanted, Mr Galloway?'

'For a start when we are alone do you think you could bring yourself to call me Edward?'

'I could try.'

'And may I call you Annie?'

'Yes,' she said, feeling deliciously happy.

'This is so frustrating, there are so few times I can get you alone and another thing you have turned down both of my invitations.' He was frowning.

'That was unavoidable.'

He had known that, in fact had counted on her being too busy. Where would he have taken her? Whatever, it would have been an evening of boredom. When he took a woman to the theatre, Edward Galloway expected some return and was seldom disappointed. Annie could never send his pulses racing. She was the type that would permit a peck on the cheek and die rather than admit she wanted more. Even so he found she intrigued him and he wondered about her dead husband. Had there been passion in the marriage? Somehow he thought not.

'Can't we sit somewhere private where we won't be disturbed? And don't be alarmed, my intentions are purely honourable.'

'I didn't doubt but that they would be.' Annie was doing some quick thinking. This was her house, there was no one's permission she need ask and she trusted Edward. Where was the harm and what was wrong with taking him along to her sitting-room? The lodgers were in their own rooms and Bridget was more than likely in hers. Annie smiled to herself as she thought about Bridget. She loved her room and her new-found freedom. There had been ructions at home apparently when she had dropped her bombshell but she had stood firm and told them that from now on they could look after themselves. It was the first time she had stood up for herself and it was a nice feeling she was finding. 'Perhaps we could go to my sitting-room but only for a short time,' she said sounding as uncertain as she felt.

'You are thinking of your reputation?'

'More important I am thinking of the Beeches' reputation.'

'As I said, you have nothing to fear from me.'

Annie wished he wouldn't keep saying it and with such conviction. She wanted him to find her attractive and irresistible instead of just someone to talk to.

'Let me take this tray to the kitchen then I'll take you along to my living quarters.'

'Sounds like the army,' he grinned.

Annie turned away to pack the tray with the dirty cups and saucers. Bridget would see to them in the morning. When she returned from the kitchen Annie wanted to change her mind but she couldn't. It would make her look such a fool.

Passing Tina's bedroom door Annie put a finger to her lips.

He shook his head. 'Kids of that age wouldn't waken if the house fell about their ears. This is very nice,' he said appreciatively as they entered the sitting-room. She was pleased to see that he was impressed and it was genuine, she knew that. Edward knew good furniture when he saw it.

'You brought all of this with you to the Beeches?'

'Yes.'

His eyes settled on the doll's house and she saw him draw in his breath.

'My God! That's a real gem,' he said going over to it.

'Everyone admires it. My husband, Hamish, made the house for Tina.' Not true but where was the harm. A little white lie.

'I am having difficulty in imagining a young man having the patience apart from the skill to produce this.' He had opened the front and was studying the furniture with the eyes of an expert.

'Hamish was older than me,' Annie said quietly.

He looked at her thoughtfully and nodded. Annie was no actress and she was hiding something. A lot older, a very mature man unless he was mistaken and he didn't think he was. Pretty much on his last legs when the marriage took place or not quite that since he had fathered Tina. Or had he? Was the child already there or on the way? Had Annie given birth to a bastard and the old boy come to the rescue? Edward was sure now that he was on to something. Whatever way it had happened she had done well for herself. There must have been a fair bit of money to enable her to buy the Beeches. Edward was almost rubbing his hands. If he played his cards right he could be on to a good thing, his future secured. Once he knew her secret she would be in his power.

He had the dining-room table in the palm of his hand. 'This, Annie, is perfection, quite, quite exquisite. You don't allow the child to play with this I hope?'

Annie was annoyed. 'Why shouldn't I since the doll's house belongs to Tina? She has played with it since she was tiny and she is very careful.'

'Even so I most certainly wouldn't permit it.'

'You would keep it purely for show?'

'I would see that it was kept in perfect condition. Annie, I am speaking as an expert and I can recognise genius when I see it. In an auction this would cause quite a stir.'

Annie laughed. 'Hamish was very clever with his hands but he would have been amused at the very idea of someone calling him a genius. In fact he would have been embarrassed, my husband was a very modest man.'

'You have my word that you have a real treasure there.'

'I wholeheartedly agree it is a treasure and a work of love. No matter it is not for sale and never will be. I wouldn't let it go and neither would Tina and it is hers.'

'When she has outgrown it she will change her mind and discover that a bit of money in the bank would be more useful.' He paused. 'If I had anything to do with it I would see that it went to a genuine collector and one prepared to give you its true value. Believe me it needs an expert to deal with these people. Sorry! Sorry!' he said when he saw her face harden. 'I do get carried away I have to admit that.'

Annie relaxed. 'So I noticed,' she said and managed a laugh.

Edward put up his hand. 'Honestly, not another word about the doll's house,' he said giving the smile that made her go weak at the knees. What a fool the woman was, he thought, all that sentimental rubbish about not being able to part with it. Still that was enough on the subject for the time being. He put the little table back in position and closed the front of the doll's house. Annie was sitting in one of the armchairs and he took a chair nearby. 'I suppose my time is running out and we haven't even begun to talk about – us.'

Had he really said that? Or was it just wishful thinking? If he had said what she thought he said then it could only mean that he was seriously interested in her. He was a widower and she a widow and it could be that he was contemplating a second marriage. But to her, plain Annie Brown, it beggared belief that he could want her. No one would take the place of his first wife who had been lovely, but a second marriage could just be for companionship. He was lonely, he had said so. That would be enough for Edward, but would it be enough for her? How difficult would it be to love someone who didn't return that love?

'What thoughts are going on in that head of yours or am I not supposed to ask?'

She smiled and shook her head. 'That's right, you are not supposed to ask.'

'Then I won't but remember a trouble shared is a trouble halved so if ever you need someone I'm here.'

'Thank you.' Could she trust him? Had she known him long enough? Did it need time or did one know instinctively whom one could trust? Or there again was she blinded because she found him so attractive? To confess would be such a relief instead of being trapped as she was in her own guilt. Edward believed her dead husband, Hamish, to be the father of Tina and she could so easily be found out in that lie. Edward had only to mention the doll's house to Tina and like as not she would tell him her grandad had made it for her.

Later she was to wonder what stopped her. She had been at the very point of blurting it all out when it was as though Hamish had spoken from the grave. Reminding her of the dangers for Tina if the circumstances of her birth were to come out. Hadn't he told her to make a clean break, to get away from Dundrinnen and make a new life for themselves.

'Annie?'

She almost jumped. 'You were nearly asleep.'

'No, I wasn't,' she said indignantly.

'You have every excuse, you have been on your feet all day.' A wheedling note came into his voice. 'Why don't we get comfortable on that sofa and don't worry, I'll behave.'

'You had better—'

'Or no more invitations?'

'I see you understand the position perfectly,' she said and only hesitated for a moment before joining him on the sofa. She wished she didn't feel so uncomfortable and was sure she must look it. What must he be thinking? Either that she was cold or lacking in experience and how could it be the latter when she was a widow?

296

'Relax,' he said gently while moving her until her head was resting on his shoulder. 'Is that comfortable?'

'Yes,' she murmured and thought how inadequate the word was. This was heaven.

They were silent for a little while and when he turned his face to kiss her Annie felt herself responding and it was he who drew away.

'You are very sweet, my dear.'

'Am I?' No one had ever called her that before.

'And a little afraid. You shouldn't be, Annie, it is only natural when two people are attracted to each other that they feel this way.'

'Are you attracted to me?' she said wonderingly.

'More than attracted, my dearest, I am in love with you. More than anything I want to protect you and your child.'

'Protect? I don't need protecting.'

'Yes, you do, a young woman on her own is very vulnerable.'

It didn't apply to her but it was nice to feel cherished and she wouldn't spoil it by saying she was well able to take care of herself and Tina. What she did say was, 'It's getting late, Edward, and I think you should go.'

He got up immediately. 'Yes, you are quite right, it is time I went. I've rushed you and I didn't mean to.'

'No, you haven't but—'

'But you need time to think it over and more important you want me away.'

'I do, Edward, I want you away. If someone were to see you leaving my rooms—'

'They would draw the wrong conclusions.'

'I don't know, but I am not prepared to risk it.'

'Then pop your head out of the door and tell me if the way is clear for me to make my escape.'

She put a hand over her mouth to stifle the giggle. Opening the door she beckoned for him to go and after brushing her cheek with his lips he left quickly. Annie closed the door and stood with her back against it. Was she dreaming or had Edward proposed?

It was another three days before they were together again. This time they were alone in the residents' lounge and talking. They weren't whispering, just talking quietly with no danger of being overheard.

'Annie, the Beeches is very important to you, isn't it?'

'Of course. I love it and it is my living.'

'You run it very well, in fact I would go as far as saying that you are doing a wonderful job.'

'Thank you, Edward, thank you very much indeed.'

'But, my dear, far too much for one person.'

'Not at all, I manage very well.'

'Only because you work practically every hour God gave you.'

'Not quite as bad as that,' she laughed. Edward did exaggerate.

His face became serious. 'Nothing would give me more satisfaction than to help you with the Beeches and I have a good business head, even though I say it myself. Together we could do so much. Much more than you do now.' His hand covered hers. 'The potential is there and there is the room for expansion.'

'Edward, your enthusiasm is catching but I am a canny soul by nature. Expansion is not on the cards and I don't see it ever happening because I don't want it. The Beeches is popular because it is not too big. People describe it as a friendly guest house and it would lose that if I were to build on to the existing building.'

'I disagree completely. You would not lose the atmosphere but the Beeches would become more profitable.'

'I don't particularly want to make large profits. A comfortable living is all I ask and all I want.'

It was becoming increasingly difficult to hide his impatience. The woman was a complete fool. 'You really do need someone to look after you.'

'And Tina?' He seldom mentioned the child.

'That goes without saying.'

She wished he would say it. For all his easy charm, Edward didn't seem to be at ease with children. Of course that could be explained by not having any of his own. Some adults were at a loss as to what to say to children and that could well apply to Edward. When she had introduced Tina he hadn't shown much interest and for that matter Tina hadn't either.

The staff were well aware of the interest Mr Galloway was taking in their employer and they had their own thoughts about it. Bridget was worried and a bit uneasy. She had seen him slipping quietly out of Mrs Brown's sitting-room quite late at night. Nobody would ever hear that from her and it could be quite innocent. It was just she didn't trust him. Gladys now had a steady boyfriend, she was happy and she wanted everyone else to be. If Mrs Brown and Mr Galloway were having a bit of romance well where was the harm? They were both mature people. The cook was the one who worried most. Mrs Archibald saw the signs, the silly lass thought herself in love. She had always been neat and tidy but now she was taking more interest in her appearance. Couldn't she see, but, of course, she couldn't, folk in love were blind. Mrs Archibald could recognise a rogue when she saw one and Mrs Brown was not his kind of woman. Not that she wasn't pleasant-looking but she was ordinary. In his eyes she would be drab and the cook didn't need a crystal ball to tell her what he did want. He wanted the Beeches and the only way to get it was by marrying the woman. Once that happened, and she would do all in her power to see it didn't, then poor Annie Brown would be putty in his hands and as for that bairn God help her. Not interfering by nature Mrs Archibald wasn't going to find it easy but by heavens she would have a good try.

She was taking a rest in the chair with her strong short legs planted apart and her eyes closed. Behind her was a string of onions hanging from a hook. The fire was low but it was pleasantly warm. Annie came in with a cup and saucer and put them on the draining-board. Mrs Archibald opened her eyes.

'I was just having five minutes.'

'A well deserved five minutes. That was a nice piece of shortbread, Mrs Archibald.'

'The praise should go to Bridget, she made it. That lass is coming on grand.'

'She is a find and I must tell her I enjoyed her shortbread.'

This was as good a time as any and the older woman straightened herself in the chair. 'If you could spare me a few minutes, Mrs Brown?'

'Of course I can. What was it you wanted to say?' Annie said as she sat down at the table.

'It is very personal.'

Annie looked surprised. 'We could go somewhere where we wouldn't be disturbed.'

'That might be better.'

Annie got up. 'Come along to my sitting-room.'

'If you wouldn't mind.' She got up stiffly.

'I don't mind at all.' She was mystified.

Once seated and the door closed Annie looked at the cook expectantly.

'I'm a great one for minding my own business as you know but there comes a time, like now, when I can't.'

'In that case you had better tell me what is on your mind.'

'I wish it were easier and I know I am going to make a hash of it but I've gone this far—'

'For goodness sake say what it is.'

'I think too much of you to let you throw yourself away on someone who is not worthy of you.'

'You are referring to Mr Galloway,' Annie said coldly.

She nodded. 'Let me be brutally frank and tell you that the man isn't after you, it's the Beeches he has his eyes on.'

Annie was on her feet, her eyes flashing angrily. 'How dare you say such a thing. Anyone but you, Mrs Archibald, and they would be out that door a lot quicker than they came in.'

'It's a true saying about having to be cruel to be kind.'

'You have been cruel and I am going to find it difficult to forgive you. How very insulting to suggest that no man as attractive as Edward could possibly be in love with me.'

Mrs Archibald saw the pain in her eyes and the hurt in her voice and felt like weeping. She had probably done more harm than good and made her own position very awkward.

'I did not say that. If he was worthy of you, Mrs Brown, you would have my blessing.'

Annie's anger evaporated. 'I know you mean well but believe me Edward is good and kind.'

'Then get him to prove it.'

'What do you mean?'

'Don't jump down my throat but make it your business to find out if it is you or the Beeches that is the attraction. And remember Tina.'

'As if I would forget Tina. Tell me,' Annie said sarcastically, 'how I would go about—'

'Proving his worth. Easy done. Try telling him that the Beeches isn't yours or that you only own a small share.'

'That would be untrue.'

'Worth a little white lie I would think.' Mrs Archibald got up slowly, feeling wearied and drained. She had done her best but it had probably been in vain. Didn't love make fools of us all?

The next few days were uncomfortable. Annie was coldly polite to Mrs Archibald who in turn became equally cold to Annie. It was obvious the two had had words and Bridget was curious but knew better than to ask. For the first time the usually friendly atmosphere in the Beeches was absent.

Annie's mind was in a ferment and it was difficult for her to concentrate. It would never do to let her personal problems interfere with the smooth running of the Beeches and there was always a smile for her guests. To her shame she had been sharp with Tina who had burst into tears and had to be comforted.

Annie was well aware what it must have cost cook to say what she had, which could only mean she was genuinely worried. She had to appreciate that. Not many people had shown concern for her in the past. Mrs Archibald was wrong, very, very wrong. She was judging a man she didn't know. Annie had met quite a number of presentable men since coming to the Beeches but none had affected her like Edward. He had made her feel like a desirable woman. Others would open a door or be helpful in other ways but Edward did so much more. He would get to his feet quickly to take the tray from her. Then he would pour the tea declaring that the teapot was too heavy for her fine wrists. If only he knew about the heavy buckets of coal she had carried up three flights of stairs. No one had considered her fine wrists then.

How could she think ill of him, this man who could make the dullest day bright just because he was there?

Chapter Twenty-Two

She was trying hard not to make it obvious but every little while she was glancing over to the window to see if he was coming. Annie was behind her desk, a pen in her hand but doing no writing. At last she was rewarded when she saw his tall figure walking briskly up the path. No one was in the entrance hall when the door opened and getting up quickly she went over to greet him.

'I would love to kiss you, my dearest Annie, but I gather this is neither the time nor the place,' he said softly.

She flushed. 'Did you have a good day, Edward?' she asked and wished her voice didn't sound so shaky.

'In my line of business we only have highs and lows. Sadly for me more lows than highs.'

'You poor thing,' she smiled while she thought how well he looked in his well-cut city suit.

Edward was thinking how the smile transformed her. She was a plain young woman but unlike most plain women she made no effort to improve herself. He felt aggrieved that she hadn't thought to do so for him unaware that she had, but the effort had been small, so small he hadn't noticed.

It was almost nine in the evening and just about his usual time of arriving. Edward only booked in for bed and breakfast saying that dinner at six thirty was too early for him. That wasn't true but it served as an excuse. The food at the Tartan Tammy might not be as good, indeed it wasn't, but the company was more to his liking. There was also the question of a refreshment and he enjoyed a glass of good wine with his meal. There was no chance of that at the Beeches.

For the first time in her life Annie felt deliciously wicked and when he looked at her questioningly she nodded. Edward could be trusted to be discreet and Annie had the feeling that he was quite happy to have their romance kept a secret for the present. Romance was putting it a bit strong if measured in kisses and hugs but for that she could only blame herself. She had been too shy to give him the encouragement he needed and he was too much of a gentleman to rush her. All that would change when they announced their engagement. She thrilled at the thought of wearing his ring and actually belonging to someone. How wonderful to know that she would always come first with Edward. That was true love and how it would be for them.

There was one niggling doubt and that concerned Tina. The child must miss not having a daddy but would they get on? Tina didn't seem to like Edward and kept out of his way which was strange when she didn't do it to any of the other male guests. Still that would all change when they got to know each other better.

'See you later,' he whispered, 'and don't worry I'll be extremely careful.' He only just stopped himself winking.

All this secrecy was beginning to make Annie feel silly. This was her guest house, she was in charge, no one else. What she did was her own business. She nodded to Edward while promising herself that from now on she would be more open about their relationship. How little she knew about him. Edward seemed reluctant to talk about himself other than that time he had spoken about his wife and her illness. Since she disliked talking about her own early life she could hardly fault him if he was of the same mind. He could, however, be a bit more open about his business if only to say how long he was to be working in this district. The occasional question hadn't brought forth anything other than a frown and a change of subject. Men were strange creatures.

Edward went up to his bedroom to deposit his case and freshen up. Believing Annie would not approve of drinking Edward had taken to sucking a peppermint to keep his breath fresh. Once downstairs he had to brace himself. His drinking companions would think it hilarious if they could see him now. There was the usual friendly chatter while tea was served and the buttered pancakes handed round. Edward made himself useful by pouring the tea and declaring to everyone that the teapot was far too heavy for Mrs Brown's slender wrists. It came as a pleasant change to be treated as though she had never known hard work, laughable too.

Annie said good night and went along to her rooms. Edward waited a while longer, said his good night and when he saw that the coast was clear went quickly along the passage and into the door Annie had left off the catch. With the door closed he took her in his arms, kissed her lightly on the mouth then taking her face between his hands looked deep into her eyes. What he saw there excited him. Her eyes were melting with love and it would be so easy, so very easy to take her. He didn't see Annie putting up much resistance. Still better to be safe than sorry and not spoil his chances. He had to remember that Annie was very different from the women he was used to. So far he had been the perfect gentleman and that would have to continue.

Putting her gently from him he sighed, 'You are very desirable and I want you quite desperately but, my dearest, I am not going to take advantage of you.'

Annie thought she was drowning in happiness. Edward loved her, she was sure of it. Hadn't she heard his quickened breathing? Her own physical longing had been strong but she could fight that, the lessons of old hadn't been entirely forgotten. Maybe she should forget them, she was over thirty and a mature woman.

'I love you Annie and I'm asking you to marry me.' He smiled. 'You don't want me on my knees, do you?'

'No, Edward, that would not suit you at all,' she murmured.

'That doesn't answer my question, in case you hadn't noticed it was a proposal.'

'I know, dearest Edward,' she said touching his face, 'I love you, but—'

'But what?' he said managing but only just, to hide his exasperation.

'This is a big step for me and I do need a little time to think about it.' Why had she said that? She didn't need time.

'Annie, we are both mature people. Neither of us will ever forget our first love but we are not put on this earth to love only once. What we have is precious, don't let us throw it away.'

'I don't intend to,' she said softly, 'but give me a little while and then you shall have your answer.' Her head suddenly went up and she looked like a startled bird.

'What is the matter?'

'Tina. I think I heard her.'

'I didn't and what of it? She isn't a baby.'

'No, Edward, Tina isn't a baby but she is still a young child. She may have been dreaming and wakened up. To put my mind at rest I'll pop along.'

'If you must.' He tried to smile.

Her absence gave him an opportunity to look more closely at the room. The previous occasion had been spent examining the doll's house. The woman had good taste, he would give her that. Not in dress – dear God, no, what she wore was drab in the extreme, but in the furnishing of a room. The colour scheme was quiet and restful with clever touches to brighten. Once he had his feet on the fender so to speak he would make changes but not too many. The shelves held some expensive books and bringing one out he felt the soft leather. He returned it and moved away. It would be unwise to show too much interest at this stage.

Annie wasn't going to be the walkover he had expected. She came in.

'Well?'

'She must have been restless, the cover was on the floor so it was just as well I went in. Do sit down, Edward.' She was surprised to find him standing. 'Why so downcast?'

'Hardly surprising if I show my disappointment. Why wait? If you love me as you say you do I can't understand why you need more time.'

Annie was smiling to herself. How wrong Mrs Archibald had been to suggest the Beeches was the attraction and not herself. Just to show cook how wrong she was she would put Edward to the test. Later she would tell him the reason and they would laugh about it.

They weren't on the sofa but sitting in chairs on the opposite sides of the fireplace.

'Edward, I have not been entirely honest with you.'

'I don't follow.' He crossed his long legs and smiled to her. This would be about Hamish, about the marriage. He had sensed a mystery, that she was hiding something. Whatever her shameful secret he was about to hear it.

'It is about the Beeches.'

His eyes narrowed. 'What about the Beeches?' He was fully alert now.

'I told you a little lie, I let you believe that the Beeches is mine.'

'And isn't it?'

'My share in it is very small.' Her eyes had been laughing, they weren't laughing now. She was afraid. Never in her life had she seen such a change in anyone. He was furious, the veins in his forehead were bulging and he seemed to be beside himself with rage. Suddenly he was on his feet, towering above her and the rage was joined by a sinister look.

'You bitch, you lying little bitch, you've been stringing me along all this time pretending to be what you are not. Swanning about like a – like a—' He stopped, unable to go on, and she saw the spittle at the corners of his mouth.

Annie could only stare and when she spoke it was as though she was having to force every word out.

'This has all been a sham, you don't love me. It was the Beeches you were after.'

'Love you? A plain little thing like you,' he said scornfully. 'Do you really think I would have spared you a second glance if all you had to offer was yourself?' he ended cruelly.

Annie flinched and her face went deathly pale. Following him with her eyes, she let him go to the door, then she spoke.

'Edward?'

He turned.

'You are going to hate yourself. The Beeches is mine, I am the owner. You see someone who had my interests at heart warned me that you were not to be trusted and implored me to put you to the test. I very nearly didn't. You almost succeeded, Edward. I shudder just to think about my narrow escape. Your bill will be on your plate. Enjoy your last breakfast in the Beeches and I hope never to see your face again.'

The door closed but not before she had seen his agonised look. It was a small satisfaction.

Annie was pleased at her composure which deserted her the moment the door shut. She had got up to give her parting shot and her legs were trembling so much that she had to grasp the back of the chair before she could trust herself to walk to the tiny kitchen without staggering. She tried to keep her mind blank, just going through the motions. Filling the kettle, putting it to boil and making a pot of tea. Concentrating on that familiar task kept the horror of the last few minutes away. Back at her chair at the fire she sipped the tea with her hands around the cup for its comforting warmth. Only then did she allow herself to think.

What a fool she had been, what a stupid, stupid fool. She had acted like a lovesick young girl and she cringed at the memory. How he must have laughed. It had been a lesson to her, a hard lesson and one she would never forget. For her this had been no infatuation, she had loved Edward and if there was anything at all to be gained, anything to thank him for, it was that for a short time he had made her feel like a desirable woman. He certainly hadn't seen her as that, but believing herself to be had given her a new confidence. She wanted to hold on to that but didn't know if she could. Pride would help her hide her hurt but she vowed in those moments never to trust another man.

Sleep wouldn't come, she hadn't expected it to and she got out of bed in the morning with a dull headache and feeling depressed. Usually she ate breakfast in her own kitchen before starting the day's work. Later, when the guests had finished breakfast and those who were departing paid their bill, she would snatch a cup of tea with Mrs Archibald. This morning she ate nothing, the food would have choked her.

Had Edward had a sleepless night? What difference did it make whether he had or not. He would eat his breakfast, settle his account and go and she would keep well out of the way until she was sure he had gone. Gladys was capable of dealing with the bills, she had done so on several occasions when Annie hadn't been available.

'Good morning, Gladys.' She was removing the breakfast dishes.

'Good morning, Mrs Brown. I see Mr Galloway hasn't taken his bill and I saw him going off in a great hurry.'

'That's all right, just give it to me.' She took it from Gladys. It wouldn't be paid but she didn't care. Just to be rid of him was all she wanted. The dull headache had worsened to a throbbing pain. Two aspirins might help, then she would go along to the kitchen and make her peace with Mrs Archibald. Admitting to have been taken in by Edward would not be easy but she wouldn't shirk it. The cook had done her a great service.

Mrs Archibald looked up from her baking bowl when Annie came in.

'Leave that just now, Mrs Archibald, and we'll both sit down.'

The cook gave another stir to the mixture, then did as she was told but her eyes were wary.

Annie moistened her lips. 'I want to apologise to you. You were right and I was so very wrong,' she said unsteadily.

'No need for an apology, we all make mistakes.'

'But for you, mine might have been disastrous. He could have ruined me and all I've worked for. I see that now.'

'He didn't succeed, that is the main thing.'

'Thanks to you.'

'You've had a shock, that's for sure and you don't look well.'

'I'm all right apart from being humiliated.' She gave a mirthless laugh. 'Fancy me being stupid enough to believe that a personable man like Edward with his charm and he had plenty of that when he chose to use it,' she swallowed, 'could be in love with me. Or as he said himself spare me a second look. You told me and I should have believed you, only I didn't want to.'

'Now just a minute, Mrs Brown – no, I'm going to call you Annie for this conversation seeing as I'm old enough to be your mother, there are a few things we need to get straight.'

'A lot of things *I* need to get straight.'

'That's as maybe. I was talking about that man Galloway and no other. He wasn't in love with you because scum like him don't know the meaning of the word. There are women for his kind who understand his greed and are no better themselves.' She sniffed. 'You, Annie, need a man worthy of you and he'll come along one of these days.'

'No,' she said firmly, 'I am better off as I am. I trusted once and I'll never trust again.'

'Never is a long time.'

'You know,' she said brokenly, 'there I was thinking about marriage, a shared life, perhaps a family, the usual order of things and all he was interested in was getting his hands on the Beeches. Dreadful to say this but I would have gone on believing in him and before I knew what was happening the Beeches would have been his with me taking orders. Until the final order came for me to get out and make way for someone more decorative.'

Cook shook her head vigorously. 'Never, you wouldn't have let him win, you would have fought tooth and nail to make sure he didn't. If not for yourself then for Tina.'

'Fighting tooth and nail, what good would that have done? We both know that this is a man's world. They make the laws and mostly they stick together,' she said bitterly.

'More's the pity but in time that will change. I see it happening in small ways, Annie, women are beginning to know their worth and not before time.'

'Women have always known their worth,' Annie smiled, 'it's men they have to convince.' She paused. 'I did what you suggested though I very nearly didn't. The change in him when I told him the Beeches wasn't mine was frightening. I truly believe he could have killed me, he seemed to have lost control.' She took a long shuddering breath. 'He wasn't good with children but I put it down to shyness where the truth was he couldn't be bothered with them. Tina didn't like him and that should have been a warning to me.'

'Don't dwell on it, just be thankful he is out of your life and let me say this, he hasn't harmed you unless you let him. Brooding on it will mean he has won.'

'No, Mrs Archibald, I won't let that happen,' Annie said determinedly. 'What a comfort you are and I desperately needed to be able to talk about it.'

'There's times we all need a bit of help and I was there.'

'No one was ever there for me, Mrs Archibald, I've always had to fight my own battles. I was a foundling, you see, and there isn't much loving goes on in an orphanage. It is mostly just survival.'

Annie saw the sympathy in the other woman's eyes and perversely she didn't want it.

'I didn't know.'

'How could you? I don't talk about it, I never want to.'

'I understand and no one will hear it from me.'

'Being alone in the world has one advantage, it does build character. You sink or swim by your own efforts.'

'You are a plucky one.'

'I was lucky, luckier than some others.'

Mrs Archibald didn't think there had been much luck. She was deeply touched. Who would have guessed that the quiet and efficient owner of the Beeches had started life as a foundling. One day she would like to hear the whole story, it would be quite a tale, but that wasn't likely. Annie had said all she was going to.

'A little luck maybe but you are a fighter, Annie Brown.'

'Yes, but there comes the day when you get tired of fighting.'

'Right now what you are is tired. Sit where you are and rest, I'll make another cup of tea. The Lord knows what we would do without a cup of tea.'

Annie put her head back and closed her eyes. It was nice to let someone else take charge for the present.

Mrs Archibald was thinking that if she could get her hands on that man she would tear him from limb to limb. Some men were such brutes, she thought savagely, and some women weren't much better. The poor lass was taking it badly. He wasn't her first love since she was a widow and once the raw pain had gone Annie would put it down to another of life's experiences.

'Mummy?'

Annie was pale but once again in control.

'Yes, dear.' She smiled as she watched Tina change out of her school clothes and into what she called her playing clothes. 'Wait a minute, is that a stain on your good skirt?'

'I didn't drop anything.'

'Well, Tina, no one else has been wearing your skirt.'

'Maybe it got there all by itself.'

'Not very likely. Leave your skirt over the chair and I'll see to it later.'

'Mummy, you know that man . . .'

'What man?'

'You know, the one who is always smiling to you.'

Dear heavens! Even the child had noticed.

'No, I don't know.'

'Yes, you do, he makes you laugh.'

'Tina, I am pleasant to all my guests, if I wasn't they wouldn't come back.'

'I hope he doesn't come back, I don't like him and I wish you didn't.'

'Are you talking about Mr Galloway?'

She nodded, then began tying her shoe lace with all the concentration that needed.

'Mr Galloway won't be coming back to the Beeches.'

'Ever?'

'Ever.' Annie was getting a great deal of satisfaction from saying that.

'That's good,' she said and lost interest. 'We got our places and Ruth is top of the class.'

'Good for Ruth, her mummy and daddy will be very pleased.'

'Ruth is cleverer than me.'

'We can't all be good at the same things. Where are you?'

'About the middle.'

'That is nothing to be ashamed of,' Annie smiled.

'Were you clever at school, Mummy?'

'Not very, just about the middle.'

'Like me?'

'No, you are cleverer because you are very good at drawing.'

'Drawing is easy.'

'Not for everyone. It is easy for you because you are good at it.'

'Ruth let her daddy see my drawings and he liked them.'

'I'm sure he did.'

'Do you know what he said?' She giggled.

'No.'

'He said I might be famous one day and when I was he would have to give a lot of money to get one of my drawings. I like him, Mummy, I wish he was my daddy.'

'Mr Forbes is a very nice man.' A very thoughtful one, too, she thought. He always showed Tina that extra bit of attention. Phyllis did too, they were a very nice couple.

Chapter Twenty-Three

Once the children in Middlefield School reached the age of nine they were taught in a mixed class with more girls than boys. The girls occupied two rows and the boys one and a half. Miss Etta Nicholson was already known to the girls who had been taught by her the previous year, but not the boys who eyed her warily. Etta Nicholson was a statuesque woman, almost six feet tall with broad shoulders and nicknamed 'Big Ben' by the older pupils. Her fiftieth birthday was only months away and she was dreading it. As she remarked to her colleagues there was a huge difference between being forty-nine and being fifty. She had experienced it from thirty-nine to forty and felt she had aged ten years in one day. Her iron-grey hair waved softly and she wore it short with a side parting. The heavy side was kept in place by a long, narrow tortoiseshell slide.

Miss Nicholson was both liked and feared by those she taught. She had her own views on the way to teach and was not of the brigade that pounced on any child who fidgeted unless it continued too long. Who amongst us, she would say, does not, from time to time move our position to one more comfortable. The mothers of the less bright children adored her since she was one of the very few teachers who concentrated more on the slow learners believing the brighter ones required only minimum attention.

The school day was drawing to an end, the last lesson was over and only a few minutes remained.

'Girls and boys, since we have a little while before the bell goes I wondered if any of you had given thought to what you would like to be when you grow up.'

A number of hands shot up, their owners eager to be asked.

'Yes, Zena, we'll start with you.' Zena was a plump, pink and white and blonde child who was seldom without a bag of sweets in her pocket. It came as no surprise that her greatest wish was to serve in a sweet shop.

'And eat all the profits,' Miss Nicholson smiled. 'Now tell me what the correct name is for a shop that sells sweets?'

'A sweetie shop, Miss,' Zena said smiling to those around her. She didn't usually get the right answer.

'No, Zena, not a sweetie shop, a confectioner's.'

Zena nodded and sat down.

'Yes, Maisie, and there is no need to snap your fingers.'

Maisie was desperate to have her say. 'I want to be a typewriter, Miss, like my big cousin,' she said importantly.

Miss Nicholson had a quiet smile to herself. 'A typewriter is a machine, Maisie, you cannot be a machine. Your cousin is a typist. What is your cousin?'

'A typist, Miss.'

'Good, try and remember that.'

'Yes, Tina, we'll have you then it will be the boys' turn.'

'I like drawing and when I'm big I want to draw pictures and sell them.'

'You want to be an artist, Tina.'

'Yes, Miss.'

The teacher turned her attention to the boys. 'Hands up any boy who does *not* want to be an engine driver.'

Two hands went up but slowly and at that moment the bell went and there was a scuffle to see who could be at the door first.

The bellow wouldn't have shamed a sergeant-major.

'Back to your seats this instant. You will leave this

classroom in an orderly fashion unless you fancy being kept behind. And may I remind you that I am in no hurry to leave.'

Once they were seated and quiet she kept them a few minutes longer then indicated they could go. They filed out, the girls first and the boys, when the teacher's back was turned, giving them a shove to hurry them on their way.

After the exodus it was peace, perfect peace. Miss Nicholson went over to where the best work was pinned to the wall. Being Friday they had to come down to allow the school cleaners to do their job properly. The drawing pins went into the box and the children's work into the wastepaper basket, all except Tina Brown's drawings. Miss Nicholson had kept the best of those in her drawer. The child interested her. Not because she was particularly clever although if she put her mind to it she could do better. Her schoolwork was average which was perfectly acceptable and Miss Nicholson didn't push her. Unless she was very much mistaken this was a gifted child and one day soon she would take Tina's drawings to an artist of her acquaintance and get his opinion. He would tell her if the child was just good or exceptional.

She thought about the mother. Mrs Brown had been a surprise. Miss Nicholson had known a little about her, that she was the owner of the Beeches Guest House and a widow. The surprise was in seeing absolutely no resemblance between mother and child. Not all girls take after their mother but there is usually something, even a very small something, that shows the bond. There was none at all that Miss Nicholson could see. Tina was a very pretty child and graceful for one so young. One day she would be beautiful, make a good marriage and whatever talent was there would be kept as a hobby or just forgotten. The thought depressed Miss Nicholson.

Their first meeting had been on a parents' day. Miss Nicholson had with her a mental picture of a pretty young woman, tragically widowed. Mrs Brown turned out to be a neat woman, quite pleasant-looking with a nice manner and she clearly adored her child.

'Tina does quite well.'

'But she could do better,' Annie persisted.

'Couldn't we all, Mrs Brown?' Miss Nicholson smiled.

Annie smiled too. 'I want her to do well and have a good life.'

'Don't you want her to follow in your footsteps?'

'Far from it. No qualifications are necessary to look after a guest house.'

'You must have had some to make such a success of the Beeches. It has a very good reputation.'

'Thank you, but I want a lot more than that for Tina. I was a maid before I was married and when I lost my husband—'

'This was the work you felt you were cut out for?'

'Yes, it is hard work but I have never been afraid of that.'

'As I said, Mrs Brown, Tina is an average pupil but she is also, in my opinion, and I must stress that it is only my opinion, a gifted child. Her drawings are quite remarkable.'

'A few people have said so.'

'Where does she get it? Have you an artist in the family?'

The same question and how best to answer it. 'Tina's father was that way inclined . . .' She hesitated.

'But he died so young,' Miss Nicholson said sympathetically. The woman wasn't comfortable talking about her late husband. Perhaps she still hadn't come to terms with his death.

'Yes.' Annie paused and looked at the woman as they stood together in the school hall. 'Could Tina be a teacher, I mean . . .' she floundered.

'An art teacher? Not very likely. There aren't many specialist teachers and most of those would be men. That said I think Tina should have lessons if you are agreeable?'

'Perfectly agreeable,' Annie said eagerly. 'I am quite prepared to pay.'

Etta Nicholson was already regretting saying so much and

raising hopes before she was sure. 'Mrs Brown, we should leave this for the present. I have an artist friend who will give me his honest opinion of Tina's drawings. I can rely on him being brutally frank. It has lost him friends.' She smiled. 'Folk ask for an honest opinion and when that is what they get they cannot accept it.'

'May I be guided by you, Miss Nicholson? If your friend thinks Tina is good enough would you advise me what to do, I mean where she should go for lessons?'

'I'll be happy to help in any way I can and as for tuition if my friend is sufficiently impressed he may well be prepared to give an hour or two of his time. He would expect to be paid but I don't see him asking too much.'

'The money won't be a problem, Miss Nicholson.' Could she ever have believed that those words would come from her lips?

David Marshall, artist and picture restorer, rented three rooms in Provost's Lane where he worked, slept and occasionally entertained young artists down on their luck and in need of a good feed and encouragement. Or it could have been one who had sold his first painting and wanted to celebrate and thank David Marshall for having faith in him and bullying him to keep on when he had been on the point of giving up.

'Well, Etta, what brings you here? Bend the head, woman, these doors—'

'Were meant for midgets,' she said crisply. She didn't have to lower her head but it was a close thing. Etta sat down on a hard, wooden chair without being asked. David Marshall and Etta Nicholson had been friends for many years and were completely at ease with one another. They didn't stand on ceremony.

'Have a look at these, David, if you will,' she said handing him half a dozen drawings.

'Who is the budding artist?'

'One of my pupils, a nine-year-old child.'

He nodded and looked at them, then spread them over the table. 'Interesting.'

'Is that all?' she said disappointed.

'What did you expect?'

'In my humble opinion I thought they were very good.'

'Who said they weren't?'

'No one, but interesting is not exactly being bowled over.'

'I never get bowled over as you call it, Etta. Here we have the drawings of a nine-year-old child – boy or girl by the way?'

'Girl and that shouldn't make a difference,' Etta said severely.

'It doesn't with me.' He paused. 'I said interesting and I do mean interesting and that, believe me, is high praise.'

She smiled with relief. 'You are an old rogue.'

'Not much older than you. Don't you celebrate your half century this year?' He raised bushy eyebrows.

'Be quiet about that, I don't like to be reminded.'

'Women are so silly about their age. It is nothing to be ashamed of. This child has a name?'

'Tina Brown.'

'I would say that Tina might well be a gifted child, it is too early to say but certainly there is promise. She is leaping ahead though, trying to do too much and that is a danger.'

'Would you be prepared to give her an hour or two of your time? Her mother is agreeable.'

'But am I?'

'David, you always have time.'

'Sadly that is true. Alas there aren't too many people buying paintings these days.'

'Then a few shillings would come in useful?'

'You could say that. The kettle is boiling. Isn't it the woman's place to make the tea?'

'Not in a bachelor's establishment, but I'll make an exception in your case.'

'Good girl. You might find some biscuits unless you came prepared and brought some?'

'Never crossed my mind,' she said getting up to make the tea.

'Have your child prodigy and her mother come to see me next week and we'll work something out.'

'Thanks, David and that milk is off.' She put down the jug with a grimace.

'How can you tell?'

'Just by looking at it.'

'No matter, I can take mine without. How about you?'

'Seems I'll have to or do without.'

'Mummy, what is his name again?'

'Mr Marshall.'

'And he's a real artist?' She had to ask that again.

'Yes, Tina, Mr Marshall is a real artist and we have your teacher to thank that he is prepared to see us.'

'Will it be like school?'

'I don't know what it will be like, but it is time we were on our way.'

'Mummy?'

'What is it now?'

'I feel sick.'

'No, you don't, it is just excitement. Take a deep breath and you'll be all right.'

Provost's Lane wasn't so far away, no more than ten minutes' walk from the Beeches. If Tina was to get tuition she would manage to get herself there and back unless in the winter when the days were short and darkness fell before the lamp lighters got round. That made Annie think again about employing a mature woman to relieve her of some of the responsibility. Gladys would shortly be leaving to get married and another housemaid would have to be engaged. The Beeches was doing very well, she knew that and so did the bank manager. She could afford to ease up if she could get the right person. Phyllis might know of someone, she had helped in the past. What was important was to spend more time with Tina and help her the best way she could.

'Is this it, Mummy?' Tina sounded disappointed.

'Yes, artists don't as a rule live in mansions.'

'Is that because they are too poor?'

'No, probably because they don't want to.'

The front door, painted chocolate brown, was directly on to the lane. Prominently placed on it was a piece of card fixed to the door by two drawing pins. In black ink were the words, KNOCK AND ENTER.

Tina giggled. 'Anybody could go in.'

'Sh-sh.' Annie gave a sharp knock then turned the knob and they went into a narrow passage with linoleum on the floor.

'In here, first door on the left.'

Annie thought it a strange welcome but did as requested.

'Mr Marshall, I'm Mrs Brown,' she said hesitating at the open door.

'Come in and you, too, Tina. Forgive my bad manners but I am just wiping the paint off my hands, not very successfully I'm afraid, so we had better forego the formality of shaking hands. Take a seat both of you and Tina, you're wee so you sit on the stool.'

David Marshall was a small man, not much taller than Annie. He wore a smock, heavily paint-stained, and in Tina's eyes that immediately made him an artist. Her eyes were huge in her small face as she looked about her. She loved the clutter, a friendly clutter while her mother was wondering how anyone could work in the midst of such chaos. The artist sat down and his expression was kindly as he watched the child.

'What makes you think you could be an artist, Tina?'

Tina looked at her mother but she was getting no help. 'Drawing is what I like doing best of all.' Was he waiting for her to say something else? 'I think I'm good at it,' she said in a rush.

'Having confidence in yourself is important and it is even more important, Tina, to realise that it takes many years of hard work before you can call yourself an artist.'

'Did it take you a long time, Mr Marshall?'

'Tina?' Annie said warningly. She wouldn't mean to be cheeky but Mr Marshall wasn't to know that.

'No, Mrs Brown, don't scold the child – that was a sensible question and one worthy of a reply. Yes, my dear, a very long time. Occasionally I used to wonder if it was all worth while but, of course, it was. There was nothing else I wanted to do.'

Tina was smiling.

'And that smile means you are of the same mind?'

She nodded happily.

David Marshall turned his attention to Annie. 'An hour twice a week should do to begin with, Mrs Brown. Let us say Wednesdays after school and Saturday mornings at ten o'clock. I'm suggesting Saturday because she will be fresh and after school she won't.' His head turned to Tina. 'You have Miss Nicholson for your teacher?'

'Yes and I like her.'

'You would have to say that, wouldn't you?' he said roguishly. 'Or who knows, I might say something.'

Tina was taking it seriously. 'It's true, Mr Marshall, I do like Miss Nicholson and I'm not just saying it.'

'I know,' he laughed.

'Mr Marshall, I would like to pay in advance.' Do that and there would be less chance of him changing his mind.

'No, that would be unwise. I'll give Tina a wee note when I want payment and don't worry I won't overcharge you.'

'Don't undercharge,' Annie said with a smile. 'I don't so why should you?'

They were moving to the door. 'One more thing before you leave. Tina will require an artist's tools.'

'How do I go about getting those?'

'I could do that for you but then again I might spend more than you bargained for.'

'Mr Marshall, buy what is necessary and don't bother about the expense.'

'A rash statement indeed.' He shook his head. 'She won't

need all that much at this stage. Tina, I will see you at ten o'clock on Saturday and do as your mother did, knock and come in.'

'You have a notice on your door.'

'Which is coming down, that was for your benefit.'

'Mummy, I like him,' said Tina as they left.

'I do too.'

'I wish he didn't have the easel facing the other way, I wanted to see what he was painting.'

'Perhaps he didn't want you to see it.'

Phyllis Forbes had called at the Beeches and was in Annie's sitting-room. They had been talking about Tina going for art lessons.

'Money well spent I would say, Annie. I don't know David Marshall personally but from what I gather he wouldn't waste his time unless he was convinced that Tina was very good.'

'He might be glad of the little extra. With artists it is difficult to know. He doesn't live in comfort if his studio is anything to go by. Honestly, Phyllis, I've never seen such an untidy room.'

'Don't get any ideas about cleaning it. Artists are supposed to work better in a muddle but enough about them, that wasn't why I came. James thinks he may know someone who would suit you.'

'Oh!' Annie brightened.

'Jemima Urquhart, maiden lady, trustworthy, pleasant manner and looking for that kind of work.'

'If James said so she must be all right.'

'I wouldn't go that far but it might be worth seeing her and then you can make up your mind.'

'Has James mentioned the Beeches to her?'

'Annie, he wouldn't do that, not until he had your permission. What he did say was that he knew of a possible vacancy that might interest her.'

'Is she local?'

'No, although she is now. She has just come to live here. If I recall correctly an aunt died and left her the cottage and rather than sell it she has decided to settle here.'

'She might be ideal, Phyllis.'

'And she might not. Shall I set the wheels in motion and arrange an interview?'

'Please do, make it any time that suits – what was the name again?'

'Miss Jemima Urquhart.'

'Whatever time suits Miss Urquhart.'

Jemima Urquhart was punctual for her appointment. She was a quietly spoken woman of medium height dressed in brown. A brown tailored suit worn with a tussore blouse, brown hat with a brown feather, brown flat shoes with a crossbar and light brown lisle stockings.

'Are you comfortable there?'

'Yes, thank you.'

'Miss Urquhart, what qualifications have you for this position?' How pompous that sounded. Was she becoming pompous?

'My parents ran a bed and breakfast – oh nothing like the Beeches but I imagine the work to be similar.'

'Yes, it would be. Did you do the cooking for your boarders?'

'My mother did that until her health failed and then it fell to me. Breakfasts I could manage but I wouldn't call myself a cook.'

'You wouldn't be called on to do that other than in an emergency. We have Mrs Archibald who is excellent.'

'What would the job entail, Mrs Brown?'

She is well-spoken, better than I am, Annie thought, and that can only be good for business. 'What would the job entail? In time I would like you to relieve me of some of the responsibility of running the Beeches.'

'You want to take it easier?'

'Yes, I suppose I do but mostly it is so that I can spend more time with my young daughter.'

'How old is your daughter?'

'Nine.'

'An interesting age.'

'Yes, I think so.' She paused. 'Among other duties I would like you to see that the maids do their job properly, that the bedrooms are spotless and the beds neat and tidy.'

'I'm particular, I can say that. Should you wish to consider me you would need references.'

'Mr Forbes speaks for you and I need no more than that.'

'Did he tell you that I inherited a small house from an aunt?'

'Yes, and I believe it isn't far from here.'

'Walking distance though I do like to cycle in the good weather. There isn't a lot I can tell you about myself other than to say I am thirty-six years of age and a good worker.'

'You can tell me why you gave up the bed and breakfast.'

'Oh, that, I was tired of it. That was where I was brought up. My father had a small job as well as helping Mother with the lodgers. With brothers and sisters it might have been easier but being an only one and a girl I had to help from a very early age. When I left school I was given no choice, it was just taken for granted that I would continue to help my parents.'

'And this you resented. It wasn't the kind of employment you wanted?'

Miss Urquhart looked surprised. 'I haven't explained myself very well. I do like looking after boarders or guests but this, the Beeches, was the sort of place I wanted. My parents had no ambition, they made a comfortable living and the thought of moving to a better district, trying to improve themselves, never entered their mind. I did my duty as a daughter, Mrs Brown, and when first my father died and then my mother I decided to sell up, have a good holiday and then consider what I should do. There was no hurry, I am not penniless and then my aunt died and as she said she would, she left me her house.'

'You are being very frank.'

'I want to be, it is only fair to you. If you are to employ me you need to know the kind of person I am.'

Honest and straightforward, Annie thought and made up her mind quickly. She liked this woman and had a feeling she could trust her. No one would take advantage of Miss Jemima Urquhart. There was a steeliness but kindness too.

'I think we might suit each other very well, Miss Urquhart, and I am offering you the position if you find the terms agreeable.'

'Perfectly agreeable and I accept,' she said simply.

'When can you start?'

'Could we say the beginning of the month, Mrs Brown? My aunt was a dear old lady and a dreadful hoarder. Nothing was thrown away and I do mean nothing. There was always the chance it could come in useful.'

'Well they do say keep a thing for seven years and you'll find a use for it,' Annie laughed.

'She certainly thought so. I'll keep a few bits and pieces for sentimental reasons and the rest will be disposed of. It's not long since I got rid of everything at home and now I'm looking forward to choosing what *I* want.'

Annie got up to show the interview was at an end and they shook hands.

'I quite envy you furnishing your house exactly as you wish.'

'Only myself to blame if I make a bad buy. Thank you, Mrs Brown, I look forward to coming to the Beeches and I'll make sure you don't regret engaging me.'

Tina would long remember her first painting lesson with Mr Marshall. A friend of Mrs Archibald's had made Tina a pale blue smock with deep pockets and she was in seventh heaven. Not only did she feel like an artist but now she looked like one. On that first visit Tina hadn't required to knock. Mr Marshall had the door open and she was just the teeniest bit disappointed. It would have been very grown-up to knock on the door then open it and go in.

'Saw you from the window, Tina.'

'Did you?' She was overcome with shyness.

'You were running, weren't you?'

'Sort of. I didn't want to be late.'

'Come in and let me get the door shut.'

Tina stepped in quickly and followed him into his studio. The first thing she saw was the plate of biscuits on the table.

'Remember this, Tina, there is no need to run. Artists are not concerned about time the way others are. This is put down to arrogance and bad manners which it is not. We can't just put the brush down in the middle of painting. There is no such thing as starting where you left off.'

Tina agreed with everything he said. Artists could be excused because — well they were different.

'I don't think it is what you said it was or bad manners.'

'You wouldn't call it arrogance, what would you say it was?'

She didn't know how to answer that. 'You can't stop, you have to finish,' she said when it became obvious he was waiting for her to answer.

'Exactly. We are going to get on splendidly I see. Help yourself to biscuits and I'll let you see what I've got for you.'

She took a biscuit and bit into it. Turning away Mr Marshall brought an old wooden box from a shelf and put it on the table.

'That was my box when I first started to paint and mighty proud of it I was. Now it is yours, Tina.'

'For keeps?' she said round-eyed.

'Yes, Tina, for keeps.'

'Thank you very much.'

'We'll keep it here. For one thing it is too heavy to carry around and for another I don't want you wasting good material.'

'I wouldn't and anyway Mummy will buy more.'

'Your mother is a very generous lady and you are a lucky lass but we are not going to put her to unnecessary expense.'

He opened the box with all its divisions. 'That's the oil paints in those tubes.'

'What is that and that?' she pointed.

'Linseed oil and the other is turpentine.'

'The brushes are all different,' she breathed.

'And all necessary,' he said, then he shut the box. 'Meantime you will make use of what I have but when you come again bring some old pieces of rag.'

'What is the rag for?'

'To wipe the paint from your hands before you go home. I'm always running out of them.'

Tina made a mental note that she would get her mummy to collect a whole lot of rags for Mr Marshall.

'Of course you have paints and crayons and sheets of paper at home?'

'Yes.'

'That is all you need. While you are here you will work to instruction but at home paint or draw whatever you fancy.' He grinned. 'That is called free expression.'

She looked puzzled.

'Never mind.'

Her eyes kept wandering to the paintings finished and unfinished and stacked against the wall. The table with the plate of biscuits was very old and had blobs of dried paint. Her mummy would have thrown it out or got someone to chop it up for firewood. There was a clutter of letters some in their envelopes and others lying open and scraps of paper. There were sketches and a broken photo frame together with a half empty cup of cold tea.

'Take another biscuit.'

'No, thank you.'

'There speaks a well brought-up little girl.'

She giggled.

'Come on we'll both have one before you get paint on your hands.'

She took one.

'Tina, what do you most like to draw?'

'Faces,' she said looking into his.

'You want to be a portrait painter?'

She nodded. 'Sometimes I draw Mummy and she doesn't mind but once I did a drawing of one of the guests and she was a little bit angry.'

'Why?'

'Mummy said it was rude and people didn't like it. Why don't they, Mr Marshall?'

'Some don't mind, in fact they might feel flattered. Others might be a bit sensitive. Drawing attention to a person's bad points would hardly endear them to you.'

She nodded as though she understood perfectly when in fact she didn't.

'Are you a portrait painter, Mr Marshall?'

'No, I wouldn't call myself that although I have done a few on request and they were well received. That is not the same as saying they were very good. Landscapes and local beauty spots are what I usually paint. Visitors buy them to take home as a souvenir of a happy holiday.' He paused and smiled. 'And so to work, this is not what your mother is paying for.'

The lessons were going well and for part of the hour she watched him at work. He worked in silence as she was quick to learn. Then when he had executed some detail to his satisfaction and knowing she was longing to ask questions, he would relent and answer them. Tina listened carefully to his explanation of colour and light, understanding some of it but not all. There was so much to learn. David Marshall was very impressed with his young pupil and gloried in her enthusiasm. He gave her every encouragement but was never lavish in his praise believing too much of it would be bad. Looking over her shoulder he would comment on what she was doing.

'Quite good, Tina.'

'I think it looks like Ruth, she is my friend.'

'A nice face but she doesn't look alive.'

'Why doesn't she?' Tina was peeved, she thought this one was by far her best.

'Because you haven't brought her to life.'

'How can I do that?'

'By giving more attention to the eyes. Look, let me show you.'

She watched but didn't quite follow what he had done. It made a difference, she had to admit that.

'I wish I could do that.'

'That will come. So much I can teach you but the rest must come from yourself. No two artists are alike, Tina, we all have our own technique.'

'If I work very, very hard will I ever be as good as you?'

'One day you may well be better.'

'When I'm a real artist I am going to have a studio just like yours and no one is being allowed to clean it.'

'And what would your mother have to say to that I wonder?'

'I know,' she said glumly. 'She wouldn't understand, only artists would.'

What a delightful child she was, he thought. Sometimes so serious that he would forget her immaturity until she came out with a childlike remark and he would realise he had been talking over her head.

'Mr Marshall, I am going to work on this until it is perfect.'

'No, Tina, you may strive for perfection but it will always be beyond your grasp.'

'But not for famous painters?'

'Yes, for them too. We recognise genius but that is not perfection. Only God's hand can produce what is perfect.'

When they were engrossed teacher and pupil would lose all sense of time and at the Beeches Annie would look at the clock and bless the day she had engaged Jemima Urquhart. The woman had settled in quickly and worked efficiently, taking over much of what Annie had done previously.

Annie put on her coat. There was no danger of missing Tina on the road since they used the direct road rather than the quicker but poorly lit lane.

That first time Tina had been distinctly annoyed. 'You don't need to come for me, Mummy,' she raged, 'I can manage on my own.'

'Now! Now! Tina, your mother is perfectly right and it is much too late for little girls to be out on their own.'

'I'm not a little girl,' she protested.

'Yes, you are and you will be for a year or two yet.'

Annie looked at him gratefully. She didn't want to appear an overprotective mother. Tina went to get her coat from the stand in the narrow lobby.

'Actually, Mrs Brown,' he said quietly, 'you can put your mind at rest. If Tina was over her time and that would be my fault, then be assured I would deliver her safely to the Beeches.'

'I couldn't have you doing that, your time is precious.'

'No more than yours I imagine.'

'I have a very able assistant and besides I enjoy the outing.'

Chapter Twenty-Four

Annie wondered just where the time had gone. The years had just slipped away and they had been good years. The loan to the bank was cleared and the Beeches was truly hers. It was a very nice, satisfying feeling. Poor Mr Cuthbert had died in hospital. Towards the end he had been too ill to know anyone, but Annie continued to spend time at his bedside holding his hand. The slight pressure she sometimes felt made her think he was aware of her presence with this his only way of telling her.

Annie was so proud of Tina. At thirteen she was a lovely girl with absolutely no airs or graces. Ruth, and most of their contemporaries, were greatly concerned with their appearance and the latest fashions which they longed to be old enough to wear. Tina had no such interests, they bored her though she was careful not to make it obvious. She had always known herself to be different and was glad to be. Only to please her mother did she occasionally go out with her school-friends.

'There is no more I can teach her, Mrs Brown. Tina would do as well working by herself at home.'

'Please don't say that, Mr Marshall, Tina would break her heart if her lessons with you were to stop. And it isn't only the lessons, she likes to talk to you about art.'

'Yes, she does and I have to admit that I would miss her coming and our talks.'

'Then carry on as you are doing and that will please me very much.'

'If you would like my advice?'

'I would.'

'We, or rather you, should be thinking about enrolling her at a good art college where she could go when she finishes school.'

'If she gets a place. Girls, I gather, are not always welcome.'

'That is true I'm afraid, but I believe that is changing although very, very slowly. The fees—'

'Not a consideration,' Annie said airily and laughed at herself. 'It wasn't always that way, Mr Marshall, there was a time when I would have looked twice at a penny before spending it. Not having to do that now gives me a wonderful feeling. Not so much for myself, my wants are modest, but for what it can do for Tina.' She frowned. 'Speaking of the little madam, she was determined she was going to leave school at fourteen and I was equally determined she was going to stay on.'

He was laughing. 'Who won?'

'A compromise I think you would call it. The best possible education was what I wanted for her but I agreed reluctantly that she could leave at fifteen.'

'Fifteen should work out well, Mrs Brown. Tina could go straight on to art college.'

'You can't be sure she will be accepted.'

'That's true but I'll put in a good word for her. Fifteen is young but they might be prepared to waive the rules if they consider she has a major talent.'

A major talent! Her Tina! Annie experienced a delicious feeling of pride and excitement.

'You really think she is that good?'

'I do, but that doesn't mean she will automatically succeed. It means years of very hard work. Tina is young and pretty and some young man may steal her heart and become more important to her than painting.'

'You mean her painting will suffer?'

'That is the likelihood. Art is a hard master and demands total commitment.'

'She is only thirteen,' Annie smiled.

'And a lot can happen before she need give serious thought to her future.' He was looking very serious.

'Surely you don't believe the rumours? We can't be on the brink of war.'

'I don't know, Mrs Brown, these are dangerous times and I just hope the powers that be know what they are doing.'

The rumours were proved to have substance and on a Sunday in August 1914 everyone knew the gravity of the situation and reacted in different ways. Annie read the newspapers and tried to make sense of it all. She just wished that countries, like folk, would mind their own business and leave others to do the same. Why should it be a concern of ours if some Archduke Ferdinand of Austria got himself assassinated in Sarajevo by a Serb? Yet that appeared to have started a whole chain of events that was going to mean war.

Everyone was affected. It could be seen in their faces, an anxiety and a feeling that they could be on the brink of an unknown terror. Men were openly discussing war and how it should be fought. The older, wiser ones kept quiet. Some had experience of war and shivered at the memory. The young showed an eagerness to get involved and fretted in case it was all over before they could don a uniform and fight for king and country. Mothers and wives lived with the constant dread of seeing their menfolk go off to war.

Annie was a spectator. She felt deeply for others, but there was no one close to her who would be going off to fight. Her worry concerned the Beeches. A guilty worry when she compared it with what so many were suffering. Was the end in sight? The end of the Beeches.

All over by Christmas, the optimists were saying and when that didn't come to pass it was to be Easter. Then they stopped trying to forecast the end of the war as the months turned into a year then two.

Perth and Dundee were seeing plenty of activity with army reservists and volunteers crowding into the barracks. Hospitals were on the alert with only emergency cases being treated. And then it was the heartbreaking sight of the wounded arriving.

There were no regulars coming to the Beeches. Annie thought about her former boarders changing their smart business suits for a uniform, an ill-fitting one unless they were officers. Mrs Archibald, less able now, was teaching a very willing and able Bridget how to cook with a view to her taking over in the not-so-distant future. Both maids had gone off to make more money in munitions. Annie had reluctantly allowed Tina to leave school and she was doing the work of a maid. Annie could have wept.

'Miss Urquhart, I'm so sorry but I am going to have to let you go. You can see for yourself how it is.'

'I am not going, Mrs Brown, the war won't go on for ever.'

'That is what it seems like,' Annie said wearily.

'Since I do very little work I can hardly expect to take a full wage. We must just look on the bright side and hope that business will improve,' she said briskly.

It did and in a most unexpected way. The comfortably-off in the large houses were finding themselves without staff or having to make do with someone totally unsuitable. The solution, they decided, was to close up the house for the duration and take up residence in a guest house. The Beeches with its reputation for comfort was the first to have its bedrooms taken. Annie and Miss Urquhart thrived on the activity and did everything possible to make their guests feel at home. They, in turn, were no longer afraid in a large empty house and in the evenings there was a family atmosphere.

Annie could have charged more but she didn't. She didn't want to be accused of making money out of another's misfortune. A small increase was necessary with food prices rocketing the way they were. The lovely flowerbeds were no longer. Two elderly men arrived one day to dig them up and plant potatoes and vegetables. The afternoon teas had ceased long ago but in their place Annie had organised working teas. Everyone wanted to help, to make a contribution, but it was lonely working on one's own. Those round the doors joined the guests to knit scarves, mitts and balaclavas and it was amazing the number that was despatched from the Beeches. Phyllis Forbes didn't come, she said she was hopeless at knitting but she went three days a week to Perth to help out in the hospital. With no nursing experience she was very often given the less pleasant tasks which sometimes turned her stomach but she never complained. Not when she saw those poor, poor boys.

With so much going on and hardly a minute to herself, Annie had completely forgotten what she had promised herself to do. First she was to tell Tina when she was twelve, then it was put off until she would be thirteen. Annie cursed herself for the coward she was. Telling a younger Tina would have been so much easier. She had no one to blame but herself. Tina must be told now.

'Tina?'

'Yes, Mother.' When she was twelve Tina had decided that Mummy was too babyish.

'Finish what you are doing, dear, then come along to our sitting-room.'

'What for?'

'A little talk.'

'Why now, can't it wait?'

'No, and no more arguments, please. I am going to make a cup of tea.'

'Here I am,' she said bursting in.

'Sit down and take this tea.'

Tina took the cup and saucer and put them on the small table. 'This gets stranger and stranger,' she muttered.

Annie closed her eyes and prayed for guidance.

'This is very difficult for me, Tina, and is why I have put it off so long.'

'Put what off?' She had been about to take a sip of tea but put it down untouched. She was going to hear something awful and suddenly she was afraid.

'You are ill, there is something wrong with you?'

'There is nothing wrong with my health.'

'Then it can't be all that bad,' she said cheering up.

'Tina, I am not your mother, not your real mother.'

She watched the colour drain from Tina's face.

'What are you saying?' she whispered.

'It's true, Tina.'

'It is not, I don't believe it.' Her voice had risen.

'Darling, I couldn't love you more if you had been my own child.'

Tina stumbled to her feet and Annie got up too. Then they were sobbing in each other's arms.

'Why did you have to tell me?' she wailed.

'I had to, Tina. Until now I haven't had to produce your birth certificate but that becomes necessary when you get married. It would be far worse for you to discover it then.' Annie gulped down some of her tea. They were both sitting. 'Will you promise me something?'

'What?'

'That you'll listen to the story, all of it and try not to interrupt. It is important to me that I don't omit anything. You need to hear it all, Tina, and my part in it. Maybe you'll hate me for it but what I did, I did for the best.'

As she listened Tina's expression kept changing but she didn't interrupt the flow of words. When she came to the end Annie was exhausted. She looked at Tina but she remained silent.

'I'm so sorry, my darling, so very sorry if you feel I have cheated you.'

'Cheated me? What are you talking about? If I'm speechless it is because I am lost in admiration. You are the bravest, most wonderful, most unselfish woman and oh, I just wish—' Her voice broke.

'What do you wish, Tina?' Annie said gently.

'That you really were my mother.'

'I am. I just didn't give birth to you, that's all. But, Tina, don't ever forget your real mother. She was the brave one. Miss Emily was so kind, so lovely—'

'Why do you keep calling her Miss Emily? Why not just Emily?'

'It wouldn't seem right to me.'

'Well, I don't like it,' she said irritably, 'it makes you sound like a servant.'

'Which was what I was.'

'You aren't now.'

'Tina, I started work as the lowest of the low, a scullery-maid and at the time I was proud to be that.'

'Where are they – Emily's parents or are they dead?' She made it sound as though she hoped they were.

'Your grandparents, Tina.'

'Never! Mr and Mrs Cunningham-Brown, that's what they are to me. They were horrible to their daughter Emily.'

'You shouldn't be calling your own mother, Emily,' Annie said in a disapproving voice.

'What else can I call her? You are my mother, always have been and always will be,' she said fiercely. 'I'm sure if she knew that, Emily wouldn't mind me using her Christian name. And you haven't answered my question.'

'As far as I know Mr and Mrs Cunningham-Brown are both alive and living in Denbrae House. In Greenhill, Tina, not so very far away.'

'You could have gone anywhere so why didn't you put a good distance between you and them?'

'This was a part of the country I was familiar with.'

'You know this, Mother, we are talking calmly about this and I am not the least bit calm, I'm all churned up inside.'

'I think you are taking it all – oh dear, what is the word?'

'Splendidly?'

'Yes, that will do.'

'What did you expect?'

'You could have been angry and upset and with good reason. I had no right to do what I did—'

'Taking a baby no one else wanted?'

'That is not true. In all probability you would have gone to a good home.'

'You couldn't know that?'

'I think I did.' Annie was trying to be honest. 'Babies from good families are carefully placed. They try to match as near as possible. You could have been the very much loved daughter of a couple denied their own child.'

'Maybe.'

Annie looked at her quickly. Now that she had had time to dwell on it, was she changing her mind and thinking that she may well have missed out?

Tina repeated, 'Maybe,' and then added, 'and maybe not. They might have given me what money could buy and like Emily I would have been given into the care of a nanny.'

'Many of them are very good.'

'Not the same though,' she smiled. 'Thank you, Mother, for stealing me.'

'What a thing to say.'

'I know. You took awful risks for me and' – the tears rolled down her face – 'more than that you gave up your chance of marriage and a family of your own. Hamish—'

'Your adopted grandfather, Tina, and a very good man.'

'I know all that, you've told me often enough, but he was very old and' – she blushed – 'he wasn't a real husband, was he?'

'No, it was a marriage in name only to make life easier for both of us, which it did.'

'Were you ever in love? Did I spoil things for you?'

Annie thought about her experience with Edward Galloway. She had thought herself in love with him and look at the narrow escape she had had.

'No, Tina, you didn't spoil anything for me. You have

given me more happiness than I thought possible and not for a single minute have I ever regretted what I did unless it was that I had denied you a better life.'

'You didn't, you couldn't. Like you I wouldn't change anything either.' They were both silent, an emotional silence. Tina broke it by saying, 'Am I like Emily?'

'Yes, very like her.'

'Don't you have a photograph?'

Annie shook her head. 'Oh, wait a minute.' She got up and went over to the book shelves. Taking down *Sense and Sensibility* she opened it, found what she was looking for and handed it to Tina.

'Is this Emily?'

'Yes.'

'Who did this sketch? It is so good, she can't have known, it is so natural. Who was the artist, Mother?'

'Can't you guess?'

'My father,' she said with awe in her voice. 'He did this?'

'Yes.'

'And you kept it all these years?'

'To show you one day.'

'What do you know about my father?'

'Very little but Miss Emily told me more than she told anyone else. She said he was tall and very attractive and I think he was quite a bit older though I can't swear to that. She was very much in love with him, that I do know.'

'Was he in love with her? No, he couldn't have been or he wouldn't have left her to face what she had to on her own.'

'He didn't know. One day he was there in his cottage and the next he was gone. And, Tina, not once did she blame him for what happened. She insisted the fault was all hers, that she had thrown herself at him.'

'You know I'm beginning to like Emily very much. I mean it takes a lot of guts to say a thing like that about yourself.'

'She was always very honest. Miss Emily told me that he had made it clear from the start that a settled life with a

341

family was not for him. He had to be free to get up and go when the notion took him.'

'A free spirit,' she said softly, 'I think I can understand that.' She gave a small sigh. 'Is that all you can tell me?'

'Yes, that is everything I know.'

'No name, not even a Christian one?'

Annie shook her head.

'I always suspected there was a mystery about my father.'

'You did?' Annie was startled.

'Mother, you might be many things but an actress is not one of them. You said he was dead and changed the subject as though you didn't want to talk about it.'

'It made me feel guilty saying he was dead when he is probably very much alive and unaware of your existence but what else could I say short of the truth and that was something I couldn't bring myself to do.'

'Poor Mother, you didn't know what you were letting yourself in for when you took me.'

'I was prepared for anything just so long as I could keep you.'

'Bless you for that,' she said huskily. 'And thank you for being the best mother any girl could have.'

Annie was too choked to answer.

Tina was suddenly all action. 'I'll make tea, that is poison.'

'No wonder it is stone cold, do you see the time? We have been sitting here for well over an hour.'

The fresh cup was welcome.

'Tina, what about your grandparents?'

'I have no grandparents,' she said coldly and clearly.

Annie didn't always read the list of the war dead, she found it too harrowing, but today she did. It was 1918 and there was a glimmer of hope that this year would see the end of the war. No one was saying very much preferring to wait and see and live a day at a time.

She was halfway down the dead and missing when her eye caught a paragraph, separate from the column of names.

It said, PROMINENT PERTHSHIRE FAMILY'S DOUBLE BLOW. Annie's heart was in her mouth as she took in the words.

Lieutenant Robert Cunningham-Brown had been reported killed on active service and his older brother Captain Michael Cunningham-Brown, previously reported missing was now known to have lost his life. There was more about them but Annie's eyes had blurred as she remembered Miss Emily's two boisterous brothers and the upheaval they caused when they were home on holiday from boarding school. Her heart went out to that old couple. What were their thoughts? Three of a family and all gone. So much suffering and surely they had been given more than their share. She went back to the paragraph. Michael had been married on his last leave and Robert had been engaged.

Mr and Mrs Cunningham-Brown had no one, no one to call family. A little voice whispered that there was Tina and another little voice said they need never know.

Chapter Twenty-Five

The fighting spirit was still alive but along with it was a great weariness. Rumours began to spread, though at first not believed, that the Germans were retreating and peace was in sight. And then it was November 1918 and it was all over, the war was done, no more fighting. In the towns they were dancing in the streets with some people hysterical. Total strangers were shaking hands and weeping unashamedly. Woodside celebrated the end of hostilities in a quieter way. They were remembering the many who would not be coming home and the tears behind closed doors.

The Beeches was celebrating. Annie, Mrs Archibald, Miss Urquhart and Bridget between them raided the larder and managed to produce a spread that gladdened the heart. Tina was helping here, there and everywhere and trying to do everyone's bidding. Old Mr and Mrs Stephenson, resident at the Beeches, had gone back to their closed-up house and returned with three bottles of champagne and some glasses in case Mrs Brown was short of them. The party spirit was there but sadness too. For some, despite the circumstances, this had been a happy period. They would miss being one big family. Speeches were said and there was a toast for Annie and another for her staff.

'Now that the war is over, Tina, we must consider your future.'

Tina had turned eighteen a month before the war ended. Being young and pretty she had been asked out many times by servicemen home on leave, but she had never been emotionally involved. Gently but firmly she had fought off those who were seeking more than a goodnight kiss. And once they knew the score most accepted it with an apology and a promise to behave themselves. If she was asked to write, Tina always agreed knowing how much a letter meant to a lad far from home.

David Marshall, too old for active service, did what he could for the war effort and carried on with his painting. Tina was still a regular visitor. Annie worried that a man on his own didn't eat. Food was scarce and it needed skill and imagination to make a tasty meal out of what was available.

'Your mother shouldn't be doing this,' he'd said on several occasions when Tina arrived with a jug of soup covered by a cloth.

'She worries about you.'

David Marshall was touched. 'She shouldn't. Heaven knows she has enough to do.' Nevertheless he did enjoy the soup or the luxury of a bowl of potted hough. Tina would make a pot of tea and have a cup with him. Sometimes she would stay and watch him painting and though David Marshall said there was nothing more he could teach her, she didn't agree. She was always learning something.

'My future?' Tina smiled to her mother.

'Yes, your future. Don't you want to go to art school?'

'Of course I do, but there is little chance of that now. The war has put paid to a lot of things, Mother.'

'What about London?' Annie said vaguely.

'What about London?'

'You might get a place there.'

Tina shook her head. Her mother didn't understand that it would take a long time for things to get back to normal if they ever did. Being a girl it was unlikely she would be considered. More to change the subject than for any other reason she said, 'You know what I would like more than anything else?'

'No, what would you like, Tina?'

'It could never happen.'

'What could never happen? You can be exasperating when you want.'

'I would like to travel abroad, perhaps visit Italy and France.'

'Your mother had a notion to go to Paris.'

'Did she? Italy appeals more to me than France. Mr Marshall talks a lot about Florence, artist friends of his have been there, that was before the war of course—'

'Florence, what a lovely name for a city.'

'Renowned throughout the world for its art and its history, Mother. I've been reading up about it.'

'Maybe we could manage a holiday there.'

'A holiday isn't what I want. If I ever went there it would be to study. Mother stop looking so serious this is just the stuff of dreams.'

'Dreams can come true and one day, you never know. The Beeches is doing very well but looking decidedly shabby and that won't attract new boarders. I really must get estimates and make a start on the redecorating.'

For Tina it had been only wishful thinking but Annie was taking it very seriously. It would be quite dreadful if Tina's gift was to be lost and end up as no more than a hobby.

In bed Annie tossed and turned and agonised over what she should do. There was no question of asking the Cunningham-Browns for assistance. But what about the money left to Miss Emily from her Great-Aunt Anne? By right that should go to Tina. It would be a small fortune and allow her to study in Florence for as long as she wished. She tried not to think of the separation, it would be very painful, but she must not be selfish. She'd had eighteen years of joy and nothing would take those away.

What she was proposing to do would take courage, a great deal of courage, and Annie wasn't sure if she had enough. Would her new-found self-confidence desert her when it came to facing her old master and mistress? Once a servant, always a servant. Had someone said that or had she made it up? Would she gain admittance to Denbrae House or would she be turned away? 'The mistress is not seeing visitors,' spoken in a haughty tone by a housekeeper or servant. Mrs Martin, the cook/housekeeper, would no longer be there. Annie didn't imagine there would be anyone left from her time. Then if she was admitted how would she introduce herself? As Mrs Brown and someone who had known the family well at one time? Annie wasn't too concerned about that. Once the Cunningham-Browns agreed to see her she would play it by ear.

Her courage kept failing her and only by reminding herself that it had been her fighting spirit that had got her where she was, did Annie finally make up her mind to take the bus to Greenhill and pay a visit to Denbrae House. Tina's future was at stake and what was rightfully hers should come to her now when it would do the most good.

Finding a time to go was the next problem. Tina was quick to notice any change of routine and she didn't want her asking questions. In the end it was Tina who made it possible. There was an exhibition of paintings in Dundee and David Marshall had invited Tina to accompany him.

Annie was up early to attend to her usual jobs and hurry Tina on her way. Punctuality was not the girl's strong point and she never allowed herself enough time.

'Enjoy yourself, dear.'

'Sure to. Cheerio, Mother.'

Annie watched her hurrying down the path with her lovely, easy, youthful walk and then turn to wave when she reached the bend where she would be out of sight of the window. Annie waved back and then went to her own rooms. She wanted to take her time and dress carefully. Annie did not have an extensive wardrobe but knew it was good sense to pay more for a garment that would retain its shape and to keep to simple lines. The extremes of fashion were not for her. She would wear her grey coat, a silver grey and her hat with the brim that toned nicely with it. Pale grey gloves, black shoes with a cuban heel and a black handbag. Looking in the mirror Annie was pleased with her appearance. Miss Urquhart was impressed too.

'If you don't mind my saying so you look very smart, I might even say very tricky, Mrs Brown.'

'Thank you very much and I don't mind in the least. A compliment is always welcome. Will it rain? Do I need to take an umbrella?'

'I shouldn't think so unless you are going far. If you take an umbrella you can be sure it won't rain.'

'I'm not sure if I understand the logic of that,' Annie laughed. 'Since I have a habit of losing umbrellas or leaving them behind I'm going to take a chance and leave mine at home. Miss Urquhart, expect me when you see me.'

'Enjoy yourself, you deserve a break, and have no fear I'll look after everything.'

'I know and it is such a relief to have you, someone I can depend upon.' Annie thought it only polite to say where she was going. 'There is a bus to Greenhill due in fifteen minutes so if I leave now I should be in plenty of time.'

The bus was up to time and Annie got on and paid her fare. No one she knew was among the passengers and for most of the time she turned her face to look out of the window. There was a ten-minute walk after she reached Greenhill. She could feel her feet dragging but this was no time to be having second thoughts and she forced herself into a purposeful walk. There had been occasions when she had thought about coming to Greenhill and having a look at the outside of Denbrae House but she never had.

The weather here was the same as it had been in Woodside. A beautiful spring day, the air was soft and the grass was the rich fresh green that only comes after a spell of rainy weather.

Denbrae house looked the same or very nearly the same. Inevitably the war had left its mark and there was a slight shabbiness, the gardens not quite up to their former glory. She admired the flowering shrubs on either side of the long drive. Almost habit had its way and she was about to go round to the back and into the servants' entrance. Instead she took the curve of the drive and went up the marble steps leading to the oak door. Memories came flooding back and she was a small anxious girl down on her knees and cleaning those marble steps.

Taking a deep breath, Annie rang the bell and heard its muffled peal and then approaching footsteps.

A stout woman with a broad face had the door open and was looking enquiringly at her.

'Forgive me calling without having written beforehand but I was in this district and felt I couldn't leave without making an effort to see Mrs Cunningham-Brown.' Annie gave a small laugh. 'It was some years ago but we knew each other very well.' Had she been too effusive, Annie worried? Was this the wrong approach?

'If you would just step inside, please, I'll see if Mrs Cunningham-Brown is available, she might be resting. Your name, if you please, I didn't catch it.'

Hardly surprising, Annie thought since she hadn't given it. 'Mrs Brown, or Mrs Annie Brown, I believe, would bring me more to mind.'

'Wait here, will you Mrs Brown?'

Annie was shown into the small room next to the dining-room, which had always been used for those who had no appointment and who might or might not be given an audience with the master or mistress. It was too early to congratulate herself.

The woman was back smartly. 'Mrs Cunningham-Brown will see you.'

'Thank you.' Annie got up and followed the stout figure with her slightly waddling walk. Would it be the upstairs sitting-room or the much more formal drawing-room? It was the drawing-room. The curtains had been partly closed against the bright April sunshine and it was a moment before Annie saw the occupants of the room. The voice guided her.

'Before you go Mrs McKenzie, open the curtains, the sun should be less troublesome now.' The woman did as she was instructed and the sunshine flooded the room. 'Not quite so much, yes, that is better. Forgive me, Mrs Brown, we complain when there is no sunshine and complain when there is too much.'

Annie smiled in agreement and stood where she was.

'Come and take this chair beside me.'

Annie went over and sat down and Mr Cunningham-Brown shuffled to the door.

'That's right, dear, go and have your rest,' then when he had gone and the door shut Maud Cunningham-Brown said softly. 'My husband is in poor health.'

'I'm sorry to hear that.' Annie had been shocked at his appearance. She hardly recognised this shambling old man as the high-and-mighty Mr Cunningham-Brown. There was a difference in her old mistress as well. Gone was the timidness and the uncertainty she remembered. The voice, everything about her, spoke of a woman in command.

'One of the drawbacks of advanced years is loss of memory. Mine doesn't fail me often but I confess I do not recall the name.'

'That is hardly surprising, the last time we saw each other was over eighteen years ago.'

'That is a very long time.'

'Yes. My maiden name was Annie Fullerton and I left Denbrae House with your daughter.'

The woman's eyes narrowed, then widened with shock. This well-dressed, nicely spoken woman could not be Annie Fullerton, yet studying her face there was a little of the servant girl who had been with Emily at the end. The audacity of the creature to cheat her way in.

'I think I am due an explanation,' she said icily.

'I quite agree.'

'If you have come here to talk about my daughter I do not

wish to hear. I mourned her death but at least I still had my two sons.' Her voice broke but she carried on bravely. 'You may or may not know that both my sons were killed in the war.'

Annie nodded. 'I was very, very sorry to read about it in the newspaper.'

'It was too much for my husband, it has finished him. The shock and pain of losing one son was dreadful but losing both was just too awful.' She closed her eyes and when she opened them some of her old haughtiness was back. 'Why have you come?'

'To talk to you about your granddaughter.'

'Emily's child was adopted,' she said harshly.

'Miss Emily changed her mind about adoption but decided against telling you in case she was forced to do so against her will.'

'You are making this up for reasons of your own.'

'I have no reason to do that. As I was saying Miss Emily had a change of heart and she was to bring up her own baby.'

'Nonsense, my daughter couldn't look after herself never mind a baby.'

'You are wrong, Mrs Cunningham-Brown,' Annie said quietly, 'your daughter was very determined and I was completely in her confidence. She said the money from her Great-Aunt Anne would buy a house and pay for staff.'

'In all this what was your position to be?' she asked with a trace of a sneer.

'Her housekeeper.'

'Then Emily died and you had to make other plans?'

'It's true I had to make other plans,' Annie said feeling a spurt of anger. 'Your husband saw fit to terminate my employment. The reason he gave was that my presence in Denbrae House would be an embarrassment and painful for you.'

'I wasn't aware of that. After Emily died I had a break-down and no doubt my husband thought what he was doing was for the best.' When next she spoke she looked directly at Annie. 'I was under the impression that you had given in your notice and had secured employment where you were.'

'That was completely untrue. I was given two months wages and permission to remain in the cottage until the end of the year.'

'That is of little importance now and can't have any bearing on you coming here.'

'As I said I came to tell you about Tina. Mrs McIntyre knew of your daughter's wishes and the adoption arrangements were withdrawn.' Annie paused and clasped her hands together to stop them from shaking. 'When Miss Emily died I made sure that her baby daughter didn't go to strangers. I brought up your granddaughter, Mrs Cunningham-Brown.'

'You? I don't believe a word of this.'

'It is the truth.'

'Are − you − saying − that you took Emily's baby and brought it up as your own?' she said incredulously.

'Yes.'

'You are married?'

'Yes, I am Mrs Brown and I am a widow.'

She nodded her head and began to smile. 'I am beginning to see it all now. How very clever, Annie.' She seemed to have slipped back to mistress and maid instead of giving Annie her married status. 'You have a daughter of your own and this is to extort money − don't you know that is a crime and you could go to prison for it?'

'Go to prison for what, Mrs Cunningham-Brown? For giving an unwanted baby a home?' Her head went up proudly. 'I wouldn't touch a penny of your money. My husband left me well provided for and apart from that I am the owner of the Beeches Guest House in Woodside.' The probability was that the woman had never heard of it but no matter, it made her point.

'Your husband left you money? A young man with money to leave I find that hard to believe.'

Annie looked at her coldly. 'He wasn't a young man. As I have discovered there are some quite dreadful people in this world and others who are very good. Hamish was the kindest, most caring person I have ever known.'

'Perhaps you were his housekeeper?'

'I was. He offered marriage, not because he wanted a wife, he didn't, but he saw it as a way to give respectability to Tina and myself. He loved Tina and she gave him a lot of happiness. He gave us his name because he couldn't bear to think of an innocent child going through what was ahead for Tina.'

'Tina?'

'The name your daughter chose.'

'Clementina! Never!'

'Not Clementina, you are quite right, she didn't like that name but she liked Tina and Tina is the name on her birth certificate.'

'Since you, by your own admission, are not in financial difficulties why these demands?'

'I don't recall making any.'

'This sudden appearance isn't about money?'

'It is, but not yours and not for me.' She paused. 'Please hear what I have to say.'

'Very well.'

'Tina is a lovely girl and a very talented artist.'

'There are no artists in my family nor in my husband's.'

'Tina's father was an artist.'

'Really! I did not know that. It would appear my daughter confided in her servant.'

Annie heard the pain and tried to be gentle.

'That was all she said, that the father of her child was an artist and she loved him very much.'

'How can I believe this girl is whom you say she is?'

'One look at Tina would tell you.'

'Why did you not bring her?'

'I didn't tell her I was coming here and when I do tell her she is going to be furious.'

'Indeed?' The eyebrows went up.

'Tina knows the circumstances of her birth. I kept putting it off, it was so difficult but when she was fourteen I told her and I kept nothing back.'

'I see.'

'I don't think you do. She has no wish to see you or your husband, she won't even call you her grandparents. The way you treated your own daughter and your cold-hearted rejection of her baby went deep. The young feel deeply you know.'

'I'm tired, this has upset me. Just say what it is you want.'

'The money that would have gone to Miss Emily from her great-aunt.'

'I suppose she is at an age when she has expensive tastes, is that it?'

'Far from it. All Tina wants to do is paint. Those who have seen her work believe that Tina has a major talent.' Annie was glad she had remembered those words, they had impressed her and hopefully they would do the same to Tina's grandmother.

'Does she take instruction?'

'Yes. Her teacher says she needs more than he can give her and Tina's heart is set on going to Florence to study there. Though I could manage to give her a holiday in Italy I wouldn't be able to afford to let her stay for any length of time. Not with fees and accommodation to provide.'

'The money from Aunt Anne is there and apart from a withdrawal my daughter made before leaving for Dundrinnen it has never been touched. One day we expected it to be shared between the boys.' She was suddenly very brisk as if just making up her mind.

'Bring Tina to see me and have her birth certificate with you. Shall we say one afternoon next week and about the same time?'

'Thank you. I'll do my best but Tina may be difficult to persuade. She can be very stubborn.'

'If she is Emily's daughter she will be.' It was the nearest Mrs Cunningham-Brown had come to a smile.

'There is a lot of Miss Emily in her daughter.'

'I am not totally convinced but some of what you say is plausible.' She touched the bell on the wall beside her.

'My housekeeper will give you tea in the kitchen before you go.'

'Mine will have something ready for me when I return.'

A maid popped her head in.

'Show Mrs Brown out.' She nodded to Annie but didn't wish her good day and Annie kept silent too.

Long after Annie had gone Maud Cunningham-Brown sat very still. Was it possible that the line wasn't finished and that this Tina was Emily's child? In her heart of hearts Maud believed it to be true. The Annie she remembered wouldn't lie but even so she had to be absolutely certain, there must be no doubt. If it was true, then Tina must come and live in Denbrae House. Once she saw the house she would quickly forget hurt and forgive and forget. Maud smiled and was in no doubt that she would win over her granddaughter. To keep her happy an art master would be engaged to give her lessons since it was a subject so close to her heart. At eighteen she should be thinking of marriage. The stain on her birth could never be removed but there was greater tolerance now, the war had made it less important.

Maud wanted to forget the past and look forward to the future. She made the decisions and was enjoying doing so. Tina would have to be taken in hand and introduced to suitable young men. A good marriage would follow and there would be children. The future of Denbrae House would be secure and she would die happy. Sadly Alfred would never know about this miracle, his mind had gone and it was unlikely there would be an improvement.

She thought back to Emily's death and his behaviour or the little she could recall. She had hidden behind the breakdown which had not been as severe as the doctor had made out. It had been her way of blocking out what she couldn't bear to think about. All the same that had been unkind of Alfred treating Annie in that fashion and the girl had every right to feel aggrieved. He had made some amends, very generous ones by the sound of them and those would have taken away any guilt feelings he had.

What a day! She must have tea, her throat felt parched. Her finger went to the bell and remained there until a maid came hurrying to find out what was required.

Annie walked away from Denbrae House with mixed feelings. She supposed the visit had been successful but it left her feeling uneasy, almost as though a threat hung over her. Then she shrugged that off as being fanciful. The money would be forthcoming and that had been the purpose for going. Tina would have the means to study in Florence and no matter how she ranted and raved, at the end of the day she would come round.

It was only this ridiculous feeling that she had put herself in the hands of her former employers. She had feared the husband once but he was harmless. The seemingly gentle one had claws and she could be dangerous. She would use every trick to woo her granddaughter into a life that did not include Annie. There were some people in this world who always got their way and the Cunningham-Browns were among those.

Annie gave herself a mental shake. This was her imagination running riot. Tina and she were very close and no one would come between them. Once the money she was entitled to was in her name, then Tina had no need to see her grandparents again unless she wanted to and that was unlikely.

The more immediate worry was how to tell Tina when she got back from Dundee.

Chapter Twenty-Six

Annie smiled to Tina. 'How did it go?' she asked as she joined her in their sitting-room. Tina had taken off her shoes and was padding around in stocking soles.

'Wonderful, I'm very glad David asked me. At times he can be quite outspoken you know. Most of the paintings got his approval but a few shouldn't have been given space. Poorly executed work was what he said and he didn't bother to drop his voice.'

'That was cruel and I'm surprised at David.'

'He was being honest. David is never intentionally unkind but he maintains it is stupid and unhelpful to say something is good when it patently is not.'

'Nevertheless he could have softened the blow.'

'You don't understand artists, Mother. But never mind that, why did you let me go out with new shoes? I've a blister.'

'Blaming me! I like that. You should have had enough sense not to put them on when you knew you were to be on your feet all day.'

Tina grimaced. 'A painful lesson. And now you can tell me where you were gallivanting to. Miss Urquhart said she thought you were catching the bus to Greenhill.'

'I did and I had every intention of telling you once we were on our own.' She cleared her throat. 'I went to Denbrae House to see your grandparents.'

Tina stared. 'You did what?'

Annie was silent.

'Why would you go to Denbrae House?' Tina said coldly. She had been wandering around the room but went over to a chair and sat down. 'Why?' she repeated.

'If you would just give me a chance I'll explain.'

'It had better be good.'

'You do want to go to Florence don't you, or have I got that wrong?'

'Oh, for heaven's sake,' Tina flung back, 'we all have dreams, impossible dreams. You must have been the same when you were young.'

Annie nodded. Years and years ago in the orphanage, she had dreamt her own secret dream that her parents would come for her and they would live in a lovely house with a garden and be happy ever after. No one had made that dream come true and the lesson she learned was that her kind, the disadvantaged, had to work hard for everything otherwise they got nothing.

'I wanted your dream to come true and I thought this might be a way.'

'Oh, no!' Tina looked shattered. 'Surely, surely you didn't ask them for money? If you say yes I'm going to die.'

'You'll live,' Annie said drily. 'I did ask for money but not theirs. All I want is what is legally yours. Are you going to find fault with that?'

'I don't know.'

'The money I am talking about was left to Miss Emily—'

'Emily,' Tina said through clenched teeth.

'Left to your mother from her Great-Aunt Anne,' Annie continued but with a small smile. 'Your mother—'

'All right, back to Miss Emily. You can be very difficult, Mother mine.'

They both laughed and the tension eased.

'The old lady was considered eccentric but in the nicest way. She was fiercely independent and believed in women having control over their own affairs. Miss Emily was her favourite and she got all the money left to her in case there came a time when she would have need of it.'

'How very true that proved to be when she was sent away.' Tina was biting her knuckle, a habit she had when she was troubled. 'You are doing this for me I know that—'

'Yes, Tina, I am doing this for you and getting precious little thanks. Believe me going to Denbrae House and facing your grandmother was an ordeal.'

'I just wish you hadn't, that's all. We were fine, just the two of us.'

'That won't change.'

'It has to complicate matters.'

'Only if you let it.'

'You haven't mentioned my grandfather.'

'He is a poor soul and we have to feel sorry for both of them. They haven't had their sorrows to seek. Can you imagine what it must have been like to lose both sons in the war? It was too much for your grandfather, his mind has gone.'

'Yes, Mother, I agree that life has been cruel to them but don't forget how cruel they were to their only daughter when she was expecting me.'

'Try not to feel bitter. They were less harsh than some parents and Miss Emily was welcome to return home—'

'Once I was born and safely out of the road. Be honest, they couldn't have cared less about me.'

Annie was surprised and perturbed to hear the bitterness in Tina's voice. She hadn't expected this amount of caring which just showed she didn't know Tina as well as she thought.

'What they did was wrong but you have to be fair. They were not completely callous, they were as sure as they could be that you would go to a good home. Tina, I am not blameless in all this. I kept you from going to a good home because I wanted you. I took a terrible chance with your life. Things might have been so different and we could have experienced real poverty.'

'Don't,' Tina said on the verge of tears. 'I wasn't deprived of anything, I was loved and surely that is more important.'

'Bless you and now I am going to be a little cruel.'

'You couldn't even if you tried, but I'm listening.'

'For your grandparents the good name of the family was everything, with you it is painting. Faced with a choice, a difficult choice, the chances are that your painting would come first. It is worth thinking about that, Tina.'

'That's different, there is no comparison.'

'Maybe not but it is worth a thought.'

'All right, you have worn me down so tell me slowly what happened at Denbrae House.' She paused and smiled. 'For a start how did you get in the door?'

'A half truth, that I had known the family very well and since I was in the district . . .'

'And that got you over the door?'

'It did.'

'Once in the lion's den did you admit your deception and introduce yourself?'

'That is about it and now, Tina, please, it would be much easier for me if you would let me tell it in my own way instead of answering your questions.'

'Sorry, I'll try and keep quiet.'

Annie related all that had taken place. 'That's it, I don't think I have omitted anything.'

'You want me to go there?'

'Yes. She needs to see you before she will believe that you are her grandchild.'

'What about my birth certificate?'

'That as well.'

'If I hadn't come on the scene what would have happened to that money?'

'In due course it would have been shared between the two boys, your Uncle Michael and Uncle Robert. With them both dead I don't know what would have happened.'

'My uncles,' Tina said wonderingly, 'if they had lived I might have had cousins.'

'Very likely.'

'Would they have accepted me do you think or would I have been shunned?'

'No one would shun you, no one could,' she said with a catch in her voice.

'Did you know them?'

'The boys? How could I? You must remember I was a maid.'

'Well, seen them then?'

'Yes, when they were home from boarding school.' Annie smiled. 'I recall hearing your grandmother say to someone that much as she loved them it was sheer heaven when peace was restored and the pair of them were on their way back to school.'

'Not having relations has not really bothered me, it was just strange hearing you call them my Uncle Michael and Uncle Robert. Kind of made them real if you know what I mean.'

Annie wasn't sure that she did but she nodded.

'I just wish you hadn't done this. We were happy as we were and this is going to change everything.'

'It doesn't have to.'

'Of course it does. Nothing will ever be the same again.'

'Nothing remains the same, Tina, but in this you have a choice. You can meet your grandmother for the one and only time' – Annie was desperately hoping that this would be the case – 'or it can be the first of many visits.'

'The one and only.' Her eyes sparkled mischievously. 'I'll take the money and run.'

'It's yours, you don't have to run. Seriously, dear, try not to hurt your grandmother. She is old and she has the worry of your grandfather. Don't heap too much blame on to her, I imagine she would have just done what she was told.'

'What her husband told her?'

'Yes.'

'The way you described my grandmother to me didn't show her as timid, quite the opposite in fact.'

'She has changed from the time I knew her. Mr Cunning-ham-Brown used to frighten me a bit but I found his wife approachable.'

'This is maybe the real woman showing herself now. With her husband the way he is she has had to take control,' Tina said.

'And finding she is well able to do so.' Annie smiled at the way the conversation was going. Tina was interested in spite of herself. Far better that they should talk it out now.

Tina squared her shoulders. 'I'm just beginning to appreciate what you put yourself through for me. Yes, we'll go and meet this formidable woman together and she shall meet Emily's daughter for the one and only time.'

Annie was pleased but wary. 'You will be polite?'

'Am I ever anything else?'

'There have been occasions. What I meant was don't spoil things for yourself. I don't know but perhaps she could make difficulties.'

'Somehow I don't think so. We will be dealing with a solicitor and he will decide if I am the rightful heir or not. Let us imagine that it is mine and think what the money could mean for us.'

'For you not me.'

'Don't be like that,' Tina said showing anger. 'Why shouldn't you share my good fortune? I've shared everything of yours.'

'That's different. I always wished it was more for your sake but life has been pleasant, hasn't it?' she said pleadingly.

'Mother, dearest, dearest Mother, life has been more than just pleasant it has been happy and for that I have you to thank.' She paused and closed her eyes. 'Just think of it, the two of us in Florence.'

'You in Florence and me in the Beeches.'

'If you think I am going without you then you are very much mistaken.'

'Tina, darling, don't count your chickens before they are hatched.'

A week went by and they were on their way to Denbrae House, both apprehensive and trying to hide their unease from the other. Tina was less successful.

'Relax, dear.'

'I am perfectly relaxed, I have never been more relaxed. You are the one who needs to relax.'

'Very well, there is no one around to think we have taken leave of our senses, so we'll stand still and take three deep breaths, I have never known it to fail.'

'What to fail?'

'Taking three deep breaths.'

They began breathing in and out, in and out, in and out, then giggled. Annie gave Tina's arm a squeeze. 'There is nothing to worry about, we can support each other.'

'Too right we can.' She slowed her steps and looked at the house ahead of them. 'I had no idea it was anything like this and so big,' Tina said sounding awed. 'It is the most beautiful house I have ever seen. No wonder Emily loved it and it must have nearly broken her heart to leave all this.'

'Yes, Miss Emily loved Denbrae House,' Annie said and felt a cold hand squeeze her heart. 'You are falling in love with it too.'

Tina heard the tremor and cursed herself for her thoughtlessness.

'In love with it as an artist, as a painter. There is so much here to delight the eye and with the ever changing seasons it would be a never-ending challenge. I wouldn't want to live here though,' she hastened to add.

'Why not? The outside is impressive but then so is the inside. The furniture and furnishings are splendid.'

'I'm sure they are. Everything coldly beautiful, a house without a soul or should that be without a heart?'

'Don't be silly.'

'A house of sorrows then?'

'I would go along with that. It was that dreadful war.'

'The war gets blamed for a lot.'

'It killed both sons.'

'Yes,' Tina said thoughtfully, 'that was a tragedy but maybe the sadness began before that. Maybe it began when Emily left never to return. I read somewhere that a house isn't just bricks and mortar, it has feelings and fanciful or not I think it might be true.'

Annie was strangely put out. Tina was changing from the carefree girl to a more complex young woman and to Annie it was like seeing a much loved object take on a different appearance. Yet was that so surprising? She must remember that Tina was not her child. She had inherited Miss Emily's beauty, her stubbornness and her lovable personality. But there was more. This unknown artist who had fathered her, what was there of him? From Miss Emily's account he had been a man who could never settle for long, who had to be a free spirit. Maybe Tina, too, had to be a free spirit.

'Come on, we are dawdling, let's get it over,' Annie said briskly and anxious to be clear of her disturbing thoughts. She went on ahead, up the marble steps and pulled at the bell. The housekeeper answered it and recognised Annie.

'Mrs Cunningham-Brown is in the drawing-room, I'll take you there.' They followed with Tina looking about her with interest. Annie wore a favourite tweed costume in a heather mixture and a brooch in the lapel. Tina had chosen a very simple dress and jacket in a shade matching her deep blue eyes. Her fair hair curled becomingly about her delicately boned face.

The gasp when they went in said it all but the woman quickly recovered.

'Thank you, Mrs McKenzie, have the maid bring in tea in half an hour.'

The housekeeper went out closing the door quietly.

Mrs Cunningham-Brown had got to her feet and her face was pale, a greyish white that showed up the crisscross lines on her cheeks.

'Forgive me, child, but that could have been Emily coming into the room. It gave me quite a start.' She took both of Tina's hands in hers and kissed her on the forehead.

'Welcome to Denbrae House, my dear. First impressions, what did you think of it?'

'The outside is very impressive,' Tina said quietly.

'And you'll agree the inside is too once you get a proper look around.' She was talking too fast and seemed to have realised it. 'I'm really quite shaken, it is like Emily come back home.'

The clear young voice rang out. 'No, it is not like Emily come back home. Your daughter is dead,' she said brutally, 'and this is me, Tina Brown.'

'Tina Cunningham-Brown,' her grandmother said reprovingly.

'No, plain Tina Brown. My middle name is Cunningham but I never use it.'

'You must, you are a Cunningham-Brown.'

'But with a difference, I was born on the wrong side of the blanket.'

Tina was trying to shock and knew she was succeeding. Unfortunately it was Annie she was shocking and not her grandmother who had a small smile playing around her mouth. The old woman had returned to her chair and gestured for Tina to occupy the one next to hers. Annie was left standing. She wondered if she should sit down without being asked to but found she couldn't. Her training wouldn't let her.

'Do find yourself a chair, Annie,' her old mistress said perfunctorily, then deliberately turned her back to give her full attention to Tina. 'Tina, my dear, I am not going to ignore what you said though it was rude and unnecessary. I don't care for the expression you used though it explains the position. Your mother was a loving and impetuous girl who made a grave mistake. When she told us she was – with child, we couldn't believe it of our daughter but, sadly, it was true and we did what all families in our position would do. Emily had to be sent away and her absence explained by pretending she had gone on holiday with her cousin. We did not abandon her, far from it, she was more than welcome to return to Denbrae House.'

'Provided I was disposed of,' Tina said flushing angrily. 'You don't have to tell me this, I know.'

'I cannot know what you were told. All I can tell you is that we made as sure as we could that you would go to a good family who would care for you.'

'Since you couldn't.'

'What Emily did upset all our lives.'

'That I don't doubt for a moment. Your lives were upset but what about Emily's?'

'Poor Emily did wrong and suffered for it. Believe me, your mother was a very much loved daughter and how were we to know that a maid in our employ would have the audacity to flaunt our wishes—'

'If she hadn't I wouldn't be here now, would I? Listen to me, Mrs Cunningham-Brown—'

'Grandmother, please.'

'Very well, Grandmother, but I'll never think of you as that. It was a very lucky day for me when Emily's companion, not maid, companion, took charge of me. No one could have done more or given me a better upbringing. She hasn't only been a mother but she is my best friend as well. I bet your daughter couldn't have said that. Emily would have had to know her place.'

Maud inclined her head. 'Kindly do not refer to your mother as Emily.'

'I'm certainly not going to call her Mother. My mother is sitting over there.' Tina turned her head and smiled to Annie.

'For such a young girl you are very bitter. We all make mistakes, Tina, and regret them, but there is no turning the clock back.'

There was a small knock at the door and a maid came in with a laden tray which she put on one of the small tables. Carefully she put the cups on their saucers, gave a little bob and said she would come back with the teapot. When she did the maid asked if she could pour.

'No, just get back to your duties.' The maid went out

quickly and Annie who hadn't uttered a single word or been spoken to found she now was.

'You could see to the tea, Annie.'

Inside Annie was seething, she longed to refuse but knew she wouldn't. It would look churlish.

Tina wasn't having it. 'How dare you order my mother about as though she was your maid. Sit still,' she said as Annie half rose. 'I'll see to the tea. And something else, Grandmother, since you pride yourself on etiquette, my mother is a married lady and should be addressed accordingly.'

Annie had difficulty in keeping a straight face. These two were a match for each other.

'I stand corrected, I was in the wrong.'

Tina was on her feet. 'I shall do the honours, Grandmother, we do it very well at the Beeches. In fact before the war our afternoon teas were very popular with the ladies of Woodside.' She gave her lovely, winning smile as she lifted a plate of tiny sandwiches and offered them first to Maud and then to Annie. When Annie took hers she gave Tina a warning look as much as to say behave yourself or I will have something to say when we get home. Tina winked, put two sandwiches on her plate and sat down.

'Grandmother?'

'Yes, dear?'

'Are you satisfied that I am Emily's child?'

'There is no doubt in my mind.'

'Then we'll get to the purpose of this visit. You will inform your solicitor of my claim.'

She nodded. 'I did that before you came. Annie – beg pardon – Mrs Brown, I knew to be an honest person. This' – she picked up an envelope and handed it to Tina – 'is for you. The address is on the front and should you need the information, Thornliehill Avenue is just off the High Street. Take your birth certificate and this letter to Mr Lennox and once everything is signed and in order the legacy will be transferred to an account in your name. Tina Brown will not be able to make a claim. Tina Cunningham-Brown will.'

'There is no hyphen on my birth certificate.'

'You must explain that to Mr Lennox and have the matter put to rights.'

'Thank you.' Tina put the letter in her bag. 'We'll go, you must be tired after all this excitement.'

'I confess I am.'

Annie was on her feet.

'Thank you, Mrs Brown, for bringing Tina. And Tina, give your grandmother a kiss before you go.'

Tina touched her lips to the woman's cheek feeling its paper dryness.

'Come back and soon.' There was pleading and anxiety in the voice.

Annie, fearful that Tina was to refuse, rushed in with, 'Of course she will, Mrs Cunningham-Brown.'

'Why did you say that?' Tina said indignantly when they were outside. 'I was going to refuse.'

'That was what I was afraid of. Don't be too hard on her, Tina, you've got what you want and in the circumstances she behaved rather well I thought.'

'Oh, did you? Well I beg to differ. She was ready to treat you as a servant and you were going to let her, weren't you?'

'Maybe I was and maybe I wasn't.'

Chapter Twenty-Seven

Tina had joined her grandmother for afternoon tea and this time they had it in the upstairs sitting-room, which in Annie's day had been known as the family room.

'Your tea, Grandmother,' Tina said putting a cup and saucer on the side table. 'I hope I haven't put in too much milk, I think I have.'

'Yes, dear, you have, but don't worry I'll drink some of the tea and then you may fill it up.'

'I like it here,' Tina said looking about her. 'Not too grand, it's got a homely look, a bit like our sitting-room in the Beeches.'

'Really?' There was a wealth of meaning in that one word. 'I don't, never have thought much of this room. I much prefer to sit in the drawing-room but being so big it is difficult to heat and during the war years, with the shortage of coal, it was little used.'

'What about Grandfather, is there any improvement?'

'No, and there won't be.' She gave a small sigh. 'How sad it is to see someone you love being reduced to this. I shouldn't say it, but there are times, Tina, when I wish your grandfather was away and at peace. It is what he would have wanted himself.'

Tina had met her grandfather several times and on each occasion she was a stranger who had to be introduced and her hand shaken. Only on that first meeting had he looked

369

puzzled as though he was searching his memory then had given up. Tina found it very difficult to know how to handle the situation and had begun to give her grandfather a beaming smile and then hurry away.

'It must be very distressing for you.'

'It is, my dear, very distressing. When the mind goes that is the end of the real person. Alfred has become like a child but without a child's endearing ways. Sadly he is like a slow child who requires everything repeated, not once, but again and again. It needs great patience, which I thought I had but find I haven't.'

'You do your best I'm sure. Before I came in I waved to him in the garden but I don't think he saw me.'

'There is nothing wrong with his eyesight but no, he might be looking your way but he wouldn't see you. Poor Alfred would be lost in a world of his own. When he started to go out and walk about the grounds I took that as a good sign and much better for him than being indoors all day. Instead of which it has become an added worry although less so than it was.'

'Why?'

'That's right, Tina, eat up those sponges and I might try one myself.'

Tina handed over the plate.

'Thank you, and now to answer your question. Why is it a worry? Because, my dear, Alfred has taken to wandering out of the gate and forgetting where he is.' She pursed her lips. 'Would you believe it, a maid, a maid mind you, brought her master home one day.'

'What was wrong with that?' Tina was genuinely puzzled. 'Surely it was kind of her to take the trouble?'

'Tina, you should know better than ask. A maid bringing her master home and arms linked if you please. Alfred, in his right mind, would have been horrified.'

'But Grandmother, it only happened because he is not himself.' Tina felt irritated. Her grandmother wasn't only unreasonable, she was impossible.

The old lady drank some tea, cut the tiny sponge into two equal pieces and ate one.

'Don't tell me you would have preferred the maid to have ignored him?'

'The correct procedure would have been for the maid or any other employee for that matter, to hurry back and report the matter to Mrs McKenzie who would have known exactly what to do.'

'Meantime poor Grandfather is wandering about and becoming more confused by the minute.'

'There are times when you can be very silly, Tina. The matter of a few minutes would have been neither here nor there.' She shook her head. 'Not altogether your fault, your upbringing is to blame or rather the lack of it.' Before Tina could make a cutting remark the precise voice went on. 'There will be no repeat performance since the head gardener has been told to lock the gates when Mr Cunningham-Brown is walking about and only to open them when he is safely indoors.' She patted the hand resting on the arm of the chair. 'Enough about your grandfather.' She smiled. 'You can't know the joy it is to have you come and see me.'

'Not for much longer, Grandmother, I'm going away, that's really what I came to tell you.'

'Going away? Where to?' Maud said faintly.

'Florence, to study art. Honestly I'm so excited at the thought and if that wonderful old lady who made it possible can hear me in heaven I hope she knows just how grateful I am.'

'Aunt Anne was a thorn in the flesh, but then we mustn't speak ill of the dead.'

Tina gathered there hadn't been much love lost. 'Your solicitor, Mr Lennox, was very helpful,' Tina said.

'Presumably he is your solicitor since he will be in charge of your affairs.'

'Yes. Such a nice man and as I said he couldn't have been more helpful.'

'Tina, he is only doing the job he is paid to do.'

'Even so.'

'So now you are a young lady of substance. Hardly a fortune but nevertheless a very substantial sum of money.'

'A fortune to me,' Tina said and added silently, and to most people. She and her mother had been nearly speechless when the solicitor read out the Will in favour of Emily Cunningham-Brown, deceased, and now in favour of Tina Cunningham Brown without a hyphen.

The solicitor had shaken hands with Tina and offered his congratulations.

'I can't believe all that money is mine,' Tina whispered and felt very near to tears. She felt sadness for the mother she had never known but joy that she could do something for the woman who had taken Emily's place.

'Take good care of the money and your legacy should keep you in comfort for the rest of your life.'

Tina was taken out of her daydream by her grandmother's voice.

'Kindly explain to me why it is necessary to go to Italy to study art when you can just as easily do it here?'

'You could be right, but I have set my heart on going to Florence. I told Mr Lennox about my plans and he thought what I was proposing was absolutely splendid. Years ago he was in Italy, though not Florence, and he said he fell in love with the country and would have been happy to stay on but sadly his money ran out and he had to return.'

Maud brushed that aside. 'It is different for a man. For a young lady it is dangerous to travel alone and unbefitting in the extreme.'

'I won't be travelling alone, my mother is coming with me. She wasn't too keen on the idea but I managed to persuade her by saying I wouldn't go without her.'

'And how is that guest house to survive without its owner?' Maud said sarcastically.

Tina ignored the sarcasm. 'That won't be a problem. Mother has a very capable assistant who will take over in her absence. Actually I wasn't finished telling you about Mr

Lennox. Once I give him all the particulars he needs he is going to pay the art school fees for me and exchange some money for Italian currency. I'm glad about that, I wouldn't have known how to go about it. Then I'll make a sizeable withdrawal, Mr Lennox will advise me about the amount and he is not in favour of us stinting ourselves. He said to make it a holiday to remember.'

'A holiday? You led me to believe you were going there to study.' She had cheered up.

'Sorry, my mistake. Mother will return at the end of the holiday but I'll be staying on for I don't know how long. A year at the very least.' She paused, moistened her lips and said, 'Mr Lennox— '

'What more did he have to say?'

'He was full of good advice.'

'I'll be the judge of that, what else had he to say?'

'That he strongly advises a smattering of Italian, just a few words or phrases, he said would come in useful. It isn't that we wouldn't get by without it, but rather because taking the trouble to learn a few words of their language is considered a compliment to your host country.'

'Nonsense, everyone should speak English. It should be compulsory in all foreign schools.'

Tina burst out laughing. 'Small wonder we have a reputation for being an arrogant race. Personally I would call us plain lazy.'

'Don't go, Tina,' her grandmother said urgently. 'If you are already booked, cancel it, I have a much better idea.'

Tina was shaking her head from side to side.

'I am *not* asking you to give up painting. Why should I when it obviously gives you so much pleasure?' Her voice softened. 'Emily dearly loved Denbrae House and all around it and I think it is working its spell on you.'

Tina knew it was true but had to be careful. 'No one could deny that you have a beautiful home, Grandmother.'

'Oh, it is much more than that and you know it. If you love it then say so.'

'Yes, I love it,' she said and immediately felt guilty. The last thing she wanted to do was hurt her mother and if this got back to her it would.

Maud was satisfied for the moment. She would be patient and in the end it would pay off.

'I'm old and I'm lonely and I no longer have your grandfather. You, Tina, are the only close family I have. This is where you belong, here in Denbrae House with me. There is much to learn and I am here to help you. For how long that might be is in God's hands but one day this will all be yours, your responsibility.' There was a note of weariness in the voice not lost on Tina who was beginning to feel trapped. Then Maud spoilt it all with what she said next.

'You belong here, Tina, not in some boarding house.' The tone could have been to suggest a house of ill repute.

'Guest house if you don't mind,' Tina said furiously. 'The Beeches is a cut above the working man's boarding house. And saying that I'm not belittling boarding houses. Most are clean and comfortable and there is a need for them.'

'Did I suggest otherwise? All I said was that your place is here with me.'

'I would never leave my mother.'

'You could visit her from time to time. And your painting won't suffer, I'll engage an art master to come to Denbrae House for as often as you wish.'

'Please don't, Grandmother, you are only making it more difficult for both of us. Nothing you say will make me change my mind. I am going to Florence and that is final.'

'Then all I can say is that you are a silly, selfish girl. Emily was born to this life but you have a very great deal to learn. To put it bluntly you are completely ignorant of the things that matter.'

'Matter to you. Yes, I would agree with that.'

'You are obsessed with Florence and your painting. Well, my child, let me tell you this, there are far more important things in life than dabbling in paints.'

'Not for me and that is what you will never understand.

Painting is my whole life and I couldn't exist without it. There is a need inside me that can't be ignored. I can't know for sure but I like to believe that my father was the same and that your daughter recognised it. She knew there was no room in his life for a wife.'

'My daughter was a fool and he a blackguard. Emily paid with her life for her mistake whereas he got off scotfree,' Maud said savagely.

'I have it from my mother that he never knew about me.'

'And you believe it?'

'Yes, I believe it. Emily would have told my mother and they were honest women. What would have been gained from lying?'

'How can I say, I wasn't in my daughter's confidence. What I do know is that you are a disappointment to me. I had hoped for better from you.'

'I'm sorry but I can't change the way I am.'

'We can all change if we have the will.'

'I don't want possessions, possessions only hold one back. When I'm older it may be different but I don't somehow think so. Like my father before me I want to be able to move on when the urge takes me.'

'The money is to blame. I wish there had been a stipulation to the effect that the legatee would be unable to benefit until the age of twenty-five.'

'By which time you would hope I was married.'

'Yes. Men understand money, women don't.'

'How narrow your outlook and I'm just so glad that my Great–Great–Aunt Anne should have held the views she did. She deplored the way women were treated as second-class citizens and letting Emily have her money at eighteen was to give her independence.'

'You'll fritter it away.'

'Depends what you mean by fritter,' Tina grinned. 'But don't worry I won't go mad, Mr Lennox will see that I don't and so will my mother. She thinks travelling first class is horribly extravagant but Mr Lennox disagreed, he recommended it and said it would make hardly a dent in the money.'

'Travel first class, I've never travelled anything else.'

'Lucky you. No, I take that back. Not so lucky you. You'll never know the luxury of first-class travel because you have never known any other. For us it will be a big thrill.' Tina's eyes were shining. 'Mother is going to have a holiday of a lifetime with no expense spared. It is my way of thanking her for all the loving care she has given me from the time I was a tiny baby.'

'You are conveniently forgetting that what Mrs Brown did was wrong and probably a punishable offence. I would be inclined to say the least said about that the better.' She pushed back her cup looking petulant and Tina immediately got up to stack the dishes neatly on the tray.

'That is the maid's job not yours.'

'She won't mind a helping hand.'

'That has nothing to do with it. My servants know their place and I just wish you did. Incidentally, just a thought, but when you are taking instruction in art what will Mrs Brown do?'

Tina had been wondering that herself but the inference that her mother wouldn't know what to do with herself, annoyed Tina. There were times when she thought she was becoming fond of the old lady, then she would spoil it by making some derogatory remark about her former maid.

'My mother is perfectly capable of occupying herself. Being quick and intelligent she has overcome her poor start in life. Your daughter, probably to alleviate boredom, took it upon herself to fill the blanks in her education. Your former maid was introduced to good books and has become an avid reader.' Tina knew she was exaggerating and stopped. Her mother enjoyed reading when she had the time but she could hardly be described as an avid reader. 'Your trouble, Grandmother, is that you can't forget my mother was once a maid.'

'Why should I forget that? Mrs Brown was a maid and a good maid, and that is and always will be as I see her.'

'Your loss. My mother is a very wonderful woman and brave. She could have married and had a family of her own but instead she devoted her life to me.'

'You could have done a lot better if—'

'If your plans hadn't fallen through. Neither you nor Grandfather bothered to check. I wasn't even worth that effort.'

'You can be so cruel.'

'Not as cruel and uncaring as you were. Emily did the unforgivable but no matter you still had the boys.'

'You forget I was ill.'

'Had I died with Emily it would have been more satisfactory. End of story.'

'Haven't you said enough?'

'Probably too much.'

'When Emily died a part of me died with her.'

'I was a living part of her. Why didn't you take me? Everyone knew by that time anyway.'

'I wish I had. Let the past go, Tina. It is time to forgive and forget.'

'I am willing to forgive and forget if only you would give my mother her place.'

'I always have.'

Tina shook her head. Her grandmother would always have the last word.

'You'll come and see me before you leave for Italy?'

'Yes, but just for a very short visit, I have masses to do and I don't know how I am going to get everything done.'

Chapter Twenty-Eight

The night before Annie and Tina were due to depart for Florence there was a surprise party at the Beeches. The staff and a few of the regular guests had got together to arrange it. Mrs Archibald, assisted by Bridget, produced a mouth-watering spread of dainty sandwiches, pastries, sponges and tarts, the like of which had not been seen since before the war. It was a very happy occasion with much laughter and high spirits and just before the end Miss Urquhart, on behalf of them all, presented Annie with a beautiful silk scarf in delicate shades of blue. Annie was deeply touched and taken aback.

'Thank you all very, very much, I shall treasure this always but why? I *am* coming back you know.'

'We sincerely hope so,' Mrs Archibald said, 'but this is just to remind you of us back home while you are sunning yourself.' There was general laughter then Tina was handed a leatherbound notebook and told it was to be used to write down her experiences. This brought more laughter and a few snide remarks about handsome, romantic Italians and had Tina blushing furiously.

Lying in bed and far from sleep, Annie felt strangely unsettled. As she tossed and turned she began to question the wisdom of accompanying Tina to Florence when she would have to return home alone. Tina was showing herself to be very capable and level-headed. It was she who was seeing to all the arrangements, the different rail tickets through France and Italy and the hundred and one things that seemed to be required.

'All those tickets and documents, Tina, how will we sort them out?' Annie asked worriedly.

'Leave it to me, Mother, I have everything organised. The tickets will be arranged in the order in which they will be required,' Tina said in a school-mistressy voice.

'You won't lose them?'

'No, Mother dear, I will not lose them nor the money so just relax and leave everything to your capable daughter.'

'I'll have to.' Her only contribution was the packing of the cases.

'Remember, Mother, we are travelling light with just enough clothes to get us to Florence. Once there we'll go on a shopping spree.'

Annie's eyebrows shot up in astonishment. 'Since when have you been interested in clothes, young lady?'

'I'm still not all that interested, but we might as well take advantage of the opportunity to get something different. Think how you will enjoy showing them off when you return home,' she added mischievously.

As the time of departure was almost on them, Annie was getting more panicky by the minute. She wanted to stay here at the Beeches, but if she had let Tina go off on her own she would never have known a moment's peace. And what could be worse than spending agonising hours imagining all kinds of terrible things? It was just as well she was going, Annie thought, looking down the stairs at the cases in the entrance hall. She was feeling better now. Fears were for the night, during the dark hours, and the shadows only exaggerated the dangers. The morning light chased them away.

Three cases with stick-on labels and one tied round the handle were ready for lifting. Two held clothes and toiletries and the other held a folder with Tina's paintings and sketches.

The weather had decided to be kind. The first days of June had been cold, showery and anything but flaming June weather. Then it changed with the suddenness that so often happened yet always seemed to surprise and catch folk unprepared. The air became warm, the rain clouds dispersed and a rainbow trembled before the colours faded into the blueness of the sky. Summer had arrived in Woodside.

Travelling first class was pure heaven, they were both agreed on that. On the train the dining-car was excellent as was the service and Annie was wishing it could be all train journeys. She wasn't looking forward to the Channel crossing having heard such dreadful accounts of mountainous seas and the ship's furniture sliding from one end to the other. Folk had been sick, almost at death's door, and this had lasted from the moment they got on board until they staggered off. Only a very few had likened the sea to a millpond and Annie wasn't inclined to believe them.

To her great relief and greater surprise, she turned out to be a good sailor and it was Tina who went pale green and had to make a dash for it.

'Mother, I feel like death,' Tina said, looking more miserable than Annie had ever seen her.

'It will pass. Sit down, dear, and I'll get the steward to give you something.'

The steward arrived, a big cheerful man who didn't give much sympathy, instead telling Tina that this was nothing and it was just a case of her getting used to the ship's movement. When his back was turned she made a face at him but whatever was in the mixture it did the trick and Tina began to think she would survive after all.

There were the show-offs as always, trying to impress first-time passengers like Annie and Tina. And thinking it entertaining to describe previous crossings when the ship tossed about in stormy conditions that had them wondering if they would ever see dry land again. Annie, who hated show-offs had the uncharitable thought that it was a pity they had. Feeling less delicate now, Tina began to enjoy herself and mix with some of the younger people. Annie only admitted it to herself that she found the endless stretches of water monotonous and wished for a more interesting view.

Later, when she looked back on the journey, Annie decided that on the whole it had been a wonderful experience. Possibly the train through France had been the most enjoyable and certainly the most memorable. The waiter in the restaurant car spoke in halting English and was most attentive to the very pretty mademoiselle and her charming maman. Annie, alarmed at what she might be eating, made a reluctant start, but was soon enjoying every mouthful. The food was different to anything she had tasted but delicious. She just wished that Mrs Archibald could have sampled it, then the Beeches could have been introduced to a French night. The thought amused her. The residents would be fearful believing French food to be mainly snails, frogs' legs and horse flesh. The coffee didn't please Annie but she wasn't a coffee drinker. She much preferred tea. It was possible to order tea but when it came it was so awful that Annie was forced to drink coffee.

'I warned you the tea would be ghastly.'

'I know you did but I didn't think it would be this bad. Why on earth don't they bring the water to the boil?'

'Coffee is never made with boiling water unless some of the stuff we produce in our country and to the French it is ghastly.'

'I wish I could go behind the scenes and show them how to make a proper cup of tea.'

'Well, you can't and they wouldn't thank you. Just remember that you are travelling first class—'

'And act accordingly?'

'Exactly,' Tina smiled.

Throughout the journey the weather had been mixed with squally rain that battered the windows then brilliant sunshine. The scenery was very different but that wasn't what made Annie realise how far from home they were. It was the jabber of foreign voices. Bold, dark-eyed young men were giving the lovely fair-haired British girl the glad eye and a great deal of attention and suddenly Annie felt afraid for Tina. The girl gave no sign of being aware of the admiring glances but she could not have been unaware. Would she fall in love, or become infatuated with a handsome Italian boy? If she did would she ever return to Scotland and Woodside?

'Won't be long now,' Tina said excitedly, 'I just can't wait to see Florence.' Her eyes were shining like twin stars and Annie's breath caught in her throat. Tina had always been pretty but now she was beautiful and her ready smile showing white, perfect teeth, captivated those around her. 'Aren't you excited?'

'Yes, and what's more I can't wait to sleep in a bed that doesn't rock,' Annie laughed.

The final leg of the journey was slow as though, unlike the passengers, the train was in no hurry to reach its destination. But at last it was journey's end, the train chugged into the station and stopped with a squealing of brakes. Stiff from sitting so long they got off and stood on the platform surrounded by three cases and a bag they had bought to carry the extras acquired on the journey. It was late at night and not the best time to arrive and Annie felt a trickle of fear. What if the hotel they were booked in had forgotten they were coming or, horrible thought, mixed up the dates? What then? What would happen if no one came to meet them? What would they do? Sit in the station until daylight?

Tina saw the tiredness and the worried look on her mother's face.

'Stop looking so worried,' she said gently, 'someone will arrive very soon. Oh, look, over there, I'm sure that's someone for us.'

'How can you tell in this half darkness?'

'I'll wave in case he hasn't seen us.'

'You'll do no such thing. Really, Tina, you don't know what you could be letting us in for.'

'Safe enough, Mother, one look at your disapproving face would send anyone packing.' Tina waved both arms and out of the gloom came an anxious-looking man dressed in what turned out to be the uniform of the Hotel Splendour. He was holding up a card on which was printed in large capital letters: SIGNORA BROWN AND PARTY.

'And party indeed, why don't I get my proper title?'

'Stop sounding so offended. "Signora Brown" means "Mrs Brown" in Italian.'

'That doesn't explain party. What was wrong with Mrs Brown?'

'I really don't know but forget that and pay attention.'

'How can I when I don't know a word he is saying?'

The porter had no English and none of the phrases Tina had learned by heart were of use. In the end it was Annie's actions that got results and a grinning, obviously relieved porter, took a case in each hand and indicated that *Signora* Brown and party should follow. Tina, who would never allow anyone to carry her precious paintings picked up her case and that left Annie with the bulging bag.

Travel weary, they were too exhausted to see much of the Hotel Splendour. All they wanted was to get their head on the pillow and sleep and sleep. The bedroom was large, cool and airy and had two single beds. Annie slept the sleep of the exhausted and wakened about half past seven on her watch and whatever time that was in Italy. She didn't get up, just lay looking up at the white ceiling. Tina was still asleep judging by her regular breathing but in less than half an hour she was awake and as she said 'rarin' to go'. They dressed and went down for breakfast which they ate at the open window. Tina said *Per favore* and *Grazie*. The phrase she really had off pat was '*Non capisco. Può parlare più lentamente?*' which was: 'I don't understand. Could you please speak more slowly?' Since that was about the extent of her

Italian it wasn't much help but it did sound fluent to her own ears. Usually someone did oblige with an English translation and were rewarded with a particularly warm smile.

The Hotel Splendour was a medium-priced hotel with lovely views of the Arno and friendly service. The dining-room was long and narrow, there were two small lounges and a wide reception hall with marble flooring. The woman behind the reception desk spoke passably good English but with a peculiar accent. She welcomed the two guests.

'Did you sleep well?'

'Very well, thank you,' Annie smiled.

'And the young lady? No need to ask, the young always sleep well because they do not have the worries of us older women. And now, please, if I can be of any help?'

'Perhaps you could advise us about shops,' Tina said, 'we would like to buy clothes.'

'But certainly, Florence has very good shops.' The woman was well-dressed herself, stylishly so. 'For myself I only go to the exclusive shops, for rich people you understand, when it is for something very special. For you perhaps it is holiday clothes?'

'Yes.'

They got detailed instructions where to go and where to avoid and after thanking the receptionist went on their way. Tina wanted done with the shopping as quickly as possible and Annie was relieved that they were going where they would not be charged the earth.

'Mother, I will not tell you again, put away your purse, this is my treat.'

'I'm taking too much from you.'

'You are not,' Tina said through gritted teeth. 'Please don't spoil this for me.'

'All right, dear, if you insist.'

'I most certainly do.'

Colours were brighter and styles a little different and both being slim they were not difficult to fit. Annie chose a linen

suit in pale lemon and with navy trimmings, several skirts
and blouses and three cotton dresses. Tina bought two long,
flowing dresses in a flimsy material that had a bohemian
look, half a dozen cotton dresses and several skirts and
blouses. A white cardigan for each of them was a necessity
for the cooler evenings and then as an afterthought a
raincoat and an umbrella. Laden with their purchases they
came to a counter with straw hats and after trying on a few
settled on two with huge brims. The shops were walking
distance from the hotel and going back they selected from
their purchases what they wanted to wear and quickly
changed into them. The hot sun called for protection and
Annie put on her straw hat before they left. Tina carried hers
ignoring her mother's warning that she would get sunstroke.

Tina had it arranged so that she would have five full days
with her mother before starting art school.

'Isn't this just perfect?' she said taking Annie's arm. 'I must
write and tell David that we have arrived and that everything is wonderful.'

David Marshall had been extremely helpful and had been
in touch with a fellow artist who knew Florence well and it
was his suggestion that Tina and her mother should stay in a
reasonably central hotel and take their time about finding
rented accommodation. He knew the art school she was to
attend and suggested they rented a house in the area
especially since a lot of the people there spoke English. A
number of them were British and they had either married an
Italian or just stayed on because they loved that part of Italy
and the warmth and friendliness of the people.

Annie and Tina happily wandered the streets of Florence,
strolled by the River Arno, and then stood for a while
looking about them and admiring the tall, elegant buildings
and from among them trying to pick out the Hotel
Splendour. They went from gallery to gallery, museum
to museum and in the Uffizi Gallery Tina stared at the
paintings as though she could scarcely take her eyes away.

Annie admired some, was less impressed with others, but took Tina's word for it that they were masterpieces. She was very conscious of her aching feet and longed for a nice cup of tea.

Rented accommodation was available in the vicinity of the art school and one apartment in particular appeared by the description to meet their requirements. Arrangements were made to view it and a middle-aged woman came with the keys shortly after they arrived. Annie had expected it to be a man; at home she was sure it would have been.

She showed them around the apartment then sat down and told them to take their time before deciding.

'What do you think, Mother?'

'Very nice, but you'll be here longer than me so it is more important that it suits you.'

'It does. I love it. First though I want to ask her something.'

The woman looked up. 'You are pleased, it is what you want?'

'It might be as long as there is someone to come in each day to clean and do the cooking.'

'*Si*, Maria come and clean.' She pointed vaguely to the window and they gathered that this Maria lived nearby.

'And the cooking?' Tina persisted.

Annie was thinking she could do it but didn't say so in case it annoyed this very self-assured daughter of hers.

She began to shake her head then changed that to a nod and they waited to see which she meant.

The woman shrugged. 'You must ask Maria.'

'Is Maria likely to say yes?'

'If she gets extra then maybe. You must ask yourself.' Her face brightened. '*Si*, you buy, Maria cook.'

They were both charmed with the apartment which was number 4. It was on the ground floor and had its own front door, painted a peachy-pink that would have looked awful in Woodside but was very acceptable here. There was a tiny courtyard with an abundance of pots, most with geraniums which made a lovely splash of colour. The door opened into a vestibule and another into a narrow passage which Annie called a lobby. The layout reminded her of the cottage in Dundrinnen she had shared with Miss Emily. The big difference being the weather, here the windows could be left wide open for most of the day and very often well into the evening.

Some might have said it was sparsely furnished but Annie liked the sense of space. In the living-room there was a handsome dresser with blue and white pottery plates displayed along the back. Annie thought they must have been bought locally and made a mental note to take some back with her to the Beeches. There was a table and chairs and a long sofa with a very colourful spread draped over it. Cotton rugs were scattered about the floor and plants covered much of the window ledges. One bedroom had a double bed and the other, only marginally smaller, held a single bed that Tina said would do her nicely. There was space for her bundle of paintings and a table with wobbly legs that would come in useful.

Chapter Twenty-Nine

Annie thought this tiny corner of Florence a haven of peace and was amazed at how easily she was settling into this idyllic life. Without housework to occupy her the days might have dragged but nothing could be further from the truth. Maria, that funny, delightful woman, who came each day to clean, was teaching Annie to cook Italian style. She knew no English and Annie no Italian yet they understood each other perfectly. Annie thought there was a lot to be said for sign language and facial expressions. To begin with Maria had done the shopping, then one morning she handed Annie a large shopping basket and a list of what was required and pointed to the door. Annie had got her orders.

In the market place there was so much laughter that Annie thought it must be the sunshine. The folk at home laughed but only when there was something to laugh about. She mentioned it to Tina.

'Of course the weather accounts for it, Mother, sunshine makes people happy and shivering in an icy blast certainly does not.'

'We do have some good weather,' Annie protested.

'Some, yes, but not in large quantities. You're loving this life, aren't you?' she said gently.

'Yes, I am, Tina,' Annie said truthfully. 'This will be a holiday I'll long remember.'

'A month isn't long enough, stay two.'

'You know I can't do that.' But already she was wondering if she could.

'I know nothing of the kind. Miss Urquhart is to keep you up to date with what is going on and you know you can depend on her.'

'I know I can but even so—'

Tina smiled. There had been a little uncertainty in the voice and perhaps it wouldn't need too much persuasion to have her stay longer. Tina hoped so. She liked having her mother here and she wasn't looking forward to returning to an empty apartment after classes.

Soon Annie was into a routine that allowed her to spend a lot of her time out of doors. She always made for the same seat in the square, the one in the shade of the trees and usually it was unoccupied. The large, raffia bag she had bought was ideal for holding everything she might need. Sometimes she would write a letter, balancing the writing pad on her knees or more often than not she wouldn't get beyond the first paragraph and put it away to be finished in the evening in the apartment. Then again she might read a chapter of her book and was always surprised at how the bright sunshine made the print so clear. Mostly she just sat and enjoyed the sunshine and the novelty of doing nothing. Hands that had seldom been idle now rested on her lap and Annie felt no guilt as once she would have done. As she remarked to an amused Tina, there was a lot to be said for being a lady of leisure.

Passersby, mostly locals out shopping, would smile and occasionally call a greeting and Annie would smile back. One man walked by most days and at about the same time and she began to look out for him. She wondered what he did and thought he was probably a local businessman by the well-cut, lightweight suit he wore. Judging by the number of times he raised his hat he was well known. About her age she thought or perhaps a year or two older. She would soon be forty-five and that was depressingly well into middle-age, yet Annie had never felt younger or more alive. The man getting all this attention was of just above average height but his slight figure made him look taller. With his jet-black hair and deep tan he could only be Italian.

The day she caught his eye, Annie looked away in some confusion. And the man, seeing the hastily lowered eyes, blamed himself. He hadn't meant to embarrass the woman yet clearly that was what he had done. To stop and apologise would only make matters worse. The truth was she intrigued him, her stillness especially. An artist would appreciate that, he thought. So many models found it almost impossible to remain in one position for any length of time. She was neatly dressed without being particularly fashionable. Probably wore what she thought suited her without being a slave to fashion. Not a beautiful woman in the accepted sense of the word yet wasn't beauty in the eye of the beholder? What he saw was a face full of character with a gentle strength. Perhaps someone who hadn't had their sorrows to seek. None of the women of his acquaintance could wear that severe hairstyle, all needed something softer. Yet on this woman it was right with her small, neat features. In the bright sunshine she should be wearing a hat, then he saw that she had one on the seat half hidden by a large raffia bag.

Who was she? A holidaymaker here for a few weeks, he guessed and then back home to wherever she came from. The thought saddened him and he couldn't think why.

Tina hid her disappointment from her mother. Her introduction to the school of art was a revelation. She was finding the conventional study tedious and in her case and in her opinion, unnecessary. David Marshall had taught her all that and taught her well. Then he had given her the freedom to express herself. Not here, though, her two Italian teachers, particularly Signor Vialli, the older one, seemed to take delight in undermining her confidence by pulling her painting apart for very minor faults. It wasn't that Tina objected to the criticism, she didn't, she welcomed it, but this was not fair criticism and inwardly she seethed. The only other girl in the class came off worse because she showed her distress and hung

her head as though in disgrace. Tina felt for her when her
work was ridiculed even though some of the criticism was
justified. The girl's work was mediocre as was the work of
some others but they were male and that made the difference.

Tina could have had a busy social life had she chosen to.
There were many invitations from fellow students but she
declined them all. She wasn't interested in young men, only
in her art and that was why she was here. The exception was
Angus McDonald, a Scottish boy.

'With a name like that you couldn't be anything else but
Scottish,' she had smiled when he introduced himself. After
lessons they would drink coffee in one of the cafés and talk
about painting and their dreams for the future. Today she
was looking glum as they left the building together.

'You shouldn't take it to heart,' he said. 'You are by far
the most talented student so have confidence in yourself.'

'I had plenty of that before I came here.'

'Then get it back and be deaf to what that pair say.'

'But why are they doing this to me?' she wailed.

'Don't you know? Can't you guess?'

'Wrong sex?'

He grinned. 'Certainly not as far as I am concerned, but
seriously, Tina, they are not ready for you yet.'

'Will they ever be?'

'It has to come but I wouldn't like to hazard a guess as to
when that would be. My advice, free for the taking, is to
ignore what you don't want to hear and work. They can't
stop you doing that after taking your fees.'

'Why did they if I'm not wanted?'

'The money, they need that.'

'I understood there was a tremendous demand.'

'There is, the top schools are always oversubscribed which
doesn't mean they are better, just that they have the name.'

They made an attractive couple, the girl fair-haired and
pretty with a long-legged graceful walk and the boy a few
inches taller. He was dark-haired, a dark brown not black
and he wore it longer than was usual. The normal length did

not apply to those attending art school. There was about Angus McDonald a lazy elegance that spoke of breeding.

'Your landscape got plenty of praise,' she said grudgingly.

'We less talented individuals need all the encouragement we can get,' he laughed.

Tina laughed too. That had been boorish of her and just as well he had taken it in good part.

For all the times they talked together Tina had learned very little about Angus and found she was curious.

'Angus, why are you in Florence?'

'Same as you, I imagine, studying art.'

'You don't try very hard.'

'How do you know? Maybe a very small effort takes a lot out of me,' he grinned.

'Why won't you be serious?'

'I am, I'm serious about you.'

Tina ignored that. 'Answer my question.'

'If you really want to know,' he said slowly, 'I'll tell you, but it will take a lot longer than five minutes and that is all the time we have.'

Time wasn't that important and it was just an excuse to avoid telling her. He would hope the matter wouldn't be raised again, only it would. She wanted her curiosity satisfied and she knew she was a little in love with him. It would go no further, she didn't want complications in her life.

'*Arrivederci*.' He gave a salute.

'*Arrivederci*,' Tina smiled and walked the short distance to the apartment.

'That smells good,' she said closing the door behind her and giving her mother a hug.

'It should, it took me long enough to prepare. Ready in ten minutes,' she said hurrying to the kitchen.

Tina went to wash her hands thinking her mother looked particularly cheerful and happy. The holiday was doing her good.

'How was your day, dear?'

'All right, I suppose, one day is much like another.'

Annie looked at her sharply but didn't say anything. Tina could clam up when she wanted and she would just have to bide her time and ask when she thought the moment was right. Maybe there would be no need to ask, the trouble might have sorted itself out by then.

'That nice boy you introduced me to—'

'Angus? What about him?'

'If you think he would like to come, ask Angus round for a meal. Give me a little warning,' she smiled, 'and I'll try and impress him with my Italian cooking.'

'I shouldn't bother with Italian cooking, Angus is from the Highlands of Scotland.'

'Meaning he wouldn't appreciate my effort?'

'Not at all, this is delicious,' Tina said taking another mouthful, 'I meant you don't have to put yourself out for Angus, he'll eat what is put down and enjoy it.'

'A boy after my own heart and speaking of hearts,' Annie said slyly, 'are you likely to be losing yours?'

'Absolutely not,' Tina said firmly, 'Angus and I are good friends and that's the way it will remain.'

'That might suit you, Tina, but it might not suit Angus. He seems a nice lad so don't hurt his feelings.'

'I'll try not to,' she muttered as she finished her plate.

'Want more?'

'Wouldn't mind, please.'

Annie thought that whatever was troubling her it wasn't affecting her appetite. She brought over the dish that had been keeping hot on the stove.

'That's plenty, give yourself some.'

Annie took a little. 'I'm eating too much and I don't want to put on weight.'

Tina looked at her critically. 'You could stand gaining a few pounds and still call yourself slim.'

'Away with you,' Annie said but she was pleased.

In the morning Angus was waiting for her just yards away from the apartment.

'Hello, have you been here long or just arrived?'

'Only a few minutes.'

'You should have knocked. We are long out of our beds you know, my mother is what you would call an early riser. Incidentally,' she said as they began to walk, 'you are invited for a meal if you want to come.'

Angus looked surprised and pleased. 'That was kind of Mrs Brown and yes I would be honoured,' he said with old-fashioned courtesy. They walked slowly in a companionable silence until they reached the art school. 'When we are alone and have a bit of time I'll tell you about myself. There isn't a great deal but I'll tell you what there is and then you can return the compliment and tell me about your early life,' Angus said.

'You'd be bored stiff, there is nothing to tell.'

'Everyone has something to tell. In any case we shouldn't have secrets from each other, not if our feelings are serious and mine are.'

Tina looked at him unhappily. They were going to be late for classes but neither seemed too concerned.

He saw her expression. 'Don't you feel the same way? I thought you did.'

Tina was guiltily aware that she hadn't moved away when the kisses that had started as a light, butterfly touch of the lips, became more demanding. She hadn't moved away because she hadn't wanted to.

'Angus, I like you better than anyone else and it may be that I am a little in love with you . . .'

'A little is maybe enough to start with and a little can grow,' he said, a tender smile on his face.

'That is just it, Angus, it mustn't.'

'Why not?'

'You won't understand this—'

'Try me.'

'When you say serious, you have marriage in mind or am I wrong about that?'

'No, you are not wrong about that, I do have that in mind, but not for a while yet.'

'I don't have it in mind at all, not ever.'

'Why on earth not? What is wrong with marriage between two people who happen to be in love?'

'Nothing, people get married all the time. I'm not one of them, that's all.' She paused. 'We're horribly late.'

'All right, come on but this has to be continued.'

After classes they went to their favourite café for coffee and cake.

'Well?' Tina said when they were served.

'Oh, that, the story of my life, I wish I hadn't promised.'

'You did, so get a move on.'

He took a large bite of cake, ate it thoughtfully and declared it excellent.

'My family have a small estate in the Highlands—'

'Landed gentry?'

'Not at all, I said a small estate.'

He couldn't hide the pride in his voice and Tina nodded understandingly.

'You love your home, nothing wrong with that.'

'The life of a laird would have suited me down to the ground but I had the misfortune to be born the second son. When Father died Douglas took over the running of the estate.'

'You must have known that would happen?'

He seemed irritated at the remark. 'Of course I did but it seemed so unfair. I was the one who had always accompanied my father, I knew the workers and their families. When roofs needed mending or other repairs I was the one they came to not Douglas and not Father once he became a semi-invalid.'

'What was your brother Douglas doing all this time?'

'Good question, enjoying himself for most of the time. Don't get me wrong, Tina, I love my brother and my sister-in-law, Ruth, is a gem. They have a couple of great kids.'

'How is he coping with the estate?'

'Very well as it happens. Most of it Ruth's doing, she is very efficient but in the nicest way.'

Tina grinned. 'In other words she keeps that husband of hers on his toes. She is the laird behind the scenes?'

He grinned too. 'That just about sums it up. She looks after Mother as well and she was pretty low after my father died.'

'You came away because you felt you weren't needed,' Tina said gently.

'No one made me feel unwelcome. Inverkyle is the family home and I am still family. I just decided it was time I moved on and made something of my life. I'm twenty-three and old enough to stand on my own two feet. Go on, have another piece of cake,' he said handing over the plate.

'Just a half, we'll share it.' She cut it and gave him his share.

'Thanks. Where was I?'

'About to set out on your travels.'

'That comes later, don't rush me. At school art was my best subject and though Father didn't think painting was a real job he put no obstacles in my way and I studied in Edinburgh for a while—'

'With what goal in mind?'

'I don't think I had a goal. Painting was a hobby, a paying hobby maybe, but you see I always secretly hoped that—'

'You might be laird, that your brother wasn't interested?'

'Stupid, but we all have our hopes and dreams.' He smiled and covered her hand with his. 'As usual Father was right. He must have known that Douglas would shape up in the end and he had a great respect for Ruth. I'm not penniless by the way, the younger brother does get his share and even if none of my paintings sell I won't starve.'

'A good feeling, isn't it?'

'What is?'

'Having one's independence. Thanks to a great-great-aunt of mine I'm not penniless either.'

'Good, neither of us will be marrying for money then.'

The waitress came over, a hint that they had been sitting there long enough. Angus gave her a huge smile and asked in passable Italian for another two coffees. She shrugged but with the hint of a smile and went to get them.

'I didn't want another coffee.'

'Neither did I, but we need something in front of us while you tell me about your interesting life.'

'You'll be shocked.'

'I'm not easily shocked.'

'I'm not what you think, I'm different.'

'That's interesting for a start.'

'I'm illegitimate and that makes me different.' She said it flippantly but he saw that her eyes had gone flat. Tina had thought she didn't care but found she did and that was only because it would make a difference to the way Angus saw her.

'Do you really think that matters to me?'

'With your background it is bound to.'

'My background is nothing special.'

'Others would disagree.'

'Tina, the top people, the real aristocracy are among the worst offenders.'

'I know and they have a way of getting rid of the disgrace.'

'Have it adopted?'

'Better with someone who wants the poor scrap than—'

'Be unwanted. You could be right.'

She paused and was silent for a few moments. 'My mother died having me.'

'Then—' He sounded very surprised.

'She isn't my biological mother.'

'She dotes on you.'

'I know. I was very, very lucky.'

'Tina, the last thing I want is to distress you. You don't have to go on.'

'I want to now that I have got this length.'

'All right, I'm listening.'

She told him everything and not once did he interrupt, only occasionally nodding his head. When she finished there was a hint of tears in her voice and she got up abruptly. 'Come on, Angus, let's get out of here, that's enough sob stuff for one day.' She went outside while he paid the bill.

Chapter Thirty

'When you have the time, love, could we go to the big shops, it's time I was thinking about gifts to take home?'

'Of course, but what exactly had you in mind?' Tina said lifting her eyes from her grandmother's letter.

'Pottery dishes, little ornaments, that kind of thing.'

'Probably get as good a selection on the doorstep. There is the Pottery Shop next to the Gallery, have you had a look there?'

'Only the window, I didn't go inside.'

'You should have. Angus and I went in one day when it was raining and I thought they had a very attractive display. We can still go to the shops but it might be worth having a look there first.'

'I'll do that, it'll save a lot of trouble.'

Tina was using her persuasive voice. 'You *have* made up your mind to stay longer?'

'I shouldn't, but maybe another two weeks.'

'Make that a month.'

'Two months away from home! Impossible,' Annie said briskly.

'No, it isn't.'

Tina only smiled; two weeks would do to be going on with.

In case she got lost and it was more than possible, Annie never strayed too far from the piazza as she now called the square. The Pottery Shop wasn't very far away and she could take her bearings from the church, Santa Maria, with its tall steeple. The morning had started dull and rainy but now the sun was out and the pavements were drying. Annie had taken the precaution of carrying an umbrella just in case she was caught in a heavy shower. The rain had cooled the air and she was enjoying the walk. A stone archway led to a narrow, cobblestoned road and the church. The solid studded black door was open and a few worshippers were going in. Annie climbed the winding road and after a sharp bend the Gallery came into view. Added on at a later date was the Pottery Shop. When she went in a few people, like herself, were there to browse around. Maybe they, too, were on the lookout for gifts or souvenirs to take home.

Tina hadn't exaggerated, there was so much here, so many lovely things to choose from. One very beautiful fruit bowl took her eye and she picked it up to feel the weight. Far too heavy for her to take back to the Beeches and she must just content herself with a few small mementoes.

'May I be of assistance?'

Hearing the English voice, Annie swung round to look into the face of the man who had passed by as she sat in her usual seat in the piazza. He saw her start of surprise and then her recognition.

'We remember each other,' he smiled. 'Was I very rude that day? I wanted to apologise to you if it appeared I had been staring.'

She shook her head. 'I didn't think that at all. I — I'm looking for small gifts, lightweight ones to take home.'

'Does that mean you are to leave us shortly? I hope not.'

Her cheeks were pink. 'I came for a month but my daughter is trying to persuade me to stay longer.'

'I hope she succeeds.'

'She usually does.'

'Is your daughter on holiday too?'

'No, Tina is an art student,' Annie said proudly.

'Is she doing well?'

'I think so. She is talented and that isn't just a proud mother talking. At home she was considered quite exceptional.'

'And here?'

'Being a girl she is meeting some prejudice.'

'She has told you this?'

'I've gathered it.'

'It exists I know but take heart it will not always be that way.'

Annie didn't know whether he believed that or was just being kind. A couple were looking across, obviously wanting attention.

'I mustn't detain you, that couple are waiting to be served,' she said dropping her voice.

'Excuse me and I'll get one of the assistants.' He disappeared for a moment and a woman in a black dress went forward to attend to the customers.

'I do apologise, you must be the manager.'

'No, I'm not the manager,' he smiled. 'I am the owner of the Gallery and the Pottery Shop.'

Annie was biting her lip. 'Oh, dear, my daughter says I can be trusted to put my foot in it and she's right. I do apologise once again.'

'No need.' He touched her arm. 'Why don't we leave the choosing of your gifts until later and have a coffee. We have a small area for refreshments.' He indicated a door between what was the end of the Gallery and the beginning of the Pottery Shop. 'Mainly it is used for prospective buyers when they are comparing the merits of one painting against another.'

Annie was nervously wondering how she could get out of this invitation without appearing rude. Had he been an ordinary assistant or even the manager she might well have accepted.

'It is very kind of you but I'm afraid I must – I mean I would rather not . . .' She floundered to a stop.

'Rather not have my company, was that what you were going to say?'

'I didn't say that or at least I didn't mean to.' She stopped and looked at him helplessly.

'Please join me, I would enjoy your company.'

'All right, thank you.'

'Forgive me I should have introduced myself. Ralph Robertson. And you are Mrs——?'

'Brown. Mrs Annie Brown,' she said shakily. 'I'm wrong about something else, I thought you were Italian.'

'Half Italian, half English. Excuse me while I get someone to bring coffee or would you prefer tea?'

He saw her face. 'You've had a bad experience I see, but fear not this will be tea as it is made in England – or should I make that Britain?'

'It would be safer. I'm Scottish.'

'I thought I recognised the twang. Tea is it?'

'Yes, please.'

The tea came, she took a few sips and smiled.

'To your satisfaction?'

'Yes, this is a good cup of tea.'

'My assistant will be pleased when I tell her.'

They were seated at a small table facing each other. It was a plain room with leather chairs and on the walls were numerous prints and maps. There was a doily-covered plate with a selection of biscuits and he pushed it towards her.

'Thank you.' She took one.

'What made you think I was Italian?'

'You look like one.'

'Do I?'

'Dark skin and that very black hair.'

'That very black hair liberally sprinkled with grey,' he smiled. 'I have my mother to thank for my Italian looks or to blame for them. As to the English side I first saw the light of day in Devon where distant relatives of my late father still live. I'm saying still live but we don't keep up so they could be dead for all I know.'

'What brought you to Florence?'

'Mother was homesick for her beloved Italy and my poor

father had little choice but to give up a promising career to teach English if the family was to remain together.'

'A bit hard on your father. Did he ever regret giving up so much?' Annie asked as she sipped tea from the fine bone-china cup.

'I'm sure he did and often but he never said so, at least not in my hearing.'

'Easy for you then to speak both languages fluently.'

'Don't you believe it. Growing up bilingual has its advantages in later life but it can be very hard on the child. Father was so afraid my English would suffer that he made a rule.' He laughed as he said it. 'One of the very few he made, my mother was the dominant partner—'

'What rule was that?' Annie asked when he stopped to drink some of his tea.

'Only English would be spoken at the table and if either my sister or I couldn't remember how to ask for something we had to do without.'

'You don't mean that.'

'It is true and I don't suppose it did us any harm. I'm boring you talking so much about myself.'

'No, you are not, I'm finding this very interesting.'

'Very well, I'll tell you a little more but I warn you I shall want a peep into your life.'

'Now that would really be boring.'

'Nothing about you could ever be boring. More tea?'

'Yes, please.'

He filled up both cups.

'If I'm not being too inquisitive tell me how you come to own the Gallery when your father was a schoolmaster.'

'The Gallery belonged to my maternal grandfather. He was a wonderful old man and I adored him.' He moved a little away from the table and crossed one leg over the other as though he had all the time in the world to sit and talk. 'Much as I loved my parents I was closer to my grandfather. With no son of his own he was training me to take his place. It was a great joy to him that I had inherited his love of art.'

'You are an artist?'

'Not in the sense you mean. I am an adviser in art and those who do not trust their own judgement seek my advice.'

Annie tried to think of a sensible question. 'You buy paintings and sell them?'

'Among other things, yes.'

'Was the Pottery Shop there or are you responsible for that?'

'I was responsible. I felt there was a demand and happily that proved to be correct. People have been kind enough to tell me that the selection here is as good as in the main shops and less expensive.'

'Which reminds me, Mr Robertson, that I came here to buy gifts and now it is too late. Thank you for the tea but I must go.' She made a movement and he got up.

'Thank you for your company, Mrs Brown, I enjoyed our little while together and I look forward to a return visit.' He went to the door with her and Annie walked home in a daze. Would she go back? She knew she would.

Perhaps if Annie had been less concerned with meeting the owner of the Gallery she would have seen the strain on Tina's face.

'I've had a very interesting day, Tina.'

'Good for you.'

'I'll tell you about it when I get this served up.' When she sat down at the table the words almost tumbled out as she told Tina all that had happened.

'I'm glad you've had such a wonderful day and wasn't it a good thing me suggesting the Pottery Shop? Think what you would have missed if I hadn't.'

'Tina, he was so kind and friendly and of course speaking English—'

'What did you buy?'

'Nothing.'

'He won't want too many customers like you. Wasn't there anything to suit you?'

'If I'd stayed any longer you wouldn't have had a meal ready for you.'

'That wouldn't have mattered, I could have waited.'

'No, I like to be here when you get in.'

'Oh, Mother—' Her voice cracked.

Annie's knife and fork clattered to the plate. 'Tina, love, what is it?' she said coming round the table.

'Nothing.'

'There is something far wrong and you are going to tell me what it is,' Annie said grimly. 'Leave the meal, I'll make something later or we can go out.' She led Tina over to the sofa and sat down beside her. 'Come on, out with it, Tina.'

'I'm just so disappointed and angry.'

'What about?'

She sniffed, searched for a handkerchief, found it in her sleeve and blew her nose. 'I told you about the assessment?'

Annie nodded. 'Someone important comes to give an opinion on the paintings.'

'Not quite. Only the best paintings are put forward for assessment and the best student gets special tuition.' She swallowed. 'We were all terribly excited because the judging is being done by two well-known painters. Jonathan Fairweather is one and Jonathan Fairweather, Mother, is the best. I've seen his work—'

'Yes, yes, I've got all that but—'

'But,' Tina said bitterly, 'he won't see mine because none of my paintings have been selected, none have apparently reached the required standard.'

'Rubbish, yours are far above the required standard,' Annie said staunchly.

'Oh, Mother, I'm not that good,' Tina said trying to laugh.

'Yes you are. What about Angus?'

'Two of his landscapes are going forward. They are very good and I'm delighted for Angus.'

'What is he saying about it?'

'He's furious, absolutely livid, I won't say what he called

them and he was all for having a showdown but I put my foot down there. It's the closest we've come to a quarrel. I told him to mind his own business, that I was perfectly capable of fighting my own battles.'

'That was rude of you. You shouldn't have been so nasty to Angus and him only trying to help.'

'I apologised and it's all right,' Tina said wearily.

'There are other art schools.'

'There is nothing wrong with this one. I am learning a lot, I just don't get praise and maybe that isn't such a bad thing. It's certainly brought me down to size. No, Mother, they will not have the satisfaction of seeing me go. I'll do my year and get my money's worth.'

'That's the spirit.' She gave Tina a quick hug.

'All this almost put it out of my mind. You must come to our exhibition, open to the public. Come and see the students at work. It'll be a chance for you to see around.'

'Will you be available?'

'No, I'll be busy behind my easel but you can come and talk to me, that is permissible, then you'll have to look around on your own. And Mother,' she said warningly, 'don't repeat a word I've told you, I need your promise on that.'

Annie gave it but reluctantly. She wanted to tell those two art teachers just what she thought of them. On second thoughts what good would it do with their limited English and her non-existent Italian.

The day was cooler than it had been and instead of a cotton dress, Annie wore her linen suit and didn't bother with a hat. No danger of sunstroke today. When she reached the school a number of people were wandering the corridors and there was the gabble of foreign tongues. She found Tina working with other students in a large room where boxes and bundles of paintings were pushed against the wall.

Annie saw Tina's fair head above the easel and went over.

'Hello, Mother, you managed then?'

'Very easily.'

'You look nice, but you shouldn't have dressed up for this.'

'Well I have.' Annie raised her eyes to the painting and gave a start of surprise.

'You recognise it then?' She smiled. 'I'm working from memory.'

'Denbrae House. Keep that one and give it to your grandmother.'

'Maybe I will.'

Angus sauntered over. 'Hello, Mrs Brown, come to see the monkeys in the zoo?'

'Hello, Angus, never mind monkeys in the zoo I feel like a fish out of water. I don't know the first thing about art and I never know what to say.'

'That is quite shocking, Mrs Brown, and you the mother of a budding genius. Oh, God, I'd better get back before you-know-who finds me missing.'

'He's hopeless,' Tina laughed, 'and what's more he couldn't care less. Sometimes I think this is all just a big joke with him.'

'Maybe he wants you to think that. He has talent?'

'Some. He isn't outstanding but then his heart isn't in it.'

'I'd better let you get on,' Annie said moving away. 'I'll take a look at some of the paintings and then I'll get back to the apartment.'

'I may be a bit late, there will be some clearing up to do.'

'That's fine, I'll see you when you come.'

There were doors leading from the main corridor and all were wide open. Most of the walls were covered in pictures and paintings. Some of the doors had brass plates but whatever was indicated by them was lost on Annie. She pursed her lips, tried to look knowledgeable as she dutifully went from one work of art to the next. Some she admired and others she wouldn't have given wall space. Funnily enough the paintings she liked least were the ones getting most attention. All this walking about and standing was hard on the feet and to Annie this was the only drawback to Florence. The pavements were too hot. At home she had never been bothered with sore feet and yet she had seldom been off them.

Wandering from room to room Annie came to one where there were no jabbering Italians and seeing a chair she sat down gratefully and eased her feet out of her shoes. The thought did strike her that she shouldn't be here. Still what harm was she doing? None that she could see. Five minutes' rest and then she would take herself back to the apartment, her duty done.

Annie closed her eyes and drifted into pleasant thoughts.

The room was not unoccupied. Had Annie looked to the floor behind the easel she would have seen a pair of very large feet. The artist had replaced his canvas with a fresh sheet of paper and he was smiling as he quickly sketched the woman resting so easily and so naturally. Afterwards Annie was never to admit to falling asleep but only to resting her eyes.

Twenty minutes later she came to with a jerk and was putting her feet back in her shoes when she almost jumped out of her skin.

'How did you get in here?' she demanded.

'This is my studio and if anyone is trespassing I would suggest it was you.' Then seeing her look of anguish he hastened in with: 'It's all right, really it is. I hope you don't mind but I did a sketch of you. I couldn't resist it, especially the feet.'

'Oh, dear,' Annie said faintly.

'Come and look.'

She got up and went round to the other side of the easel. What she saw had her laughing and laughing. Annie couldn't help it. She should have been furious but it was just so funny. It was her to a T, as Mrs Archibald at the Beeches would have said.

He joined in the laughter. 'I'm glad you aren't offended.'

The pencil sketch reminded Annie of another. Rather

than leave the one of Miss Emily between the pages of *Sense and Sensibility* and risk one of the maids dusting the books and perhaps losing the envelope, Annie carried it with her in her bag.

'I'm not offended though perhaps I should be, but let me show you something.' She rummaged about in her bag until she found the envelope. 'It's worn with age but it is the same sort of pencil sketch,' she was saying as she took it carefully out of the envelope and put it on the table. Annie wasn't prepared for his bark of shocked amazement.

'Where on earth did you get that? That's mine, I did that God knows how many years ago.' He had been leaning over her shoulder and when she looked up and into his face it was her turn to be shocked. Annie's heart gave a leap. Deep blue eyes, so like Tina's, were holding her own in a steady gaze. There was a buzzing in her ears she supposed was the result of shock and she knew without a shadow of doubt that this big, broad-shouldered man was the same man, the artist, Miss Emily had fallen in love with all those years ago.

'You haven't answered my question, how do you come to have this sketch?'

'Let me put a question to you first. What do you remember about the girl in the sketch?'

He shook his head.

'Perhaps I can help you,' Annie said unsteadily.

He was still shaking his head. 'Whoever she is won't be very young now. That must have been done – let me think – nineteen or twenty years ago.'

'Nearer twenty-one. I can tell you this much. You sketched that girl in a field in Greenhill, Perthshire. You had rented a cottage from a farmer and the girl was from nearby Denbrae House.'

He was smiling. 'It's coming back.'

'The girl was Miss Emily Cunningham-Brown.'

'How do you know all this?'

Annie brushed that aside. 'You do remember?'

'Not in detail, I haven't that kind of memory. What I

seem to recall is a girl, a pretty little thing who wouldn't stay away. She was coming between me and my work and if I can put it bluntly making a nuisance of herself.'

'That is very possible, she was used to getting her own way.'

'Where is she now?'

'Miss Emily is dead,' Annie said quietly.

'I *am* sorry, she was quite a bit younger than me.' He paused. 'You were a friend?'

'I like to think so and that was true later when she was banished from the family home. You see I was a maid at Denbrae House and I went with her to Dundrinnen up north.'

'Banished? What had the poor girl done?'

'Enough to disgrace the family name. Do you mind if I ask yours, your name I mean?'

'Jonathan Fairweather.'

The name sounded vaguely familiar and Annie remembered then that one of the artists to do with the assessment was called that.

'Mr Fairweather, you have another shock coming to you. Miss Emily died giving birth to your child, your daughter.'

He was on his feet and his face had gone pale. 'How dare you suggest such a thing.'

'Think back, Mr Fairweather, a long way back I know, but think back and hand on heart can you deny that the possibility was there?'

He was silent for a long time. 'I can tell you this Mrs—'

'Brown.'

'Mrs Brown, that I have never forced myself on any woman.'

'I believe you.' He was still a handsome man and in his younger years must have been attractive to women. 'Miss Emily was in love with you. She was a very honest person and said she had shamelessly pursued you, that what happened was entirely her own fault. I think she took too much guilt on herself, it does take two after all.'

He gave a crooked smile. 'Emily took all the blame?'

'Not once did she say who was responsible for her condition although her parents did everything to try and force it out of her. She told me a little, just that he was an artist who had to be free to go where he wanted and that there would be no question of marriage – ever.'

'I can't accept this, you know, a popular, pretty girl like Emily would have had many admirers and a busy social life.'

'Not after she met you.' Her face flushed as the next words came out. 'You cannot know for sure if you were the last but you must know that you were the first.'

She saw him swallowing and looking uncomfortable. 'Now that you have got this length you had better go on with the rest.' He got up to close the door properly, then took a chair.

'The baby was to be adopted and Miss Emily to return home after supposedly having had a holiday abroad with her cousin.'

'Was that what happened?'

'No. Miss Emily decided she wanted to keep her baby and without telling her parents she made the necessary arrangements. She had her own money and I was there to help her.'

'Then she died,' he said softly and she thought she caught a look of pain.

'Yes. I couldn't see the baby going to strangers, I won't go into the details, just let me say I brought her up as my own.'

'Does she know you are not her mother?'

'She knows everything. I waited until she was fourteen before telling her.'

'How did she take it?'

'Very well. We are very close and I think if anything that brought us even closer.'

'Was she curious about her – father?'

'Not especially. Tina is a very unusual young woman. All she really lives for is painting and for that gift she thanks her unknown father. Tina is here, Mr Fairweather, she is a student.'

'Then I will be seeing her work.'

'No you won't. Tina tells me that none of her paintings have been put forward for this assessment.'

'I'm afraid, Mrs Brown, that speaks for itself. If her work wasn't selected then it was not of a sufficiently high standard. That doesn't mean it is poor, just not good enough to be considered.'

'You are wrong to think that. Tina's work is well up to the required standard and beyond it. She is very talented, Mr Fairweather, but because she is a girl her work is not taken seriously.'

'You cannot be a judge. This has all been very interesting, Mrs Brown, and all because of a sketch I did long ago. To use a time-worn cliché, it is a small world.'

'Yes, it is and you, Mr Fairweather, are afraid of the truth.'

'The truth as you think you see it. I am not accepting this girl as my daughter.'

'That doesn't upset me in the least.'

'Are you going to tell her?'

'No.'

'Because you don't really believe it yourself?'

'Wrong, I do believe it. However there is one thing I ask of you.'

'And that is?'

'Look at Tina Brown's paintings and make your own judgement.'

'I can promise that.'

'However you go about it please make sure that Tina gets no hint that I was involved.'

'No problem and will you accept my verdict whatever it might be?'

Annie didn't immediately answer, then she said quietly, 'Yes, Mr Fairweather, I will accept your verdict.'

'Thank you and before you go I would like to leave you with this. You may think it selfishness on my part and I don't deny there is some of that.' He smiled. 'If Tina should, indeed, be my daughter it is better for her that she shouldn't know. If she was to make a name for herself the satisfaction would come from knowing she had made it on her own and not because she was—'

'The daughter of a renowned painter. Yes, I would agree with that.'

He walked with her to the door and opened it. They shook hands.

'Tina is your daughter, there is no doubt in my mind, but should she ever find out the truth it won't be through me.'

'I won't claim her, Mrs Brown, though the day may come when I wish I had.'

She liked him for that. 'One more thing I ask of you. I want you to tell me yourself, face-to-face your true opinion of Tina's paintings.'

'How can we do that? Not here, that could be awkward, but I am in my own studio Thursdays and Fridays. Make it afternoon and you'll find me there.'

'Where is there?'

'In Via Marco. You know it?'

'I don't know anywhere. Write it down and someone will show me where it is.'

He turned back and she followed him.

'I'll give you my card.'

'No, don't do that. If Tina saw it how would I explain it? No, a piece of paper I can destroy.'

'You do know your own mind, Mrs Brown.'

'I have to when it is something as important as this.'

Long after she left, Jonathan Fairweather was deep in thought and then true to his word he went along to have a word with Signor Vialli. They spoke about matters of general interest then he said casually that he would have a look at the work of the less successful, that sometimes a word of encouragement did wonders.

Signor Vialli smirked that it would need more than that and Jonathan nodded and began his round. He spoke to each student and made a remark on the work produced for his benefit.

Tina knew that someone had come into the room but didn't look up. Jonathan could see only one girl and she was a disappointment. He didn't know what he had expected but certainly not someone so drab. She was very nervous and, what made it worse, the girl was so piteously grateful for his few encouraging words.

If this was Tina Brown, and there was no sign of any other female, then it was small wonder her work hadn't been singled out. The poor lass tried hard, he would give her that, but she would never be better than mediocre. If the essential something was missing no amount of teaching would alter that. Feeling his duty done, Jonathan was about to have a few words with Signor Vialli before he departed when he saw a fair-haired girl at the far end of the room. Approaching her, Jonathan saw that this girl was totally absorbed in what she was doing and didn't spare him a glance. She was lovely and Jonathan felt strangely excited. It was like opening the door on a lost memory.

'Very good,' he said quietly and felt a lump in his throat.

She turned round, her blue eyes lighting up. 'Is it good? Do you really think so?'

'I do.'

'It's my grandparents' home in Scotland and this is from memory.'

He nodded. 'Show me your other paintings if you will?'

'Of course.' She was flushed with excitement and a bit embarrassed at not immediately acknowledging his presence. She had been aware of someone but hadn't wanted to stop what she was doing. From the corner of her eye she could see Signor Vialli looking over and frowning. With a toss of her head for his benefit Tina displayed her work against the wall. A few of the students were looking over, curious as to what was going on.

Tina's eyes never moved from his face but Jonathan

Fairweather showed nothing, not a spark of interest and her last hope fled. She was angry, very, very angry. Why say Denbrae House was good if he didn't mean it? For the first time in her life she knew complete dejection and only just stopped herself walking out never to return.

Jonathan Fairweather was equally angry, he didn't know when he had been so angry and it made his voice curt.

'Tell me your name?'

'Tina Brown,' she said woodenly.

How could Signor Vialli fail to recognise a major talent when he saw one. The girl was outstanding but she shouldn't be wasting her time with landscapes, not when she showed such a flair, such skilfulness with life drawings. Unless he was very much mistaken Tina Brown was destined for great things as a portrait painter. She had that rare gift of bringing her subject to life. A huge excitement was battling with a terrible anger. Because of a stupid, bigoted teacher, Tina's work might have been lost. He wouldn't show him up in front of the students though he had a mind to. No doubt they knew that Tina's paintings were far superior to their own painstaking efforts. He muttered thank you to Tina and signalled to Signor Vialli to follow him out. When they were far enough along the corridor, Jonathan turned on him.

'Why? Just tell me why?'

The raised bushy eyebrows were meant to show surprise and ignorance of what was being asked.

'That girl's work, why wasn't it put forward?'

'In my opinion—'

'Which counts for very little if you can't recognise a gifted student when you see one.'

'I am well aware the paintings in question show promise but why waste time and effort for nothing? The girl is pretty, she will marry, have children and the painting is something that will be brought out in odd moments when she can spare the time.'

'You can't know that and you could be very far wrong. I

would say that girl is dedicated to art, that marriage and motherhood have no place in her plans.'

Signor Vialli's eyes narrowed. 'You seem to know a lot about Signorina Brown.'

'I never set eyes on the girl until a few minutes ago.' He paused. 'Ask the girl to select three of her paintings, one a life drawing, and have her bring them along to me.' He gave a curt nod and walked away.

Annie had no difficulty finding someone to direct her to Jonathan Fairweather's studio in Via Marco. A woman pushing a pram, who said she was going that way, took her to the door.

'*Grazie*,' Annie said gratefully then added for good measure, 'thank you very much.' The young woman disappeared round the corner and Annie took time to study the building in the narrow Via Marco. To Annie it looked ancient, like stepping back into history. A brass plate with his name confirmed that she was at the right place and she climbed the winding, much worn stone stairs. There were two doors on the first landing and two nameplates on the wall. One gave his name with an arrow pointing to a door which was half open. She gave a small tap.

'If that is someone knocking, come in.' Annie recognised the voice and went in.

'Thought it might be you. Had I not been listening I might not have heard that apology of a knock.'

'Then I would have knocked louder,' Annie said with a smile.

'I'm sure you would.' He came over to shake her hand, cleared a chair and asked her to be seated. His paint-stained smock was torn under the arm and she wondered if he had anyone to look after him. 'A disapproving look if I am not mistaken but I make no apology for the chaos, we artists work better surrounded by clutter.'

'I know, we have one like you at home.'

He wiped his hands on a towel and drew over a chair for himself.

'I'll come straight to the point. Tina will be taking tuition from me as from now.'

Annie beamed. 'She is that good?'

'She is that good,' he smiled.

'Just what I expected you to say, but tell me what is that Mister Villain saying about it?'

He threw back his head and roared with laughter. 'For your information Signor Vialli was severely reprimanded or if you are familiar with the expression, went away with a flea in his ear.'

She nodded. 'Seriously, I am very grateful to you and you can't even begin to know what this will mean to Tina.'

'I think I do,' he said quietly. 'It might have taken her longer, but she would have got there in the end.'

'I'm not so sure. Tina was trying to hide her disappointment from me but I knew that inside she was weeping and that a lot of her confidence in her own ability had gone.'

They both got up. Annie made to shake hands but he took her hand in both of his. 'Tina is very lucky to have you and Emily knew who to choose for a friend.'

'Thank you.'

Nothing more was said but the look that passed between them convinced Annie that Jonathan Fairweather was acknowledging to her that Tina was his daughter and he was proud of her.

Chapter Thirty-One

After seeing Jonathan Fairweather, Annie was in such a state when she got back that she burnt her finger lifting a hot dish out of the oven and was rubbing soap on it when Tina came bursting in. She looked flushed and happy with her fair curls in glorious disarray and rushed over to give Annie a huge hug.

'Mother, you'll never guess, never in a million years,' the words were falling over each other in her haste to get them out.

'No point in trying then, is there?' Annie smiled.

'I can't believe it, it's just so wonderful.' Tina managed to say before her eyes filled and the tears rolled down her cheeks.

Annie patted her shoulder and gave her time to recover.

'Sorry about that, stupid to cry when we're happy, isn't it?' She sniffed, blew her nose and smiled through the tears. 'You remember me telling you my paintings were not to be assessed?'

'I do, blind as a bat that teacher you have. You are going to tell me he has seen sense and they are to be assessed after all?'

'Better than that, in fact far better than that,' Tina laughed excitedly. 'Jonathan Fairweather, you know who I mean, *the* Jonathan Fairweather, likes my work, was high in his praise and – wait for it – I've been selected for special lessons. Not in the school but in his own studio.'

Annie sent up a silent prayer that she had wandered into
that room and all this had come about because of that sketch
of her. Worth making a fool of herself. Fate, she thought,
sometimes did take a hand.

'Which only goes to show he must have been very
impressed.'

'Signor Vialli apologised and in the end he was rather
sweet. He said he very much liked my paintings and had I
been plain' – Tina giggled – 'he would have put them
forward.'

'Likely story.'

'No, let me finish. He said he thought it would be a waste
because he was sure I would get married, have lots of babies
and forget all about painting.'

'And you put him right, I hope?'

'No, I just smiled and we shook hands. Far better to part
with no bad feelings.'

With Tina wrapped up in happiness, Annie could think
about her own situation. This had been an unforgettable
holiday but holidays couldn't go on for ever and it was time
to return to the Beeches. Leaving Tina, leaving Florence,
was going to be hard, but the thought of leaving Ralph
Robertson for ever made her want to weep. She didn't deny
to herself that she was in love, what was the use, but no one
else must know, she must be very careful about that. A few
weeks, that was all the time she had known him, yet how
long did it take to fall in love? She had been attracted from
that first moment their eyes met. How could she ever have
believed herself in love with that dreadful Edward Galloway? Just to think of him had her shuddering. Ralph was his
complete opposite, he was kind and good and a gentleman
in every sense of the word.

Annie sighed. Dreaming impossible dreams that's what
she had been doing. Italians set such store by the family and
she didn't have one. They were poles apart. The days were
few when they didn't see each other and it just seemed to
have happened naturally. Sometimes Ralph would sit beside

her in the piazza. At other times they would take a stroll and drink coffee at one of the cafés. People were noticing the friendship developing between Signor Robertson and the quiet English lady who so often sat under the shade of the trees in the piazza. They smiled but it was in a nice way. They were all very fond of Signor Robertson.

Tina and Angus had been introduced to Mr Robertson and both agreed he was 'all right' which from them was high praise. Ralph had a quiet, friendly way with him that made conversation easy. Back at home Tina would tease her mother about her Italian boyfriend but was scornful when Angus suggested it might be serious.

'Don't be daft, Angus, my mother is forty-five and Mr Robertson is probably a few years older.'

'Age matters not, my darling, he is a widower, she a widow. Can it be that you are not prepared to welcome a stepfather?'

'As it happens I wouldn't mind, I like him, but it won't happen. Mother is perfectly happy as she is,' Tina said in a voice that said she knew best.

When Ralph joined Annie for their stroll, he remarked about her being unusually quiet.

'Do I detect a little sadness, Annie?'

'I was just thinking how much I am going to miss all this when I leave.'

'Tina tells me there is absolutely nothing hurrying you back, that your second-in-charge is managing very well.'

'That may be so, but I can't stay away too long. I came for a month, you know, and it will soon be two.'

'It would be a great pity to return before I have had the opportunity to show you Florence, not the visitors' Florence, Annie, but the real city. I had hoped to take a few days off from the Gallery and to be your escort.'

'Were you? Were you really going to do that?'

'I was and I still am if you don't run away. Please stay.'

She shook her head.

'Annie, there is so much I wanted us to do together. Tina

is busy for most of the day which leaves you a lot on your own.'

'I don't mind, I was prepared for that and I *have* managed to see quite a lot,' Annie protested.

'Museums and art galleries and not much more apart from some of the shops,' he chuckled. 'All very interesting but a very small part of what there is to see. There is the beauty of the countryside, the Cypress trees that are very often planted as a windbreak in the fields. Did you know that?'

She shook her head.

'Many of our families make their own wine and the farms sell home-produced olive oil. Still interested?'

Annie laughed. 'Still interested.'

'Let me see. Ah, yes, the sunflowers, now that is a sight to gladden the heart. Each season has its wonders—'

'Just as in Scotland.'

'Granted but this is different. Spring brings out the window boxes, hardly a house without them. We celebrate John the Baptist day which you may or may not know is the 24th June.'

'I didn't know.'

'So much to learn. We have many festivals, Annie, all to be celebrated with local food and wine—'

'And a happy time had by all,' Annie laughed. 'Don't, please, you are only making it worse for me.'

'Which is exactly what I am trying to do. You have only seen the outside of my house since I couldn't persuade you to have lunch with me. My housekeeper would have been delighted to make your acquaintance.'

'If you ask me again I may manage to accept. I would like to see the inside,' she admitted and saw him smile. The tall house quite close to the Gallery was very imposing with its ivy-smothered walls and the curving stone steps leading to the door. It would be another memory to take back with her. 'Living so near to your work gives you no excuse for being late,' Annie smiled.

'A bit like living over the shop and that can have its

disadvantages. Grandfather had the house built to his specifications and possibly in the hope of having a large family which sadly wasn't to be. After my wife, Isabella, died, Gabriella said I should get rid of it and get something smaller and easier to manage but I couldn't bring myself to do that. My needs are simple and I only use the ground floor. It is only when my sister and her brood descend on me that we use the dining-room. You would like Gabriella and Luigi and their four adorable, boisterous, very wearing children. To be honest I love to see them and I love to see them go. I'm afraid I value my peaceful existence.' He smiled. 'Does that make me sound very ancient?'

'Not at all and I wouldn't call you ancient.'

'I'm about to celebrate my half century.'

'I'm forty-five.'

'Just nice for each other.'

Time to change the subject. 'Where do they live, your sister and family?'

'Siena. Not very far away and well worth a visit. You simply cannot leave Firenze with so much still to see.' There were a few seats around and they made for one that had just become vacant. Once they were seated he turned to face her. 'Maybe it is time I told you what is in my heart. Before you entered my life, Annie, I didn't realise how lonely I was. The truth, if you don't know it, is that I have fallen in love with you.'

She was shaking her head and blinking back embarrassing tears. 'You will soon forget me once I'm gone.'

'Never. Is this your way of saying that you don't love me? You are a very honest person, Annie, it is one of the many things I love about you. If you don't love me say so. None of this letting me down gently, I prefer to be told the truth.' He forced her to look at him.

Annie swallowed. He deserved the truth.

'Has it something to do with Tina?' he asked.

'No, nothing to do with Tina, she is very fond of you. Since you insist on the truth, Ralph, I do love you.'

'That is all I need to know.'

'It isn't. You know nothing about me.'

'Enough to know that I want to spend the rest of my life with you. Annie, I'm asking you to marry me.'

'You just don't understand. Ralph, I don't even know who I am.'

He looked puzzled.

'I don't and I never will.' She blinked to keep away the tears and tried to steady her voice. 'Let me tell you about myself and when I'm finished you don't need to say anything, I'll understand.' Then she told him the story of her life from the orphanage to the Beeches and by the end her voice had sunk to almost nothing. She kept her face averted not wanting to see the expression on his.

'Look at me, Annie! What kind of man do you think I am?' It was the first time she had heard anger in his voice.

'All Italians care about family,' she said shakily.

'They do, I don't deny that. You have Tina and she couldn't have a better mother. Really, Annie, for an intelligent woman you surprise me and I'm torn between wanting to kiss you or shake you. Maybe I'll do both. No right-minded individual would be shocked or disgusted by what you have told me, far from it. Being a foundling is nothing to be ashamed of. I am thinking of a tiny babe getting a poor welcome into this world.'

'You are honestly saying it doesn't matter?'

'Of course it doesn't matter. You are a very wonderful woman and a courageous one. Not many would have done what you did. If what you have told me makes any difference at all it is to make me love you all the more.' Looking into those soft brown eyes he saw the love there and uncaring whether they were seen or not, he took her in his arms and held her close. 'From now on I will look after you, my darling, and you must do something for me.'

'Anything,' she said huskily.

'You must learn Italian.'

'Is it very difficult?'

He shook his head. 'No, not at all difficult. Italian is a beautiful language and I shall teach you.'

'You won't be so hard on me as your father was on you?' she laughed.

'Now I hadn't thought of that but, no, I could never be hard on you.'

'You'll be patient?'

'Oh, very patient and now I think you will agree there is no question of you returning to the Beeches.'

'The Beeches seems so far away, like in another life. I'm just so happy, Ralph, the two people I love most in the world will be here. Regarding the guest house, Miss Urquhart may want to buy it, I'll ask her first and if she doesn't it will go on the market.'

Annie wondered how she was going to tell Tina her news and kept worrying about it as she prepared the meal they would eat at six o'clock. Tina and Ralph got on well together but that was a far cry from being asked to accept Ralph Robertson as the man her mother had promised to marry. There was a fear growing in Annie that Tina would be shocked and upset. Would she see her mother as silly, believing as so many of the young did, that romantic love was for them and not for someone her age? How could she make Tina understand that she loved Ralph so much that if she were to lose him now her life would be meaningless?

When Tina breezed in just before six o'clock, she chattered on about the day's events and Annie heard enough to be able to smile and put in the occasional word. She had decided that news, good or bad, was better given after a meal rather than before it. Tina had a hearty appetite and enjoyed what was put before her and didn't notice how little Annie ate. Only when the dishes were cleared away and they were having coffee at the low table, did Annie begin to talk about what was on her mind.

'Tina, you do like Ralph, you do like Mr Robertson?'

'You know I do. I think he's a pet and very fond of my mother,' she teased.

'What would you say if I told you it was more than fond?'

'Am I supposed to answer that?'

'Yes.'

Tina was thoughtful. 'Then I would say you would have to be careful not to hurt him. Poor Mother, is life becoming complicated?' she said gently. 'This wasn't something you bargained for when you came to Florence.'

Annie could only agree with that. She swallowed. The difficult part was still to come. 'And if I was to tell you that it wasn't all on one side?'

Tina looked worried then disbelieving. 'Mother, are you trying to tell me something?'

'I am and I'm not doing it very well.' Her hands were gripped together. 'Ralph has asked me to marry him and I have accepted.'

'You are joking, you have to be?'

'Why should I be joking?'

'Then you are serious?'

'Yes, very serious. A shock for you, Tina, but you like Ralph you said so and you are pleased for us, aren't you?'

Tina saw the pleading in those soft brown eyes and pulling her mother out of the sofa she gave her a big hug.

'Of course I'm pleased. Your happiness means everything to me and if you are sure this is right for you—'

'I am.'

'Then there is no more to be said except to say that you deserve to be happy and I hope Mr Robertson – heavens I can't keep calling him that – would he object if I addressed him as Ralph?'

'I'm sure he wouldn't.'

'As I was saying I just hope he realises how lucky he is.'

'I'm the lucky one.'

Tina hid her anxiety but she was troubled. She had thought this to be no more than a holiday friendship and had ridiculed Angus when he had suggested there might be more to it. What should she do? Nothing she supposed. She had no right to interfere. On the other hand she couldn't just do nothing and let her mother make what might turn out to be the biggest mistake of her life. She would have to tread very carefully.

'Mother, this is all very exciting but I wonder if you have given this enough thought. No, don't answer that, let me say what is on my mind. After all I am your daughter and your welfare and happiness are my concern.'

Annie smiled and nodded.

'You would be far from home, you would be living here in Florence.'

'I already love Florence.'

'So do I but that isn't the point. This is Italy, a foreign country.'

'It will become home to me.'

'Then there is the language, I haven't noticed you making any attempt to learn it.'

'I intend to do so or do you think that is beyond me?' Annie said tartly.

'Mother, nothing is beyond you.'

'Tina, I can see you are concerned but truly you have nothing to worry about. Every marriage is a risk, every marriage has to be worked at but with love, respect and a sense of humour I think, I know, that Ralph and I will make a success of it.'

Tina smiled, feeling much happier now. Her mother wasn't going into this blindly. Ralph and she were mature people who knew their own mind. She was beginning to think that this could be a very happy marriage, she certainly hoped so.

Relieved that the telling was over Annie felt she could relax. 'With my future more or less settled am I allowed to ask about Angus and you?'

'Nothing to tell you except to say he was right and I was the one slow off the mark.'

'What are you talking about?'

'Angus thought you and Mr – you and Ralph were in love and I ridiculed him.'

'Why did you do that?'

'I'm not altogether sure,' Tina said slowly, 'maybe I just didn't want to share you. I didn't say that to Angus.'

'What did you say?'

'That I thought you were both too old.'

Annie bristled. 'What a cheek, I hope Angus didn't agree?'

'He didn't and I didn't think it either. It was just as I said that I didn't want to lose you.'

'Tina, my darling, that could never happen. You will always be my precious child.' Her face lit up with what she was to say next. 'I'm so happy to think we won't be parted, that we'll be together in Florence.'

Tina was shaking her head. 'No, Mother, that isn't going to happen.'

'But I thought—'

'I know what you thought, that I would settle here and paint. I'll do my year, Mother, and Jonathan says that is all I need. The rest is up to me, to make my own mark.' She was looking carefully at Annie when she said, 'I'm going home.'

'Home?' Annie felt a tightness in her chest.

'Yes, I'm going to live with Grandmother in Denbrae House.'

'I see.' Annie felt as though she had been dealt a physical blow. The Cunningham-Browns had won and it was all her own fault. If she hadn't been so anxious for Tina to claim her inheritance none of this would have happened. Yet how could she regret coming to Florence and meeting Ralph Robertson? She was experiencing the kind of happiness she had never imagined for herself.

'No, you don't.' Tina took a deep breath. 'I would never have left you, never. You must believe that.'

'I do believe it. You would have stayed at the Beeches out of a sense of loyalty and all the time wishing you were with your grandmother.'

'That must be the most hurtful thing you could have said to me.'

'I'm sorry,' Annie whispered.

'And so you should be. You are going to have Ralph to look after you, you won't need me, Grandmother does, she says so in every letter.'

'I'm being selfish. She is a lonely old woman and I should remember that.'

'She is also a very cold, calculating besom,' Tina said with a laugh. 'And you are wrong to believe Grandmother is the reason. She has no hold over me but Denbrae House has. I can't explain it properly but it seems to be calling me.'

'Perhaps it is calling you, Tina,' Annie said softly. 'Your own mother loved that house and I know that nothing would have pleased her more than to know her own daughter was there.'

'Maybe she did leave me that part of herself.'

Annie nodded. 'Tell me this, Tina, I would really like to know, do you love Angus?'

'Of course I love him.'

'Enough to marry him?'

Tina moved impatiently. 'Why is marriage so important?'

'It was invented for a very good reason,' Annie said severely, 'it is a commitment.'

'We don't need that.'

'Meaning artists are different?'

'I think we are, we don't live by a certain set of rules. Angus and I understand each other. He accepts that my painting will always come first.'

'You could lose him if you aren't careful.'

'That is always a possibility. Who knows what the future brings? We may well tie the knot some day but for the present we are happy as we are. Grandmother knows about Angus and being the awful snob she is, he is to be welcomed. I don't know but I wouldn't put it past her to have checked up on the family estate in the Highlands.'

Annie wouldn't put it past her either. 'What does Angus want to do with his life?'

'Good question he would say. Painting, he'll do a bit of that but Angus always wished that he had been the elder son and the one to take over the running of the estate. We do talk about the future you know.'

'I'm sure you do and I am interested.'

'Angus knows all about Denbrae House, all about me as it happens.'

'That made no difference?'

'Only to make me more interesting, he said.' Annie swallowed the lump in her throat. Who said that young people were thoughtless? Angus had said just the right thing. 'He knows that Denbrae House will be mine one day and all the land that goes with it. Such a waste—'

'They were beautiful grounds.'

'At one time I've no doubt but they could be put to better use. Angus is full of ideas, some plain daft I told him, but others—'

'Not so daft. I'm glad, Tina, I didn't think I would be, but I am. Denbrae House needs youth and laughter and you and Angus will provide that.' She looked at her lovely daughter and felt so proud. She would miss Tina but it was time to let go.

'You and Ralph will come and spend long holidays,' she laughed. 'And, oh, I meant to tell you, Jonathan as you know couldn't be more helpful, he is marvellous to me. And would you believe, once I am back home he wants me to keep in touch. Wasn't it nice of him to suggest it?'

'Very nice,' Annie said with a quiet smile. Life was full of wonders.